Selections From Liao Zhai

【汉英对照·图文本】

聊斋精选

::马德五/编著

世界图书出版公司

上海·西安·北京·广州

SO-BFC-298

图书在版编目（CIP）数据

聊斋精选（汉英对照·图文本）／马德五 编著—上海：
上海世界图书出版公司,2005.8
ISBN 7－5062－7486－8

Ⅰ.聊… Ⅱ.马… Ⅲ.英语—对照读物,小说—汉、英 Ⅳ.H319.4：Ⅰ

中国版本图书馆 CIP 数据核字（2005）第 045097 号

聊斋精选 （汉英对照·图文本）

马德五 编著

上海世界图书出版公司出版发行

上海市尚文路 185 号 B 楼

邮政编码 200010

上海竟成印务有限公司印刷

如发现印装质量问题，请与印刷厂联系

（质检科电话：021－55391771）

各地新华书店经销

开本：889×1194 1/24 印张：9.5 字数：294 000
2005 年 8 月第 1 版 2005 年 8 月第 1 次印刷
印数：1－6 000
ISBN 7－5062－7486－8/H·601
定价：25.00 元
http://www.wpcsh.com.cn

自　序
Preface

千百年来,鬼神的存在与否一直是个争论性的问题。

For thousands of years, the existence of spirits has been always a controversial subject.

虽然人们在超自然的探讨上从来没有获得具体的答案,每一个国家都有很多的鬼故事。

Although mankind's inquiry into the supernatural has never produced substantial answers, every country abounds in ghost stories.

中国是世界上最古老的具有高度文化的国家之一,有数不清的超自然故事一代又一代地流传着。清朝蒲松龄(1640～1715)的《聊斋志异》是一致公认不论在通俗上抑或学术上都是中国文学领域中最杰出的经典巨著之一。

China is one of the oldest highly civilized nations in the world. There are countless supernatural tales told generation after generation. *Liao Zhai Zi Yi* by Pu Songling (1640～1715) from the Qing Dynasty is unanimously acknowledged, both popularly and academically, as one of the most remarkable works of this sort in the canon of Chinese literature.

在"聊斋"的四百多个故事里,这些鬼怪和精灵们都被活生生地拟人化了。他们与人们生活在人的世界里,同时也生活在他们自己的世界里。他们往来于这两个世界是非常地容易和频繁。虽然他们都具有超自然的能力,这本书中的精灵却都喜欢以人的形象出现。当他们居住在人的世界中时,他们的形象及举止动作都和人一模一样。因此,在书中的故事里有时候就很难分辨出谁是人而谁又是精灵。当这个秘密在精巧的设计下被披露时往往也就是这整个故事的高潮。

In the more than four hundred short stories in *Liao Zhai*, ghosts and spirits were all vividly personified. They lived with humans in the human world, and also in their own world. They traveled from one world to the other easily and frequently. Although they had the advantage of supernatural powers, the spirits in the book still liked to show themselves in human form. They looked and acted like human beings when they lived in the human world. Thus, in the stories of the book, it is sometimes hard to distinguish which one was human and which was spirit. The ingenious revelation of that secret, therefore, often becomes the most exciting part of the story.

当你发现中国鬼故事是如此地神秘动人时,你可能又回到了那个争论性的老问题:谁又真正地看见过鬼了?

As fascinating as one may find the Chinese ghost stories, one may still return to the old controversial question: Who has ever really seen a ghost?

在回答这个问题以前,请让我来先问你几个问题:

Before answering this question, let me ask you a few questions first:

每年秋季,总有百万只以上橘黄色的蝴蝶飞向那百里以外遥远的山边森林,可这些蝴蝶中没有一只曾经去过那儿。它们是如何找到路的?

Every fall, how do millions of tiny monarch butterflies find their way to remote mountain forests, hundreds of miles away, where none of them have ever been before?

每年冬季,那些5000磅重的海象都会穿越数百哩长的公海游回到它们当年出生地的海岸。它们又是如何找到路的?

Every winter, how do those five-thousand-pound elephant seals navigate hundreds of miles of open sea and return to the beaches where they were born?

这不过是自然界中无数的难以回答问题中的两个举例而已。动物的美妙世界里充满了很多的神秘,迄今尚没有一个科学家能够给我们一个满意的答案。正因为我们找不到答案,同样地我们也不能回答"聊斋"故事中的很多问题。

These are only two examples of the countless unanswerable questions about how the natural world works. The marvelous world of animals is full of so many mysteries that no scientist so far has yet been able to give us satisfactory answers how and why. Just as we cannot find those answers, neither can we answer the questions in the stories of *Liao Zhai*.

你的一生是一个故事,我的一生是一个故事。故事就是故事,只要是好的故事,我们就不必要太过分去怀疑这些故事的真实性，而毋宁去重视这些故事中的真理性。

Your life is a story. My life is a story. Stories are stories. As long as they are good stories, we should not question too much the truthfulness of the tales, and would rather concentrate on the truth in the tales.

在读了很多遍"聊斋"后，我必须要说绝大多数的故事都是没有意义的怪异事件之报告而已，而那其余的很多故事又都是典型的中国式故事，是很难会引起西方世界里非中国人士的兴趣的。

Having read *Liao Zhai* many times, I have to say that the majority of the stories are but meaningless reports of strange happenings. And many of the rest are typical Chinese stories, which would hardly arouse the interest of non-Chinese readers in the Western world.

本书里的聊斋故事是经过我审慎挑选过最有兴趣的部分。为了使说英语的读者们有最大的满足和兴趣，我将每一个故事予以修订后重新写过。

This book contains a careful selection of the most interesting stories in *Liao Zhai*. In order to best satisfy and entertain English-speaking readers, I have revised and rewritten each of them.

"聊斋"的原作者蒲松龄死于三个世纪以前。现在我尽自己的能力将他的部分作品以英文重新写过，显然地我没有获得他的同意。我只希望他在那鬼的世界里对我在人世间所做的工作不要过分的反对。如同他在他的故事中所说的每一位男女主角一样，他可能也具有超自然的法力了，甚至于也许会决定重现到人的世界里来拜访我，也许还会感谢我将他的故事介绍给说英语的读者们呢！

Pu Songling, the original author of *Liao Zhai*, died three centuries ago. I have now rewritten parts of his works in English using my best judgment obviously without obtaining permission from him. All I hope is that he will not object too much to my work, which is done in the world of humans, while he is in the world of ghosts. Like the heroes and heroines in his book, he may also have supernatural powers. He might even decide to show up in the human world and pay me a visit, perhaps to thank me for introducing his tales to the English-speaking readers!

所以我在耐心地等待着这一刻的到来。

So, I patiently wait for that moment to come.

"爱听秋坟鬼唱诗"

我如何将《聊斋志异》改写为英文的心路历程

自从 2000 年我的《英文聊斋精选译本》在美国出版以后,很多中国朋友就曾经问我当初是如何想写这本书的? 如今我的汉英对照本聊斋精选又在中国正式问世了,让我趁机来回答这个问题吧。

这话似乎还得从一个多甲子以前来说。六十多年前我还是一个十岁左右的小孩子时,我和我的家人住在江苏省北部灌云县老家。那个时候的苏北是个穷乡僻壤的地方,尤其是乡间,我们从来没有看见过电灯和自来水等所谓"洋"玩意。每年夏天太阳下山了吃过晚饭后,全家四代老小便会聚集在我们是庄主的"马前河庄"门前广场上纳凉聊天,人手一把芭蕉扇子,说东说西的一直聊到我们感觉全身都凉透了方才回到房间里去睡觉。

我的本家璞斋大伯时常来我们家看望我的祖母和我的二伯父。璞斋大伯喜欢逗我们小孩子玩,每次来时,我和我的两位堂姐德容和德宇就会央求他老人家在晚间纳凉时为我们讲故事,于是他就讲了很多奇奇怪怪的故事,把我们迷得七荤八素。因而每天起身后就盼望天快点儿黑了好在广场上听璞斋大伯的神奇故事。

以后我进了中学,慢慢地明了当年璞斋大伯所讲的好听故事原来都是出自一本名叫《聊斋志异》的书上的,我乃将这本最负盛名的中国鬼怪传奇短篇小说集一读再读,不知道读了多少遍。

1949 年我到了台湾,数年后考进了国立台湾大学中国文学系就读,我对聊斋作者蒲松龄的生平和他的其它著作又作了一番研究,还准备去写一篇论文,后来论文没有写成便毕业了,又数年后我就来到了美国。

1980 年我和我的家人住在美国怀俄明州。1987 年 9 月我开始为当地一家英文日报 *The Riverton Ranger* 撰写每周专栏,内容可以完全由我自己决定,于是有时候我就写一些极短篇的小说放在我的专栏上。

我们都知道每年 10 月底是美国的"万圣节",也就是俗称的所谓"鬼节"。在这天里,很多美国人特别是儿童们都喜欢穿着像妖魔鬼怪一样的衣服,把面孔画得怪模怪样地装成魔鬼的形象。为了适应节日的气氛,我就从聊斋中选出一篇鬼怪故事将它改写为英文,作为我那一周的专栏。我的本意是想告诉我的美国读者们我们中国的女鬼是多么地美丽和温柔,不但不可怕,简直是可爱极了。连续好几年,每年万圣节时我都写这么一篇应景文章,每次都收到很多读者们的热烈反应,告诉我他们是多么地盼望万圣节能够早日来临。一些读者们更建议我在不是万圣节时也写些这类的中国神奇鬼怪故事。我于是与报纸编辑戴夫·佩里(Dave Perry)商量,戴夫不太同意,他说这就好像不是万圣节时我们没有人去穿那些像魔鬼一样的衣服一样。

于是有几位读者乃建议我索性将这本中国鬼怪故事书多翻译一些出版成为一本专集,相信一定会有很好的销路的。这就是我当初想翻译聊斋为英文的直接动机。

于是我将蒲松龄的这本旷世杰作再度重头去读,虽然以往我曾经读过聊斋很多遍了,可是从没有像这次读得那么仔细。慢慢地我发现聊斋里虽然有四百三十多个故事,可是真正能够算得上有情节有现代短篇小说结构的还真不多,绝大部分可以说不过是些怪异事件的叙述而已,根本不配叫做短篇小说。还有一些虽然也算是故事,可是那些故事都是纯粹中国式的,如果将之译为英文是无法能被西方人士所了解所欣赏的。因此,真正算得上有现代短篇小说结构而且能为西方人士所接受的故事并不是非常地多。

据说蒲松龄当年曾经在路边摆个茶亭请过往客商喝茶,由每个喝茶人向他讲个鬼怪故事。因为他的故事来源很杂,所以书中也就有很多自相矛盾的地方。

譬如人死了后变成了鬼,鬼在阴间"照理"是永远不会像人们一样由少年慢慢地长大为中年最后成为老年的。因为鬼也会像人一样生病的,那么病重了以后怎么办?因此蒲松龄又编造了一个鬼死后成为聻的说法。不错,中国的古书上也的确有"鬼死为聻"的记载。鬼的世界好写,聻的世界就难了,可能蒲松龄也很快就发现把"聻"写得更玄的困难,所以在聊斋中关于聻的故事只有数篇而已。

在我们那个古老的中国,一个男子娶一个以上的女子是很普遍的事情,事实上不管多少个女人被娶进门,仍然只有一个叫做妻子,其余的都是侍妾。因此在聊斋里如果一个男子对他死去的妻子非常忠诚,往往便会终身不再娶妻,可是他仍有很多的娇美侍妾和他共同生活,对于现在的西方英文读者们来说,这一点是无论如何也不能使他们赞同的。

所以当我在选择聊斋故事翻译为英文时,我真是谨慎又谨慎把这些不为西方人士所能接受的部分都予以剔除或将其整个改编。譬如"莲香"这个有鬼也有狐两女一男的故事的确很动人,可是这个故事的结尾实在太荒唐得"不近人情"了,于是我将它重写。其它如"公孙九娘"、"书痴"、"伍秋月"、"小翠"、"凤仙"、"阿英"、"梅女"等也都被我差不多整个儿重写了。蒲松龄一再说鬼是不能在阳光下出现的,可是他在"聂小倩"中竟又让女鬼在大白天和人们共同生活在一起,所以我把这些都改写了,表示前后一致。有时候我更将两三个故事中的精华部分合并为一个故事,譬如我把"荷花三娘子"、"董生"和"胡四姐"合并为一个完整的短篇小说。有时没有女主角而这又是一个很特别的故事,譬如"二斑",我就为它创造了一个女主角和一段哀艳的爱情。诸如此类,几乎每一篇我所采用的聊斋故事都被我改编得"体无完肤"。为什么?因为我要我的英文聊斋能为现代的说英语的人士所接受。所以严格说来,我不是照着原书翻译的,不过是将聊斋故事中比较精华的部分改写为玄之又玄的一本英文短篇小说集。不过话又说回来,不管我如何地改写,这种凡人与鬼怪精灵恋爱的精神仍然是属于蒲松龄的。以上就是我如何撰写英文聊斋的整个经过。

这本书我是写了又改,改了又写,就这样地写写改改了好几年,方才稍稍满意,由曾经出版过我一本英文散文集的纽约 Barricade Books 出版公司于 2000 年予以出版了,书名也是他们决定的,就叫做 *Chinese Ghost Stories for Adults*(《成年人阅读的中国鬼故事》)。事实上我认为我的英文聊斋应该是更适合青少年们阅读的书,于是我和他们交涉告诉他们"成年人阅读的"几个字委实没有必要。出版公司回答我他们之所以特别说明"成年人",因为我在好几个故事中有关"性爱"的描写有点儿露骨了,恐怕小孩子们在不知情的情况下读了后他们的家长会提出控诉。事实上,我对所谓"性爱"的描述也只是点到为止,根本没有如出版公司所说的露骨。我想这不过是他们的一个促销的噱头而已。不管怎么说,由于合约中订明出版公司有权更改书名的,所以我也就不再去和他们争论了。

2003 和 2004 年上海世界图书出版公司分别出版了我早先在美国出版过的两本英文书加上我自己的中文翻译,由于这两本汉英对照书在中国的书市上似乎还蛮受欢迎的,所以这家出版公司又和我再度合作签约出版我的第三本汉英对照书《聊斋精选》。

亲爱的读者朋友们,如果你认为这本书的可读性很高,那这个功劳仍然是属于蒲松龄的;如果觉得不堪一读,那这个责任就完全是我的了。

不管如何,我对四百多年前的蒲松龄先生仍是非常感激的。如果没有他,哪有我今日的一再丰收!
(作者的个人写作网站为 www.tomtewuma.homestead.com,欢迎文友上网沟通指教)

马德五

注:清朝最负盛名的文学批评家王士祺的聊斋读后诗:"姑妄言之姑听之,豆棚瓜架雨如丝。料应厌作人间语,爱听秋坟鬼唱诗。"

目　录
(Contents)

一、

莲

香

The Lover, the Murderess?

任桑晓是他所住的乡里公认为最英俊的一位年轻男子。由于他的外表和相貌,他有很多女友,可没有打算和任何一位女友结婚。他告诉她们也许他会娶一位不嫉妒他有别的女人的女友。因为每一个女子都不能忍受她的丈夫有另外的女人,所以他一直保持着单身的身份。

Ren Sangxiao was known as the most handsome young man in the area he lived. Thanks to his looks, he had many girlfriends, but no intention of marrying any of them. He told his girls that perhaps he would marry the one who was not jealous of his other sweethearts. Since no woman could stand the situation of her husband's keeping another woman, his bachelorhood was safe.

一天,桑晓认识了一位名叫周莲香的美丽女子。他邀请她到他的家里,他是一个人单独住在一栋房子里的。他们立刻陷入了情网。莲香留宿一夜,第二天早晨便离开了。

One day, Sangxiao made the acquaintance of a pretty girl named Zhou Lianxiang. He invited her to his house where he lived alone. They fell in love immediately, and Lianxiang stayed overnight and left in the morning.

从此莲香开始每隔四五天就来拜访桑晓一次。每次来后他们都会做爱,双方均能得到性爱的乐趣。他要求她搬来和他同住,或者至少来得勤快一点,可是被她拒绝了。根据她的解释,像他这样健康的青年男子,每四五天有一次性爱是无伤于身体的。因此,她希望他们的亲密关系就限定在这样一个日程上。

Since then, Lianxiang visited Sangxiao every four or five days. Every time she came they would make love and have a wonderful time. He asked her to move in, or at least come more often, but she declined. According to her opinion, as a healthy young man he could have sex every four or five days without affecting his health. She wanted to limit their intimate relationship to that schedule.

一天夜晚,莲香不在身边,桑晓非常思念她。突然间他听到敲门声,他去开门,看见了一位靓丽动人的女子站在他的房门外。他邀请她进入屋内。女子含羞地自我介绍名叫李婉。然后坦率地告诉他自己是一个妓女,她想毛遂自荐作为他的一个情妇。

One late evening when Lianxiang was not there, Sangxiao began to miss her badly. He suddenly heard a knock on the door. He opened the door and saw an attractive girl standing outside of his house. He invited her to come in. The girl shyly introduced herself as Li Wan. After that, she told him frankly that she was a prostitute, and she wondered whether she could offer herself as his mistress.

桑晓大喜过望。天快亮时,李婉说她必须赶回妓院。临走时她留给桑晓一条粉红色的绣花手帕,她说如果他在夜晚想念她时,他就可以把手帕拿出来代替她。

Sangxiao was overjoyed. Before dawn, she said that she had to go back to her brothel. She presented him with a pink silk handkerchief embroidered with delicate flowers. She said that whenever he missed her in the late evening, he could be with the handkerchief in her stead.

聊斋精选

奇怪的是每当桑晓玩弄手帕时,李婉便会立刻出现在他的房间里面。莲香每隔四五天就来一次,而在其余的晚间李婉便夜夜都来了。他的性生活从没有如此之美好过。

The strange thing was that every time Sangxiao played with the handkerchief, Li Wan would immediately appear in the room. Lianxiang visited every four or five days and Li Wan came on all the other nights in between. His sex life was better than ever.

不久,莲香发现桑晓另有新欢。她询问他,可是他不承认。莲香说他和她并不是夫妻,她没有权力去干涉他的性生活。不过她警告他太多的每日纵欲会伤害一个男子健康的。她说她将暂不再来,而于一个月后再来查看他的情况。于是她没有过夜就走了。

Soon Lianxiang discovered that Sangxiao had another sweetheart. When she inquired, he denied it. Lianxiang said that since he and she were not husband and wife, she had no right to intervene in his personal love affairs. But she warned him that too much daily carnal conduct would eventually ruin a man's health. She said that she would stop coming for a while, and return to check on him a month later. Then she left without even staying overnight.

莲香不来了,李婉于是每天晚间都来。这两个爱人便夜夜从事那荒唐的淫荡欢乐。

In Lianxiang's absence, Li Wan came every evening. The two lovers indulged in wild debauchery every night.

三个星期后,桑晓发觉自己对食物的胃口一天天逐渐减退,同时他也发觉自己的体重也在减轻。可是他毫不在意,仍然每天夜晚与李婉在追逐肉欲之乐。

Three weeks later, Sangxiao felt that he was gradually losing his appetite for food, and he was losing weight, too. However, he did not worry too much and still sought carnal pleasure with Li Wan every evening.

一个月后,莲香回来了。当她注意到桑晓的健康已经日益恶化,她再度警告他:必须立刻断绝与那另一个女人的疯狂性行为;否则,他的性命难保。

A month later, Lianxiang came back. When she noticed that Sangxiao's health had been deteriorating, she gave him another warning: He must terminate his carnal gluttony with the other woman right away; otherwise, his life would be in jeopardy.

桑晓漫应着,心想莲香不过是嫉妒他有另外的女人罢了。当他邀她上床时,她拒绝了。她告诉他,她必须再度离开他,但将在六个月后回来挽救他的性命。于是她突然不见了。

Sangxiao answered heedlessly, figuring that Lianxiang was just jealous of his other woman. When he invited her to bed, she refused. She told him that she had to leave him again, but she would return in six months to save his life. Then she disappeared suddenly.

莲香说的不错,桑晓的健康一天坏似一天。可那更糟的是即使他愿意,他也无法摆脱李婉,她坚持每晚来看他。而每次李婉一来,他就无法拒绝她的色情诱惑而不与她做爱。不久,他在痰中发现了血。后来他连走路也不稳当了。这时候他想起了莲香的警告,但此时太晚了。

Lianxiang was right. Sangxiao's health worsened daily. And the worse thing was that even if he wanted, he could not get rid of Li Wan, who persisted in visiting him every night. Once she showed up, he could not resist engaging in sensual pleasure with her. Soon, he found blood in his saliva. Later he developed a stumbling gait. By the time he remembered what Lianxiang had warned him about, it was too late.

一天下午,桑晓病卧在床,喃喃地叫着莲香的名字,追悔不听她的劝告,最后昏迷过去而失去了知觉。

One late afternoon, while sick in bed, murmuring Lianxiang's name and feeling much sorrow for not accepting her advice, Sangxiao finally lost consciousness.

一只柔软的手摸在他的脸上,把他摸醒了。他睁开眼睛一看,惊喜地发现莲香坐在他身边的床上,用手轻抚着他。桑晓立刻想坐起身来,可他已经弱得力不从心了。莲香拥抱着他,两个人都哭了起来。

He was awakened by a person's soft hand touching his face. Opening his eyes, he was overjoyed to find Lianxiang sitting beside him on the bed, caressing him. Sangxiao immediately tried to sit up, but was too weak to make it. Lianxiang hugged him and they both began to cry.

她告诉他她回来是为挽救他的性命的。她也承认了她不是人类,她是一只雌狐。她和他在前世原来是夫妻,所以她感觉有责任来救他。因为他的性生活放纵以及这种种的事故,使得她看破了人生的虚幻。她已决定一等他的健康恢复了,她就回深山去过苦行的修炼生活,寻求修成正果。

She told him that she was back to save his life. She also admitted to him that she was not a human. She was a female fox. She and he had been husband and wife in their previous lives. Thus, she felt obligated to save his life. Meanwhile, his sexual recklessness and what it had done to him made her understand the vanity of a human's life. She had decided that after restoring his health, she would go back to a wild mountain to live an ascetic life in order to achieve immortality.

在这以往的六个月中,她到昆仑山上日以继夜地去采集那世上最稀罕的植物叶片用以制造特别的药丸来恢复他的健康。于是她拿出了一个小瓶子,里面装满了褐色药丸,她吩咐他立刻先服两粒。

Over the previous six months, she had stayed on the Kunlun Mountain where she worked day and night to collect the world's rare medicinal plant leaves to make special pills to restore his health. Then she took out a small bottle full of brown pills and ordered him to take two immediately.

一个小时以后,桑晓神奇般地感觉见好了点。他不用莲香的帮忙在床上自己坐了起来,同时告诉她他开始有点胃口想吃点东西。她于是烧了一碗米汤,喂他在床上吃了。

An hour later, Sangxiao miraculously felt his health returning. He sat up on the bed without Lianxiang's help and told her that he had regained some appetite. She cooked a bowl of rice soup and fed him in bed.

吃完了米汤以后,桑晓把李婉的故事一五一十地告诉了莲香,并自枕头下面将李婉的手帕拿了出来,懊悔地要求莲香将它烧掉。突然间李婉出现在房内。

After eating the soup, Sangxiao told Lianxiang about Li Wan in details. He took Li Wan's handkerchief out from under his pillow and regretfully asked Lianxiang to burn it. Suddenly, Li Wan appeared in the room.

看见莲香,李婉想逃走,可是莲香已经挡住了门户的出口,同时用手指急忙指向李婉,李婉立刻跌倒在地上不能动弹。于是莲香询问她的出处,这个女子终于坦称她不是人而是个女鬼。

Upon seeing Lianxiang, Li Wan tried to flee. But Lianxiang blocked the door and hastily pointed her finger at Li Wan. Li Wan immediately fell to the ground and paralyzed. Lianxiang interrogated her about her background. The woman finally admitted that she was not a human but a ghost.

她一边痛哭一边诉说,她爱桑晓,而他也爱她。爱到后来他们沉溺在性爱中不能自拔。她从来没有想到她是在谋杀她的恋人。因为她几乎害死了他,她愿意负担起一切的责任,接受莲香及桑晓的任何惩罚。她对莲香说只要能使桑晓的健康恢复,不管什么她都愿意牺牲。

She said through tears that she loved Sangxiao and he loved her. Because of love, they kept seeking carnal pleasure and finally could not control it. She never realized that she was actually murdering her lover. Since she had almost killed him, she wanted to take the full responsibility for her actions and receive whatever punishment Lianxiang and Sangxiao deemed appropriate. She told Lianxiang that she would sacrifice whatever she could to restore Sangxiao's health.

听了李婉的故事后,莲香不由得长长地叹了一口气。她告诉桑晓这一切的一切都是命运的安排,所以他们也不要再去责备李婉了。于是她又用手向这女鬼一指,李婉立刻可以站起身子和移动了。可是她不再想逃跑,相反地,她竟跪倒在莲香的面前请求惩罚。莲香让她站起身来,要她每天晚上来帮助她一同照顾桑晓。

Having heard Li Wan's story, Lianxiang sighed a long heavy sigh. She told Sangxiao that everything must has been arranged by fate. They should not blame Li Wan anymore. Then she pointed at the female ghost again, and immediately Li Wan could stand up and move freely. Instead of trying to escape again, she knelt down before Lianxiang begging for punishment. Lianxiang stood her up and asked her to come every evening to help her take good care of Sangxiao.

聊斋精选

聊斋精选

在这两个女子的细心照顾下，以及服用莲香的药丸，桑晓恢复得很快。不到一个月，他的饮食及行动差不多都正常了。在夜晚，这两个女子睡在一张床上，桑晓单独一个人睡。当他见好多了时，他便会和这两个女子拥抱及接吻，莲香不准他有其它的亲密举动。她告诉他至少在四十九天以内他是不可以有性行为的。

Under the two women's constant care and taking Lianxiang's pills, Sangxiao improved rapidly. Within a month, he could eat and walk almost normally. At night, the two girls slept on one bed while Sangxiao slept alone. When Sangxiao was better, he started to hug and kiss the two girls. Lianxiang prohibited him from engaging in further intimacies. She told him not to have sex for at least forty-nine days.

莲香日夜都留在桑晓处。李婉因为是个鬼，只能在夜晚来而天亮前又必须离开。有一晚，她没有出现，而且在第二晚也没有来。这是很不平常的。不管桑晓怎么去玩弄她的手帕，她仍然没有出现。桑晓和莲香很困惑，可又无法去寻找她。

Lianxiang stayed with Sangxiao every day and night. As a ghost, Li Wan could only come in the evening and must leave before dawn. One night, she did not appear. And she was absent the following evening. This was unusual. No matter how much Sangxiao tried to play with her handkerchief, she still did not show up. Sangxiao and Lianxiang were stumped, but they had no way of finding her.

三天后，一个陌生的中年男子来拜访桑晓。他告诉桑晓他的家中最近发生了一件使人难以相信的事情。他的十九岁的女儿死了，可是死后第二天又复活了。复活后，她声称不是他们的女儿，是另一个女孩名字叫李婉，她有一个男友名叫任桑晓，他住在这儿。她说她要和她的男友立刻结婚。她的父母认为她的神智混乱，极力劝她把这个奇怪的念头打消。可是她扬言如果她的要求不能达成，她就自杀。她的父亲没有办法只好来拜访桑晓，希望能找出原因为什么他的女儿会有这个奇怪的行为。

Three days later, a strange middle-aged man came to visit Sangxiao. He told Sangxiao that an unbelievable thing had recently happened in his home. His 19-year-old daughter had died, and the next day she revived. After coming back to life, she declared that she was not his daughter but another girl named Li Wan and that she had a boyfriend named Ren Sangxiao who lived at this address. She said she wanted to marry her boyfriend right away. Her parents thought that she might be mentally confused and tried hard to convince her to drop the crazy idea, but she threatened to commit suicide if her request could not be met. Her father had no choice but to visit Sangxiao to try to find out why his daughter was acting so crazy.

桑晓立刻明白他的鬼友李婉一定是进入了这个死了的女子的身体里面复活了。他将李婉的整个故事以及他们的关系告诉了他的访客。看起来桑晓是个良好的青年，于是这个父亲便愉快地同意让他的"女儿"嫁给桑晓。一个正式的婚礼不久就举行了。

Sangxiao immediately realized that his ghost girlfriend, Li Wan, must have entered the dead girl's body and revived as a person. He told the visitor the entire story about Li Wan and her relationship with him.

Seeing that Sangxiao appeared to be a nice young man, the father happily agreed to let his "daughter" marry Sangxiao. A formal wedding ceremony was soon held.

婚后,李婉把经过的事情告诉了桑晓及莲香。在那天天亮以前,当她离开他们后,她再度检讨这整个事件的发生,不由得深深地自责。在深切自责下,她突然决定不像以往一样地回坟墓去休息,以此作为一种自我惩罚。到了白天,她被强风从一个地方吹到另一个地方。到了夜晚间,她完全迷失了方向而不知道身在何处。于是她听到了一个人家悼念亡者的哀泣。顺着声音,她进入了一家人家,接着她看到了一个女子的尸体。她于是一头钻入尸体内。等她明白时,发现她已经是一个人了。

After marriage, Li Wan told Sangxiao and Lianxiang what had happened. Before dawn that night, after she had left them, she examined the whole thing once again and blamed nobody but herself. The more examination she made, the more she blamed herself. Suddenly she decided not to return to her grave to rest as she usually did as a form of self-punishment. When the daylight came, she was blown by a fierce wind from one place to the other. By late evening, she was totally lost and did not know where she was. Then she heard the bitter cries of a family in mourning. Following the sound, she entered a house and found a dead girl's body. She rushed into the corpse and the next thing she could remember was that she had become a human.

现在,桑晓和李婉已经是一对正式的夫妻了,于是莲香要求永远离开他们。

Now that Sangxiao and Li Wan had formally become husband and wife, Lianxiang asked to leave them for good.

可是桑晓和李婉不让她走。这对夫妻双双跪倒在她的面前恳求她留下。他们哭泣着说没有她,哪会有他们的快乐今日,他们声泪俱下长跪不起除非她答应不走。最后莲香应允暂且留下。

But Sangxiao and Li Wan would not let her go. The couple knelt down in front of her, begging her to stay. They claimed, through tears, that without her they could not have had their present happy life. They cried and refused to get up unless she promised them not to go. Finally, Lianxiang agreed to stay for a while.

于是李婉安排她和莲香各居一室,桑晓隔日分睡一女房间。可是,奇怪的事情是每次当桑晓睡在莲香的房间时,而他第二天早上醒来则总会发现还是在李婉的房间与李婉睡在一起。

Li Wan arranged two bedrooms for Lianxiang and herself to sleep. Sangxiao would be with each one every other night. But the strange thing was that every time Sangxiao slept with Lianxiang, he always woke up in Li Wan's room with Li Wan beside him on the bed.

同时,莲香开始呈现虚弱。当她每次生病时,桑晓和李婉都会尽心尽力去服侍她就如同当初她们两女服侍桑晓一样。可是不管他们如何服侍,莲香还是时常生病,而且每病一次,人就显得苍老多了。不到

聊斋精选

一年光景,莲香就苍老得像个老妇人了。可是桑晓和李婉还是对她敬爱如初,毫不稍减。

Meanwhile, Lianxiang began to waste away. Every time she was ill, Sangxiao and Li Wan would take good care of her as carefully as the two women had taken care of Sangxiao before. Despite their efforts, Lianxiang still often became sick and every time she seemed to recuperate, she would also appear greatly aged. In less than a year, Lianxiang appeared like an old woman. But Sangxiao and Li Wan still loved and respected her as deeply as before.

莲香终于亡故了。死后,她的尸体又变为一只雌狐。桑晓和李婉把她的尸体放入一口精致的棺材里,尽其全力以最恭敬的葬礼把她安葬了。嗣后每年忌日两人都到她的坟前祭祀。

Finally, Lianxiang died. After death, her body changed back into a female fox. Sangxiao and Li Wan put her body in a fine coffin and gave her a very respectful funeral spending as much as they could afford. Every year on the anniversary of the date she died, they would offer sacrifices to her grave.

李婉与桑晓生了三个女儿一个儿子。这个男孩长大了以后开始经商。因为业务的关系,他经常旅行在外。

Li Wan bore Sangxiao three daughters and one son. When the boy grew up, he became a salesman. For business, he often made out of town trips.

一天,这个年轻的商人外出到一个不知名的小镇后得了一种奇怪的疾病。当地惟一的医生对他的病症束手无策,他病得一天比一天严重,最后连行走都困难了。他害怕会死在这个不知名的地方,害怕他的家人也无法找到他的尸体了。

One day, the young businessman traveled to an unknown small town and was stricken by a strange disease. The only doctor in the town could not help him and his condition worsened daily. Finally, he could not even walk well. He was afraid that he might die in this unknown place and his family would not even find his corpse.

他是一个虔诚的佛教徒,于是在午夜后,他艰难地挪到旅店后院跪倒在地上,向着冥冥的天空祈求观世音菩萨的帮助。在月光下,他看到了一位年轻美貌的女子从空中飞落下来。她说她不是观世音菩萨,不过凑巧路过这儿,听到了他的祈求。她说她还是他父母的一位老友。于是她取出一个小瓶子,从里面倒出来两粒棕色药丸,她要他服下去治他的病。她告诉他这些药丸还是多年前她用来救他父亲的性命时所留下来的。她要这个商人代她问候他的父母亲。说完了以后,她就飞回天空而不见了踪影。

As a dedicated Buddhist, he dragged himself after midnight to the backyard of the hotel where he stayed. He knelt down facing the sky and praying for help from the Goddess of Mercy. In the moonlight, he saw a pretty young lady fly down from the sky. She said that she was not the Goddess of Mercy, but happened to be passing by and heard his request for help. She said that she was also an old friend of his parents. Then she took out a small bottle and poured out two brown pills. She wanted him to take the pills to cure his disease. She told him that the pills were left over from the ones she had used to save his father's life years ago. She asked the salesman to give his parents her best regards, then, she flew back into the sky and disappeared.

年轻人服下这两粒药丸后,病果真好了。

The young man took the two pills and, indeed, recovered from the disease.

回到家后,他把事情的经过一五一十地告诉了父母。桑晓和李婉立刻怀疑这位神秘女子可能是莲香,可是她早已在多年前死了。于是他们将莲香的坟墓挖开,并又打开棺材,果然发现里面空无一物,他们方才相信莲香早已经真的修炼成为正果了。而她原来的那些时常生病、日见苍老,以及后来的病故等等都不过是她的幻化,目的是要离开他们可以去专心修炼。她终于成功了。

Upon returning home, he told his parents the whole story. Sangxiao and Li Wan immediately suspected that the mysterious lady might be Lianxiang, but she had died years ago. They dug out Lianxiang's grave and opened her coffin. Inside, they found nothing. The coffin was empty. They began to believe that Lianxiang had finally become an immortal. Her getting sick often and appearing older day after day, even her death, were all but her tricks in order to leave them, so she could concentrate on her quest for immortality. And she had finally made it.

二、

陆

判

Judge Lu

朱尔旦的左脚自幼就变了形,脚背弯曲。他曾经请教过很多医生,可就是没有一个人可以帮助他。虽然他仍不放弃,总希望有一天他可以找到一位脚科专家能够把他的脚纠正过来,使他能和别人一样地正常行走。

Zhu Erdan's left foot had been deformed since birth. The instep was crooked. He had consulted with many doctors but never found one who could help him. Yet he would not give up, hoping that someday he might be able to find a foot specialist who could fix his foot to make him walk as normally as everyone else.

虽然尔旦不能如正常人走得一样地快,可是他是当地众所公认胆量最大的男子。他可以单独地在任何时间不论白天或黑夜去任何地方,不管那儿是如何的荒凉。换言之,他不相信有鬼魂的存在。

Although Erdan could not walk as fast as a normal man, he was well known as the most courageous man in the area he lived. He would go anywhere, alone, at any time of day or night, no matter how desolate the area was. In other words, he did not believe in the existence of spirits.

他和他的妻子住在一个村庄的西面。他们没有小孩。在村庄的东面有一座佛教庙宇,在大殿里面有很多尊木头雕刻的鬼像。除了阎罗王坐在大殿的后面外,他的旁边站立着四位官员,一位判官站在前面,八个卫士面向着他站立。这些和真人一样大小的木像雕塑得非常地精致,再加上彩色的油绘,远远看去,真的像活人一般。

He lived at the western area of a village with his wife. They had no children. A Buddhist temple stood at the eastern end of the village. Many painted wooden statues of ghosts were installed in the main hall of the temple. Besides the grand ruler of the ghost world sitting in the back, there were four officials standing next to him, and a judge stood in the front with eight soldiers standing to face him. The life-size statues were delicately carved and colorfully painted to make them appear like real humans if they were seen from a distance.

聊斋精选

在这些雕像中,以这个判官雕得最为凶神恶煞了。一对特别大的眼睛怒目圆睁,似乎是在注视着每一个胆敢向他看望的人。他的鼻子奇高而且嘴巴又特大,那从不曾梳过的红色长发以及那白色的短须看起来就令人毛骨悚然。他的右手紧握着一根粗糙的皮鞭,好像是要去惩罚歹徒。据说每到夜里,当人们从庙前经过,总会时常听到一些严厉的叱责声及残酷的鞭打声,夹杂着绝望的呼叫声以及凄厉的求饶声直接从庙里传出来。因此妇女和小孩在天黑了以后都不敢单独经过这座庙宇。

Among the statues, the judge appeared most repulsive and fierce, with a pair of extra-large eyes widely and angrily opened toward any onlookers if daring to stare back at him. His nose was rather high and his mouth was unusual big. His uncombed long red hair and white short beard seemed electrified. His right hand grasped a rough leather whip as if he was ready to punish evildoers. It was said that whenever people were passing through the temple at night, they would often hear severe scolding and cruel whippings, followed by hopeless wails bitterly beseeching mercy, directly from the inside of temple. Because of this, women and children alone dared not pass by the temple after dark.

一天晚间,尔旦和几个朋友在家里喝酒。当大家谈到鬼魂时,他坚持世上根本没有什么所谓鬼魂的东西。他说当一个人说他曾经看到过鬼,那完全是这个人的幻觉,因为幻觉就可以产生幻影,一切就是如此地简单。

One evening, Erdan was drinking with several friends at home. When they talked about spirits, he insisted that there were absolutely no such things called ghosts. He said that when a person said that he had seen a ghost, that was but the person's imagination, for the imagination would create the phantoms. It was so simple.

于是,一个朋友提到他们这儿庙里在夜间发出来的奇怪声音。尔旦大笑,并告诉他的朋友们,他在夜里路过这座庙宇无数次,可他怎么从来不曾听到过任何奇怪的声音从里面发出来? 所谓听到什么完全是这个过路人的幻觉罢了。他说那些雕像都是木头做的,木头是无生命的,怎么可能有什么灵魂在木头里面呢? 他的回答使得他的朋友们哑口无言。

Then a friend mentioned the nearby temple and the strange sounds heard from the inside of the building at night. Erdan laughed and told his friends that he had passed through the temple countless times at night, and why hadn't he heard any strange sounds from the inside? The claims were clearly the products of imaginations of the people who were passing by. He said that all the statues were made of wood and wood was inanimate. How could a piece of wood have a spirit in it? His conviction rendered his friends speechless.

于是一个朋友向尔旦挑战此时单独去庙里把那座像貌最凶恶可怕的鬼判官雕像背回来,如果他能做到,他们就在第二天晚间请他到城里最昂贵的饭店内吃饭。

Then one friend challenged Erdan to go to the temple alone that night to bring back the most fierce-looking ghost judge statue. If he could accomplish the task, his friends promised to honor him with a dinner next night at the most expensive restaurant in town.

"好,就这么办!"尔旦毫不犹豫愉快地回答。他把他的酒一口喝完,便立刻走了出去。

"It's a deal," Erdan answered happily without any hesitation. He finished his drink and went out immediately.

半个小时以后,尔旦把那尊像貌最凶恶的木雕鬼判官背在身上回家来了。他把鬼判官雕像放在桌子旁边。在那暗淡的油灯下,这位极讨人厌怕的鬼判官的两只特大的眼睛似乎是怒目圆睁对着在座的每一个人。一时间,尔旦的每一个朋友都感到不寒而栗。他们请求他赶快把鬼判官雕像背回庙里去。他们答应第二天晚间一定请他吃饭。

Half an hour later, Erdan returned home with the wooden statue of the most fierce-looking ghost judge on his back. He put the ghost judge statue down by the table. Under the weak light of the oil lamp, it seemed that the most repulsive ghost judge's two extra-large eyes were angrily staring at everyone in the house. It made every one of Erdan's friends cringe in horror. They begged him to carry the ghost judge statue back to the temple right away and promised him they would honor their words to have dinner the following evening.

聊斋精选

在背回去这尊木雕以前,尔旦斟满了一杯酒倒进鬼判官的嘴里,并以开玩笑的方式向鬼判官敬酒,"请原谅我今天晚上的粗鲁行为。我的家离你的庙不远,哪一天晚上你不工作的时候,欢迎来我家做客,我们一起喝两杯。"说完后他把这尊鬼判官木雕像背回庙里去了。

Before carrying back the wooden statue, Erdan filled up a glass of liquor and poured it into the ghost judge's mouth. He jokingly toasted the judge, "Please excuse me for my rude behavior tonight. My home is not too far from your temple. You are welcome to drop in as my guest, and we shall have a few drinks together when you have a night off." Then he put the ghost judge wooden statue on his back and left for the temple.

第二天晚间,尔旦在城里一家最豪华的饭店里享受了一顿精美的晚餐,由前天晚上在他家喝酒的朋友们付的账。他很愉快,喝了很多酒。当宴会结束时,他已经是半醉了。回到家后,他就想立刻上床睡觉。

The next evening, Erdan had a good time at the most expensive restaurant in the town. The dinner was held in his honor and paid for by his friends who had drunk at his home the night before. He was happy and had many drinks. When the dinner was over, he was half drunk. After reaching home, he planned to go to bed right away.

就在他要脱衣服时,他听到了有人敲他家的前门。他去开了门,一下子惊吓得呆了。访客正是他在前一天晚间背回家去的庙里那位相貌最凶恶的鬼判官。不过今天晚间鬼判官以人的形态出现了。

Before he took off his clothes, he heard a knock at his front door. He went to open the door and was shocked. The visitor was the most fierce-looking ghost judge from the temple whom he had carried home the night before. Tonight the ghost judge appeared in human form.

"你是因为我昨天晚间的无礼行为而来鞭打我吗?"尔旦极度恐惧地询问道。
"Are you coming to whip me because of my impolite behavior last night?" Erdan asked in great fear.

"不是的,"鬼判官带着微笑和气地回答,"你看我并没有带鞭子来。我是应你的邀请来这儿和你喝两杯的。"
"No," the judge answered kindly with a smile, "you see I don't have my whip in my hand. I'm here to accept your invitation to have a drink with you."

尔旦立刻放下了心。他邀判官进入房内并请他坐下。
Erdan was instantly relieved. He invited the judge to enter the house and asked him to sit down.

他到卧室去告诉他的妻子庙里的鬼判官到他们家来和他喝酒,他要她去给他们热壶酒。这个女人害怕见鬼判官,不敢出来。尔旦只好自己去热了酒来招待判官。于是他们俩一人一鬼边饮边谈起来了。

He went to the bedroom and told his wife that the judge from the temple had come to their house to have a drink with him. He asked her to heat a bottle of liquor for them. The woman was frightened to see the ghost judge and dared not come out. Erdan had to heat the liquor himself and serve the judge. Then the two started to drink and talk.

慢慢地，尔旦发现鬼判官虽然相貌长得非常吓人，可他还是很友善的。而且他也发现这个判官和他是同一类型的男人，那就是他们两个都很爽直，都很诚恳，也都喜欢喝酒。不到一个小时，他和这个判官便成了朋友，而忘掉了他们之间的不同点：一个是人，一个是鬼。

Gradually, Erdan found that although the ghost judge's appearance was very fierce, he was actually quite friendly. And he also discovered that he and the judge were the same type of men: straightforward, honest, and fond of drinking. Within one hour, he and the judge became friends and forgot the difference between them, a human and a ghost.

自从那天夜晚以后，鬼判官便经常来拜访尔旦。他们一同喝酒聊天，引以为乐。几次拜访后，尔旦的妻子便也就习惯于鬼判官的凶恶外貌了，并且有时候也来参加他们的谈话。

From that night on, the ghost judge visited Erdan frequently. They enjoyed drinking and talking together. After a few more visits, Erdan's wife became accustomed to the ghost judge's fierce appearance, and sometimes she joined in their conversations, as well.

鬼判官告诉尔旦他姓陆。他生前一直都在做法官。死后，由于他有这么多年的经验，阎罗王便也派他为判官。陆判官现在阴间被公认为最公正无私及最受尊敬的判官之一，很得阎罗王的信任。

The ghost judge told Erdan that his last name was Lu. As a human, he had been a judge his whole life. After death, since he had so many years of experience, the grand ruler of the ghost world also appointed him a judge. Judge Lu now was well known as one of the most impartial and honorable judges in the world of ghosts and had won the trust of the grand ruler.

"作为一个判官，我总是尽一切可能不惩罚无辜者。"陆判官告诉尔旦。
"As a judge, I always try my best not to punish the innocent," Judge Lu told Erdan.

"可是，为何人们时常在夜间听到庙里传出残酷的鞭打声及哀求声呢？"尔旦问道。
"But, why do people often hear the cruel whippings and crying for mercy in the temple at night?" Erdan asked.

"我从来没有下令严厉惩罚一个疑犯，除非我获得充足的证据证明这个疑犯的确是犯过重罪。"然后陆判官又说："对于某些罪犯，只有沉重地鞭打才能使他们明白他们所犯罪恶的严重性。"
"I have never ordered a severe punishment unless I have found sufficient evidence of the suspect's crime." Then Judge Lu added, "Only severe whippings could make the sinners realize the consequences of their wrongdoings."

由于尔旦仍然不能完全同意他这个朋友，陆判官进一步解释："如果一个人在生时从不曾犯过任何罪恶而相反地曾经做了很多善事，死了后变成了鬼，这个鬼将受到阎罗王的仁慈礼遇而很快地便将之安排投生在富贵的人家。换言之，只有那些严重的罪犯鬼才会受到我的鞭打。"

聊斋精选

As Erdan still did not fully agree with his friend, Judge Lu further explained, "If a person has never committed a crime and instead done many good deeds while he or she was a human, after death, the person will become a ghost and the ghost will receive nice treatment from the grand ruler of ghost world. The ruler will immediately arrange for the ghost to be reborn to a wealthy and dignified family. In another words, only the truly criminal of the ghosts receive my whippings."

这两个朋友愉快地喝酒聊天几乎无所不谈。尔旦告诉陆判官他一生中从未犯过罪行,他对他现在的一生也非常满意。
The two friends happily drank and talked about many subjects. Erdan told the Judge Lu that in his entire life, he had never committed a crime, and that he was wholly satisfied with his present way of life.

"如果一定要说有遗憾的话,那就是我的左脚了。我的左脚天生变形使我不能和别人一样正常地走路。"尔旦告诉他的判官朋友。
"If there must be something I might still feel regret about, it would be my left foot. It is deformed. I can't walk as normally as other people," Erdan told his judge friend.

"也许有一天我可以帮助你,使你能够正常地走路。"陆判官回答说。
"I might be able to give you a help to make you walk normally one of these days," Judge Lu replied.

"如果真能如此的话,我就感激不尽了。"尔旦说。
"If it could be done, I would appreciate it very much," Erdan said.

这以后,尔旦就把这段谈话完全忘记了。
But soon afterwards, Erdan forgot the conversation completely.

几个星期后的一天夜里,尔旦被一种在他左脚上的压力弄醒了。他睁开眼睛一看,非常震惊地发现他的鬼友陆判官正用左手紧紧地抓住他的左脚,而他的右手拿着一把奇怪的长刀企图把他变形的左脚切下来。在尔旦还没有开口要他停止时,陆判官急忙解释他正将他的变形左脚换上只好脚,因为他刚找到一只完好的左脚。他要尔旦不要移动,换脚的工作马上就要完成了。
A few weeks later, one night Erdan was awakened by a pressure on his left foot. He opened his eyes and was shocked to find that his ghost friend, Judge Lu, was using his left hand to hold his left foot tightly, and that his right hand was grasping a strange long knife trying to cut his deformed left foot off. Before Erdan could ask him to stop, Judge Lu quickly explained that he was replacing his deformed foot with a normal one that he had just found. He wanted Erdan not to move, as he was just about to finish the switch.

一分钟后,陆判官高兴地告诉尔旦:"我的工作已经完成了,你现在可以站起来试着走走,看是不是行了。"

聊斋精选

One minute later, Judge Lu told Erdan happily, "My work has been done. You may now stand up and try to walk to see if it is all right."

尔旦下床着地后,惊喜地发现他果然有了一只和右脚一样好的左脚,于是他在房间内走了一圈。

Erdan got out of his bed and onto the ground. He was elated to find that he indeed had a perfect left foot as good as his right one. He started to walk around the room.

"真是妙极了!"他兴奋地告诉他的鬼朋友,"我现在能和其他的人一样正常地走路了。真是非常感激你,我的好朋友。"

"Great!" he said excitedly to his ghost friend, " I can now walk as normally as everybody else. Thank you very much, my good friend."

这个换脚手术前后不过是几分钟光景,连一滴血也没有流出,一点儿也不感到疼痛,而且还一点看不到伤口。这刚换的左脚就好像右脚一样正常。

The foot transplant took only a few minutes without a single drop of blood being spilled and with zero pain. And not even a scar could be seen. The replaced foot appeared just like the other natural one.

自从这次出乎意料的成功换脚手术后,尔旦开始相信陆判官的神功可以完成世间凡人所不能做到的甚至于想都不敢想的事情。

After the unexpected successful foot transplant, Erdan began to believe that Judge Lu's supernatural power could accomplish the work a normal human could not do or even imagine.

一天夜里,当他们喝了差不多一整瓶的酒后,他问他的鬼判官朋友:"我是否可以再请你帮我一个大忙? 我的妻子和我已经结婚多年了,她对我很好,我们相互恩爱。惟一不太满意的就是她的脸蛋儿不是很美丽。以前我有一只跛脚,我还能批评什么呢。现在我的左脚正常了,我不知道能否请你把她的脸蛋也弄得漂亮?"

One night, after having finished almost an entire bottle of liquor, he asked his ghost judge friend, "May I ask you to do me another big favor? My wife and I have been married for many years. We love each other very much, and she is nice to me. But the only unsatisfactory thing about her is that her face is not very pretty. When I had a deformed foot, I could not criticize too much. Now that my left foot is normal, may I ask you to do something to make her face pretty?"

陆判官回答他可以做到,不过这要等一段时间。他要尔旦耐心地等待,同时也不要告诉他的妻子他们已经达成了这个秘密协议。

Judge Lu answered that he could do it, but it would take a little while. He wanted Erdan to have patience and not to tell his wife about the secret deal they had made.

几个月后,有一天半夜,陆判官来拜访尔旦,手里提着一只很重的袋子。他悄悄地告诉尔旦,他已经为他的妻子找到了一个漂亮的年轻女子头颅,这个女子刚死才一天。

One midnight several months later, Judge Lu came to Erdan's home carrying a heavy bag. He whispered to Erdan that he had found a pretty young woman's head for his wife. The woman had died only a day earlier.

当这两个朋友像往常一样地喝酒聊天时,尔旦的妻子到卧室里去睡觉了。当她熟睡之时,尔旦把他的鬼判官朋友带到他们的卧室里。陆判官拔出了刀立刻把这个熟睡中的女人的头切了下来,就好像人们用刀切西瓜一样。然后他赶快从袋子里拿出了一个美丽女人的头,迅速地将头安装在尔旦妻子的脖子上。一切就是这样的简单,和他上次替尔旦换脚一样,没有血也没有疼痛,而这个刚换过头的女人还在熟睡中什么也不知道呢。

While the two friends were drinking and talking as usual, Erdan's wife went to bed. When she was soundly asleep, Erdan took his ghost judge friend to their bedroom. Judge Lu took out his knife and quickly cut off the sleeping woman's head just as easily as people use a knife to cut watermelon. Then he swiftly took out the pretty woman's head from his bag and connected it to Erdan's wife's neck. That was it. As he did with Erdan's foot-replacement before, there was no blood and no pain, and the woman, who had just had a head transplant, was still soundly asleep, unaware of anything unusual.

第二天早上,尔旦的妻子起身后到洗手间去。当她和往常一样地照着镜子时,她突然吃惊地尖声大叫,"啊,天呀! 这镜子里面的美丽女子是谁啊?"

The next morning, when Erdan's wife woke up and went to the bathroom, she checked herself in the mirror as usual. She suddenly screamed sharply, "Oh, my goodness! Who is the pretty woman in the mirror?"

尔旦赶快走到她的身边,向她解释了昨天夜晚所发生的事情。当她明白了整件的事情后,她对换头的结果非常地满意和欣喜,并深深地感激她丈夫的精心设计。

Erdan quickly went to her side and explained what had happened last night. Once she understood, she was very delighted with the head-transplanting and deeply thanked her husband for his deliberate idea.

同时,在附近的一个集镇里发生了一件骇人听闻的案件。当地一位富有的中年男子的年轻美丽女儿死了。死后第二天的夜间,她的头突然被换为一个普通女人的头,可是她的身体却仍然是原样没有丝毫变形。换言之,头是别人的,而身体仍是他的死去的女儿的。在头与身体的接缝中也看不出任何痕迹。于是,这位男子赶快向当地官府报告要求调查这个神秘事件。可是官府人员也不知道应该从何处着手去调查。

Meanwhile, a horrible thing happened in a neighboring town. A wealthy middle-aged man's pretty daughter died. The next night, her head was suddenly exchanged with a homely looking woman's head, while the body remained in original condition as if nothing untoward had happened. It meant that the body was still his daughter's, but the head was not. And the connection between the newly dead girl's head and her body was seamless. The man quickly reported the event to the local government asking them to investigate the mysterious case. But the government had no clues with which to start the investigation.

不久,尔旦的邻居们发觉尔旦的妻子和以前不一样了。她的声音身材以及行动都没有变,可是她的脸蛋完全不同了。他们都感到困惑不已。几天后,当官府人员听到了这件奇异的事情时,他们立刻把尔旦妻子的容貌变化与邻镇的神秘换头事件相联系,于是控告尔旦和他的妻子以巫术来调换人头。

Soon, Erdan's neighbors noticed the difference in his wife. Her voice, figure, and actions was still the same, but her face was not. They were all confused. A few days later, when the government officials also heard of the strange occurrence, they immediately connected Erdan's wife's face change to the mysterious head-exchanging in a neighboring town, and charged Erdan and his wife using witchcraft to exchange heads.

尔旦和他的妻子吓坏了。那天夜里鬼判官来看望他们,他告诉他们不要担心,他已经安排好了,由这个女孩的鬼魂直接在梦里告诉她的父母。

Erdan and his wife were frightened. When the ghost judge came to visit them in the evening, he told them not to worry about it. He said that he had already arranged to let the dead girl's spirit tell her parents directly in a dream.

那天夜里,这对富人夫妇有一个相同的梦。在梦中,他们死去女儿的鬼魂告诉他们关于换头事件的整个经过。她说她对这件事情很高兴。她已经死了,可是她那美丽的脸蛋竟仍可留存在人世。她建议她的父母亲去把这个换头的女人认为义女,如此,每当他们思念她时就可以去拜访这个女人。

That night, both of the wealthy man and his wife had the same dream. In the dream, their dead daughter's spirit told them how the two heads had been exchanged. She said that she was very happy with the exchange. She had died, but her beautiful face would still exist in the human world. She advised her parents to adopt the head-exchanged woman as their daughter, so that whenever they missed her they could visit the woman.

梦醒后,这对富有夫妇接受了他们女儿的建议。他们要求官府撤销了对尔旦夫妇的指控,然后把尔旦的妻子认为义女。尔旦和他的妻子都自幼就没有了父母,如今尔旦突然变成了这对富有夫妇的女婿,他的妻子也有了义父义母。

After waking up, the wealthy couple took their daughter's advice. They asked the government to drop the charge against Erdan and his wife. They adopted Erdan's wife as their daughter. Erdan and his wife had both lost their parents when they were young. Now Erdan suddenly become the son-in-law of the wealthy couple and his wife had adopted parents.

陆判官仍时常在夜里来拜访尔旦。他现在不但被尔旦也被他那美丽的妻子热情欢迎,有时还会被他们那富有的义父母及岳父母所欢迎。

Judge Lu continued to visit Erdan in the evening. He was warmly welcomed by not only Erdan but also by his pretty wife, and sometimes even by their wealthy adoptive parents and parents-in-law.

三、

聂

小

倩

The Demon's Girl

夜色已经降落大地。宁采臣,一个孤单的旅行者,在这个完全陌生的小集镇里到处找不到旅店或者任何可以栖身的地方。所有的店铺和住宅在这个时候都关门了。他尽力寻找,只发现在一条很窄的死巷内一座古老的佛教庙宇门还是开着的。他敲了门,可是没有人回应。于是他走了进去。在那七月的皎洁月光下,他发现满院长着野草,到处都是脏物,显然这是一座荒庙,没有僧侣或任何人居住于此。

Darkness had already descended over the land. Ning Caichen, a lonely traveler, could not find a hotel or lodging of any kind in the unfamiliar small town. All the shops and dwellings were closed. As much as he had tried, he only found an old Buddhist temple with the door still open at the dead end of a narrow lane. He knocked on the door, but nobody answered. So he entered. In the bright July moonlight, he found that the weeds grew wild in the yard, and dirt abounded everywhere. Obviously, it was an abandoned shrine with no monks or anyone else living there.

采臣进入了一间空屋。他把两片破木门板拼在一块儿作为临时的床。

Caichen went into an empty room. He put two broken wooden doors together to fashion a temporary bed.

"虽然睡在上面并不太舒服,可是总比睡在那野草丛生院子里的肮脏地上好多了,"他自语着说。

It will not be very comfortable to sleep on, but it is much better than sleeping on the dirty ground in a yard filled with wild weeds, he told himself.

就在刚刚躺下时,他听到了脚步声。他坐起身,看到了一个有胡子的男子提着一个大旅行袋子走进庙来。他立刻站起来走去向这个人打招呼。这个人说他也是一个旅行者,已经于前一天在这庙里住了一晚了。他告诉采臣不必担心睡在这儿,因为这是一座多年不用的荒庙,没有人会在乎他们在这儿留宿的。这人向采臣道了晚安后便去另一个房间睡觉了。

After he had lain down, he heard footsteps. He sat up and saw a bearded man carrying a large traveling bag enter the temple. He immediately stood up and went to greet the man. The man said that he was also a traveler and had spent a night there the night before. He told Caichen not to worry about sleeping there, as the temple had been abandoned for years and nobody would care. The man wished Caichen a good night and went to the other room to sleep.

采臣回到他的房间再度躺在这个临时凑合的床上。

Caichen returned to his room and lay down again on the makeshift bed.

刚闭起眼睛时,他听到了窗外有人说话的声音。于是,他站起身来走到窗前向外窥视,他看到三个人坐在院中一个水塘旁边讲话。在那皎洁的月光下,他看到两个年长的女人和一个年轻的女子。女子有着姣好的身材,穿着红色的衣服。一个年长的女人问这个女子近来找到情人没有,女子冷冷地回答她还在寻找中。

As he closed his eyes, he heard a conversation outside the window. He got up and moved to the window to take a peek. He saw three people sitting and chatting by a pond in the yard. In the bright harvest moonlight, he saw two older women and one girl. The girl had a delicate figure and was dressed in red. One of the two older women asked the girl whether she had found a sweetheart lately. To which she coolly replied that she was still lookingfor.

采臣是一个正派的人,他不喜欢去偷听别人的私话,更何况是女人间的事情。所以他就回到床上去睡觉了。

Caichen was a decent man. He disliked overhearing other people's private conversations, especially women's affairs. So he went back to bed to sleep.

刚睡着不久,他被人弄醒了。睁开眼睛一看,他很惊讶地发现一个穿着红色衣服的女子站在他的床边,采臣立刻认出她就是刚才他所看到的院子里那个年轻女子。因为她站得离他很近,他发现这个女孩长得很美,大约十八九岁或二十岁刚出头。这个女孩甜甜地自我介绍是这座庙宇的邻居。然后,她用一只光溜溜的脚趾去轻戳采臣的私处。

The moment he fell asleep, he was awakened. He opened his eyes and was surprised to find a girl dressed in red standing by his bed. Caichen immediately recognized her as the girl he had spied on in the yard a little while before. As she stood close to him, he noticed that she was a very pretty girl in her late teens or early twenties. The girl sweetly introduced herself as a neighbor of the temple. Then she reached out with one of her naked feet and gently brushed against Caichen's private parts.

"喂,"这个美丽的女子以极其挑逗的口吻直接问道,"要不要和我在这么美丽的夏夜里做爱?"

"Hey," the pretty girl said directly and seductively, "how about letting us make love on such a lovely summer night?"

当采臣因为太惊讶了还没有来得及回答时,她又说:"这是没有人会知道的。"

While Caichen was too surprised to answer, she added, "Nobody will know it."

这后加的一句使得采臣更为愤怒。他坐起身来,推开这女子的脚。"不,"他大声地告诉她,"如此的淫荡行为将有损你我两人的名誉。夜已深了,年轻女子,你还是回家去吧。"

The last comment made Caichen even angrier than the first suggestion. He sat up, pushing away the girl's foot. "No," he answered loudly, "Such a casual action would ruin both your and my reputation. It's getting late, young lady. You would better go home."

"你真是一个愚蠢的乡巴佬，"这个女子淫猥地笑着说，"在这荒郊野庙里有谁会知道你做事规矩与否？"

"You are indeed a stupid peasant," the girl giggled sexily, "This is a deserted temple. Who would know if you do something immoral or not?"

接着她就要脱掉衣服爬上他的床。采臣立刻阻止她的举动。他对这个无耻的女子大发雷霆。

Then she tried to take off her clothes and get on his bed. Caichen stopped her immediately. He was furious with the shameless woman.

"天和地会看到，菩萨和鬼魂会看到。你怎么可以说没有谁会知道？"他尖厉地斥骂这个放肆的年轻女子，指着门厉声要她离去。

"Heaven and Earth would see. Buddha and ghosts would see. How could you say nobody would know?" He sharply scolded the wanton young woman and pointed at the door harshly demanding that she leave.

突然间，女孩低下了头，将那淫荡的表情转为严肃，缓缓地走了出去。

Suddenly, the girl hung her head and her lustful expression changed to one of gravity. She left the room slowly.

没有几分钟后，她又回来了，手上拿着一把银币。她把银币放在采臣的床上，告诉他愿意以这些银币来交换性行为。

A few minutes later, she came back with a handful of silver coins in one hand. She set the money on Caichen's bed and told him that she wanted to trade it for sex.

如此的一个邪恶要求使得采臣相信这个女孩真是卑鄙得不可救药了。于是他捡起银币向她甩去，并且向她吼道："滚！滚开，你这个无耻的女人！"

The vile offer forced Caichen to believe that the girl was even more despicable and hopeless. Picking up the coins and throwing them at her, he yelled, "Go! Go away, you, shameless woman!"

女孩收拾起银币，可还在犹豫是否要走，采臣威胁着说如果她再不走，他就去叫醒睡在另一个房间里的有胡子的男子，请他帮忙赶走她。听了这个威胁，女孩立刻跑走了。

The girl gathered up the coins but still hesitated. Caichen threatened that if she refused to go, he would wake up the bearded traveler in the other room to help him expel her. Upon hearing this threat, the woman ran out immediately.

聊斋精选

第二天早晨,采臣起身后去城里办事。因为事情没有办完,他决定再在这里停留一天。虽然睡在破门板上并不舒服,可这是免费的。为了省钱,他计划在这庙里再住一个晚上。

The next morning after getting up, Caichen went downtown to conduct business. Because he did not finish his business, he decided to stay in town for one more day. Although sleeping on the broken wooden doors was not comfortable, it was free. In order to save money, he planned to spend one more night in the deserted temple.

当他刚躺下准备睡觉时,这个女子又回来了。这一次,她的举止可是庄重多了。她直接告诉采臣她不是人,她是鬼。她的名字叫聂小倩。她含泪地说她被一个强有力的妖魔所控制,妖魔强迫她色诱狐媚孤单的旅客使其昏迷,然后妖魔来吸食这个男子的血液直到这人死亡为止。她前一晚用来诱惑他的银币并不是真正的银币,那些都是被妖魔吸光血后的死人的磨光骨头。因为她没有达成迷惑采臣的使命,她很肯定这个妖魔今夜会亲自来取采臣的性命。她建议采臣立刻去到另一个房间和那个有胡子的男子同住,因为那个人是一名剑客,妖魔可能不敢跟他交手。

As soon as he lay down to sleep, the same girl returned. This time she behaved much more decently. She told Caichen directly that she was not a human. She was a ghost. Her name was Nie Xiaoqian. She said in tears that she was under the control of a powerful demon that forced her to seduce and bewitch any lone traveler to make the man lose consciousness. After that, the demon would come and suck the man's blood until he died. The silver coins she had used to try to tempt him the night before were not real coins, but the reshaped bones of the demon's victims. Since she had failed to seduce him, she was sure that the demon himself would come to take his life that night. She advised him to move in and share the room with the bearded man immediately as that man was a swordsman. The demon might not dare to approach him.

这下子采臣恐惧了。他感谢这个女鬼救了他的一命,并问她他如何可以报答她的大恩。

Then, Caichen was frightened. He thanked the female ghost for saving his life and asked her how he could repay her favor.

"我一直企图逃脱妖魔的掌控,可是没有成功,因为我的坟墓在这庙宇的后院子里。"她向他哭诉她的悲惨经历。

"I have been trying hard for a long time to free myself from the demon's control but I could not get free, because my grave is in the backyard of the temple." She cried bitterly as she was telling him her sad story.

她恳求他:"如果你能打开我的坟墓将我的棺材挖出,在你回家的时候把我的棺材带回家去,葬在你家的后院,我就可以逃脱这个妖魔的控制了。"

She begged him, "If you could dig up my grave and take my coffin with you when you leave for home

聊斋精选

and rebury it at your backyard, I would be safe from the demon's control."

采臣当即应允,于是这个女鬼快乐地含着眼泪走了。
Caichen promised without hesitation. And the female ghost left happily, with tears still in her eyes.

采臣立刻去到那另一个房间,他叫醒了有胡子的男子,把女鬼所说的话告诉了他。这个男子同意采臣留在他的房间里,同时,他从他的旅行袋中掏出了一只陈旧的皮制剑鞘子,里面有一支短剑,他把剑鞘放在窗台上,就又去睡觉了。但是采臣因为太恐惧了而不敢入睡。他躺在床上,两眼圆睁,恐惧地望着窗户。
Caichen immediately went to the other room. He woke up the bearded man and told him what the female ghost had told him. The man allowed Caichen to stay with him. Meanwhile, he took out an old leather sheath with a short sword in it from his traveling bag and left it on the windowsill. Then he went back to sleep. But Caichen was too frightened to do so. He lay on the bed with eyes wide open watching the window in fear.

午夜刚过,采臣看到一个丑陋的男子在窗口出现,眼睛大如鹅卵,两颗长牙从血盆大嘴中外露出来,蓝色的头发几乎根根竖立。采臣想,这一定就是小倩所说的妖魔了。
Shortly after midnight, Caichen saw an ugly guy show up at the window. His eyes were as big as goose eggs and two long teeth protruded out from an enormous bloody mouth. His blue hair stood at end. *It must be the demon Xiaoqian mentioned*, Caichen thought.

在采臣还没有叫醒他的同室男子时,他发现一道闪电从皮剑鞘中射出,几乎是同时,闪电又射回鞘中,而妖魔已消失得无影无踪了。一切都发生在一霎那间。
Before Caichen could wake up his roommate, he noticed a flash of light shooting out of the sheath. Almost instantly, the light flashed back into the sheath, and the demon disappeared. The whole thing happened in seconds.

就在这个时候,这个有胡子的男子醒来了。他站起身来从皮鞘中拔出短剑,就着月光一看,他告诉惊魂未定的采臣这个狡猾的妖魔逃掉了,可是他相信这妖魔一定受了重伤。
Just at this moment, the bearded man woke up. He stood up and took out the sword from the sheath, and checked it in the moonlight. Then he told the frightened Caichen that the crafty demon had escaped, but he was sure the demon must have been badly injured.

采臣感激这个男子的救命之恩,并问道他是否可以跟他学习剑术。男子告诉他这是很不容易的,而且采臣也不是属于学剑术的这一类人。他把短剑放在袋子里的一个新的鞘子里,而把这个旧皮鞘子送给

聊斋精选

了采臣。

Caichen thanked the man deeply for saving his life and asked if he could learn swordsmanship from him. The man told him that it was not easy, and Caichen was not the sort of person to learn it. However, the man presented him with his old leather sheath as a gift and he put his sword in a new sheath he had in his bag.

"这个陈旧的剑鞘曾经浸过了无数妖魔鬼怪的血液,是有神力可以镇伏鬼魂之类的妖怪的,假如这个逃脱的妖魔再来找你麻烦的话,它就可以保护你。"他告诉采臣。

"This old leather sheath has been soaked with the blood of countless devils and demons. It has the power to quell evil spirits and protect you in case the escaped demon finds you in the future," he told Caichen.

采臣收下了礼品并再度深深地感谢。

Caichen accepted the gift with many thanks again.

第二天早晨,采臣去到庙宇的后院子里找到了小倩的坟墓,他把坟墓打开,雇了一辆拖车,假称棺材里的尸体是他死去的妹妹,他要把妹妹的棺材运回家去。到家后,他把小倩的棺材重新安葬在他家的后院里。

The next morning, Caichen went to the backyard of the temple and found Xiaoqian's grave. He dug up the grave and hired a carriage man to take Xiaoqian's coffin to his home, pretending that the coffin held the body of his dead sister. After reaching home, he reburied Xiaoqian's coffin in the backyard of his house.

那天晚上,小倩出现在他的书房窗子外面。采臣出去邀请她进来。她犹豫着说房间里面有一件非常神秘具有威力的东西,她不敢进屋。采臣明白了一定是那个有胡子的剑客送他的旧皮剑鞘子。于是他赶快把剑鞘放在另一个房间,然后她走了进来。进得门后,她向采臣跪下,感激他把她带出了魔掌。采臣立即把她扶起。小倩说为了报答他的恩情,她愿意当他家一个不要报酬的婢女。

That evening, Xiaoqian appeared outside of the window of his den. Caichen went out inviting her to enter, but she hesitated, saying that she dared not as something very strange and powerful was hidden in the room. Caichen realized that it must be the bearded swordsman's old leather sheath. He quickly removed the sheath to another room, and she appeared in the room. After entering, she knelt down in front of him to thank him for bringing her out of the demon's control. Caichen helped her up. In order to return his kindness, Xiaoqian offered to be a maid for his family without pay.

采臣已经结婚好几年了,他的妻子玉玲一年来经常生病,近来更是大多数的时间都躺在床上。家务几乎都是采臣的寡母担当。当他告诉母亲及妻子关于小倩愿意做他们家的婢女时,这两个妇人都害怕见这个女鬼。

Caichen had been married for several years. His wife, Yuling, had often been sick in the past year, and

聊斋精选

27

lately she spent even more days in bed. Caichen's widowed mother did most of the housework. After he told his mother and his wife about Xiaoqian's offer to be a maid, the two women were afraid to meet the ghost girl.

一天晚上,当这两个妇人偶然在采臣的书房里遇见了小倩时,她们一致认为这真是一个可爱的女孩。从此以后,小倩每天晚上都来帮助他的母亲和妻子处理各项家务,而且每一件事情都做得很好。采臣的母亲非常喜欢小倩,并把她当作女儿一样看待,小倩也把老妇人当做自己的亲生母亲一样地孝顺,玉玲非常感激小倩代她做家务及孝敬婆婆。换言之,这三人一鬼就好像一家人似的亲密地生活着。

One evening, when the two women happened to meet Xiaoqian at Caichen's den, they felt that she was indeed a very lovely young girl. Since that time, Xiaoqian came in every evening to help his mother and his wife do the household chores and she did everything very well. Caichen's mother loved Xiaoqian very much and treated her like her own daughter. Xiaoqian also respected the old lady like her own mother. Yuling deeply appreciated Xiaoqian's helping her do the housework and taking care of her mother-in-law. In other words, the three people and one ghost lived as closely as a happy family.

因为小倩是个鬼,她只能在晚间出现。每当这三个人要睡觉了,她就依依不舍地回到她的坟墓里去。

As a ghost, Xiaoqian could only appear after dark, and she would leave unwillingly for her grave when the three people were ready to go to bed.

一天,采臣的母亲也生病了。晚间小倩来后,她必须单独去做所有的家务,还要照顾两个生病的妇人。当睡眠的时间来了,小倩又准备像往常一样地回到她的坟墓里去时,采臣的母亲把她留下了,要小倩和她同睡在一张床上,如果她在夜间需要什么时,小倩也可以照顾她。

One day, Caichen's mother became sick, too. In the evening, Xiaoqian came and she had to do all the housework alone, as well as take care of two sick women. When bedtime came, as usual, she was ready to return to her grave. Caichen's mother asked her to stay and sleep with her on the same bed so that when she needed help in the night, Xiaoqian would be there.

可是第二天早上,当采臣的母亲醒来后,她发现小倩早已在天未亮前回到她的坟墓里去了。老太太告诉她的儿子,如果小倩能在白天也留下,那该多好。

But when Caichen's mother woke up in the morning, she found that Xiaoqian had already left for her grave before dawn. The old lady told her son that it would be truly wonderful if Xiaoqian could also stay with them in the daytime.

一年后,玉玲的健康一天比一天坏。终于,她完全不能起床了。小倩细心照顾,包括每日的床上喂饭及擦洗她的身子和清洁床铺,不管如何肮脏,她都毫无怨言。玉玲感激小倩不已,经常拉着她的手说她真不知道如何去报答她的恩情。

A year later, Yuling's health worsened daily. Finally, she could not get up at all. Xiaoqian took care of her as carefully as possible including feeding her in bed and bathing her and cleaning the bed every evening without complaint, no matter how dirty they were. Yuling appreciated her help greatly, often holding her hand saying that she did not know how to repay her kindness.

当玉玲的病情危急时,她知道她是活不长久了。她要求她的丈夫和婆婆及小倩来到她的床前,她说她知道她的生命快到尽头了。她请求他们为她祈祷,不是为她的健康祈祷,而是向阎罗王恩求在她死后让小倩借她的尸体还魂重新为人。假如她的恩求能够实现的话,她请求采臣和小倩结婚,如此这三个人的家庭在她死后仍能够延续下去。这也是她惟一能够报答小倩的方式。她很肯定小倩将来一定会是个贤良的妻子和媳妇。如此她将死而无憾了。

When Yuling's condition became critical, she knew that she would not live long. She asked her husband and mother-in-law and Xiaoqian to come by her bedside. She said that she realized that her life was going to end soon. She asked them to pray, not for her health, but to the grand ruler of ghost world to allow Xiaoqian to be revived in her body as a human again after she died. If her wish could be met, she asked Caichen to marry Xiaoqian, and the family of three would survive without her. That was the only way she could think of repaying Xiaoqian's favor. She was sure that Xiaoqian would be a nice wife and daughter-in-law. If this could happen, she said she would die without any regrets.

这个将死妇人的请求把三位都感动得热泪盈眶,他们告诉玉玲,如果能实现,他们将尽力照着她的愿望去做。

The dying woman's request moved all the three to tears. They told Yuling that if it could be done, they would do their best to fulfill her wishes.

不久,玉玲安详地过世了。小倩跪下向死者致她最后的敬意,然后站起身来向尸体扑去。小倩果然借尸还魂又成为一个人了。

Soon Yuling passed away peacefully. Xiaoqian knelt down to pay her last respect to the dead woman. Then she stood up, rushing toward the corpse. And she was indeed revived in the newly dead woman's body as a human again.

复活后,其身体和形象都还是玉玲的,可是她的思想和声音则是小倩的。而最重要的是她现在是一个健康的妇人了。采臣的母亲迅速为她的儿子和小倩举行了一个简单的婚礼,以后他们便是一对夫妇了。两人恩爱得就像一般的新婚夫妇一样。采臣的母亲也很高兴,因为从此以后,小倩便不必再回到坟墓里而在白天也可以和她一起生活了。

After reincarnation, the body and appearance were Yuling's, but the mind and voice were Xiaoqian's.

Most importantly, she became a healthy woman. Caichen's mother quickly held a wedding ceremony for her son and Xiaoqian. After that, they started a new life as husband and wife. They loved each other just like a couple of newlyweds. Caichen's mother was happy, too, as Xiaoqian did not have to leave for grave and could also stay with her during the daytime.

一天，小倩对采臣说不知道为什么她就是突然感觉非常心神不安，她很害怕那个在破庙里的妖魔可能已经找到了她在何处，而赶来惩罚她的背叛和逃跑。她要采臣把那个神秘剑客送给他的旧皮剑鞘子放在他们卧室的窗台上，然后再上床睡觉。那天夜晚，这两个人都不敢真的睡着，他们眼睁睁地望着窗户。

One day, Xiaoqian told Caichen that she did not know the reason why but suddenly felt terribly uneasy that day. She was afraid that the demon in the abandoned temple might have discovered where she was, and was coming over to punish her for her rebellion and escape. She asked Caichen to take out the old leather sheath that had been given to him by the mysterious swordsman. They put the sheath on the windowsill in their bedroom before going to bed. Neither of the two dared sleep that night. They kept their eyes on the window.

午夜刚过，这个妖魔真的来了。当他冲向采臣和小倩的卧室时，他突然发现了窗台上的皮鞘子，于是立刻停止前行并退回了几步。一会儿，他又冲了过来，并且想用手去抓这皮鞘子。就在这个时候，采臣和小倩看见了一道闪电从皮鞘中射出，然后又退回鞘内，同时这对受惊的夫妇听到了一声刺耳的尖叫，接着一切又归于平静，就好像什么事情也不曾发生过似的。

Soon after midnight, the demon did come. As he was rushing into Caichen and Xiaoqian's bedroom, he suddenly noticed the leather sheath. He stopped advancing and retreated a few steps. After a while, he rushed forward again and tried to grab the sheath. At the same time, Caichen and Xiaoqian saw a flash of light shoot out of the sheath then retreat back to the sheath, and the frightened couple heard a sharp scream. After that, everything became quiet, as if nothing had happened.

采臣和小倩一同起身，走到了窗前。把皮鞘子拿过来一看，发现里面装满了恶臭的血。小倩兴奋地告诉采臣这个妖魔终于被杀死了。夫妻两人紧紧地相抱，很长时间一句话也说不出来。

Caichen and Xiaoqian got up and walked to the window. Picking up the sheath, they found it was filled up with foul blood. Xiaoqian told Caichen excitedly that the demon had finally been killed. The couple hugged each other tightly without saying a word for a long time.

一年后小倩生了一对双胞胎儿子。采臣高兴地发现一个男孩长得像玉玲，另一个长得像以前的小倩。等两个儿子长大了以后，他们告诉儿子们关于他们母亲的故事，这两个年轻人非常高兴地说他们有两个母亲可又是同一个人。

聊斋精选

聊斋精选

A year later, Xiaoqian gave birth to twin sons. Caichen happily found that one boy looked like Yuling and the other one looked like what Xiaoqian used to look. When the two boys grew older, they told their sons about their mother's story. The two young men were glad to say that they had two mothers but in one person.

聊斋精选

A year later, Xiaoqian gave birth to twin sons. Caichen happily found that one boy looked like Yuling and the other one looked like what Xiaoqian used to look. When the two boys grew older, they told their sons about their mother's story. The two young men were glad to say that they had two mothers but in one person.

聊斋精选

四、

梅女

An Avenging Spirit

从 6 世纪的隋朝开始,直到 1912 年清朝被推翻建立民国为止,中国的王朝一直都是以公开的科举考试方式去任用政府官吏的。由于考试的内容完全取材自中国的经典,因此,在那个年头里,凡是有抱负的年轻男子都勤奋地攻读经书。

Since the Sui Dynasty in the sixth century, the Chinese monarchy had always employed government officials by way of public examinationsuntil 1912 when the Qing Dynasty was overthrown and the republic was founded. As the subjects on the examinations were all derived from the Chinese classics, all the ambitious young men studied the classics as diligently as they could in those years.

封云就是其中的一个年轻男子。为了可以专心读书,他在京城里租了一栋房子,准备参加来年朝廷举办的考试。

Feng Yun was one of those young men. In order to concentrate on his studies, he rented a house in the capital to prepare for the coming year's examination held by the imperial court.

一个阴雨的晚间,当封云在油灯下研读经书时,突然发现在他坐着的对面白色粉墙上有一个人的影子。起初他认为这只不过是一个幻觉罢了,并没有把它放在心上,仍去继续读他的书。一会儿后,当他抬起头来再看时,很惊奇地发现这个人影子仍在,而且比刚才还更清楚。

One rainy evening, while Feng Yun was studying by the light of an oil lamp, he suddenly noticed a person's shadow on the white wall opposite where he was sitting. At first, he thought it might be an illusion, so he ignored it and kept studying. After a while, when he lifted up his head and looked again, he was surprised to find that the shadow of a person remained there and that it was even clearer.

他把书放下,站起来走近墙边再看,果然发现这是一个女人的影子。她的舌头长长地伸出嘴巴外面,颈子上还挂着一根绳子。假如是一个普通的人在这么一个夜深人静时看到了这么一个情景,一定会把魂都吓掉了。可是封云是一个很有胆量的人,他一点儿也不害怕。从他所看到的,他明白这是一个吊死的女鬼。

He put down his book, stood up, and moved a little closer to the wall to look again. Sure enough, it was the shadow of a woman with her tongue extended and a rope around her neck. If an ordinary person had seen this so late in the evening, that person might be scared to death. But Feng Yun was a very courageous man. He was not afraid at all. From what he had seen, he realized that it must be the ghost of a woman who had died by hanging.

"我知道你是谁,"封云对着影子大声地说,"显身出来告诉我你有什么困难,也许我能够帮助你。"

"I know who you are," Feng Yun said to the shadow loudly, "Show yourself, and tell me your problem, Maybe I can help you."

影子投到地上立刻变成了一个美丽的年轻女子。

聊斋精选

The shadow fell to the ground and immediately turned into a pretty young woman.

"谢谢你要我显身，"她感激地轻声说，"十七年前因为一件冤案使我在这栋房子里上吊自杀。多少年来我一直在寻找帮助，可是所有住在这栋房子里的人在看到了我的影子后都吓得赶快搬走。你是惟一的一位要我显身说出我困苦的人。"

"Thank you for asking me to show up," she said gently and appreciatively. "Seventeen years ago, a great grievance made me hang myself in this house. Since then, I have been looking for help, but all the people in the house were scared and moved away soon after I showed them my shadow. You are the first person asking me to appear and tell you my problem."

她恳请封云去要求房东将天花板上她上吊处的横梁烧毁而换上一根新的。如果能够实现的话，她的舌头就不必经常伸出嘴巴外面，而围在她颈上的那根绳子也就会脱落了。

She requested that Feng Yun ask the landlord to remove and burn the beam in the ceiling where she had hung herself, and replace it with a new one. If it could be done, her tongue would not have to extend out of her mouth most of the time, and the rope around her neck would be released.

封云毫不犹豫立刻应允为她一试，这个女子道谢了以后便不见了踪影。

Without hesitation, Feng Yun promised that he would try. Then the woman thanked him and disappeared.

第二天，当封云和房主提起这件事情时，房主承认这栋房子的确闹过鬼，不过他不愿意将横梁换新，因为这将花费太多的钱。于是封云威胁如果不办，他将向官府要求重新调查当年那个女子上吊自杀的神秘案件。房主害怕了，只好答应办理。旧的横梁终于被拆下烧毁而换上一根新的。

The next day, when Feng Yun discussed this matter with his landlord, the owner of the house admitted that the house was haunted, but he was reluctant to replace the beam, as it would cost him too much money. Feng Yun threatened to ask the government to reopen and reinvestigate the mysterious case of a woman's hanging if the beam could not be replaced. The landlord was frightened and gave in. The old beam was finally removed and burned, and replaced with a new one.

当新的横梁被换上的那天晚上，这个女鬼又出现在这栋房子里。她对封云的帮助深深地感激。她告诉他她的闺名叫梅女。十七年前，她和父母住在这栋房子里。有一天夜晚，一个小偷潜入她家偷东西，被她的父母发现抓住了，他们迅即把贼送交官府。这个罪犯贿赂县官说是来她家私会他的情人梅女的，因为梅女的父母不赞成他们相会。贪官受贿后把小偷无罪释放了。不公的判决使梅女感觉极大的羞辱，愤而自缢，表示抗议。一年后，她的父母双亡，这个贪官也被调到别的省份去了。她的灵魂则长留在这栋房子里遭受一年又一年的劫难，一直到她遇见了封云帮助她解除了她的苦痛。

聊斋精选

The evening after a new beam had been put up, the female ghost appeared again in the house. She deeply thanked Feng Yun for his help. She told him her name was Meinü. Seventeen years ago, she and her parents lived in the house. One night, a thief snuck into the house looking for items to steal. The thief was discovered and caught by her parents, who promptly turned him over to the government. The criminal bribed the judge, saying that he had sneaked into the house to meet his sweetheart, Meinü, as her parents objected to their dating. The corrupt judge took the bribe and released the thief. The false judgment made Meinü feel terribly humiliated. She hanged herself in protest. A year later, both her parents died, and the corrupt judge was transferred to another province. Her spirit had since been left in the house to suffer year after year until she met Feng Yun who helped her release her pain.

从此,梅女每天夜晚都来。她帮助封云烧饭洗衣服及做其它的所有家务,完全负起了一个贤良家庭主妇的责任,如此封云可以专心去读书。

After that, Meinü appeared every evening. She helped Feng Yun do the cooking and washing as well as all the other household chores, acting like a nice housewife so Feng Yun could concentrate on his studies.

终于,他们坠入了爱河,他们时常拥抱和接吻。一天夜晚,当封云企图将她抱到床上去,她突然悲伤地哭了起来。

Gradually, they fell in love. They often hugged and kissed. One evening, when Feng Yun tried to take her to bed, she suddenly cried out bitterly.

"如果我让你和我做爱,"她含着眼泪说,"那么我以往多年的冤情将永远无法洗清了。"

"If I let you make love to me," she said with tears in her eyes, "the cause of all those years of my grievance will never be redressed."

梅女的眼泪终于浇冷了封云的欲火。他告诉她他尊重她的决定,并向她保证以后再也不会如此了。于是她向他保证,当时候到来时,她定会满足他的要求的。封云问她这个时候何时到来,她娇羞地回答:"请耐心地等待。"

Meinü's tears finally made Feng Yun cool down. He told her that he would respect her decision and assured her he would never try to do it again. Then she assured him that when the time came, she would let him do whatever he wanted. But when Feng Yun asked her when, she replied shyly and sweetly, "Please wait with patience."

夏天过去,秋天来了。封云去参加三年才举办一次的最激烈的考试,结果落榜了。对于一个像封云这样有政治抱负的年轻人来说,这当然打击很大,一时意气消沉。

After summer, when the fall came, Feng Yun went to take the most grueling examination that was held once every three years. He failed. For a young man with political ambitions like Feng Yun, he was naturally crushed and upset.

梅女安慰他说,"你有很多才华,仍可以做很多有意义的事情。世界上有很多成功的人都没有通过任何的官府考试。反言之,很多的人通过了考试得到了官位,却做尽了各种坏事,就像那个贪官一样逼得我去上吊。因此,只因为你落选了,这并不就是说你不会成为一个正直和受人尊敬的人。"

Meinü comforted him, "You have many talents. You are able to do many meaningful things. Many people, who have been successful, never passed any kind of government examinations. On the other hand, many people who have passed the government examinations and become government official, committed all kind of evils, like the corrupt judge who made me hang myself. Therefore, just because you failed, it does not mean that you will not become a just and respectable person."

终于封云听从了她的解说,又提起了精神。
Finally, Feng Yun heeded her words and became cheerful again.

因为考试已经结束了,他没有继续留在京城的必要。他必须回家和他的家人团聚,他们住在另一个省份。
Now that the examination was over, he had no reason to remain in the capital. He must go home to be with his family in another province.

"可是,"他对她说,"我实在不愿意再让你单独留在这栋房子里。"
"But," he said to her, "I hate to leave you alone in the house again."

"我也早已想到了这点,"她说,"在你回家以前,可否再帮我一个大忙?"
"I have thought of it, too," she said, "Before going home, would you do me another big favor?"

她说她已经找到了那个贪官现在的住处,因为距离京城尚有数百里之遥,她无法走去,她要求他带她去那儿,好让她亲自报仇雪恨。她拿出了一个小瓶子,她告诉他,白天他旅行时,她可以藏在瓶子里,晚上他住进了旅店后,她就可以从瓶中出来与他共度一宵。
She said that she had found out where the corrupt judge was. It was several hundred miles away from the capital, too far for her to walk. She asked him to take her there so she could avenge her own death upon him. She showed him a small bottle and told him that she could hide in it while he traveled during the daytime. In the evening after he checked into a lodging, she would come out of the bottle and spend the night with him.

聊斋精选

聊斋精选

封云愉快地答应了。
Feng Yun promised happily.

经过了好多天的旅程,他们终于到达了梅女所说那个贪官居住的地方。封云向当地的人士打听了一下,发现大家都痛恨这个为非作歹的县官。
After many days of travel, they reached the place where Meinü said the corrupt judge had relocated. Feng Yun checked around and found that all the local people hated the judge for his evil behavior and unjust rulings.

在封云和梅女到达后的第二天,当地就传说这个遭人痛恨的县官在前一天夜晚被人神秘地扼死了,没有人知道这是谁做的以及如何做的,可是人人称快。
On the second day after Feng Yun and Meinü had arrived at the place, news spread among the local people saying that the loathed judge had been mysteriously strangled to death the night before. Nobody knew who had murdered him or how, but everybody was happy about his death.

报了大仇以后,梅女深情款款地问封云:"你仍爱我吗?"
After the revenge had been taken against her enemy, Meinü asked Feng Yun affectionately, "Do you still love me?"

封云把她紧紧地抱在怀中,以坚定的口吻告诉她:"只要能使你快乐,我愿意为你做任何事情。"
Feng Yun hugged her tightly in his arms and told her positively, "I would like to do whatever to make you happy."

"那么,"她神秘地回答,"现在是你实现诺言的时候了。"
"Well," she said mysteriously, "now it is the time to make your words good."

根据梅女所说,在她吊死后不久,阎罗王就安排她重新投胎成为一对富有夫妇最小的女儿。因为她一心想亲自报仇,所以她压根儿就没有去到那个女孩的身体里。现在这个少女虽然长得很美丽,却是个没有灵魂的白痴。这对富有的夫妇曾经带她看过很多医生,可是没有一个人可以找出她的病因。这个女孩现在已经十七岁了,她的父母亲非常担心他们女儿的终身大事,因为没有一个男子愿意去娶一个如此智力不足的女孩。
According to Meinü, soon after she had hanged herself, the grand ruler of the ghost world arranged for her to be reborn as a wealthy couple's youngest daughter. Because she planned to take revenge on her tormentor, she never actually went to the young girl's body, so the girl, though pretty, lacked spirit and intelligence, and acted like a fool. The wealthy parents had taken her to see many doctors, but no one could

39

find out what was wrong with her. The girl now was seventeen years old. The parents were worried about their daughter's future all the time, as nobody wanted to marry such a mentally deficient young woman.

梅女建议封云去拜访这对富有的夫妇,向他们表示愿意娶他们的小女儿为妻。她告诉他这对富有的夫妇一定会很愉快地接受他的求婚的。在结婚的当天夜晚,当没有别的人在房间时,她要他把小瓶子的盖子打开,用瓶子去打这个女孩的头顶三下,她就可以进人这个女孩的身体了。

Meinü suggested that Feng Yun visit the wealthy couple and propose marriage to their youngest daughter. She told him that the wealthy couple would surely be very glad to accept the proposal. On the wedding night, when nobody else was present in the room, she wanted him to open the bottle and use it to hit the girl's head three times so she could then enter into the girl's body.

"然后我就是这个女孩,你的新娘。"接着她羞答答地又说,"到了那个时候你就可以像我以前答应过你的要求那样做了。"

"And I'll be the girl, your bride." Then she added shyly, "By that time, you can do whatever you want like I promised you before."

封云大喜过望,紧抱着她狂吻不已。

Feng Yun was elated, hugging and kissing her fervently.

梅女的话一点儿也不错,当封云去拜访这位富有的男子,表达了他愿意娶他的小女儿为妻的意愿时,这位男子果然欣喜地立刻答允。一个简单的婚礼便很快地举行了。

Meinü was right. When Feng Yun visited the wealthy man and expressed his desire to marry his youngest daughter, the man accepted the proposal joyfully and immediately. And a simple wedding ceremony was soon held.

第二天早上,当新娘从卧室内走出来时,她的一切言行举动都和一个正常的新婚妇人一样。她娘家的每一个人都对她的正常举动惊讶不已。于是封云走出房来暗地里把秘密告诉了他的岳父母。

The next morning, when the bride emerged from the bedroom, she spoke and acted like a normal newlywed. Every member of her family was surprised at her normal behavior. Then Feng Yun came out telling his parents-in-law the secret in private.

当封云将他的新妇带回家后,他的家人和朋友们都为他的良配惊赞不已。

When Feng Yun brought his bride home, all of his family and friends were happily surprised at his having found such a fine and pretty match.

聊斋精选

五、

织

成

The Poet and Pearl Flower

鄱阳湖位于江西省境内,是中国的五大湖之一。

Poyang Lake, located in the Province of Jiangxi, is one of the five largest lakes in China.

多少年来,人们相信如果一条停泊在码头的空船突然自动浮泛湖中,而在数小时后又回到原位,那就是说鄱阳湖神借用过这条船了。如果船主在船上发现了一颗珍珠或者什么值钱的东西,他就会相信这是湖神故意留给他抵作租船费用的。

For many years, it was believed that if an empty ship moored at a pier in the lake suddenly floated away all by itself and several hours later floated back to its original place, it meant that the god of Poyang Lake had borrowed the ship. And if the owner of ship happened to find a pearl or something valuable left on the vessel, the owner would consider it as a substitute for payment by the god for renting his ship.

刘义是一位很有才气的年轻诗人。他喜欢喝酒,时常喝醉。他也喜欢和朋友辩论。因为有智慧和辩才,他时常语出惊人,没有人可以把他驳倒。

Liu Yi was a young talented poet. He liked to drink and often became drunk. He also liked to debate with his friends. Because of his intelligence and strong eloquence, he often made shocking comments that nobody could refute.

一天,刘义参加了一个旅游团,他们租了一条刚装潢好的大船去游览鄱阳湖。这是一个舒适的暮春季节,刘义为美丽的景色所陶醉,喝了很多杯酒,也做了很多首诗。当这个旅游团的人员和船上的工作人员都下船时,刘义已经醉得站不起来,而一不小心跌倒地板上躺在桌子底下酣睡,完全没有被人发现。

One day, Liu Yi joined a tourist group that rent a newly decorated large ship to tour the Poyang Lake. It was a pleasant day in late spring. Being entranced by the beautiful scenery, Liu Yi had many drinks and composed many poems. By the time all of the tourist group and the crew were leaving the ship, Liu Yi was too drunk to stand up, instead carelessly lying on the floor under a table and sleeping, totally unnoticed by others.

终于,刘义被很大的音乐声及讲话声吵醒了。他睁开眼睛一看,非常惊讶地发现这条船又在湖上移动。从桌子底下向外望去,他发现很多年轻女子忙碌地来回于厨房和大餐厅中。同时一个小型的乐队在大厅的一角演奏着美妙的音乐。这一切的一切就好像是一个尊贵的人家正在湖上游览风光。几乎是立刻地,他想起了这位尊贵的人可能就是传说中的湖神在借用这条船。于是他继续藏在桌子底下思考着如何现身。

Finally, Liu Yi was awakened by loud music and conversation. He opened his eyes and was surprised to find that the ship was again floating on the lake. Peeking out from under the table, he discovered many girls coming and going between the kitchen and the large dining room. He also saw a small band playing nice music in a corner. It seemed that a dignified family was entertaining themselves on the lake. Almost

聊斋精选

immediately, he thought that the dignitary might be the god of lake who was borrowing the ship as it was often said. Liu Yi remained hidden under the table, trying to figure out how to make his appearance.

突然，一双女子的腿挡住了他的视线。一个年轻的女子站在他躲藏的桌子旁边。这个女孩没有穿袜子只穿着一双用手绣制有珠花系在上面的便鞋。在明亮的日光下，刘义可以清晰地看到她粉红色的丝裙和那裙里的一切，他不由得获得了灵感而就在此时此地赋成了一首诗。

Suddenly, a pair of female legs blocked his vision. A young girl came to stand by the table under which he was hiding. The girl wore a pair of hand-embroidered slippers with pearl flowers fastened on the top. She did not wear socks. Under the bright sunlight, Liu Yi could see her pink silk skirt and everything wrapped in skirt. He had an instant inspiration and immediately composed a poem right then and there.

当他在心中默诵他的诗篇时，他另有一种冲动而去偷了这女子鞋子上的一朵珠花放在口袋里作为纪念。

As he was reciting his poem to himself in silence, he had another impulse and stole one of the pearl flowers fastened on the girl's shoes and put it in his pocket as a souvenir.

这个意想不到的偷珠花动作吓了这个女子一跳，她弯下身子去察看究竟是怎么一回事，而她的同伴们也在帮她寻找。在这种情况下，刘义不得不从桌子底下爬了出来。

The unexpected action to steal the pearl flower startled the girl and she bent over to find out what had happened, joined by her companions all looking down for the strange thing. Under such circumstances, Liu Yi had no choice but to crawl out from under the table.

两个卫士立刻把刘义带去见那位单独坐在上席具有威严相貌的中年男子。显然地这个人就是这条船上的主子，也很可能就是传说中的所谓鄱阳湖的湖神。听了卫士的报告后，这位主子对于刘义藏身船上大为震怒，一句话也不问，就下令卫士："把他扔到湖里去。"

Two guards took Liu Yi to see a dignified-looking middle-aged man, sitting alone at the table of honor. Obviously, the man was the master on the ship, probably the so-called god of Poyang Lake. After hearing the guards' report, the master was furious over Liu Yi's hiding on the ship. Without questioning, he ordered his guards, "Drop him into the lake!"

"等一下，"刘义立刻大声抗议，他向这位主子大吼，"不管按照天律或是人间法律或是什么地方规定，处我死刑是绝对不公平的。"

"Wait a minute!" Liu Yi protested loudly and immediately. He yelled at the master, "It is totally unfair to murder me according to the laws of every land no matter in the human world or heaven or anywhere."

聊斋精选

43

听了这么一个大胆的抗议后,这个主子于是又下令暂缓执行,他要听听这个人的陈情。

Upon hearing such a daring protest, the master ordered to delay of the execution, as he wanted to hear the man's petition.

刘义向前走上一大步,面对着这位中年男子,他毫无惧色地以他那一贯的雄辩而富有条理的方式作了如下的陈辞:

Liu Yi moved forward one big step and stood straight in front of the middle-aged man. He fearlessly made the following statements with his usual eloquence and logic:

"第一,我是在你们一伙人之前登上这条船的。所以说我是先来而你们是后到的。"

"First, I boarded the ship much earlier than your group. So I'm the first to come, and you're the second."

"第二,我是付了船费再上船的,因此我有权利停留在这条船上。"

"Second, I have paid for boarding this ship. I have the right to stay aboard."

"第三,是这个女孩来到我的面前,而不是我去到她的面前的。"

"Third, it was the girl who came to me. I did not come to her."

"第四,因为这个女孩是如此的美丽诱人,没有一个健康的男子能够不被迷住的。"

"Fourth, the girl is so irresistible that no healthy man could avoid being charmed."

"第五,我是一位有名的诗人,所有的诗人都会努力把握灵感去作一首好诗的。"

"Fifth, I'm a famous poet. All poet knows he must catch a good inspiration for composing poetry when it comes to him."

"因此,我是完全无辜的,你如何可以处死我?"

"Therefore, I'm totally innocent. How could you murder me?"

刘义的大胆又机智的陈辞使得这个主子一时哑口无言。

Liu Yi's bold and intelligent statements made the master speechless.

他立刻改变那傲慢的态度,下令将刘义释放。并邀请刘义与他同桌作为他的来宾。他告诉刘义他是湖神。然后他要那个穿着粉红色丝裙的女孩为客人斟酒。湖神告诉刘义这个女孩是他的侍女名叫织成。他要她每当刘义喝完了杯中的酒后就立刻再为他斟满。织成恭敬地应从。于是刘义注意到了这个侍女,是他一生中所看到过的最美丽的女子。

He immediately reversed his haughty attitude and ordered Liu Yi's release. He invited Liu Yi to sit with him at his table as his guest. He told Liu Yi that he was the god of the lake. Then he wanted the girl who wore the pink silk skirt to pour wine into the guest's glass. The god told Liu Yi that the girl was his maid whose name was Zhicheng. He ordered her to keep filling up Liu Yi's glass whenever he finished. She complied respectfully. Liu Yi noticed that the maid was the most beautiful woman he had ever seen.

因为刘义曾经自称他是一个有名的诗人，湖神问他是否可以把这天游湖的情景写成一首诗。刘义在这天早上早已写了好多首诗，所以他要来纸笔后一挥而就，当场写了很多首诗。写好后他把诗呈现给湖神。湖神为刘义的杰作所吃惊，赞为奇才。他高兴地宣布将赐送刘义一件礼品作为奖励。

As Liu Yi had said that he was a famous poet, the god asked him if he could write a poem to describe the events of the day. Liu Yi had already composed many poems that morning. Without hesitation, he ordered to bring over a pen and the paper and immediately wrote down many poems. He showed his poems to the lake god. The god was stunned by Liu Yi's quick composition and highly applauded his literary talent. He happily announced that he would present Liu Yi a gift as a reward.

刘义一口气喝了三杯酒，然后谦卑地问湖神是否可以让他自己来选奖品。湖神慷慨大度地答应了，并且还说不管刘义想要什么，他都可以赠送。

Liu Yi polished off three glasses of wine. He humbly asked the god if he could choose the reward himself. The god agreed generously, adding that whatever Liu Yi wished to have, he would give it to him.

于是刘义站起身来，深情款款地望着这个美丽的侍女织成，他问湖神："我可以得到你的准许娶她为妻作为我的奖品吗？"

Then Liu Yi stood up, staring affectionately at the pretty maid, Zhicheng, he asked the god, "May I have your permission to marry her as my reward?"

这真是一个怎么也想不到的要求。湖神爽朗地大笑着回答："我是没有问题的，可是织成是我妻子最钟爱的侍女，我必须征求她的同意。此外我也必须要问织成本人是否愿意嫁给你。"

This was a totally unexpected request. The god laughed loudly and replied, "It is all right for me, but Zhicheng is my wife's most favorite maid. I must ask for her agreement. Besides, I must also ask Zhicheng herself if she is willing to marry you."

这话使得这个侍女非常害羞，她立刻红着脸含羞带笑、低下头来一语不发。由于湖神的妻子不在船上，无法获得她的同意。所以刘义自选奖品一事也就这样地没有答案结束了。他继续陪伴湖神喝酒和吃东西。

聊斋精选

The conversation made the maid very shy. She quickly hung her head, blushing and smiling without saying a word. As the god's wife was not on the ship, there was no way to get her agreement. So Liu Yi's self-selection of reward thus ended without a definite answer. He continued to drink and eat with the lake god.

当宴会结束后,湖神带领他的一群人下船。他们在水面上行走,很快便全不见了踪迹。刘义再一次地一个人留在船上。他望着这似乎是无边的湖水与往常没有任何分别。他揉了揉眼睛,开始怀疑这整个的一切是否仅仅是一个梦。于是他连忙检查他的口袋,很高兴地发现他从织成的鞋子上所偷来的那朵珠花仍在。这就证明了他的确曾经见到了湖神和他的美丽侍女。

When the banquet was over, the god led his group off the ship. They walked on the water and soon all disappeared. Liu Yi was once again alone on the ship. Watching the wide lake seemingly without an end with nothing different than usual, he rubbed his eyes and started to wonder whether the whole thing was but a dream. Then he quickly checked his pocket and was glad to find that the pearl flower he had stolen from Zhicheng's shoe was still there. This meant that he had really met the lake god and his pretty maid.

他上岸后走回了家。

He went to the shore and returned home.

从此以后,这个美丽侍女织成的倩影就深深地印在他的脑海里。他想念这个他在船上曾经提出婚约的女孩,他不知道湖神和他的妻子谈起过这件事没有以及她是否同意了,而最重要的是织成本人是否也同意这件婚姻? 他无从找到答案也无人可问。

Since that time, the image of the pretty maid, Zhicheng, was indelibly stamped in his mind. He missed the girl to whom he had proposed marriage on the ship. He did not know if the god had mentioned his proposal to his wife and if she had given her agreement, and more importantly, if Zhicheng herself had agreed to marry him. He had no way to check and nobody to ask.

时间就在焦急中一天天度过。

He lived in daily anxiety.

终于一件奇怪的事情在刘义所住的区域内发生了。

Finally, a strange thing happened in the area where Liu Yi lived.

就在他从那神奇的鄱阳湖之旅回来后的半个月,一个中年妇人和一个年轻女孩来到这个区域,她们自称是母女。妇人公开声明如果有个男子能拿出一朵珠花可以和她女儿一只鞋子上的那一朵完全相配,她就把女儿许配给他。

About half a month after his fantastic voyage to Poyang Lake, a middle-aged woman and a teenage girl came his region saying that they were mother and daughter. The woman publicly announced that if a man could bring a pearl flower to match the other one on her daughter's shoe, she would marry her daughter to him.

这个妇人和她的女儿居住在一家本地旅店内。凡是看到过这个女孩的人都说她真是一个绝色美人。因此很多年轻男子特别是那些富家子弟,都拿着一朵美丽的珠花来请见这个妇人。结果没有一个人的珠花是和她女儿鞋子上的那朵相配。

The mother and daughter stayed at a local lodge. Every person who had seen the girl said that she was a rare beauty. Many young men, especially the ones of wealthy families, had presented the woman with a very nice pearl flower. But none of them matched the other one on her daughter's shoe.

当刘义听到了这个消息时,他怀疑这个女孩可能是织成。他立刻去拜访这位妇人并给她看珠花。妇人把珠花拿进内室与女儿的那朵相对,发现完全一样。女孩走了出来,她果然是湖神的美丽侍女织成。两个年轻恋人紧紧握住对方的手,高兴得热泪盈眶。

When Liu Yi heard the news, he suspected that the girl might be Zhicheng. He immediately paid a visit to the woman and showed her the pearl flower. She took it inside to check with her daughter's. It matched perfectly. The girl came out. She was indeed the lake god's pretty maid, Zhicheng. The two young lovers held each other's hands tightly with joyful tears in their eyes.

"啊,织成,"刘义兴奋地告诉她,"我是多么地想念你! 我真害怕可能永远没有机会再见到你了。"

"Oh, Zhicheng," Liu Yi told her excitedly, "I have missed you so much and was afraid that I might never have a chance to meet you again."

"我也是的,"织成含羞地说。然后她告诉刘义,"起初,湖神的妻子是不同意我嫁给你这个凡夫的。可是我坚持要嫁,同时湖神也从旁协助,他说你是一位伟大的诗人,也必将是一个很好的丈夫,终于她同意了。然后她指派一个年长的侍女陪同我上岸来寻找你。为了安全起见,我们对外假称是母女。我是多么地高兴我们终于找到了你了。"

"Me, too," Zhicheng said shyly. Then she told Liu Yi, "In the beginning, god's wife did not agree to let me marry you, a mortal man. But when I insisted, and with the help of god saying that since you were a great poet you would be a nice husband, she finally gave her permission. Then she appointed an older maid to accompany me to the shore to look for you. For safety, we pretended we were mother and daughter. I'm so glad we have finally found you."

刘义感谢了这个年长的侍女,邀请她留下参加他们的婚礼。可是她谢绝了,她说既然她们已经找到了他,她必须赶紧回去向湖神和他的妻子报告这个喜讯。临走时,她提醒织成不要忘记她曾经答应过湖

聊斋精选

神夫妇在婚后一年一定要回去拜见他们的。织成说她不但要回去,而且还要带着刘义一同去。

Liu Yi thanked the older maid and asked her to stay to attend their wedding ceremony, but she turned down the invitation, saying that since they had found him, she must return to the god and his wife to report the happy news. Before departing, she reminded Zhicheng to visit the god and his wife a year later after their marriage as she had promised. Zhicheng said she would, and she would ask Liu Yi to go with her.

刘义把织成带回家去,他们迅速举行了一个婚礼成为夫妇,愉快地生活在一起。

Liu Yi took Zhicheng home and they soon held a wedding ceremony to become husband and wife, and happily lived together.

结婚一周年后,这对快乐的夫妇来到了鄱阳湖,准备去拜见织成的老主人湖神夫妇。当他们到达湖边时,织成拔下头上的一根发针抛向湖中,湖上立刻现出了一条道路。于是她牵着丈夫的手向前走去,一直走到了一座以纯白色大理石砌成的豪华宫殿。

After their first anniversary, the happy couple went to the Poyang Lake planning to visit Zhicheng's former masters, the lake god and his wife. When they reached the lakeside, she dropped one of her hairpins into the water and suddenly a road showed up in the lake. She held her husband's hand and they walked along the road that took them directly to a splendidly tall building made of pure white marble.

刘义一辈子从未见过如此宏伟的建筑物,织成告诉他这就是湖神的宫殿。当刘义回过头来再看他刚才走过的道路时,惊讶地发现它早已完全不见了。而且在这么一处深水底下,竟然没有一滴水,只有空气而且还是和岸上人们所呼吸的一样新鲜,这真是一个多么神奇的世界,简直无法使人相信,可这又都是真的。

Liu Yi had never seen such a huge, stately building in his life. Zhicheng said that it was the palace of the lake god. When Liu Yi turned his head, he was surprised to discover that the road on which they had traveled had already disappeared. He was also amazed to find that under such deep water, there was no water at all, but the same fresh air that people breathed on the shore. What a wonderful world it was! These phenomena were absolutely unbelievable, but they were true.

当织成去敲大门时,一个身着蓝色制服的年轻男子出来开门,他亲切地告诉织成说主人夫妇早已等候她们多时了。这个男子带领这对夫妇进入了一间大的客厅,遇见了很多宫里的侍女,每一个人都来和织成愉快地紧紧拥抱,就好像亲生姐妹久别重逢一样,织成连忙为她们介绍了她的夫婿,大家都对刘义表示热诚欢迎。

When Zhicheng knocked on the door of the entrance, a young man in blue uniform opened the door. He warmly told Zhicheng that the masters had been waiting for them for a long time. The man led the couple to a large living room and they met many other maids. Everybody came over to hug Zhicheng tightly and joyfully

聊斋精选

聊斋精选

like sisters having a happy reunion after a long separation. Zhicheng quickly introduced her husband to them and they warmly welcomed Liu Yi.

不久,湖神夫妇出现了,织成连忙上前跪下想以大礼参拜,可是被湖神及他的妻子所阻止,他们笑容满面地告诉织成,她早已不是他们的侍女了。事实上他们是以接待女儿回娘家一样来接待织成的,没有让织成再干任何活,只希望她去尽情享受。湖神又命令一个低阶官员带领刘义游览湖底的各处美景。

Soon, the lake god and his wife appeared. Zhicheng walked forward trying to kneel down to pay respect to her former masters, but was stopped by the god and his wife. They joyfully told her that she was not their maid anymore. In fact, they treated Zhicheng like a daughter returning her parents' home after marriage. They would not let her do any kind of work but asked her to enjoy whatever she wanted. The god even ordered a lower official to show Liu Yi all the marvelous places under the lake.

织成与刘义和湖神一家欢聚了一周才回家。临别时,湖神夫妇送了她们一袋子湖底珍宝作为礼品。

Zhicheng and Liu Yi stayed with the god family for a week, then, returned home. Before they departed, the god and his wife presented them with a bag of sea treasures as gifts.

以后他们每隔数年就会到湖底去拜候湖神夫妇,而每次均带回来很多湖底珍宝。由于这些珍宝在人间都很值钱,最后刘义和织成变成了富有的人。

Every few years, they would pay the lake god and his wife a visit and every time they would bring back some sea treasures. As those treasures were valuable in the world of human beings, Liu Yi and Zhicheng finally became wealthy people.

聊斋精选

六、水莽草

Replacement Killer

在中国湖南省中部某一个山区地带生长一种有毒的植物名叫水莽草。因为水莽草的叶子很像茶树叶子,而且煮出来的味道也和一般茶的味道很相近,一些从外地来的人往往误把它当茶来喝。据传说,如果有人喝了水莽草叶煮的茶后,三天内一定毒发身亡。

Shuimang was said to be a poisonous plant that grew only in a certain mountainous area located in the central part of the Province of Hunan, China. Because the Shuimang leaves looked pretty much like the tea leaves and tasted similar as well, some visitors from other places often mistakenly drank it without knowing it was not tea. It was rumored that if a person drank the water of boiled Shuimang leaves, the drinker would be poisoned and die in three days.

很久以来,住在这个地区的人们相信一个人中了水莽草毒死后变的鬼便叫做水莽鬼。水莽鬼是不能投胎为人的,除非这个鬼去毒死另一个人做他(她)的替身。

For a long time, the people in that area believed that when a person died of Shuimang poisoning, he or she would become a ghost called Shuimang ghost. This ghost could not be reborn as a person until the ghost poisoned another person to die as his or her substitute.

祝生是从中国东部沿海来的一位年轻武术师。他毕业于一家武术学校后,就在湖南中部找到了一个工作,便举家搬来定居。

Zhu Sheng was a young martial arts instructor from the east coast. After being graduated from a martial arts school, he found a job in the central part of the Province of Hunan, and moved his family to live there.

一个夏天的晚上,他去拜访一位刚认识不久住在山脚下的朋友。在大热天走了一段长路后,他感到非常口渴。四下一望,他看到了在路边不远处有一个很小的茶亭。他决定走过去喝一杯茶。

One summer evening, he went to visit a newly acquainted friend who lived at the foot of a mountain. After a long walk in hot day, he felt very thirsty. Looking around, he saw a small tea booth not too far from the roadside. He decided to go there to have a cup of tea.

卖茶的是两个女子。年长的在烧茶,年轻的在招待顾客。

The tea sellers were two women. The older one was making the tea and the younger one was serving it to the customers.

当这个年轻的女子把茶送来时,祝生发现这个女侍是个绝色美女,她头上戴着一朵野花,越发觉得其妖媚无比。在她为他倒茶时,祝生给了她很好的小费,并乘机碰了下她的手腕。女孩回报他一个迷人的微笑,这给祝生一个鼓励。

When the young woman brought the tea to him, Zhu Sheng noticed that the waitress was a very pretty girl, wearing a wild flower in her hair to make her even more attractive. After the girl poured tea for him,

Zhu Sheng gave her a nice tip and had a chance to touch her delicate hand. The girl responded with a bewitching smile. This encouraged Zhu Sheng.

"我可以知道你的名字吗?"祝生问她。
"May I have your name?" Zhu Sheng asked her.

"我的名字叫三娘。"女孩甜甜地回答。
"My name is Sanniang," the girl replied sweetly.

"何不坐下来?"祝生指着他旁边的座位,"现在并没有别的客人。"
"Why don't you sit down?" Zhu Sheng pointed at a seat beside him, "There are no other customers right now."

她羞答答地坐在了他的身旁。
She sat down by him shyly.

然后这两个年轻人便愉快地交谈着。祝生为她的美貌所迷恋,而她也似乎很喜欢和他谈话。
The two young people talked pleasantly. Zhu Sheng was charmed with her beauty and she seemed to enjoy speaking to him as well.

谈话中,他愈来愈被这个女侍的美色所吸引,他问她:"我明天拜访过朋友后,想请你到城里最好的一家饭店里吃顿晚饭,怎么样?"
As their conversation continued, he was even more bewitched by the pretty waitress. He asked her, "Why don't we have dinner tomorrow evening at the best restaurant in town after I have paid a visit to my friend?"

"什么时候?"她似乎有兴趣。
"What time would that be?" She seemed to be interested.

"就在这个时刻是不是太早了点?"
"Is this time too early?"

"我在这儿等你。"
"I'll be waiting here for you."

握手后,祝生重新上路,女孩向着他含情地挥手道别。他对于这么快速就和这个美丽的女侍建立了友谊而感到很高兴。

After shaking hands, Zhu Sheng went back onto the road while the girl waved at him affectionately. He was glad to have established a quick friendship with the pretty waitress.

等到祝生赶到他的朋友家后,他感觉头和胃都剧痛,而且全身发痒得厉害。他告诉他的朋友他在那天曾经吃过和喝过什么东西。朋友是本地人,从祝生的症状看来,他很担心祝生在茶亭里喝的饮料可能是水莽草烧的。如果是真的,那么这两个在路边茶亭里卖茶的女人便就是在找替身的水莽鬼。

Soon after Zhu Sheng reached his friend's home, he felt severe headache and stomachache. And his whole body was itching badly. He told his friend what he had eaten and drunk earlier that day. The friend was a local man. Judging from Zhu Sheng's symptoms, he was afraid that Zhu Sheng might have drunk the broth made from Shuimang leaves. If it was true, the two women selling tea at a booth by roadside might be Shuimang ghosts looking for substitutes.

当祝生告诉他的朋友这个漂亮女侍的名字以及她的相貌后,朋友益发害怕他倒了霉,因为三娘是本地一位富有男子女儿的名字,她是在一年前中了水莽草毒亡故的。未死前她是当地最美丽的女孩。

After Zhu Sheng told his friend the pretty waitress' name and described what she looked like, the friend was even more afraid of his having bad luck, as Sanniang was the name of a local wealthy man's daughter who had died of Shuimang poisoning a year ago. She used to be the most beautiful girl in the area.

这个年轻的武术师顿时惊得目瞪口呆。
Suddenly, the young martial arts instructor was shocked and speechless.

"有一个方法也许可以救你一命,"朋友告诉惊骇的祝生,"根据当地的传言,当人中了水莽草的毒后,如果能够及时弄到这个水莽鬼生前穿过的一件内衣煮水喝,就可以把毒解掉而可以不死。换言之,如果你能够从三娘的父母处弄来一件她生前曾经穿过的内衣煮水喝,非常可能你的毒就可以解除而不会死亡了。"

"There might still be a way to save your life," the friend told the frightened Zhu Sheng. "According to the local legend, a person who has been poisoned with Shuimang leaves may be released from the poison if he can drink the broth made by boiling a piece of underwear that belonged to the former person before he or she has become a Shuimang ghost. In other words, if you can get a piece of Sanniang's underwear from her parents and boil it and drink the broth, very likely your poison will be released and

54

you'll not die."

听了这个信息后,祝生于是立刻去拜访三娘的父母,告诉这对富有夫妇他遇见了他们死去女儿鬼魂的整个经过,并恳求他们赐给他一件他们女儿生前穿过的内衣,好让他去煮水喝。

Upon hearing this message, Zhu Sheng hurriedly paid Sanniang's parents a visit. He told the wealthy couple the whole story of having met their dead daughter's spirit and begged them to let him have a piece of their daughter's underwear to boil and drink its broth.

他的恳求被一口拒绝了,这使得祝生极为难过。这对年长夫妇非常高兴知道他们女儿的鬼魂终于找到了替身并可以投胎为人了。

To Zhu Sheng's great sorrow, his request was immediately turned down. The senior couple was very happy to know that their daughter's spirit had finally found a substitute and would be reborn as a person.

祝生没有办法只好回家。他将这个可怕的消息悲伤地告诉了他的妻子和他的寡母,特别请求他妻子的原谅。起初他的妻子对他的不忠行为很是生气,后来想到他就要死了,也就感到非常悲伤。第三天他死了。

Zhu Sheng could do nothing but return home. He sadly told his wife and his widowed mother the horrible news, and begged for their forgiveness, especially his wife. In the beginning, his wife was angry for his unfaithfulness to her, but seeing that he was going to die soon, she felt very sad. On the third day, he died.

祝生死后一个月,他的岳父母把他的妻子接回家去,他们告诉祝生的母亲说只是把他们惟一的女儿接回家去散散心,不久就把她送回来,他们要求祝生的母亲在她的媳妇不在家时暂时带养她儿子同他们女儿所生的一个两岁大的小孙子。

A month after Zhu Sheng's death, his parents-in-law came to pick up his wife and told his mother that they just wanted to spend some time with their only daughter to make her feel better, then they would send her back. They asked Zhu Sheng's mother to temporarily take care of her two-year-old grandson Zhu Sheng and his wife's child, while the boy's mother was away.

事实上这老两口把女儿接回家后,就赶紧安排把她又嫁给了另一个男子。

Actually, after the old couple had brought back their daughter, they quickly made arrangements for her remarriage to another man.

祝生的妻子又结婚了,祝生的母亲必须独力去照顾她的小孙子。在这种毫无帮助的情况下,这个可

聊斋精选

怜的老妇人真不知道她和她的小孙子如何可以生存下去。她日夜都在哭泣。

So Zhu Sheng's widow got remarried. Zhu Sheng's mother now had to take care of her baby grandson all by herself. Without help, the poor old lady did not know how she and her grandson could survive. She cried day and night.

在一个孤寂的夜晚,当这个可怜的老太太抱着她的小孙子在绝望地哭泣时,她忽然看见了一个人影子冲进房子里来。在油灯下,她立刻认出了那是她死去的儿子祝生的鬼魂。

One lonely late evening, when the poor old lady was holding her grandson in her arms and crying desperately, she suddenly noticed a figure rushing into the house. Under the lamplight, she immediately recognized that it was her dead son, Zhu Sheng's spirit.

祝生告诉他的母亲他实在不能忍受母亲日夜的绝望哭声,而不得不从阴间出来给予他母亲所急需的帮助。他又告诉母亲,在他变成了鬼后第一件事就是去寻找三娘,那个卖给他水莽茶使他毒发身亡的漂亮女鬼。在她就要去投胎为人之前被他找到了。因为他是一个受过训练的武术师,他很容易地阻止了她去投胎,并使她成为他在阴间的妻子。

Zhu Sheng told his mother that having heard her desperate crying day and night, he just could not restrain himself from leaving the ghost world and coming back to give his mother the help she so badly needed. He also told his mother that after he became a ghost, the first thing he did was to look for Sanniang, the beautiful female ghost, who had sold him the poisonous Shuimang tea to make him dead. He found her just before she was going to be reborn as a person again. Being a trained martial arts instructor, he easily stopped her from going and made her his wife in the ghost world.

获得了母亲的同意后,祝生到户外把三娘带了进来。她要三娘向母亲行了拜见婆婆的礼节。三娘娇羞地行了礼。祝母愉快地握住三娘的手盛赞她是她所见过的最美丽的女子。现在这个老太太高兴了,她不仅看到了儿子回来,同时更带回来一个比以前那个媳妇还要漂亮的新媳妇。

With his mother's permission, Zhu Sheng went outside and brought in Sanniang. He asked her to pay his mother due respect as her daughter-in-law. Sanniang did shyly. Zhu Sheng's mother joyfully held Sanniang's hand, praising her as the most beautiful woman she had ever seen. Now the old lady rejoiced to see her son back together with a new daughter-in-law who was even much prettier than her former daughter-in-law.

祝生与三娘立刻帮助母亲操持各种家务并喂孩子吃饭,老太太发现她的鬼媳妇每一件事情都做得很好。

Immediately, Zhu Sheng and Sanniang started to help his mother take care of the household affairs including feeding the boy. The old lady found that her ghost daughter-in-law did those things

聊斋精选

very well.

因为是鬼，祝生和三娘只能在夜晚出现，又必须在天亮前离开。因此，夫妇俩尽可能把家务事，特别是繁重的家务事，在夜晚间都去做好，如此省却了祝母的精力。对于这个老妇人来说，日子突然比以前好过多了。

As ghosts, Zhu Sheng and Sanniang could only appear after dark and they had to leave before dawn. So the couple tried to do everything, especially the jobs consisting of heavy labor, in the evening sparing Zhu Sheng's mother. Suddenly, things went on much easier for the old lady.

不久，三娘的父母亲听到了他们的女儿时常来祝母家的消息，于是问祝生母亲他们可否在夜晚来她家会见他们的女儿。祝母同意后，他们在天一黑就来到了她的家里。当他们看到了他们那做了鬼的女儿，大家抱在一起高兴地哭泣着。

Soon, Sanniang's parents heard the news of their daughter's frequent visits to Zhu Sheng's mother's house. They asked Zhu Sheng's mother if they could meet their daughter at her home at night. With the old lady's permission, the senior couple came after dark. When they met their ghost daughter, they hugged each other, crying happily.

当初三娘的父母亲曾经拒绝将女儿的内衣交给祝生煮水喝解去水莽草的毒，使得祝生亡故。祝生仍然记得这件残酷的往事，因此他不愿向三娘的父母行子婿之礼，这使得三娘非常难过。

As Sanniang's parents had refused to let Zhu Sheng have a piece of their daughter's underwear to make the broth to release the Shuimang poison, Zhu Sheng had died. Remembering the bitter past, Zhu Sheng was reluctant to pay Sanniang's parents the due respect as a son-in-law. It made Sanniang very sad.

"如果你没有死亡，你如何可以和我在阴间结婚？"三娘哭着说。她又说，"我已经向你的母亲行了媳妇之礼了，你如何可以不向我的父母行子婿之礼？"

"If you had not died, how could you have married me in the world of ghosts?" Sanniang cried. Then she added, "I have paid your mother the due respect as a daughter-in-law, how could you not respect my parents as their son-in-law?"

终于祝生让步，向三娘的父母亲行了子婿之礼。
Finally, Zhu Sheng gave in and paid Sanniang's parents the respect they were due.

当三娘的父母亲发现他们的女儿和祝生是如此之相配及相爱，就和人间的恩爱夫妻一样，他们也就放下了心。

聊斋精选

When Sanniang's parents found that their daughter and Zhu Sheng was such a good match that they loved each other just like any loving couple in the human world, their worry was alleviated.

他们发现祝母家的房子是如此地陈旧和简陋,这对富有的夫妇便帮助祝母将住房整个重新装修得像一栋新的房子一样。

And when they noticed that Zhu Sheng's mother's house was so old and humble, the wealthy couple helped Zhu Sheng's mother remodel her house to make it look like a new one.

祝生痛恨这个规定为了可以重新投胎做人,一个水莽鬼必须谋杀一人作为替身。所以每当他听到了有这样的一件谋杀事件又要发生时,他就会立刻到现场去阻止事件之发生。因为祝生是个武术教练,没有一个水莽鬼可以打得过他。祝生因此救了很多人的性命。慢慢地阎罗王也听到了这件事,便下令将这一不合情理之规定予以废除。从此以后,水莽鬼和其它的鬼一样可以重新投胎为人了。

Zhu Sheng hated the rule that in order to be reborn as a human again, a Shuimang ghost must murder a person as a substitute. Whenever he heard that such a murder was going to happen, he would immediately go to the spot to prevent it from happening. As a martial arts instructor, Zhu Sheng could beat any Shuimang ghost in a fight. He had saved many people's lives. Gradually, when the grand ruler of the ghost world heard of the story, he ordered the unfair rule to be rescinded. After that, the Shuimang ghosts were able to be reborn as people just like the other ghosts

若干年后,祝生的儿子长大成人也结婚了,因为有了第三代的帮助,老祖母就不太需要她的鬼儿子和媳妇的帮助,这对鬼夫妇也就不像以前一样每天晚间都来了,不过在重大的家庭节日时,他们还是会回来的。

Many years later, Zhu Sheng's son grew up and got married. With a third generation helping out, the grandmother did not need much help from her ghost son and daughter-in-law. The couple of ghosts would not appear every evening as they used to, but still showed up on some important family occasions.

一天夜晚,祝生和三娘以盛装出现。他们愉快地告诉他们的家人,因为他曾经救过很多无辜人的性命,阎罗王认为他是一个正直的鬼,指派他为一个很远省份的鬼省长,管理那个省内所有的鬼。他们是来向家人辞行后去就任的。

One night, Zhu Sheng and Sanniang appeared in formal dress. They happily told their human family that as he had saved many innocent people's lives, the grand ruler of the ghost world considered him a very fair ghost and appointed him as the ghost governor in a faraway province to rule all the ghosts in that province. They came to say goodbye to their human family before going to take the official appointment.

聊斋精选

聊斋精选

　　祝母过世的那一天,祝生和三娘回来了,自此后,这对夫妇就没有再回来。

Since then, Zhu Sheng and Sanniang did not come back except when Zhu Sheng's mother passed away. After that, the couple never showed up again.

聊斋精选

Dr. Ying and His Wife

应成果是一位医生。他精通针灸和外科手术。他住在一座高山脚下的一个都市里。因为他曾经做过很多次几乎神奇的成功手术,他不但在本地就是在临近的城镇甚至于山那边的地方都享有盛誉。

Ying Chengguo was a medical doctor who specialized in acupuncture and surgery. He lived in a city at the foot of a high mountain. As he had performed many miraculously successful surgeries, he had a great reputation in his city as well as in the neighboring towns including those on the other side of the mountain.

一天,一个男子来到他的诊所,他请应医生到山那边他的家里为他的老父亲动手术。

One day a man dropped by his clinic. He asked Dr. Ying to come to his home on the other side of the mountain to perform surgery on his aged father.

"我父亲的背上生了一个很大的肿瘤,因为病得厉害他无法翻越这座高山到你的诊所,在山那边的医生都看了,可是没有一个能为他开刀割除肿瘤。"这个男子说。

"My father has a large tumor on his back. He is unable to come to your clinic because he is too sick to travel across the mountain. Doctors on the other side of mountain have checked, but none of them are able to remove the tumor," the man said.

应医生在犹豫着是否要去,因为这要花费他几乎一整天的时间才可以翻过高山到达他的家里,而且这条山路崎岖不平。这个男子突然跪倒在他的面前央求着说,"应医生,如果你能来,我们全家人都会非常感激你的。我还要付给你比平时出诊多一百倍的诊费。"

Dr. Ying hesitated, as it would take him a whole day to climb over the mountain and the route was rough. The man suddenly knelt down before him, begging, "Dr. Ying, my whole family would deeply appreciate your efforts, and I would pay you a hundred times more than your regular fees if you could come."

这个男子很富有,也是个出名的孝子。终于应医生答应走这一趟。

The man was very wealthy and well known for treating his parents with filial respect. Finally, Dr. Ying agreed to go.

他到了这个病人的家中,又完成了一次成功的手术,把这个老人背上的肿瘤割除掉了。

He made the trip, and performed the surgery on the old man's back, which was successful.

由于天色已晚,无法翻山回家,应了这个男子的要求,应医生决定在这家住一晚。第二天早上,他准备走回家去时,老人要他的儿子像接他来时一样护送他的医生穿过山去,可是被应医生谢绝了。他说他已经熟悉山路,很有把握可以自己走回去。

Since it was too late to climb over the mountain to return to his home, the man offered Dr. Ying the hospitality of staying one night at his home. The next morning, when he was about to leave, the old man wanted his son to accompany his doctor over the mountain as he had done earlier. Dr. Ying turned down the

聊斋精选

offer, saying that he was now familiar with the mountain trail and was sure he could find the way back alone.

走到半途,应医生出乎意料地遇到了一只狼。他立刻捡起了一根粗树枝当作武器来保卫自己。不久,又来了两只狼。这批狡诈的动物围住他企图从三个不同方向同时攻击。应医生明了自己必死无疑了,悔恨当初不接受他病人的建议让他的儿子护送他。

Halfway across the mountain, Dr. Ying unexpectedly met a wolf. He quickly grabbed a rough tree branch as a weapon to protect himself. Soon, two more wolves appeared. The crafty animals surrounded him, positioning to attack him from three different directions at the same time. Dr. Ying realized that his death was inescapable. He was very sorry for not taking his patient's suggestion to let his son accompany him.

就在这个时候,一只老虎出现了。这只猛虎迅速扑杀了一只狼,那其余的两只狼立刻逃跑了。应医生想这下子他一定会被老虎杀害。出乎他意外,老虎竟没有想去伤害他就跑掉了。

Just at that moment, a tiger appeared. The mighty tiger swiftly killed one wolf and the other two immediately fled. Now Dr. Ying feared that he would be surely killed by the tiger. But to his great surprise, the tiger did not try to hurt him and instead ran away.

抓紧树枝,应医生又重新上路。不久他遇见了一个年轻男子,拦住了他,很有礼貌地问他:"你是应医生吗?"

Gripping the branch, Dr. Ying resumed his journey. Soon he came across a young man who stopped him and politely asked, "Are you Dr. Ying?"

"是的,我是。"应医生回答着。

"Yes, I am," Dr. Ying answered.

"好极了,"这个人说,"我是一个猎人,我的名字叫胡大。我可否请你去我家医治我生病的母亲?"

"That's great," the man said. "I'm a hunter. My name is Hu Da. May I ask you to come to my home to treat my sick mother?"

当应医生还没有回答时,男子继续说:"我母亲的颈子上长了一个大瘤。如果你能把它割除,我将陪同你走完这段山路。这里经常会有野兽出没伤害行人。"

Before Dr. Ying answered, the man continued, "My mother has a large tumor on her neck. If you could remove the tumor for her, I would join you for the rest of the routes on the mountain. There are often wild animals to attack the travelers."

由于狼的出现已经把他吓坏了,应医生立刻答应去帮助。

Since the wolves had nearly scared him to death, Dr. Ying readily promised to help.

胡大和他的寡母及一个妹妹住在一个巨大的山洞里。他将应医生介绍给他的母亲。这个老妇人的颈子上长了一个差不多有鹅蛋大的肿瘤,使得她日夜痛得无法睡眠。因为他们住在这座荒山上,很难找到像应医生这样的好医生。

Hu Da lived with his widowed mother and a younger sister in a huge cave. He introduced Dr. Ying to his mother, an older woman with a tumor as big as a goose egg growing on her neck. The tumor hurt her day and night making it impossible for her to sleep. As they lived in the wilderness, it was very difficult for them to find a good doctor, like Dr. Ying, to help.

男子的妹妹是个十八九岁的女孩子。她长得很美而且看起来体格非常强壮。

The man's younger sister was a late teenager. She was very pretty and looked very strong physically.

应医生要老妇人躺在一张石床上,他为她做检查。检查完了,他告诉这家人,这个瘤必须拿掉而且要愈快愈好。他说他可以做这个手术。

Dr. Ying asked the woman to lie on a stone bed and gave her an examination. After that, he told the family that the tumor must be removed as quickly as possible and he could do the job.

在获得了家人的同意后,应医生先用长针在这个妇人颈子周围的穴位上扎下去麻醉这个地方,然后拿出了一把刀子开始割除手术,由这个妇人的女儿在一旁充当助手。

With the family's agreement, Dr. Ying put a few needles into the woman's acupuncture points around the neck to anesthetize the area. Then he took out a knife and started the operation, with the woman's daughter at his side acting as an assistant.

一个小时内,应医生将肿瘤完全割除,并用药粉撒在创伤的地方。他告诉这家人手术很成功。

Within an hour, Dr. Ying removed the tumor. Then he sprinkled medical powders on the wound. He told the family the surgery was a success.

当应医生坐在一条石墩上休息时,这个女孩开始烧饭。饭烧好后放在一张石桌上。应医生发现所有的菜肴都是由各种肉类烹做的,没有米饭,也没有蔬菜。他尝了后发现味道都很可口。

Dr. Ying rested on a stone seat as the girl cooked a meal. When the meal was placed on a stone table, Dr. Ying found that all the dishes were made of different kinds of meats, with no rice or vegetables. Yet after tasting them, he thought that they were all delicious.

饭后,这个老妇人要应医生坐在她的床边上。"我非常感激。你的手术使我重生。"她说。

After the meal, the old woman asked Dr. Ying to sit at her bedside. "I deeply appreciate your surgery. You gave me a new life," she said.

聊斋精选

然后,她又突然问他,"你结婚了没有?"
Then she suddenly asked him, "Are you married?"

"还没有。"应医生回答。他在奇怪她怎么问他这个私人问题。
"Not yet," Dr. Ying answered, wondering why she asked him such a personal question.

这个妇人对他的回答似乎很满意。然后她指着她的女儿说:"我的女儿斑斑的胸部也长有一个瘤。问题是一个少女的胸脯除非是丈夫是不能让别的男子看到的。"
The woman was seemingly happy at his reply. Then she pointed at her daughter and said, "My daughter, Banban, also has a tumor on her chest. The problem is that a young girl's naked chest is not supposed to be shown to a man unless the man is her husband."

当应医生还没有说话时,妇人又郑重地问他:"你可否愿意和我的女儿结婚,然后为她割除胸部的病瘤?"
While Dr. Ying did not say a word, the woman asked him again seriously, "Would you like to marry my daughter, then cut her tumor off on her chest?"

这真是一个最直接和最出乎意料的婚约了!
What the most direct and unexpected marriage proposal it was!

应医生向着斑斑望去,发现她正在深情地望着他,转过头来,发现胡大也正在焦急地等着他的回答,而这个老妇人更是那么急切地希望能听到他的肯定回音。
Dr. Ying took a look at Banban and found she was affectionately staring at him. Turning his head, he discovered Hu Da was anxiously waiting for his answer, and the older woman was also eagerly wishing to get a positive reply from him.

应医生仍是单身未婚。很多媒人来到他家想为他介绍一个合适的好伴侣。他希望娶一个女子不但美丽而且要有强壮的身体。他相信只有身体强壮的母亲才能生出身体强壮的小孩。在那些他所看到的女孩中竟没有一个达到他的标准的。可是在今天这个荒山洞穴中这个名叫斑斑的女孩竟正是他所要寻找的对象。
Dr. Ying was still single. Many matchmakers had approached him, hoping to find him a nice match. He wished to marry a girl who was not only pretty but also physically strong. He believed that only a strong mother would bear a strong child. None of the candidates he had seen had met his qualifications. But today, in this wild mountain cave, he had found that the girl named Banban was exactly the type of young woman he wanted.

"好的,我愿意和你的女儿结婚。"他愉快地告诉这个妇人,接受了婚约。
"O. K. I'll marry your daughter," he happily told the woman, accepting the proposal for marriage.

这个山洞里的其它三个人立刻都兴奋了起来,斑斑羞红着脸迅速地低下了头,而她的母亲则是开怀大笑。

Immediately, the other three people in the cave became excited. Banban shyly hung her head, blushing, while her mother laughed aloud in delight.

胡大迅速走过来向他的妹妹及应医生道喜。他要这对新人一起面向他的母亲站好,然后向母亲跪下磕三个头。当应医生和斑斑站起身后,他高声宣布:

Hu Da quickly came over to congratulate his sister and Dr. Ying. He asked the couple to stand together, facing his mother, and kneel down to bow their heads three times. When Dr. Ying and Banban stood up, he loudly announced,

"恭喜恭喜,应医生和斑斑,你们两人现在是夫妻了。"

"Congratulations, Dr. Ying and Banban, you two are now husband and wife."

这个婚礼是如此地简单和愉快。

The ceremony was so simple and joyful.

成为夫妻以后,应医生带着他的新娘到她的房间里为她检查胸脯上的瘤。因为瘤很小,所以他很快地便把它割除了。

After becoming husband and wife, Dr. Ying took his bride to her room to examine the tumor growing on her chest. Because it was a small lump, it did not take long for him to remove it.

应医生很愉快地在山上度过了三天。当斑斑的母亲也就是他的岳母的伤口快要愈合时,他带着他的美丽又强壮的新婚妻子回家,把他的家人和朋友们都吓了一大跳。

Dr. Ying spent three happy days on the mountain. When Banban's mother, his mother-in-law's wound began to heal, he took his pretty and strong bride home and surprised all of his family and friends.

斑斑是一个勤奋的家庭主妇。她除了操持家里的各种事务外,更把家庭农场经营得有条有理,使得应医生可以专心一意地去发展他的医务。

Banban was a diligent housewife. Besides handling the household affairs, she also operated the family farm very well, so Dr. Ying could concentrate on his medical practice.

她的身体也和男子一样地强壮,应医生承认她的体能比他还强多了。

Physically, she was also as tough as a man. Dr. Ying had to admit that she was indeed stronger than he.

因此,每当她回山上去探望她的母亲和哥哥时,她都拒绝她丈夫陪同她一起去的建议。她告诉丈夫,"当我年轻时,我时常跟随我的父亲和哥哥去狩猎,我所获得的猎物总是比我哥哥的还要多。"

Whenever she went back to the mountain to visit her mother and brother, she always turned down her husband's offer to accompany her. She told her husband, "When I was young, I often joined my father and

聊斋精选

brother's hunts, and I always killed more animals than my brother did. "

尽管应医生反对,可是斑斑每次都是安全地独来独往。
Despite Dr. Ying's protests, Banban always traveled alone and returned home safely.

有一天,当她从山中回家后不久,人们发现有一个男子死在山中的路旁。一看就知道这个人是被野兽咬死的。可是奇怪得很,除了胸脯被咬穿以外,这个人的尸体还很完整。显而易见这只野兽只是想杀害他而并不想去吃他的肉。
One day after she had returned home from a visit on the mountain, a man was discovered dead along one of the mountain trails. It appeared that the man had been attacked and killed by a wild animal. Strangely enough, the man's corpse was still in good shape, except that his chest was broken. For some reasons, the animal just killed him, evidently not intending to eat him.

死者的家庭很富有,他平时就以喜欢调戏漂亮的单身妇女而臭名昭著,曾经好几次是强奸未遂嫌疑犯。因为他富有的家庭背景及与官府的一些贪官有勾结关系,被害的妇女和她们的家人都不能将他绳之以法。
The dead man was from a wealthy family. He was notorious for harassing pretty single woman and had been suspected of several attempted rapes. Because of his wealthy background and close association with certain corrupt government officials, the assaulted women and their families had not been able to win any legal judgments against him.

因此,当他的神秘死亡消息传出去以后,除了他的家人没有别人为他悲伤。甚至于传言说因为那个恶贯满盈的人这一回想去强暴一只雌老虎而被这头野兽咬死的。当应医生告诉斑斑这个消息及传言后,她笑着说:"我相信这个传说。"然后她又说:"这个恶人应受恶报。"
Therefore, when the news of his mysterious death spread, nobody except his family really felt sad. It was even rumored that the vicious man had tried to rape a female tiger this time and had been killed by the wild animal. When Dr. Ying told Banban the news and the rumor, she smiled and said, "I believe the rumor." Then she added, "I think the vicious man deserved the death. "

两年后,斑斑生了一个儿子。当这个小孩一周岁时,应医生和斑斑将他们的小儿子带到山上去拜访斑斑的母亲和哥哥。快乐的外婆特别为她的小外孙办了第一个庆生会。
Two years later, Banban gave birth to a son. When the boy was one year old, Dr. Ying and Banban took their little son to visit Banban's mother and brother. The happy grandma held a party to celebrate her grandson's first birthday.

在酒席中,斑斑的母亲和哥哥喝了很多杯酒,两个人都喝醉了。应医生和斑斑也喝了好几杯。
At the party, Banban's mother and brother drank many cups of liquor and both got drunk. Dr. Ying and Banban had a few drinks, too.

饭后,应医生出去到附近一座森林里散步。当他刚走入森林后,他惊讶地发现了一头老虎睡在一块大石头旁,并且还有一股强烈的酒气从这头野兽身上发出。应医生立刻悄悄地溜了回来。他告诉了他的妻子。斑斑笑着说:"也许老虎偷了我母亲的酒喝,来庆祝我俩儿子的周岁生日的。"

After dinner, Dr. Ying wanted to take a walk in a nearby forest. There he was surprised to discover a tiger sleeping by a large rock, a strong odor of alcohol emanating from the wild animal. Dr. Ying quickly sneaked back and told his wife. Banban said with a smile, "Maybe the tiger stole my mom's liquor to celebrate our son's birthday, too."

渐渐地有很多人说他们在山上发现了老虎,可是没有人报道有人曾经被这种凶猛的野兽所伤害。相反地,有些人还说他们曾经遇到过老虎帮助他们把野狼吓跑。一个爬山人更说,一头颈子上有个大疤痕的雌老虎还将他从野狼的爪牙中救了后又跑掉了。

Gradually, more and more people reported that they had seen tigers on the mountain, but nobody knew of anyone who had been hurt by the fierce animals. Instead, people said that the tigers had often helped them frighten away the wolves. According to one mountain climber, an old female tiger with a scar on its neck had saved him from the attacks by wolves. After that, the tiger ran away.

斑斑经营家庭农场照顾小孩及处理家务都很成功,应医生全力发展医务。不到几年,这对夫妇的家便成了一个富裕的人家了。

All this time Banban managed the family farm, taking care of her baby and household affairs and she did all of them very well, while Dr. Ying concentrated on his medical practice. In a few years, the couple became wealthy.

然而成功也为他们带来了一个意想不到的大灾难。一股强盗绑架了他们的儿子,索要一笔很大的赎金。因为赎金的数字委实太高他们难以一次付出,应医生与绑匪接头要求降低赎金数字以便救出儿子,结果被绑匪拒绝了。斑斑建议由她溜进绑匪的藏地把他们的儿子救回,应医生不同意因为那太冒险了。

But their success brought them a horrible misfortuhe. A gang of bandits kidnapped their only son and demanded a huge ransom. As it was too much for them to pay one time in cash, Dr. Ying tried to negotiate with the bandits, asking them to decrease the amount so he could free his son. The negotiation failed. Banban suggested that she sneak into the bandits' hiding place to get their son back. Dr. Ying rejected the idea as too dangerous.

在此同时,绑匪警告应医生不可将此案件报告官府,否则将立刻杀害他的儿子。可是官家早已风闻此一秘密非法勾当,官家准备在应医生付与绑匪赎金时,发动突如其来的袭击,把绑匪绳之以法。

Meanwhile, the bandits warned Dr. Ying not to report the case to the government or they would kill his son. But some government officials got news of the secret anyway. The officials planned a surprise military strike while Dr. Ying went to deliver the ransom in exchange for his son.

在一个很晚的午后,应医生和斑斑去一个隐蔽的地方向绑匪的头子送上双方同意的赎金。当绑匪头子

聊斋精选

聊斋精选

收到赎金下令放人时,官兵突然一拥而上。绑匪首领大怒,立刻准备将小孩杀害作为报复,然后逃跑。

Late in one afternoon, Dr. Ying and Banban went to the hideout and paid the leader of bandits the ransom they had finally agreed on. As the leader received the ransom and ordered the release of the boy, the government troops suddenly appeared. The leader was furious and tried to kill the boy in retribution then flee.

就在这个时候,斑斑突然就地一滚变成了一头猛虎向绑匪扑去,把他们吓跑。事情发生得快如闪电。结果孩子被救回来了,斑斑也变回了一个女人,可是她已身受重伤,命在旦夕。

Just at that moment, Banban rolled over and changed herself into a tiger, rushing over to attack the bandits and frighten them away. Everything happened in a flash. The boy was rescued and Banban changed back into a woman, but she was fatally injured in the skirmish.

事件的发生吓坏了应医生,他把受伤妻子及饱受惊吓的儿子带回了家。

The action shocked Dr. Ying. He took his injured wife and frightened son home.

到家后,斑斑含泪地向应医生说:"我必须向你承认,我不是人类,我与我的母亲及哥哥都是老虎。虽然我们是老虎,我们从没有伤害过人类,除了有一次那个无恶不作的男子想在山中强暴我,我才把他杀了。"

After reaching home, Banban tearfully said to Dr. Ying, "I have to admit to you I'm not human. My mother, brother and I are all tigers. Although we are tigers, we have never hurt any person except the notorious man who tried to rape me on the mountain."

应医生将他的妻子抱在怀中,回答她:"我不管你是谁以及你的出身是什么,我只知道你是我最亲爱的妻子和我们儿子的母亲。"

Dr. Ying held his wife in his arms and replied, "I don't care who you are or what your background is. All I know is that you are my dearest wife and our son's mother."

斑斑终于死在她亲爱的丈夫怀抱中。

Banban finally died in the arms of her beloved husband.

应医生非常悲恸。他以最正统和最豪华的葬礼把他的妻子安葬了。他深深怀念他的爱妻而终生不再另娶。

Dr. Ying was very sad. He gave Banban the most formal and expensive funeral he could afford. He deeply missed his beloved wife. For the rest of his life, he never remarried.

这个小孩长大以后,他成为一个强壮的男子。然后他从军,不到十年就升为一位将军。在战场上,他勇猛得如同一头老虎,因而赢得老虎将军的称号。

When the boy grew up, he became a very strong man. After serving in the army for ten years, he was promoted to a general. In battle, he was so fierce and relentless like a tiger that he had been well known as the Tiger General.

聊斋精选

八、

翩
翩

Penance

罗子浮五岁时,他的父母亲先后亡故,幸得他那富有的叔叔收养他。叔叔和婶母待子浮如亲生。子浮长大后成为一个英俊的少年。他开始结交了一些放荡不羁的朋友,一个邪恶朋友更引导他逛妓院,子浮被一个年轻妓女的美色所迷醉。

When Luo Zifu was five years old, both of his parents died. His wealthy uncle adopted him. The uncle and his wife took good care of him like their own child. Zifu grew up to be a handsome young man. Gradually, he started to associate with some wayward young men. One wicked friend tempted him to go to a whorehouse. There, Zifu was charmed with the beauty of a young prostitute.

他把从叔父那儿偷来的钱全花在这个年轻的女人身上。当他的叔父发现了这件事后,将他狠狠地痛责一番。可是,子浮已经被这个妓女迷恋得不能自拔,于是他从叔父处偷了一大笔钱,离家出走,他要和这个妓女生活在一起。

He stole his uncle's money and spent it all on the young woman. When his uncle discovered this, he punished him severely. However, Zifu was so attracted to the prostitute that he could not refrain from sinning. Finally, he stole a large sum of money from his uncle and left his uncle's home for good. He wanted to live with the prostitute.

为了躲避他的叔父,他终于说服了这个年轻的女人和他一起离开这个城镇,他们搬到了一个很远的地方。这两个年轻恋人什么事也不做,整天去享受人生。不久,子浮的钱花光了,而他们又找不到工作。终于这个女人又回到当地的一家妓院重操旧业,子浮就变成了一个流浪汉。

In order to hide from his uncle, Zifu convinced the young woman to leave the town with him. They moved to a faraway place. The two young lovers did nothing but enjoy a good life. Soon Zifu's money ran out, and neither of them could find a job. Finally the woman went to work for a local brothel, and Zifu became a wanderer.

更糟糕的是他在这个时候又发现得了性病,由于没有钱去看医生,他的全身都被病毒所侵犯,与他整天在一起讨饭的乞丐也不愿意和他再在一起了。子浮于是去妓院向那个妓女求助,可是这个女人拒绝见他。子浮知道自己以往做了什么,因而实在没有这个脸面回到他的叔父家。

Worse still, he learned that he had a venereal disease. Without money to see the doctor, the syphilis soon infected his whole body. Even the beggars he went with everyday were reluctant to be near him anymore. He went to the brothel trying to beg the prostitute for help, but the woman refused to see him. Realizing what he had done, he was too ashamed to go back to his uncle's home.

在这种极度苦难和绝望的情况下,他决定自杀。于是他来到一座高山上计划在那儿了此残生。他坐在一株大树下,他在想,是在这株树上上吊、还是简简单单地去附近跳崖。突然间,他悲从中来,不由得放声大哭。他深深地后悔他的错误行为。假如事情能够重新再开始,他一定不会再犯这同样的错误了。如今一切都晚了,他毁了自己的一生。他站起身来缓缓地走向峭壁准备就从那儿跳下去。

Under such a great torment and despair, he decided to end his life. He went up to a high mountain, planning to commit suicide. Sitting under a tree, he pondered whether he should hang himself from the tree or

聊斋精选

simply jumped off a nearby cliff. Suddenly, he felt very sad and cried out loud. He bitterly regretted his wrongdoings. If he could have started over, he would not have repeated the same mistakes. But it was too late. He had ruined his life. Standing up and walking slowly toward the edge of the cliff, he planned to jump.

就在这个时候,他感觉到有人在拉扯他的上衣。回过头一看,他惊讶地发现了一位美丽年轻的女子正拉住他。女子问他为什么要自杀。

Just at that moment, he felt someone tugging on his shirt. Turning his head, he was surprised to find a very pretty young lady trying to hold him back. The woman asked him why he wanted to end his life.

由于决定自杀了,子浮就不理会这个女子而准备再度冲向峭壁。可是,事情很奇怪,有一种东西竟然阻挡了他,而且还把他又推回到原来的大树边,他跌坐在地上。因为这里除了他和这个神秘的女子外,没有任何其它的人。他向她望去,发觉她所站的地方离他还有好几尺远,根本没有碰到他,然而子浮可以肯定那一定是她阻止他的,虽然他并不知道她是如何办到的。于是,他站起来再向前冲去,结果他又被推倒跌坐在大树旁的地上。就这样他一再试了好几遍,他终于放弃了。于是他回答了这个女子询问他为何要自杀的问题。

Determined to die anyway, Zifu ignored the lady and started to rush forward to the edge of the cliff again. But strangely enough, something stopped him and instead pushed him back to the tree, where he fell to the ground. There was nobody else around but the mysterious woman. He looked at her and found that she had not touched him at all and was still standing a couple of feet away. Yet Zifu was sure that it was she who had prevented him from jumping, although he did not know how. So he stood up and tried again and again, and fell on the ground every time. After a while, he gave up and replied to the woman's question inquiring why he wanted to commit suicide.

"我是一个仙女。"这个年轻美丽的女子说道,"如果我能把你的病医好使你又成为一个全新的健康的人了,你是否还想去自杀呢?"

"I am a fairy." the pretty young woman said, "If I can cure your disease and make you a completely new and healthy man again, would you still want to die?"

因为子浮不能如他的计划去死,这个神秘有力的阻力使他无法冲向峭壁,他已经是无能为力了,于是他告诉她,"如果你能把我的健康恢复了,我就不再去自杀。"

Since Zifu could not go to die as he had planned, because he was powerless against the mighty, mysterious force that prevented him from rushing off the cliff, he told her, "If you could restore my health, I would not try to kill myself."

"好的,"这个女子说,"跟我来。"

"Good," the woman said, "just follow me."

聊斋精选

她把他带入不远处的一个山洞里。这个山洞的进出口并不是太大,只能容纳一个人通过。可是进得洞后,子浮惊奇地发现里面竟是宽大得像一栋大的房子,而且是座豪华的房子。虽然没有蜡烛也没有窗子,可是里面的光线和外面一样地明亮,一套漂亮的家具玲巧地摆放着。

She led him into a cave not too far away. The opening of the cave was only wide enough for one person to fit through at a time. After entering, Zifu was surprised to find that the inside was as big as a house, and a splendid one. It was as bright as the outside although there were no candles or windows. A set of nice furniture was artfully displayed.

女子没有要子浮坐下,她指着浴间要他先去洗个澡。当子浮坐在浴池里用那山上流进来的温泉水向他的身上淋去时,他很惊讶地发现每淋一次,自己的病情就减轻了一些。

The woman did not ask Zifu to sit down but pointed at the bathroom, wanting him to take a bath first. As he was taking a bath in the bathtub with the running water coming from the spring on the mountain, he was shocked to find that with every splash of water over his body, he could see his disease disappearing a little bit.

当他沐浴完了后,他发现健康已经完全恢复了。他兴高采烈,同时在想他如何还能再穿那些他刚才脱下来的脏衣服呢? 他用浴巾围着身体走出了浴池,看见这个女子用手指着几片树叶,那些树叶就立刻变成了漂亮的衣服,她让他去穿。

When he finished his bath, he discovered that he had completely regained his health. He was elated, but wondered how could he still put on the dirty clothes he had taken off? Walking out of the bathroom in a towel, he saw the lady point at some tree leaves that immediately turned into fine clothes for him to wear.

衣服穿好后,子浮又成为一位英俊的男子了。这个女子又用手指向几片树叶,这些树叶立刻变成了佳肴,有鱼有肉,还有蔬菜和米饭及一瓶美酒。她邀他共进晚餐。席间,他们互问了姓名。她的名字叫翩翩。她说她住在这座山上已经有很多很多年了。

After he dressed up like a handsome young man again, she pointed at some leaves to turn them into a delicious meal with fish, meat, vegetables and rice, plus a bottle of wine. She asked him to have dinner with her. While they were enjoying dinner, they exchanged names. Her name was Pianpian. She said she had lived in this mountain for a great number of years.

享用了这么一顿好久未吃到的精美的晚饭后,子浮感觉好极了。他现在是没有疾病,没有疼痛,穿着如此华美的衣服,坐在这么一栋豪华的屋子里,面对着这么一位美丽的年轻女子。突然间,他怀疑这整个的一切都不是真的,可能只是一个梦而已。翩翩似乎早已看透了他的心思,告诉他:"你不必怀疑,这一切都是真的。"

Having finished a good meal, which he had not had for a long time, Zifu felt great. Now he had no disease and no pain. He was wearing nice clothes and facing such a pretty young lady in such a splendid living room. He suddenly wondered whether the whole sequence of events was real, or a dream. Pianpian seemed to read his mind and told him, "You don't have to doubt. Everything is real."

聊斋精选

于是,他们相互介绍自己的世界。翩翩告诉子浮:"当一个人悔悟了他以前所做的一切都是错误时,上天往往会再给他一个机会。只有那些一而再再而三不停犯罪永不悔悟的人,才是没有救药必须遭受惩罚的。"接着她又笑道,"根据命运的安排,上天有意要我来帮助你的。"

They started to tell each other about their own worlds. Pianpian told Zifu, "Once a person realizes what he has done before was a great mistake and regrets his wrongdoing, Heaven will often give that person one more chance. Only the person who repeats the same mistake again and again without regret can be called hopeless to rocaive punishmente." Then she added with a smile, "According to fate, I was sent by Heaven to give you help."

当他们谈话时,翩翩从屋角的水池中取了水后,水马上变成了酒,于是他们一边喝酒一边聊着笑着,不久他们就愉快得像两个非常亲密的老朋友。

As they talked, Pianpian took some water from a fountain at the corner and it soon turned into wine. They drank and laughed pleasantly. Pretty soon, they felt like they had been intimate friends for a long time.

睡眠的时间到了,子浮问翩翩,"这里只有一张床,我怎么去睡觉呢?"在她含情默默地看着他时,他要求她,"我可以和你睡在一起吗?"

When bedtime came, Zifu asked Pianpian, "Since there is only one bed here, how and where am I supposed to sleep?" As she was looking at him affectionately, he begged, "May I sleep with you?"

"你怎么要求得这么多呢?"翩翩带着微笑回答他,明显地表示她是愿意的。
"How could you expect so much?" Pianpian replied with a smile, indicating that she was willing.

"我欠你的真是太多了。"子浮解释道。
"I owe you too much," Zifu explained.

翩翩大笑,于是他们开始拥吻。
Pianpian laughed as they started to kiss and hug together.

做完了爱后,她告诉他,他们前世原来是夫妻,因此命运才会安排她来救他。他们就可以再续夫妻前缘。
After making love, she told him that they had been husband and wife in their previous lives. Therefore, the fate had arranged for her to save his life, so they could resume their conjugal relationship.

两人开始住在一起像新婚夫妇一样地亲密。
The two began living together as newlyweds.

一天,另一位美丽的年轻女子来访翩翩。翩翩介绍给子浮说这是山上的另一位仙女,她的名字叫花城。花城带来了一篮水果作为庆贺他们团聚的贺礼。看起来花城年长翩翩几岁。她的美和翩翩的美不一样。和花城相比,翩翩好像还是一个大孩子,一个淑女,一个尚未成熟的美女,而花城是个迷人的美妇人,一个新婚的美丽少妇。子浮立刻被花城的美所迷惑。

One day, another pretty young woman came to visit Pianpian. Pianpian introduced her to Zifu as the other fairy on the mountain. Her name was Huacheng. Huacheng brought in a basket of fruits as a gift to congratulate them on their reunion. Huacheng looked a few years older than Pianpian, and her beauty was different from Pianpian's. Compared to Huacheng, Pianpian looked like a late teenager, an elegant girl, a premature beauty, while Huacheng was a bewitching beauty, like a newly wedded pretty woman. Zifu was immediately fascinated by Huacheng's beauty.

这两个年轻女子相互大胆地调侃,根本无视于子浮的在场。从她们的谈话中,子浮知道花城也有一个男友同居。

The two young women teased each other boldly and totally disregarded Zifu's presence. From their conversation, Zifu realized that Huacheng also hod a boyfriend living with her.

当这两个女子在嬉笑时,他故意将一个橘子掉在地上。当他弯下身子去捡橘子,从桌子底下,他偷看到了花城那双光溜溜的玉腿及脚面子,他不由得用手去轻摸一下花城的脚面。花城好像是毫无感觉,仍然与翩翩谈话和嬉笑。

While the two women were teasing and giggling, he purposely dropped an orange on the ground. As he bent over to pick up the fruit, he peeked under the table at Huacheng's naked legs and insteps, and he could not control himself from using a hand to softly touch one of her insteps. It seemed that naked legs and Huacheng did not feel it at all, as she was still talking and laughing with Pianpian.

可是,当子浮坐回到他的座位时,他恐惧地发现了他所穿的衣服都变回树叶子了。他知道是什么原因,立刻端正他的好色心态,慢慢地树叶子又变成了衣服。自从这次事情发生后,花城再来拜访翩翩时,他对她再也不敢怀有任何不正当的念头了。

But when Zifu sat back on his seat, he was scared to find that his clothes had been turned back into leaves. He knew the reason why. He immediately suppressed his lustful thoughts, and the leaves slowly turned back into clothes again. After this accident, Zifu dared not have any improper thoughts about Huacheng when she came to visit Pianpian.

一年后,翩翩和花城都生了小孩。翩翩生了一个儿子,花城生了一个女儿。因为她们是山上仅有的两位仙女,所以两家往来得很密切。当这两个小孩长大了以后,很自然地便恋爱起来了。翩翩和花城就决定让她们的子女结为夫妇。新婚夫妇住在另一个山洞里,距离他们的父母处也不太远。

A year later, both Pianpian and Huacheng gave birth. Pianpian had a son and Huacheng had a daughter. As they were the only two fairies on the mountain, the two families visited each other often. When the two children grew up, they naturally fell in love. Pianpian and Huacheng agreed to let their children get married. The two young newlyweds lived in another cave on the mountain, not too far from their parents.

聊斋精选

这时,子浮已经进入中年了,可是翩翩和花城几乎还是保持着当初的花容月貌,岁月在她们的身上似乎不留任何痕迹。

By this time, Zifu had entered middle age. But Pianpian and Huacheng still looked as young as ever. It seemed that the passage of time did not affect them at all.

当子浮日渐苍老后,他开始想念他的故乡以及他的叔父和婶母。他告诉翩翩他想回去看望他们。翩翩听了后深深地叹了一口气,苦笑着告诉他:"我不能阻止你去看望你的叔父和婶母,同时我也了解到按照天律,我们的夫妻缘分也到了终了的时候了。"

As Zifu grew older, he missed his native home and his uncle and aunt. He told Pianpian that he would like to pay them a visit. Pianpian sighed with a bitter smile and told him, "I cannot prevent you from visiting your uncle and aunt, but I realize that it is about the time to end our conjugal relationship, according to the heavenly rules."

子浮说他仍要回来的,翩翩没有再说什么,只能以眼泪回答了。

Zifu said that he would come back, but Pianpian said nothing, only responded with tears in her eyes.

翩翩使一根树枝变成了一匹马供子浮坐骑。她又把一些树叶变成干粮供他在路上吃,同时,她又使一些小石头变成银子供他在旅途中使用。若干日后,子浮终于回到了他叔父母的家。

Pianpian took a tree branch and turned it into a horse for Zifu to ride. She also turned some leaves into dried foods for him to eat on the way. And she turned some small stones into silver for him to use when he traveled. It took Zifu quite a few days to reach his uncle and aunt's home.

他的叔父母非常惊喜地看见那失去消息的侄子又回来了。当他们要仆人将子浮的马牵到马厩时,这匹马突然倒在地上变成了一根树枝。于是子浮连忙向他的叔父要了一身干净衣服,当他换好了后,那原来穿来的衣服都变回树叶子了。同时他所带来尚未吃完的食物和银子也都变回成树叶子和小石子。于是,子浮乃将他以往数十年来的奇遇告诉叔父婶母一家人,可是没有人相信他的故事。

His uncle and aunt were happily surprised to see their missing nephew back. When they ordered their servants to lead Zifu's horse into the stable, the horse suddenly fell on the ground and turned back into a tree branch. Zifu quickly asked his uncle to give him some clothes so he could change. After changing, the clothes he had just worn turned into leaves, and the food and the silver left with him all turned back into leaves and stones. Then Zifu told his uncle and aunt and their family about his miraculous experience over the past years, but nobody believed him.

一个月后,他终于说服了他叔父的两个儿子跟着他又回到了山上。可是,不管他们如何努力去找,就是找不到子浮和翩翩居住过多年的山洞,也找不到花城家和他们孩子们的家。

A month later, he convinced his uncle's two sons to follow him back to the mountain. No matter how hard they tried, they just could not find Pianpian's cave where he and she had lived for many years, neither the ones Huacheng and their children had lived.

聊斋精选

九、

书痴

The Pretty Girl in the Book

聊斋精选

自从公元 6 世纪开始到 1912 年,中国历代皇朝任用高级官员都是采取公开考试的方式。因此,在那长达一千四百多年的岁月里,一个出身低微的年轻男子一旦读书勤奋通过了官府的考试后,高官厚爵附有华厦可住和富贵人家的美丽女子的婚约都会在等待着他。所以民间就有这么一种说法:"书中自有黄金屋,书中自有颜如玉。"

Since the sixth century, the Chinese monarchy's government had always hired its senior officials through open examinations until 1912. During that long period of more than fourteen hundred years, it was very common that once a humble young man studied books hard enough and passed government examinations, a senior position in the government with a free and splendid official house to live in plus a marriage proposal to a pretty girl from a wealthy family would all come to him. That was the reason why this proverb prevailed in those days: *There are splendid houses in the books. There are pretty girls in the books.*

郎玉柱就是一个非常相信这种说法的年轻男子。他单独一个人生活,因为他的父母都已亡故,又没有兄弟姐妹。他从父母处继承了二十亩耕地和一栋陈旧房子。除了在田地里干活外,他把其余的时间都用在读书上,一心想有一天可以中榜而功成名就。

Lang Yuzhu was a young man who strongly believed in this proverb. He lived by himself for his parents had died. And he had no brothers or sisters. He inherited twenty acres of agricultural land and an old house from his parents. Aside from working in the field, he spent all his time reading books in a wish to pass the examinations and obtain the abovementioned benefits.

可是,年复一年,他什么榜都未中过。人们讥笑他,可他从不在乎,仍然日夜不停地研读书籍。

But year after year, he did not pass any examinations. People laughed at him, but he did not care. He continued to study day and night.

时间一天天过去,他已经到达婚娶的年龄了,媒婆们来到他家说要为他找一个妻子,可是他拒绝了。他说他会在书中找到一个美丽女子的,因为一向都是这么说的。这个回答使得人们愈加觉得他真是个傻瓜。

As time went by, he reached marriageable age. A few matchmakers approached him offering to help him find a match to be his wife. He turned down the suggestion, saying that he would find a pretty girl in the books as the proverb said. The reply made people further believe that he was indeed a fool.

一天,他偶然在一本书中发现了一张美丽女子的画片。女子穿着一件粉红色的丝质衣服,上面绣着玫瑰花朵,似乎直对着他微笑。他一下子乐坏了,告诉他自己,"我终于找到她了。"

One day, he happened to find a picture of a pretty girl in his book. The girl wore a pink silk dress with embroidered roses on it. Her smiling face seemingly looked directly at him. He was elated, telling himself, "I have finally found her."

他把画片贴在墙上。从此以后,每当他吃饭时,他就会盛一碗饭放在画片前面的一张桌子上。他从田里采来最美丽的花朵插入瓶子后也放在桌子上。只要他有时间,他就会坐在画片的对面,默默地向着画片中的美女一望就是几个小时。对他来说,这是他一天中的最高的享受了。一天又一天,一个月又一个月,他一直如此地爱恋着这张画片中的美女。

He posted the picture on the wall. Since then, whenever he ate, he would put a bowl of food on a table in front of the picture. He collected the most beautiful wild flowers from the field and put them in a vase on the table too. When he had time, he would sit down facing the picture, doing nothing but staring at the beauty silently for hours. For him, it was the most enjoyable moment in his day. Day after day, month after month, he continued to admire the beauty on the picture.

一天午后,一件奇迹发生了。当玉柱干完了田地里的活及读了两个小时的书后,他搬了一张椅子又坐在画片的对面。就在他目不转睛地望着墙上的美女时,美女突然从画片上走了出来,站在地上。她羞答答地告诉玉柱,"我是天上的仙女,上天派我下凡来做你的妻子的。我的名字叫媚宁。"

One late afternoon, a miracle happened. After Yuzhu had finished his work in the field and read his books for a couple of hours, he took a chair to sit facing the picture again. While staring at the beauty, he saw the pretty girl suddenly walk out of the picture and stand on the ground. She told Yuzhu shyly, "I'm a fairy sent by Heaven to come to the world of human to be your wife. My name is Meining."

玉柱自从父母亡故后,就没有一个家人。如今突然有了一个妻子,他真不知道如何去处理新生活。幸而媚宁是个很好的家庭主妇,她立刻开始去操持家务。

Since his parents died, he had never had a family. Now he suddenly had a wife. He did not know how to manage his new life. Luckily, Meining was a good housewife. She quickly started to take care of the household.

他们快乐地生活在一起就像任何一对新婚的夫妻一样。

聊斋精选

聊斋精选

They happily lived together, just like a couple of newly married ordinary people.

不久,媚宁又发现了玉柱读书时根本没有完全明了书中的含义,不过是背诵而已。于是,媚宁又一个字一个字地为他讲解每一段书中的意义。在媚宁的悉心指导下,玉柱的学业突飞猛进。一年后,他通过了当地县府所举办的考试。

Soon Meining also discovered that when Yuzhu read the books, he did not completely comprehend the meaning of words. All he did was memorize them. Under Meining's deliberate tutelage, Yuzhu's comprehension of the Chinese classical books improved tremendously. A year later, he passed the examination held by the local county government.

因为媚宁的突然出现,使得玉柱的一些邻居们产生了怀疑。没有人知道她从何处来,以及如何嫁给了这个穷农夫。她是如此地一个绝色美女,把家务操作得又是如此地好,一个嫉妒的邻居暗中向官府密报说她一定是个女巫,不是一般的平凡妇人。

Because of Meining's sudden appearance, some people in Yuzhu's neighborhood became suspicious. Nobody knew where she came from or why she had married the poor farmer. She was so beautiful and so nice in handling the household that a jealous neighbor secretly reported to the government that she must be an enchantress, not an ordinary woman.

媚宁被传唤出庭。在法庭上,她要求法官给她一个单独会谈的机会,她可以私下报告她的出身。法官认为她不过是个弱女子,不怕她逃跑,便要其他的人离开,于是媚宁告诉法官她是从天上下来的仙女。为了证实她有神通,她把法官所做那些见不得人的脏事连他的妻子都不知道的种种非法勾当都一一说出。这下子把法官吓坏了,立刻下令以查无实据,将她释放,了结此案。

Meining was summoned to appear in court. She asked the judge to let her tell him in private about her background. As she was such a delicate young lady, the judge was not afraid of her fleeing. After all the other people had left the courtroom, she told the judge that she was a fairy from Heaven. To prove that she had supernatural powers, she revealed all the judge's illegal records, which were supposed to be his most personal secrets that even his wife was not aware of. The judge was scared and quickly ordered her release and closed the case due to insufficient evidences.

因为媚宁是个绝色美女,每当她和玉柱外出时,都会招致很多好色之徒的不愉快的困扰。她便告诉玉柱以后必须出远门时,她将藏身在画片中而由他将画片放在一本书里,如同当初一样,然后他携带着书去旅行。当到达目的地住进了旅店后,她就从画片中走出与玉柱共度良宵。

As she was a great beauty, whenever she went out with Yuzhu, she would always attract many admirers and often caused some unwelcome unpleasantness. She told him that when they had to make an out of town trip again, she would hide herself in a picture and let him put it in a book as she had been before. All he had to do was carry the book to travel. When they reached their destination and checked in to a lodge, she would come out of the picture and spend the night with him.

一年后,他们用这种方法去了省城,玉柱去参加省府举办的考试。接着他又考取了。三年后,玉柱又通过了京城里的最高考试,并被派任为京官。于是,他携同媚宁住到京城里去了。

They used this method to go to the capital of the province a year later, when he went to attend another examination administered by the provincial government. And he passed that examination as well. Three years later, he passed the highest central examination in the capital of nation. He was appointed to a senior position in the central government. He and Meining moved to the nation's capital to live.

玉柱个性耿直,他看不惯朝廷里的很多贪官污吏,特别是那些经管财务的官员,更与他格格不入。慢慢地,这批贪官也害怕玉柱从中泄露他们的不法行为,计划将玉柱贬逐出朝政,就诱骗他进入了一个陷阱。一个恶毒的计谋终于把玉柱弄进了大牢。不管他如何为自己辩护,都无法上奏皇帝使他洗脱罪责。

Yuzhu was a man of integrity. He could not tolerate the corruption in the central government. So he did not get along well with his bureaucratic colleagues, especially the ones who held the financial positions. Gradually, those corrupt officials feared Yuzhu might disclose their illegal activities. They tried to oust him from government service by way of framing him with a false charge. A sophisticated vicious plot finally put Yuzhu in jail. No matter how much he struggled trying to clear himself of the phony charge, he could not make his appeal reach the emperor.

当玉柱被捕时,媚宁告诉他不要害怕。她说她会设法让皇帝了解真相的。

When Yuzhu was arrested, Meining told him not to worry too much. She said she would try to let the emperor know the truth.

在一个夜深的晚上,当皇帝在御书房阅读奏章时,一个身着黑色衣服的陌生女子突然走进了书房,并将一份奏书呈交给了皇帝。在皇帝还未来得及询问她是谁时,这个神秘女子就迅疾不见了踪影。这一切发生得如此快速和出人意料。皇宫是一个警卫森严的地方,然而这个女子仍然能够随便进出而无阻挠。皇帝大怒,立即下令仔细搜查,结果仍无她的踪迹。

One late evening, when the emperor was reading documents in his den, a strange young woman in

聊斋精选

black clothes suddenly appeared and left him a written report. Before the emperor had a chance to inquire who she was, the mysterious woman disappeared right in front of him. Everything happened swiftly and unexpectedly. The royal palace was always tightly secured against break-ins, yet the woman still entered and left without being stopped. The furious emperor ordered an immediate search, but no trace of her could be found.

　　于是皇帝开始阅读这个送来的奏文,读后更加大怒了,因为报告内列举了财务大臣的诸多贪污劣迹,以及诬陷一个忠臣郎玉柱的事实。

The emperor then read the report and he was further furious at his financial officials' corruption and the false charge against his most upright officials, Lang Yuzhu.

　　但是这个进出大内的神秘女子又是谁呢? 以及她如何可以在这警卫森严的皇宫内来去自如呢? 因为找不到答案,皇帝只能猜想这一定是上天派来信使帮助他整顿朝政的。于是他下旨彻查,把那些贪官污吏都予以严办,玉柱非但获得昭雪释放,还得到晋升。

But who was this mysterious female messenger and how could she come and leave so freely in his tightly secured palace? As he could not find the answer, he presumed that maybe the messenger was sent to him from Heaven to help him rule his kingdom. He demanded a thorough investigation and severely punished all the corrupt senior officials. Yuzhu's case was cleared. He was not only freed from prison but also promoted.

　　从此玉柱的仕途非常顺遂。当他六十岁时,他辞退朝政,携带全家人荣归故居。此时玉柱和媚宁已经有很多儿女及孙辈。可是,媚宁仍然看起来像当初一样地年轻貌美,岁月对她毫不留痕,不认识的人往往误认为她是她的媳妇的妹妹。这一大家人看待她不仅是一个敬重的母亲和祖母,更恭敬如神明。

Since that time, Yuzhu's political career proceeded smoothly. When he reached age of sixty, he retired from the government service and took his family back to his native home. By this time, Yuzhu and Meining had had many children and grandchildren. Yet, Meining still looked as young and pretty as ever. The years did not mark any change upon her. People who did not know her often mistook her for the younger sister of her daughter-in-law. The big family treated her not only as a respectful mother and grandmother but also as a goddess.

　　玉柱享有长寿,一直活到95岁方才无疾而终。当一切安葬事宜办妥后,媚宁召集子孙齐聚在大厅中,她告诉大家这是她返回天上的时候了。她向天空呼哨了一声,立刻飞来一只巨大的白鹤,停在前院。

聊斋精选

于是她骑在鹤的背上，在全家人的跪拜下，白鹤载着她飞向天空，终于没有了踪影。

    Yuzhu enjoyed a long life. He died a natural death at the age of ninety-five. After the funeral, Meining gathered all of her offspring in the splendid family hall. She told them that it was time for her to go back to Heaven. She whistled at the sky and a huge white crane flew down and landed in the front yard. She sat upon the bird's back and it took her flying far into the sky, while her human family knelt down in the yard and watched her fly away.

The Heart Eater

虽然他的妻子是个美丽的女子,可是好色的王生仍然喜欢拈花惹草,只要有机会,他是从不放弃的。

Although his wife was a beautiful woman, Wang Sheng, a lewd man, still liked to dally with young pretty girls' affections whenever he had a chance.

一天,王生骑着一匹马走在一条荒凉的路上,他注意到一个纤弱女子独自一人靠着路边一株大树哭泣。他停下马来,走到她的身前,发现那是一个非常美貌的年轻女子,不过二十岁刚出头而已。王生当然不会放弃与这么一个绝色美女接近的机会,他便竭尽同情的姿态询问这个女子,"姑娘,这究竟是怎么一回事? 能让我知道你为什么如此伤心吗? 我可以帮助你吗?"

One day, when Wang Sheng was riding his horse on a deserted road, he noticed a delicate woman crying sadly, leaning against a tall tree by the roadside. He stopped and approached, finding her a very pretty young woman in her early twenties. Naturally, he would not want to miss the opportunity to deal with such a rare beauty. As sympathetically as he could, he asked the woman, "What's the matter with you, young lady? May I know why you're so upset? And may I offer you some help?"

"我的丈夫在几个星期以前死了,"女子一边抹着眼泪一边说,"我正准备去前面的城里找他的亲戚要求帮助,但我不知道他们是否愿意帮助我。如果他们不愿意,我真不敢想像我以后如何独立谋生。我的父母早已亡故,我又没有兄弟姐妹可以依靠,我哭因为我实在是无助啊。"

"My husband died a few weeks ago," the woman replied, wiping her tears, "I'm going to visit his relatives in the town ahead to ask for help. But I do not know if they will help me or not. If they won't, I can't imagine how I can make a living all by myself. Both my parents have died and I have no brothers or sisters to depend on. I'm crying because I am helpless."

王生不花多少时间,就说服了这个纤弱无助的孀妇接受他的帮助。他们交换了姓名,她的名字叫静静。他请她上马和他一起去到城里,在城里的另一头他的妻子不会去的地方,他给静静租了一间小房子,又为她买了点家具及食物。为了表达她的感谢,她轻轻地拥抱了他一下,于是他吻她,发现她没有拒绝,他便将她抱上了床。这个美丽的女子静静就这样成了王生的秘密情人。

It did not take Wang Sheng too long to convince the delicate and helpless young widow to accept his offering of help. They exchanged names. Her name was Jingjing. He invited Jingjing to ride with him on the horse and took her back to his town. He rented a small house for her at the other side of town where his wife would not go. He bought some furniture and groceries for her. In appreciation for his help, she gave him a slight hug. He kissed her and met little resistance. He took her to bed. Thus the pretty young woman, Jingjing, became Wang Sheng's secret mistress.

王生很高兴这么容易就弄到了一个如此美丽的情人。他尽可能把时间都用在这女人身上,而没有一个人知道他的秘密。

Wang Sheng was very happy at having found such a pretty sweetheart so easily. He spent as much time as he could with the woman, with nobody else knowing his secret.

可是有一天,他在街上被一个道士挡住了,道士在中国据说是有某些神通的。这个道士警告他命在旦夕,因为他现正被一个妖魔所迷惑,这个妖魔计划要他的性命。王生是个无神论者,他一笑了之不予理会,就准备走开,对于这个警告他是掉以轻心的。道士就把他的名字及道观地址告诉了王生,"如果有危急,可以来找我。"然后道士就走开了。

But one day, a Taoist priest stopped him on the street. Taoist priests were widely known in China as having some supernatural powers. The priest warned him that his life was in jeopardy for he had been bewitched by a demon that was planning to take his life. As an atheist, Wang Sheng laughed and ignored him, trying to walk away. He made light of the priest's warning. The priest told Wang Sheng his name and where his temple was located. "Come and see me if you feel you are in danger." Then the priest departed.

王生这天下午正巧无事可做,便又溜到他的秘密情妇那里,准备将一个下午好好地消磨在那儿。当他到达这栋小房子时,发觉前门从里面锁了,这是很不寻常的。他就到后院里去,想从后门进入。可是后门也从里面锁上了。他便走近窗户偷偷地张望他的情人大白天在家做什么。突然间,他被惊吓住了。

As Wang Sheng had nothing to do that afternoon, he went to his secret sweetheart again. He planned to have a wonderful time with her the rest of day. When he reached the small house, he found that the front door was locked from inside which was unusual. So he went to the backyard trying to enter from the back door. But the back door was also locked from inside. Then he approached the window, taking a peek to see what his sweetheart was doing during the daytime. Suddenly, he was shocked.

他没有看到他的情妇,可他看到了一个凶恶的妖魔正弯下身子用一支笔在桌子上面画什么东西。王生继续看下去不敢发出一点儿声音,他看到了这个妖魔正在一张人皮上画一个美女的脸。画完之后,这个妖魔站起身子把人皮向身上一披,立刻变成了一个妖艳美女,他的秘密情人静静。

Instead of seeing his sweetheart, he saw a fierce demon bending over a table using a pen to paint something. He kept watching, daring not make any sound, and he found the demon was painting a pretty woman's face on a piece of human skin. After finishing the painting, the demon stood up and put the skin over his body and he suddenly became a delicate beautiful girl, his secret mistress, Jingjing.

王生这下子真的惊骇极了,他迅速地溜出后院,向道观跑去。

Wang Sheng was scared. He quickly sneaked out of the backyard and ran to the Taoist temple.

"道士的话是对的,静静是个妖魔变的,我的性命真是危在旦夕。"他自言自语道。

The priest is damn right. Jingjing is a demon, and my life is in jeopardy, he told himself.

聊斋精选

89

他冲进了道观恳求道士帮助。听了王生诉说的关于他的神秘情妇的情形后,道士给了王生一道符,要他在晚间将符挂在他的卧室门上。道士说这道符可以阻止妖魔再来找他。王生拿了符后急忙回家。他把全部经过告诉了妻子,并请求她的原谅。

He rushed into the temple, begging the priest for help. After hearing what Wang Sheng had told him about the mysterious woman, the priest gave Wang Sheng an amulet and told him to hang it on the door of his bedroom. The priest said the amulet would be able to stop the demon from coming to him again. Wang Sheng took the amulet and hurried home. He told his wife the whole story and begged for her forgiveness.

妻子是又惊又气。她告诉他,她将到孩子的卧房去和孩子同睡一床。王生只好独睡并面对这个危险情况。

Wife was shocked and furious. She told him she would move to the other bedroom to share a bed with their child. Wang Sheng had to sleep himself to face the dangerous situation.

到了晚上,当全家的人都上床睡觉后,王生躺在床上两眼圆睁向着门望去。午夜刚过不久,他听到了房门外面有脚步声。他不敢开门,从门眼中偷看,发现这个妖魔仍然装扮成他的情妇模样向着他的卧室走来,王生在房内吓得全身发抖。

During the night, when everybody else in the family had gone to bed, Wang Sheng lay awake with his eyes open on the door. Shortly after midnight, he heard footsteps outside his bedroom. He dared not open the door, but peeked through the keyhole. Indeed, he found the demon, still disguised as his secret mistress, walking toward his room where he was shivering inside.

突然间,她停下了脚步,向着挂在门上的那道符望了一眼,然后很不情愿地退却了几步就不见了。王生松了一口气,可仍盯着外面望。不多久这个女孩又回来了,手上拿了把怪形的锤子。她开始与符上发射出来的光芒奋战。终于,她把光芒逼退回符中,然后她走上前去,将符撕下扔在地上,在大笑声中走进了房间,同时她已经变回了原来的妖魔样子。王生此时早已吓得跌倒在地上昏了过去。

Suddenly, she stopped and took a look at the amulet hanging on the door, then, she retreated a few steps reluctantly, and soon disappeared. Wang Sheng relaxed a little bit, though still keeping an eye on the outside. A few minutes later, the girl returned with a strange hammer in hands. She started to fight against the bolts of lighting shooting out from the amulet. Finally, she pushed the bolts of lighting back into the amulet, and she stepped forward, tearing off the amulet and tossing it on the ground. Meanwhile, she had turned back into a demon, walking into the room laughing loudly. By this time, Wang Sheng had been greatly terrified lying on the ground in a dead faint.

妖魔弯身用他那像利爪一样的手指割开了王生的胸膛,挑出他的心脏,当场就活生生地吃了,鲜血从他嘴巴的两边一直流下来。然后他在狞笑声中走了出去。

聊斋精选

The demon stooped down and broke through Wang Sheng's chest with his sharp talons. He ripped out Wang Sheng's heart and ate it right on the spot with blood running down both sides of his mouth. Then he left, laughing wickedly.

王生一家人被这场凶杀吓坏了。当妖魔走后,大家围了过来,王生的妻子扑在他的身上哭得死去活来。她边哭边诉说着这是她丈夫自己找来的惨死,是他不忠于她愚笨地带来了凶手。他是该死的。可是作为他多年的妻子,她也不想再去多责备他了,只有悲恸。

The murder was a great shock to Wang Sheng's family, who came to him after the demon left. Wang Sheng's wife cried over her husband's dead body. She blamed him for the tragedy. It was he who had been unfaithful to her and unwittingly brought in the murderer. He deserved it. But having been his wife for many years, she did not want to curse him further but cried sadly.

突然,她想起了王生在生前曾经告诉过她关于道士的事情。是这个道士送给王生这张符来保护他免遭妖魔毒手的,明显地,这张符的力量还是不够。很有可能这个道士还有神通能挽回她丈夫的性命。于是,她来到道观一把鼻涕一把眼泪地把这事情的经过告诉了道士。

Suddenly, she remembered what Wang Sheng had told her about the Taoist priest. It was the priest who had given Wang Sheng the amulet to protect him from the demon's attack. Obviously, the amulet was not strong enough. And very possibly, the priest might have some supernatural ability to bring back her husband's life. She went to the Taoist temple and tearfully told the priest what had happened.

道士听了这个悲惨的故事后大怒。他要王生的妻子带他去她家察看。检查了以后,道士告诉她这个妖魔还藏身在这附近。他要王生的妻子带他逐门逐户去查问是否有陌生人在这天出现在这附近。终于有一家女主人告诉道士说她刚在那天早上雇了一个年老的女佣,因为这个女佣说她没有家人,需要一份工作来养活她自己。

Having heard the sad story, the priest became angry. He asked Wang Sheng's wife to take him to her home to check. After checking around, he told her that he had sensed that the demon was still hiding in the neighborhood. With the help of Wang Sheng's wife, the priest searched the entire neighborhood, house by house, to see if any stranger had appeared that day. Finally, the female master of a house told the priest that she had just hired an old maid who had said she had no family and needed a job to support herself.

当这个年老女佣发现了道士时,她立即想调头逃走,道士立即拔出宝剑阻止了她,并逼着她退到后院中,要她变回原形。在这种情况下,老妇人没有办法,只好变回了妖魔,跪倒在神通广大的道士面前,要求饶命。

When the old maid laid eyes on the priest, she immediately tried to turn away and flee. But the priest drew out his sword to stop her. He forced her to retreat to the backyard and demanded her to turn back to

聊斋精选

what she was originally. Under the circumstances, the old maid had no choice but to turn back into a demon kneeling before the powerful priest, begging for mercy.

妖魔辩解说是王生自己好色找死的。道士说虽然王生对他的妻子不忠,也不至于要他的性命。于是,道士强询妖魔一共杀害了多少人。当道士知道妖魔已经杀死了十多个人时,道士毅然决然地用剑将妖魔的头砍了下来。奇怪的是妖魔的颈上竟无一滴鲜血外流,只有一股烟雾冲出无头的脖子。道士便急忙用一个小瓶子将烟雾吸进了瓶内然后将瓶口封好,准备离去。

The demon tried to defend himself insisting that it was Wang Sheng who had been lewd first so he deserved what he had gotten. The priest replied that even though Wang Sheng was not loyal to his wife, he did not deserve death as a punishment. Then the priest harshly demanded that the demon confess how many other people he had murdered. When the priest found that the demon had murdered more than ten people, without hesitation he used his sword to cut off the demon's head. Strangely enough, there was no blood, but a string of smoke rose up the headless neck. The priest quickly used a small bottle to absorb the smoke and sealed the bottle. Then he was ready to leave.

王生的妻子目睹了道士的神通。她拦住了他,恳求他救回她丈夫的性命。道士告诉她,他的法力还办不到,但是他建议她到城西找一个要饭的年老流浪汉。他说那个乞丐不是凡人,他的法力比他强多了。

Wang Sheng's wife witnessed the priest's supernatural powers. She stopped him, begging him to restore her husband's life. The priest told her that his power was not strong enough to do that. But he suggested that she seek help from an old vagrant who begged for food everyday in the western part of town. According to the priest, the beggar was not an ordinary man. His supernatural power was much stronger than his.

这个可怜的女人遵照道士的忠告到了城镇的西部。她很快地找到了这个乞丐,恳求他救回她丈夫的性命,可是老乞丐根本不承认他有什么法力,然后就想脱身。王生的妻子立即挡住了他,并跪倒在他的面前恳求他无论如何要大发慈悲。尽管乞丐再三说他无能为力,她还是从早上一直跪到下午,最后老乞丐向肮脏的地上吐了一口痰,向着王生的妻子说,如果她能将这口痰吃了,他就设法救她丈夫的命。

The poor woman took the priest's advice and went to the western part of town. She easily found the beggar, and asked him to restore her husband's life. But the beggar denied having any power at all and tried to escape. Wang Sheng's wife quickly stopped him, and knelt down in front of him pleading for his mercy, no matter how much the beggar said he was unable to do it. From morning till the afternoon, she continued until finally the beggar spat on the dirty ground telling Wang Sheng's wife that if she could eat his spit, he would try to restore her husband's life.

看在能救回她丈夫性命的分上,这个勇敢的女人真的趴下去将老乞丐的脏痰吃了。殊不知当她刚站起身子后,这个乞丐就在大笑声中突然跑走了,并说她被他骗了。不久就跑得无影无踪。

For the sake of having her husband's life back, the brave woman bent and ate the old beggar's dirty spit. But when she stood up, the beggar suddenly ran away, laughing and saying that she had been cheated. Soon, the beggar disappeared from sight.

王生的妻子伤心极了。她一无所获回到了家中,而且嘴巴里还有臭味。在极大的悲痛中,她准备将王生的没有了心脏的胸膛折合起来,然后计划安葬。

Wang Sheng's wife was crushed. She returned home empty-handed but with a foul taste in her mouth. In great dismay, she tried to close Wang Sheng's broken chest without a heart inside and planned to bury him.

坐在她丈夫的尸身旁边,她痛苦地回想这一天的事情。又想起了那一口脏痰,面对着丈夫满腔肮脏的血斑,突然间,她突然有一种想呕吐的感觉。她想转过头去不要呕吐在丈夫的胸膛里,可是迟了,她把胃里所有的残羹完全呕吐进了她丈夫的空腔内。一时间,她惶恐得不知如何是好。可就在这个时候,她不胜惊讶地发现她刚才所吐的东西变成了一个跳动的心脏在剖开的胸腔里。她便急忙把王生的胸腔缝合起来。王生竟然神奇一般地又活了过来。

Sitting by her husband's body, she bitterly recalled the day's events. Thinking about the dirty spit while seeing the dirty bloody spots in her husband's empty chest, she suddenly had a feeling of needing to vomit. Unable to avoid turning her head over, she vomited whatever the food had been left in her stomach directly into her dead husband's open chest. While she was terrified at how to clean up the big mess, she discovered in great astonishment that whatever she had just vomited had become a beating heart in the broken chest. She quickly stitched up Wang Sheng's chest. Miraculously, Wang Sheng revived.

经过了好几个月的休养,王生终于复原了。终其余生,他永远不再想去动一个年轻女子的歪脑筋了,不管这个女子是多么的美丽,他忠于他的妻子,这个救了他性命的女人。

After several months of rest, Wang Sheng regained his health. For the rest of his life, he would never have any lascivious thoughts about any young woman again, no matter how pretty she was. He remained loyal to his wife, the woman who had saved his life.

十一、

黄英

The Chrysanthemum

菊花有很多种颜色及大小样式。
Chrysanthemum plants bear flowers in many colors and sizes.

马子才自幼就是一个菊花迷。长大了以后,他想在他的花园里种植各式各样的菊花。只要听说在某一个地方有一种珍稀品种的菊花,他就会去买些种子回来种植在他自家的花园内。有时候这些种子长大成树,有时候他没种成。

Ma Zicai had been an admirer of chrysanthemums ever since he was a child. When he grew up, he tried to grow as many of these plants in his garden as he could. Whenever he heard of a certain rare chrysanthemum at a certain place, he would go there and buy the seeds to try to grow them at home. Sometimes, the seeds grew up to be healthy plants, but sometimes, he failed.

有一天,子才在一处公共花圃里遇到了一个名叫黄近的年轻男子。他很快发现黄近对于菊花的知识比他渊博多了。他便邀请黄近到他的家中,请黄近观看他所种植的各种菊花,特别是那些没有成功的品种。黄近把那些萎谢的幼苗及已经枯萎了的树根子拔掉,重新种植,他对子才说,如果这些菊花活过来的话,就告诉他。子才漫不经心地应诺着,因为他认为这是不可能的事情。

One day, Zicai happened to meet a young man named Huang Jin at a flower nursery, and he soon discovered that Huang Jin had much more knowledge about the chrysanthemums than he. He invited Huang Jin to his home and showed him what he had grown, particularly the ones that had not succeeded. Huang Jin picked up the withered branches and dead roots and re-planted them. He asked Zicai to let him know if they revived. Zicai answered in a roundabout way, as in his mind he doubted it would happen.

大约十天后,出乎子才的意料,所有重新种植的已经萎谢了的幼苗及枯萎了的树根子都活了。这真是奇迹!子才赶紧跑到黄近的家中,兴奋地告诉他这个好消息。黄近只是微笑一下,显然他一点也不惊讶,好像是理所当然似的。

About ten days later, to Zicai's great surprise, all of the withered branches and dead roots came back to life. What a miracle! Zicai hurried to Huang Jin's home at the address he had given to him and excitedly told him the happy news. Huang Jin smiled, but seemingly was not surprised.

黄近与他的姐姐黄英同住在一栋租来的小房子里。他告诉子才他们是双胞胎姐弟,父母已于数年前去世。当黄近将子才介绍给他的姐姐黄英后,黄英就以茶点招待子才。子才发现黄英长得很美,他们谈得也很愉快。

Huang Jin lived with his sister, Huang Ying, in a small rented house. He told Zicai that he and his sister were twins. Their parents had passed away several years ago. After Huang Jin introduced Zicai to Huang Ying, she treated Zicai to tea and homemade cakes. Zicai noticed that Huang Ying was a very pretty young woman. They had a pleasant conversation.

和子才一样,这对姐弟都喜欢种菊花。黄近告诉子才他们现在所租的房子很小,没有花园或后院,因此他们正在找寻一栋房子能有个大的后院,可以种植他们所喜爱的菊花。

Like Zicai, both the brother and sister were fond of growing chrysanthemums. Huang Jin told Zicai that because the house they rented was very small without a garden or backyard, they were looking for a house with a big backyard so they could grow their favorite chrysanthemums.

子才和他的妻子张凤住在一栋很大的房子里,房子是他的父母过世后继承下来的,后院里有一座好几亩大的花园,种植着数百种菊花,园子一角还有一栋很小的房子,原来是供园丁住的。子才和张凤常觉得房子太大了难以照料,特别是这座大花园,而他们又没有孩子。

Zicai and his wife, Zhang Feng, lived in a large house, inherited from his parents, with a huge garden in the backyard covering several acres. They grew hundreds of kinds of chrysanthemums in their garden. At the corner of garden, there was a small house for the gardener to live originally. Zicai and Zhang Feng always thought the house was too big for them to take care of, especially the huge garden, and they had no children.

由于子才的大部分时间都消磨在花园里,张凤便时常感觉很寂寞。所以当他和她商量邀请黄近和黄英搬到他家后院子的那幢小房子里居住,不收房租只是帮忙他们照料花园时,她立刻同意了。

As Zicai spent most of his time in the garden, Zhang Feng often felt lonely. So when he discussed with her about the idea of inviting Huang Jin and Huang Ying to live at their small house in their garden, with free rent but helping them take care of the chrysanthemums, she quickly agreed.

妻子既已同意,子才便到黄近家当面邀请。姐弟两人欣然接受,并于数天后就搬了过去。

With his wife's consent, Zicai came back to Huang Jin and delivered the invitation. The brother and sister happily accepted and moved in a few days later.

张凤和黄英几乎是一见如故。白天里,当这两个男子在花园中忙碌时,这两个女子便像亲姐妹一样在屋子里一同料理家务。两家人虽然住在两栋不同的房子里,他们都在子才和张凤的家里吃饭。他们相互照顾就好像是快乐的一家人。

Almost immediately, Zhang Feng and Huang Ying got along very well. In the daytime, when the two men were busy in the garden, the two women took care of household affairs as intimately as sisters. The two families lived in separate buildings, but they ate together at Zicai and Zhang Feng's house. They treated and cared for each other like a happy family.

慢慢地子才发现黄英对于菊花的了解似乎比她的弟弟还要深。

Gradually, Zicai found that Huang Ying's knowledge about chrysanthemums seemed even better than her brother's.

聊斋精选

因为子才也不是个非常富裕的人，而且他在菊花上又花费了太多的钱财，黄近便建议子才将他的菊花园子对外界开放公开卖花。子才接受了这个建议。因为有了黄近和黄英的帮助，不多久，子才的菊花生意竟是一天比一天兴隆。

Since Zicai was not a very wealthy man and he was spending so much money on the chrysanthemums, Huang Jin suggested that Zicai open his garden to the public to sell the flowers. Zicai accepted his advice. With the help of Huang Jin and Huang Ying, Zicai's chrysanthemum business became very prosperous.

人们从各地来到子才的花圃里买花、花种子及花秧回家去种。更重要的是子才的菊花种子和秧苗保证可以长得出来。有的顾客甚至于把他们家中那些已经枯萎了的珍稀品种菊花幼苗或枯根拿来问子才是否能重新成活，子才就将这些交给黄近和黄英去重新种植。十天后，这些死了的幼苗和枯根就都又活了过来，于是这些顾客就会很高兴地时常付给子才比原先同意的价钱还要多的钱。

People from all over the places came to buy flowers, seeds and seedlings from Zicai. Most importantly, Zicai's chrysanthemums seeds and seedlings were guaranteed to grow. Some customers even brought in their already withered seedlings or dead roots of the rare species asking Zicai if he could revive them. Zicai would then give them to Huang Jin and Huang Ying to replant. And ten days later, those dead ones would all come back to life. The customers were so happy that they would often pay Zicai much more than the original prices agreed upon.

子才也注意到黄近和黄英如何将死了的幼苗培植活过来的方法，可他照着去做后，就是不成功。他问这对姐弟为什么他们培植的就会活而他的就不会。黄近和黄英微笑着说他们也不知道。

Over time, Zicai watched the methods Huang Jin and Huang Ying used to revive the dead seedlings and he tried to emulate them, but he never succeeded. He asked the brother and sister the reason why their plants lived and his did not. Huang Jin and Huang Ying smiled and said they did not know, either.

子才乃将卖菊花所得的收入一分为二，自己保留一份，另一份交给黄氏姐弟。因为没有黄氏姐弟，他是不可能赚这么多钱的。

Zicai divided the income from sales of the chrysanthemums into two parts. He kept half and let Huang Jin and Huang Ying keep the other half, as without the brother and sister, he would not have made such a good profit.

现在，他们有了大笔固定的收入了，子才和张凤建议黄近和黄英找个媒婆为他们各寻一个终身伴侣。这个建议被这对双胞胎姐弟拒绝了。

Now that they had a large and steady income, Zicai and Zhang Feng suggested that they hire matchmakers to find mates for Huang Jin and Huang Ying. But the twins turned down the suggestion.

聊斋精选

黄近说:"我很满意我现在的独身方式。"
"I enjoy my bachelorhood." Huang Jin said.

"我也不要,谢谢你。"黄英含羞而又神秘地说,"我的婚姻时间还没有来到。"
"No, thank you." Huang Ying said with a shy mysterious smile. "My marriage time has not come yet."

一年后,张凤生病,日渐严重,子才带她去看了很多位医生,可是没有一位可以治好她的病。数月后她就病故了。子才非常哀伤。
A year later, Zhang Feng became sick. And her condition worsened daily. Zicai took her to see many doctors, yet no doctor could help her much. After a few months, she died. Zicai was very sad.

等到一切丧葬事宜都办妥了,子才单独住在房子里开始感到寂寞,日夜怀念已故的妻子,可是她已去世永不会回来了。惟一与他早晚仍旧在一起的年轻女性就是黄英。黄英早已达到婚嫁的年龄而且还是单身。于是子才向黄英求婚,她含羞地接受了。
After the funeral, Zicai lived alone and felt very lonely. He missed his wife day and night, but she was gone and would never return. The only young woman he still met with every day and evening was Huang Ying. As Huang Ying had already reached marriageable age and she was still single, Zicai courted Huang Ying for marriage. She shyly accepted.

婚后,她告诉子才她有预测一个人前途的才能。当他们第一次见面时她就测知张凤会在何时逝世。
After marriage, she told Zicai that she had a talent for forecasting a person's future. She had forecasted that Zhang Feng would die at a certain time when they first met.

"所以我当初不接受你们的建议去找媒婆为我寻找终身伴侣。"她甜甜地对子才说。
"That was the reason why I turned down your suggestion to let a matchmaker find a match for me," she said sweetly.

因为黄英成了子才的妻子,她搬去和她的丈夫同住。黄近单独住在花园旁的小房子里,他仍没有成婚的念头,每天还是到子才这边吃饭。
Since Huang Ying became Zicai's wife, she moved to live in with her husband. Huang Jin lived at the small house in the garden all by himself. Yet he still had no intention of getting married. He ate at Zicai's house as usual every day.

子才和黄近不仅都是菊花迷,而且又都热衷于喝酒。子才有时会喝醉,可他从没有见到黄近喝醉过。子才另外有个喝酒的朋友,他夸口自己是天下第一酒客,因为不管他喝多少杯,从未醉过。于是子才把他

聊斋精选

介绍给黄近,两个酒量大的人立刻变成了好朋友,他们一有时间就在一块儿喝酒。

Both Zicai and Huang Jin were not only fond of chrysanthemums, but also crazy about drinking. Zicai sometimes got drunk, but he never saw Huang Jin get drunk. Zicai had another drinking friend who boasted he was the number one drinker in the kingdom because no matter how many cups he drank, he had never been drunk. Zicai introduced his friend to Huang Jin. The two heavy drinkers immediately became good friends. They drank together whenever they had time.

有一天,正值举国假日之际,没有人工作,子才的花圃也打烊一天。这个酒友来到子才家。黄英为他们准备了一顿精美的午餐。饭后这三个酒友开始饮酒。不久,子才退出。这个朋友便向黄近挑战,谁再退出,谁就是输家。黄近大笑,将满满一杯茅台一口干了。他告诉这个朋友他接受挑战。

One national holiday, since nobody worked on that day, Zicai closed his flower nursery for one day too. The drinking friend came to Zicai's house. Huang Ying prepared a nice lunch for them. After the meal, the three men started to drink. Soon, Zicai quit. The friend challenged Huang Jin that whoever quit again would be the loser. Huang Jin laughed and finished off a full cup of Maotai, the strong Chinese whisky. He told the friend he accepted the challenge.

一个下午,这两个男子喝完了三瓶茅台。终于这个朋友说他不要再喝了,他要回家。黄近问他:"你……你可……承……不承认你是个输输输家了?"

As the afternoon progressed, the two men finished three bottles of Mao-tai. Finally, the friend said that he just did not want to drink anymore and wished to go home. Huang Jin asked him, "Do you… admit… you are… a.. looooser?"

这个朋友还没有作出回答就倒在地上睡着了。于是子才和黄英安排他在他们的家中过夜。

Before answering, the friend dropped on the ground and felt fast asleep. So Zicai and Huang Ying arranged to let him stay the night at their home.

黄近站起身子,大笑地说:"我……我……我没有……喝……醉。"
Huang Jin stood up claiming with a loud laugh, "I'm … not… drunk."

可是从他那走路和说话的样子看来,很明显地他也已喝醉了。因为天色已渐晚,黄近跌跌撞撞地走回小房子去睡觉,子才怕黄近在路上跌倒,便紧跟在他的后面。

From the way he was speaking and walking, it was obvious that he was drunk, too. As it was getting dark, Huang Jin began to stumble back toward his small house. Zicai was afraid that Huang Jin might fall on the way, so he followed after him closely.

就在经过花园时,黄近终于跌倒了。当子才上前准备躬身去扶起他时,突然间,子才惊吓得目瞪口呆,他发现黄近已经变成了一株菊花树,扎根在地中,而且满树都散发着一股强烈的酒气。

Passing through the garden, Huang Jin finally fell down to the ground. When Zicai tried to lean forward and help him up, he was shocked to find that Huang Jin had turned into a chrysanthemum plant with its roots going into the ground, and a strong odor of alcohol emanating from the plant.

子才急忙冲进房间去告诉他的妻子,她的弟弟所发生了什么情况。黄英走到了现场,把菊花树连根拔了起来,抛在地上,然后又用一条毯子盖在树上,于是她督促子才和她一起回到房间去而不要忧愁。

Zicai rushed into the inside of building and told his wife what had happened with her brother. Huang Ying went to the spot, pulled out the plant, and laid it on the ground. Then she covered it with a blanket and urged Zicai to return to the house without further worry.

子才明了黄近可能是一个菊花精灵,因此他怀疑黄英可能也是的。他问她,黄英神秘地回答:"你真在乎这个吗?"

Zicai realized that Huang Jin might be a spirit of chrysanthemum plant and he suspected that Huang Ying could also be. He asked her. Huang Ying replied mysteriously, "Do you really care?"

子才把她紧抱在怀中,告诉她:"我一点儿也不在乎。"
Zicai hugged her tightly in his arms, replied, "Not at all."

然后这对夫妻就好像什么事也不曾发生过似的。
Then the couple were just like nothing had happened.

第二天一大早,子才就到黄近跌倒的地方去察看,很惊讶地发现黄近躺在地上。他叫醒了黄近,扶着他走回到他的卧室。

Early the next morning, Zicai went to the spot where Huang Jin had fallen, and found Huang Jin lying on the ground. He woke up Huang Jin and helped him walk back to his room.

自从这件事情发生后,黄近喝起酒来就更不加限制了。在喝了太多酒以后,在走回家的路上就会又变成了一株菊花树。每次发生时,子才就会去告诉他的妻子,黄英就会走来把树连根拔起放在地上并盖上毯子,第二天,黄近就会醒过来又变成了一个人,行动如同一个正常的男子一样。慢慢地,子才也就习惯了而不以为奇。

After this incident, Huang Jin drank more heavily without restrictions. After too much drinking, he would sometimes turn into a chrysanthemum plant again on the way back to his room. And every time it happened, Zicai would inform his wife, and Huang Ying would come and pull out the plant and cover it with a blanket,

聊
斋
精
选

and the next day, Huang Jin would wake up as a human and act like a normal man. Gradually, Zicai got used to it.

八月十五日是中国的传统中秋节。那一天,家家户户都在家里以盛宴庆祝。子才和黄英也在家办了盛宴。黄近在饭后喝了很多的酒并且又喝醉了。当他走在回卧室的途中,他又变成了一株菊花树。

The fifteenth day of August on the Chinese lunar calendar was the traditional Chinese moon festival. On that day, all the Chinese people would celebrate with a big dinner at home. So did Zicai and Huang Ying. Huang Jin got drunk soon after dinner. On the way back to his place, he turned into a chrysanthemum plant again.

这时黄英正在房子里忙于清理晚餐后的工作,子才懒得再到房子里去打扰他的妻子,就把这株树连根拔了起来,然后放在地上,又用一条毯子盖在上面,一切就如同黄英以往所做的一模一样。然后他到房间里把刚才发生的事情告诉了他的妻子。

As Huang Ying was busy to clean up after the big dinner in the house, Zicai did not want to go inside to bother her this time. He simply pulled up the plant and laid it on the ground, then covered it with a blanket exactly the way his wife had done before. After that, he went inside and told his wife what had happened.

黄英愕然大惊,然后流出了眼泪。她哭着说子才杀死了她的弟弟。不管子才如何道歉,黄英只是不停地哭泣。她告诉他,她并不责怪他,她泪流满面地说:"这一切都是命中注定的!"

Huang Ying was stunned, then, she broke into tears. She cried and told Zicai that he had killed her brother. No matter how much Zicai tried to apologize, Huang Ying just kept crying. But she told him that she would not blame him. "It was fate," she said tearfully.

黄英说得不错,第二天一早,子才就到花园里去察看,结果很伤心地发现他昨天夜间拔起来的菊花树已经开始枯萎了,那里根本没有黄近。他对黄英感到非常抱歉,可是她告诉他这不是他的错,并且要他不要再自责了,因为每个人的命运是一生下来就被安排好了的。

Huang Ying was right. Early next morning, Zicai rushed into the garden. He found that the plant he had pulled out the night before had started to wither. There was no Huang Jin there at all. He felt very sorry for Huang Ying, but she told him it was not his fault. She even told him not to feel too bad, as everybody's life had been arranged by fate since birth.

从此以后,每天夜半,黄英就到花园里去,她跪倒在黄近死去的地方向上苍祷告如何可以挽回她弟弟的生命。在第七天后的晚上,她兴奋地告诉她的丈夫现在终于有了希望了。她用小刀把手臂割破,使血流在那枯萎的菊花树根上,然后她重新培植这株死了的菊花树。

Since that night, Huang Ying went to the garden every midnight. She would kneel down at the place

Huang Jin had died to pray to Heaven for a way to revive her brother's life. After seven nights, she told her husband excitedly that there was a hope. She used a knife to cut her arm and let her blood drop on the withered chrysanthemum root and re-planted it.

　　在黄英的每日细心照料下,就像她和黄近以往为顾客们重新培植那些死了的菊花幼苗一样,这株死了的树终于又活了过来。一年后,它长成了一株巨大的菊花树,可是没有长花朵。

Under Huang Ying's daily care, the dead plant gradually revived just like the others she and Huang Jin had saved before for their customers. A year later, it grew up into a big healthy plant but it bore no flowers.

　　一天,当子才一个人在他的书房内看书时,房门突然被人推开了,黄近,那个一年前已经死了的他妻子的弟弟一手拿着一瓶茅台酒,走了进来。他邀请子才和他痛饮几杯来庆贺他的重生。

One day, while Zicai was studying alone in his den, the door was suddenly pushed open and in walked Huang Jin, his wife's brother, the man who had died a year ago. He held out a bottle of Mao-tai, inviting Zicai to have a few drinks with him to celebrate his rebirth.

聊斋精选

十二、

伍秋月

Fugitives

安葬好了爱妻后,丁原,一个才不过三十出头的人,请他的哥哥和嫂嫂代为照顾他那五岁大的女儿,因为他要去度一个短暂的休假来拂抹他对亡妻的悲恸。

Having buried his beloved wife, Ding Yuan, a man in his early thirties, asked his elder brother and sister-in-law to take care of his five-year-old daughter for him. He wanted to take a vacation to ease the sorrow of his wife's death.

丁原与他的妻子结婚有七年,婚姻生活一直很美满。他们从小在同一个地区长大。她是方圆有名的美女,他是当地一位出色的剑士。所以当他们两人结婚时,人人称颂这是一对最佳配偶。

Ding Yuan and his wife had been happily married for seven years. They had grown up together in the same district. She had been known as a great beauty, and he as an outstanding swordsman. When they were married, everybody admired the couple and agreed that they were perfect match.

当一场疾病突然夺走了他的妻子的生命时,丁原简直不能接受他那最亲爱的伴侣竟然永远不会回来的事实。可是,他那年幼女儿的不停啼哭使得他又时时面对着这个悲剧。他的哥哥和嫂嫂答应会好好地照顾他的小女儿,要他安心去度假不要担心他的女儿及家。

When an illness suddenly took away his wife, Ding Yuan could not accept the fact that his dearest companion was gone forever. But the constant crying of his little daughter reminded him of the tragedy all the time. His brother and sister-in-law promised him to take good care of his daughter while he was on vacation, and told him not to worry about his daughter or home.

丁原来到了他所居住的江苏省内最有名的太湖边。他计划在那儿住上七至十天好好地轻松休息一下。他住进了一家上等的旅馆,并选择了一个面对湖光山色的舒适房间。

Ding Yuan went to the famous resort by the Lake of Tai located in the Province of Jiangsu where he lived. He planned to stay there for a week or ten days to relax completely. He checked into a nice hotel and chose a comfortable room with a good view of the lake.

第一天,他乘着一艘新近装潢的大船,尽情游荡太湖的美景。到了晚上,他便与一批年长的旅客在旅馆游艺室内下棋打牌,一直玩到筋疲力尽方才回房去睡。

On the first day, he took a large newly decorated ship touring around the lake. In the evening, he played cards and chess with some senior travelers in the hotel recreation room until he was tired. Then he went to his room to sleep.

就在他刚合上眼睛不久,他看见了一个身着黄色丝绸衣服的年轻美丽女子朝他走来并和他做爱。醒来后,他发觉那不过是一场春梦。

Not too long after he closed his eyes, he saw a pretty young woman in yellow silk dress coming to him

聊斋精选

and made love to him. He woke up and found he had had a pleasant dream.

早上起身后,他继续游览,而很快地便把前一天夜晚的那场梦忘了个一干二净。
When he got up in the morning, he continued his excursion and completely forgot the previous night's dream.

在第二天夜晚,这个同样的春梦又发生了。他感觉到有点不对头,可又无人可以询问,也无从去打听。所以在醒来后他也并不十分在意。当这个春梦第三晚又发生时,他很肯定在这个房间里一定有件奇异的事情在作怪。两次也可以说是碰巧,可是不会有第三次。丁原是个剑士,他一点儿也不惧怕。他自言自语道,"我一定要把这件事情查个水落石出。"
But the pleasant dream was repeated the second night, He felt that something might be wrong, but he had nobody to ask and no way to investigate. So he did not worry too much once he had woken up. After the pleasant dream was repeated once again the third night, he was sure a strange thing was happening in this room. Twice could be explained as a coincidence, but not three times. Ding Yuan was a swordsman. He was not scared. *I will find out the answer*, he told himself.

于是,在第四天夜晚,他上了床,闭上眼睛,假装入睡了。午夜刚过,他听到了轻微的脚步声。他微睁眼睛成一条缝,果然看到了这个前三天夜里所梦到的身穿黄色衣服的同一个女子轻轻地溜进了房间,并向着他的床走来。当她走近时,丁原突然睁开眼睛并紧紧地把她抱在怀中,大声地喝问:"你是谁?"
On the fourth night, after he went onto the bed, he closed his eyes, pretending he was sleeping. Soon after midnight, he heard light footsteps. He opened his eyes a crack and sure enough, he found the same girl in yellow dress during his previous three dreams sneaking into the room and walked toward his bed. when she came closer, Ding Yuan suddenly opened up his eyes and held her tightly in his arms, demanding loudly, "Who are you?"

他的突然行动吓坏了这个女孩。她便急想逃跑,可是无法挣脱丁原强有力的拥抱。终于,她放弃了,娇羞地承认:"我是一个女鬼,我的名字叫伍秋月。"
His sudden action frightened the girl. She tried to escape, but she could not get free from Ding Yuan's powerful embrace. Finally, she gave up and admitted shyly, "I'm a ghost. My name is Wu Qiuyue. "

"你怎么每天夜晚来到我的梦里?"他问她。
"How can you come into my dreams every night?" He asked her.

"三年前当我还是十六岁时我淹死在这湖内。"这个女鬼流着眼泪说,"在我淹死前,一个道士曾经告诉过我,我在命中注定将在十九岁时嫁给一个名叫丁原的鳏夫。这个道士甚至还对我说这个鳏夫会在什么时候一个人来到湖边。

聊斋精选

"I was drowned in the lake three years ago when I was sixteen years old." the female ghost said tearfully, "Before I died, a Taoist priest had told me that I would be fated to marry a widower named Ding Yuan at the age of nineteen. The priest even told me when the widower would come to the lake resort by himself.

"我已经死了并变成了鬼,可我仍记得那道士的预言。因此,最近半个月来,我每天夜晚都来检查湖边的每一个旅店,因为道士说你将在这个期间来到这儿。

"Now I have died and become a ghost. I still remember the priest's forecast. For half a month, I have been checking every hotel around the lake, since the priest said you would come during this period.

"当我发现了你时,我胆怯得不敢面对你。我知道使你相信这道士的预言是几乎不可能的事情,于是我决定在你的梦中与你相见。"

"When I finally found you, I was too timid to face you. And I knew it would be very difficult to convince you to accept the priest's forecast. So I decided to appear in your dreams."

在这么一个可爱的夜晚,听着这么一个浪漫动人的命运故事,丁原接受了这个预言而把她抱得更紧了。他不在乎她究竟是人还是鬼。

On such a lovely night, hearing such a romantic story of fate, Ding Yuan accepted the forecast and held her even more tightly. He did not care whether she was a human or a ghost.

自那以后,每当夜色低垂时,秋月便出现在丁原的房间里和他共度良宵,如同一对新婚夫妇那样在这有名的湖边胜地度蜜月。

Since then, every evening shortly after dark, Qiuyue would show up in Ding Yuan's room and spend the night with him. They acted like a pair of newlyweds spending their honeymoon in the famous lake resort.

当她问他的家中还有些什么人,丁原告诉她他的妻子刚死不久,留给他一个五岁大的女儿。他问她在阴间是否看到过他的妻子。她回答阴间有千万个鬼魂就像人间有数不清的人一样。不过她答应丁原如果他能把他的妻子的情况告诉她,她会尽一切可能去替他打听她的下落。

When she asked him about his family, Ding Yuan told her about his newly deceased wife and his five-year-old daughter. He asked her whether she had met his wife in the ghost world. She replied that there were hundreds of thousands of ghosts in the world of ghosts, just like the countless number of humans in the world of human. However, she promised Ding Yuan if he gave her enough information about his wife, she would try her best to find out where she was.

两天以后,秋月告诉丁原她终于打听到了,他的亡妻现在已被安排即将投生在一个很远的省份内为一个女婴。丁原便问秋月为何她没有被安排投胎。她解释道当她死后,她没有去向阴曹地府报到,因为她相信那个道士的预言而等待见到这个鳏夫。假如这次她找不到这个鳏夫,她就去向阴曹地府报到要求安排投胎。

A couple of days later, Qiuyue told Ding Yuan that she had finally found out that his wife had been assigned to be reborn as a baby girl in a faraway province. Ding Yuan asked Qiuyue how it could be that she had not been granted such an arrangement of rebirth. She explained that after her death, she did not report to the ghost government, because she believed the priest's forecast and wanted to meet the widower. If she could not meet the widower this time, she would then report to the ghost government asking for such an arrangement.

"我非常高兴终于找到了你。"她甜甜地说。丁原被她的故事所感动,把她紧紧地抱住。

"I'm very happy that I have finally found you," she said sweetly. Ding Yuan was moved by her story, and hugged her.

有一天夜晚,丁原问秋月阴间究竟像个什么样子。她说基本上阴间和人间很相近的。出于好奇,他问她是否可以带他到附近的阴间集镇一游。她答应了。于是她带领他来到荒郊野外一座小山旁边,她说他们已经进入了一个阴间集镇。

One night, Ding Yuan asked Qiuyue to describe what the world of ghosts looked like. She said that basically, it looked similar to the world of human. Out of curiosity, he asked her if she could take him to a nearby ghost town to have a quick tour. She promised. Then she led him to a wild field by a small mountain. She said that they were now entering a ghost town.

因为丁原眼前一片漆黑什么也看不见,秋月便要他闭上眼睛,她用舌头在他的眼皮上舔了一下。当丁原再度睁开眼睛后,他很惊讶地发现他们果然正在一个繁华的商业区。购物者来来往往而商家出售各种商品一如人间的任何一个都市。

As Ding Yuan could not see anything but darkness, Qiuyue asked him to close his eyes, and she licked his eyelids. When Ding Yuan opened his eyes again, he was surprised to find that they were indeed in a busy commercial area. The shoppers coming and going and the businesspeople selling merchandise all appeared no different from those in any city in the world of human.

当他们在这个鬼镇上漫步时,丁原突然看到一个执法士兵用链条拖着一个男子。士兵的链条一端锁在这个男子的颈子上,他一手紧握着另一端强力拉着这个男子向前走去。这个可怜的男子无法违抗只能被士兵拖着走,就好像一个畜生被它主人拖着一样。秋月告诉丁原这个士兵是冥府官员派去锁拿刚死的人的鬼魂向冥府报到的。

As they were leisurely walking around in the ghost town, Ding Yuan noticed a law enforcement soldier

冥府

聊斋精选

pulling a man in chains. The soldier was forcefully tugging the chain that was locked around the man's neck. The poor man could not resist but followed the soldier like an animal pulled by its master. Qiuyue told Ding Yuan that the soldier was sent by the ghost officials to bring the newly deceased human's spirit to report to the government.

丁原再仔细一看,他很惊吓地发现这被链条锁着的男子正是他的哥哥。于是他上前阻挡这个士兵,并大声呼叫他哥哥的名字。当丁原的哥哥发现了丁原时,他便高声呼救告诉丁原这个士兵把他如同畜生一样地虐待。

Ding Yuan took a closer look and was shocked to discover that the man in chains was his elder brother. He immediately stopped the soldier and called his brother's name. When Ding Yuan's brother saw him, he yelled for help, telling Ding Yuan that the soldier was treating him like an animal.

因为丁原阻挡他的前进妨碍他执行公务,士兵大怒,便拿起军棍威吓要打丁原。丁原的勇敢是出了名的。为了营救他的哥哥,他迅速地拔出了佩剑刺中了士兵的右臂。士兵抛下了军棍,连忙逃跑。丁原救下了他的哥哥。

Infuriated by Ding Yuan's interference with his official duties, the soldier drew his truncheon and threatened to beat Ding Yuan. Ding Yuan's reputation for bravery was well deserved. In order to save his brother, he swiftly drew his sword and struck the soldier on his right arm. The soldier dropped his truncheon and fled. Ding Yuan freed his brother.

这场意想不到的打斗吓坏了秋月。她说攻击执法士兵在阴间是一种严重的罪行,她催促丁原和他的哥哥逃跑得愈快愈好。她劝他们到家后要立刻在家的周围焚香七天七夜,如此阴间的鬼兵鬼卒就不敢来家逮捕他们了。七天以后,他们就会平安无事了。

The unexpected fighting frightened Qiuyue. She said that assaulting a law enforcement soldier was a serious crime in the ghost world. She urged Ding Yuan and his brother to run away as fast as possible. She advised them that when they reached home, they should burn incense all around the house, day and night, for seven days. This would hold off the ghost soldiers coming to arrest them. After seven days, they would be safe.

丁原和他的哥哥到家后,发现他们全家人都仍在为丁原哥哥的逝世而痛哭不已。丁原的哥哥找到了他的尸体躺在家中的大厅里,他进入了他的尸体,于是又复活了。两兄弟连忙在家屋的四周焚香七天七夜。

When Ding Yuan and his brother reached their home, they found that their whole family was still crying over Ding Yuan's brother's death. Ding Yuan's brother found his own corpse lying in the family hall. He entered into his corpse and he revived. And the two brothers quickly burned incense sticks all around their

聊斋精选

house for seven days and nights.

七天后，危机过去了。丁原告诉他的哥哥他很担心秋月的安危，因为她在他攻击阴间执法士兵的时候也在场。于是，他立刻赶回太湖边的住地。

Seven days later, the crisis was over. Ding Yuan told his brother that he was worried about Qiuyue's safety since she had been present when he stabbed the ghost law enforcement soldier. Ding Yuan rushed back to the lake resort.

他住进了同一个旅馆里的同一个房间。可是天晚后秋月没有出现。丁原无从去寻找。突然间他想起了秋月曾经带他去过的一个阴间集镇。他来到了野外的那座小山旁。因为没有秋月用舌头去舔他的眼皮，所以除了一片漆黑外他什么也看不到。

He checked into the same room of the same hotel. But Qiuyue did not show up in the evening. Ding Yuan had no way to find her. Suddenly, he thought of the ghost town where Qiuyue had taken him there. He came to the wild field by a small mountain, but without Qiuyue's licking his eyelids, he could see nothing but the darkness.

非常失望中他回到了旅馆的房间，思索着如何可以找到她。他绕室徘徊，一个小时又一个小时过去了，仍然一筹莫展。终于因为太疲倦了而倒在一张椅子上睡着了。

Desperately, he returned to his hotel room, wondering how to find her. Pacing around the room for hours, he still could not figure out a way. Finally, exhausted, he fell asleep in a chair.

不久，一个老妇人走进了他的房间。她告诉丁原她是秋月的邻居，她知道秋月现在何处。她说秋月现在已经有了极大的麻烦。自从那次丁原刺伤了士兵并和他的哥哥逃走后，冥府派了一队士兵来追捕他们。因为找不到丁氏兄弟，他们便将秋月捉进牢里。

Soon an old woman walked into his room. She told Ding Yuan that she was Qiuyue's neighbor and knew her whereabouts. She said that Qiuyue was in big trouble. After Ding Yuan had stabbed the soldier and fled with his brother, the ghost government sent a squadron of soldiers to chase after them. Since they could not find Ding Yuan and his brother, they arrested Qiuyue and put her in jail.

应丁原的要求，老妇人将他带到阴间牢旁。看起来这里就像是一栋破旧的公寓。有很多房间关着很多犯人。老妇人用手指向一个小房间，说秋月就被关在这里面。

At Ding Yuan's request, the old woman led him to the ghost prison. It looked like an old, poorly built apartment. There were many small units to hold many lawbreakers. The woman pointed to a small unit, indicating that Qiuyue was locked inside.

聊斋精选

　　丁原透过窗户向里面窥视,他发现秋月正被两个丑陋的牢卒调戏因而伤心地哭泣。她在尽力躲避着,可是这两个牢卒却不停地调戏她。

Ding Yuan took a peek through the window. He discovered that Qiuyue was sadly weeping while two ugly jail guards were molesting her. She was trying her hardest to escape, but the guards kept molesting her.

　　丁原愈看愈是气愤填胸。终于他再也无法抑制自己,拔出了佩剑,将窗户捅破而跳进了屋里。在这两个牢卒还没有来得及反应前,丁原把这两个家伙刺杀了,救出了秋月。

The longer Ding Yuan watched, the more furious he became. Finally, he could not restrain himself. He drew his sword, smashed the window, and jumped into the room. Before the two guards could react, Ding Yuan killed both of them and rescued Qiuyue.

　　突然间,丁原从梦中醒来,发现他仍坐在旅馆房间内的椅子上。可是,当他转过头来时,他很惊讶地发现秋月坐在另一张椅子上,仍然穿着囚服。她泪流满面地向丁原道谢在梦中拯救了她。

Suddenly, Ding Yuan woke up from his dream, finding he was still sitting on a chair in his hotel room. But when he turned his head, he was surprised to find Qiuyue sitting on the other chair, wearing her prison uniform. She tearfully thanked Ding Yuan for rescuing her in his dream.

　　接着秋月告诉丁原,他已经杀死了两名牢卒,阴曹地府一定会很快地派来大队士兵逮捕他们。丁原没有办法,只好将秋月带回到他自己的家中。

Qiuyue told Ding Yuan that since he had killed the two guards, the ghost government would soon send a large squadron of soldiers to arrest them. Ding Yuan had no choice but take Qiuyue home to hide.

　　到家后丁原立刻又在房子的四周点起香来,防止鬼兵入内。同时他和他的哥哥商量秋月的处境,因为秋月是一个鬼,七天后,鬼卒们仍可以来把她逮捕归案的。

After reaching home, Ding Yuan immediately burned incenses all around his house to prevent the ghost soldiers from entering. Meanwhile, Ding Yuan discussed Qiuyue's situation with his brother. As Qiuyue was a ghost, after seven days, the ghost soldiers could still come to arrest her and put her back in prison.

　　惟一能使她脱离鬼卒们迫害的办法就是让她借尸还魂重新作为一个人,可是她已经死了三年,她的尸体早已腐烂。丁原突然想起了他那最近刚死不久的妻子的尸体,于是兄弟两人将她的坟墓打开,发现她的尸体仍然完好。

The only way to escape the ghost government's persecution was to revive Qiuyue as a human being. But she had been dead for three years and her corpse had already decayed. Then Ding Yuan suddenly thought of his recently deceased wife's body. He and his brother immediately dug up her grave. Luckily, her body was still in good condition.

聊斋精选

　　在丁原同意下,秋月向丁原的妻子尸体恭敬地跪下磕了三个头,然后站起身来向着尸体冲去,于是秋月借尸还魂又重新成为一个妇人了。

With Ding Yuan's permission, Qiuyue respectfully knelt down and bowed to Ding Yuan's wife's corpse three times. Then she stood up and entered the corpse. Qiuyue revived in Ding Yuan's wife's body.

　　在相貌上,秋月完全像丁原的前妻,可是其灵魂是秋月自己的。丁原的哥哥迅速为他的弟弟及秋月举行了一个简单的婚礼。当年那个道士的预言果然很灵,秋月真的在这一年命中注定地嫁给了一个鳏夫。

Although her appearance was that of Ding Yuan's former wife, the spirit was Qiuyue's. Ding Yuan's brother quickly held a simple wedding ceremony for his younger brother and Qiuyue. The Taoist priest was right after all. Qiuyue was fated to marry a widower this year.

聊斋精选

十三、

阿英

Violating Fate

甘笔是他父母亲的小儿子,他的哥哥甘玉比他大十九岁。当父母亲过世时,甘笔才五岁大,而甘玉已经二十四岁,并且早已结婚了。所以甘笔是甘玉和他的妻子秀珍一手带大的。因为甘玉夫妇没有小孩,他们照顾小弟无微不至,待他就好像是自己的儿子一样。

Gan Bi was his parents' younger son. His elder brother, Gan Yu, was nineteen years older than he. When their parents died, Gan Bi was only five years old and Gan Yu was twenty-four and already married. So Gan Yu and his wife, Xiuzhen, brought up Gan Bi. As Gan Yu and Xiuzhen had no children, they took good care of the younger brother, treating him like their own son.

甘笔长大后成为一个英俊的年轻男子。当他达到成婚的年龄时,很多媒人来甘玉夫妇处为甘笔说媒。因为甘玉挑选很严,媒人所提的人家他没有一个看得上眼。

Gan Bi grew up into a handsome young man. When he reached the marriageable age, many matchmakers came to Gan Yu and Xiuzhen and offering their service for finding a good match for Gan Bi. Gan Yu interviewed the candidates for his younger brother very strictly. None of them met his requirements.

一天,甘笔经过一处小森林遇到一个年轻美丽的女孩,她和很多女孩在一起愉快地玩耍。这个女孩挡住甘笔问他的名字是否叫甘笔,他的哥哥名字是否叫甘玉,他们家是否住在某处。甘笔很惊讶地作了肯定回答以后,女孩含羞地质问他,"为何你的哥哥现在反悔你与我已定的婚约,而计划为你另找一个女子成婚?"

One day, when Gan Bi was passing by a small forest, he met a pretty young lady who was happily playing with many other girls. She stopped Gan Bi and asked him if his name was Gan Bi, and his brother's name was Gan Yu, and if they lived at a certain address. Gan Bi was surprised and answered yes. Then she shyly blamed him, "How could your brother try to repudiate your marriage arrangement to me and plan to find another girl to be your wife?"

这个问题使得甘笔很困惑。"我从没有听说过这么一个婚约。"他坦诚地告诉她。望着她那美丽的面孔,他立刻接着说:"我今天一回家后就问我哥哥。"

The question confused Gan Bi. "I have never heard of such a marriage arrangement," he told her honestly. Seeing her pretty face, he quickly added, "I'll inquire my brother about this subject when I return home today."

"你最好去问他。"她甜美地笑着说。

"You better do it," She said with a sweet smile.

"可是,我如何回复你? 你叫什么名字?"

"But, how can I get back to you, and what's your name?"

"我的名字叫阿英。"她回答道。在她还没有来得及把她的住处告诉他时,她的玩伴们就来把她拉走而且很快地便都没有了踪迹。

"My name is Aying," she replied. Before she could keep telling him her address, her playmates came to pull her away, and soon they all disappeared.

回家之后,甘笔立刻向他的哥哥提起此事,并问这是怎么一回事。甘玉回答他也从来没有听到过这个婚约。假如有的话,那一定是他们的父母亲订的。接着他又说,"这是不可能的,因为当父母亲去世时,我已经二十四岁了,如有此事,他们一定会告诉我的。"

After returning home, Gan Bi immediately mentioned this to his brother and asked for details. Gan Yu replied that he knew nothing about any marriage arrangement. If there was one, it must have been made by their parents. Then he soon added, "This was unlikely, because when our parents died, I was twenty-four years old. If there was one, I should have been told of this."

于是,秀珍问甘笔这个女孩长得如何? 甘笔含羞脸红地低下了头没有回答。

Xiuzhen then asked Gan Bi what the girl looked like. Gan Bi shyly hanged his head and blushed without saying a word.

聪明的嫂子笑道:"我相信这个女孩一定长得很美,否则小弟是不会如此关心的。"

The smart sister-in-law smiled and said, "I believe that she must be a very pretty girl, otherwise, our younger brother would not be so interested."

因为他们除了知道一个短短的名字外,对于这个女孩的其它方面一无所知,所以他们对女孩或其家人也就无从打听了。

Since they had no other information about the girl except a short name, they could not find anybody to ask about her or her family.

甘笔从此以后就日夜思念这个名叫阿英的美丽女孩。他告诉他的哥哥他对媒人所提的其它女子都没有兴趣。换言之,除了阿英外,他谁也不娶。他的哥哥对此是爱莫能助,因为无法帮他找到这个神秘女子。

But Gan Bi missed the pretty girl named Aying day and night. He told his brother that he was not interested in any other young women the matchmakers had offered. In other words, he would marry nobody else but Aying. But his brother could not help him find the mysterious young lady.

一个月后,有一天,甘玉拜访一个住在邻市的朋友后于回家的途中,他凑巧看到一个女子单独一人靠在路边一株大树旁哭泣。他走上前去一看,发现这个女孩长得非常美丽。甘玉问她为何啼哭。她回答:

聊斋精选

117

"我的父母早已亡故,又无兄弟姐妹。更糟的是我的未婚夫家现在又要悔婚,我真不知道今后何去何从。"

A month later, when Gan Yu was returning home from visiting a friend in a neighboring town, he happened to find a girl crying by a tree alone by the roadside. He approached her and found she was a very beautiful young woman. When Gan Yu inquired why she was crying, she answered, "My parents were dead, and I have no brothers and sisters. The worse thing is that my fiance has repudiated the marriage proposal to me. I'm sad because I don't know what I'm going to do with my future."

当甘玉问她的名字以及她的夫家是谁时,他很惊讶地发现她正是甘笔曾经遇到过的而现在日夜思念的女孩! 甘玉问她关于婚约是怎么一回事。她说这是他们的老父亲当年答应过的。既然老父亲早已过世,这事也就无从查证了。甘玉告诉她自己是谁,毫不犹豫地就把阿英带回了家。

When Gan Yu asked her name and who her fiance was, he was surprised to learn that she was exactly the girl Gan Bi had met and longed for day and night. Then he asked her about the marriage arrangement. She said that it had been made by their fathers years before. Since the old man had died, nobody could confirm it. Gan Yu told her who he was, and without a second thought, he took her home.

甘笔当然大喜过望,而秀珍也很喜爱这个女孩。由于甘笔与阿英如此相配,甘玉与秀珍便愉快地为他们主持了一个婚礼。

Naturally, Gan Bi was overjoyed. And Xiuzhen was fond of the girl, too. As Gan Bi and Aying was a pair of perfect match, Gan Yu and Xiuzhen happily held a wedding ceremony for them.

婚后,阿英与甘笔小夫妻恩爱有加,朝夕不离。阿英对甘玉和秀珍敬如公婆,秀珍和阿英两人也亲密得如同母女又如同大姐和小妹一样。他们一家四口快乐地居住在同一栋房子里。

After their marriage, Gan Bi and Aying loved each other so much that they just wanted to stick together every minute. Aying treated Gan Yu and Xiuzhen respectfully as parents-in-law. And the two women got along as intimately as mother and daughter, or an elder sister and a younger sister. They happily lived together under one roof.

一年后的一天下午,当甘笔与阿英正在他们家的花园内欣赏初秋的美景时,秀珍派来一个婢女邀请阿英到她那儿去饮茶和下棋。甘笔很舍不得让他的爱妻离开,可又不愿拂逆长嫂的美意,阿英明了丈夫的心意,于是她告诉婢女说她等会儿就到她的女主人那儿去。

One early afternoon, a year later, when Gan Bi and Aying were enjoying the fall scenery in their family garden, Xiuzhen sent a maid over inviting Aying to come to her side to have tea and play chess. Gan Bi did not want his beloved wife to leave, but he did not want her to reject his elder sister-in-law's kind invitation either. Aying read her husband's mind. She told the maid that she would join her mistress in a few minutes.

聊斋精选

可是,半个小时后,她仍和甘笔在一起。甘笔不时提醒她曾经答应了敬重的嫂嫂之邀,可是,她只是微笑地要他不要为此发愁,她说她会妥善处理,不会让嫂嫂不愉快的。

Half an hour later, she was still with Gan Bi. Gan Bi kept reminding her of her promise to his respectful sister-in-law, but she smiled telling him not to worry. She said that she would manage it and not make his sister-in-law unhappy.

事实上,这整个的下午,她一直和甘笔在一起而没有去应秀珍的邀请,这使得甘笔感觉不安。

As a matter of fact, she spent the whole afternoon with Gan Bi without attending to Xiuzhen's invitation at all, which made Gan Bi feel uneasy.

第二天早上,当甘笔遇到秀珍时,他连忙为阿英昨天的失信而道歉。秀珍很惊讶地告诉他,阿英昨天陪她饮茶下棋了整整一个下午。这下子把甘笔弄糊涂了,因为阿英昨天下午一直和他在一起而片刻未离。

So the next morning when Gan Bi met Xiuzhen, he mentioned her yesterday's invitation and apologized for Aying's not coming to her. Xiuzhen was shocked and told him that Aying had spent the whole afternoon with her yesterday. Now Gan Bi was confused, as Aying had never left him the entire afternoon.

于是叔嫂两人来到阿英的面前,要她解释她如何可以同时出现在两个不同的地方。阿英只是微笑而没有说一句话。

Then they both went to Aying, asking her to explain how she could be in two places in the same time. Aying just smiled, not saying a word.

不久,甘玉回家了。秀珍连忙告诉他阿英有分身术。于是,甘玉和秀珍两人来到甘笔和阿英处,联同甘笔,三个人一起要阿英解释这个神奇法术究竟是怎么一回事。

Later when Gan Yu returned home, Xiuzhen immediately told him about Aying's being able to be at two places in the same time. Then Gan Yu and Xiuzhen both came to Gan Bi and Aying's place, joined by Gan Bi, inquiring into the cause of Aying's supernatural power.

终于阿英承认她不是人类。她深深地叹了一口气,然后对甘笔说:"这是命运的安排,我们的夫妇关系只能到此为止了,我很抱歉,我必须离开你们了。"

Finally, Aying admitted that she was not a human being. She sighed a long sigh and told Gan Bi, "I realize that our relationship as husband and wife has come to an end, according to the fate. I'm sorry to tell you I must leave you now."

当这三个人还很惊讶地坐在那儿时,阿英突然化为一只美丽的鹦鹉,飞向天空,很快就不见了踪影。

聊斋精选

While the three other people sat there in shock, Aying suddenly turned into a beautiful parrot and flew away into the sky and soon disappeared.

于是甘玉想起来了,很多年前,他的父亲曾经养过一只美丽的雌鹦鹉,那时甘笔还不过是个岁数不大的小孩子,他非常喜爱这只小鸟,每天一有空就和它玩在一起,因此,他们的父亲就时常开玩笑地对他的小儿子说:"你既然这么喜欢这只鸟,等你长大了,我就把它许配给你做媳妇。"

Gan Yu then remembered that long ago his father had had a beautiful female parrot at home when Gan Bi was only a few years old. As Gan Bi was very fond of the bird and tried to be with it all the time, his father often teased his little boy, promising, "Since you are so fond of the bird, I'll let you marry the bird when you grow up."

以后他们的父亲过世了,没有人注意到这只鹦鹉是如何逃脱了的。甘玉终于明了为什么阿英当初责怪他们毁弃婚约的缘故。

After their father died, nobody noticed how it happened that the bird had taken the opportunity to fly away. Gan Yu finally understood that this was what Aying had meant when she blamed them for repudiating the marriage promise.

三个月后,甘玉催甘笔再婚,可是被甘笔拒绝了。他仍然怀念他的爱妻阿英,他希望有朝一日她能回来和他团聚。他告诉哥哥,他不在乎她是人还是鸟,他只爱她,只有是他的爱妻。然而,阿英一直没有回来。

Three months later, when Gan Yu urged Gan Bi to get remarried, Gan Bi refused, as he was still missing his beloved wife, Aying, and wished that maybe one of these days, she would come back. He told his brother that he did not care if she was a human being or a bird. He just loved her and treated her as his dear wife. Yet Aying did not return.

又是一年过去了,甘笔明白阿英是不会回来的了。于是他答应他的长兄考虑再婚。不久,他就又结婚了,妻子名叫叶明。

One year passed. Gan Bi finally realized that Aying would not return. He told his brother that he would consider getting remarried. And soon he remarried a girl whose name was Yeming.

叶明也是个年轻美丽的女子。虽然她也努力去讨好每一个人,特别是丈夫和那几乎是婆婆一样的长嫂秀珍。可是,不知道为什么,甘笔和秀珍就是不太十分喜欢她而仍是非常怀念阿英。这使得叶明真不知道如何去改善与他们两人的关系。

Yeming was a pretty young woman, too. And she tried hard to be nice to everybody, especially her husband and his sister-in-law, Xiuzhen, the woman who acted as her mother-in-law. But nobody knew the

聊斋精选

reason why Gan Bi and Xiuzhen just did not like her as much as they should. The two still missed Aying very much. It made Yeming confused and she did not know how to improve her relationship with them.

一天,阿英突然归来,这使得甘笔和秀珍非常兴奋。他们告诉阿英他们是如何地想念她。阿英说她也是非常地想念他们的。她说她此次回来是看望他们,不是回来居住的。她恭贺甘笔的再婚。于是甘笔把他现任妻子叶明介绍给阿英。

One day, Aying suddenly returned. Gan Bi and Xiuzhen were excited. They told her how much they had been missing her, and she told them she had missed them, too. But she said that she was coming back to visit them only, not to stay. She congratulated Gan Bi for his remarriage, and Gan Bi introduced her to his new wife, Yeming.

这两个年轻女子竟一见如故。阿英要叶明带她到她房间里去。两人关起房门一谈就是几个小时。天黑了,阿英与秀珍同房,因为甘玉那天适逢出城去了。

The two young women immediately became friends. Aying asked Yeming to take her to her bedroom, and they closed the door to speak in private for several hours. In the evening, Aying stayed with Xiuzhen as Gan Yu happened to be out of town that day.

第二天,阿英告诉他们她必须又要走了。不管甘笔和秀珍如何挽留甚至于叶明也希望她能多留几天,阿英说当命运要她和甘笔分离时,她必须服从。不过她答应他们,她以后将会时常回来看望他们的。说完了她又像上次一样,化成一只鹦鹉飞向天空去了。

The next day, Aying told them that she must leave them again. No matter how much Gan Bi and Xiuzhen asked her to stay a little longer, with Yeming chiming in, she said that when the fates wanted Gan Bi and her to be separated, she must obey the law. However, she promised them that in the future, she would drop in to see them once in a while. Then she turned into a parrot and flew away as she had done the previous time.

阿英走后,一件奇怪的事情发生了。叶明突然像变成了另一个妇人。她的言语和行动与阿英非常相似,这使得甘笔和秀珍开始也喜欢她了。

After Aying left, a strange thing happened. Yeming suddenly became a different woman. She acted and talked just like Aying, and Gan Bi and Xiuzhen began to love her much more.

阿英真的不时地回来。每次她都受到家里的每一个人的欢迎,叶明对她更是亲热得如同长姐。每次她来时都适逢甘玉出城,这就好像她能预知而故意挑选那一天来似的,如此她便可以和秀珍同房过夜。虽然她对每个人都很好,她总是尽量避免和甘笔单独相处,而甘笔则非常渴望。

Aying did come back every once in a while. She was warmly welcomed by every one of the families.

Yeming especially treated her as intimately as an elder sister. Every time she came, Gan Yu would happen to be out of town. It seemed that she could forecast it and purposely chose that day to come, so she could stay with Xiuzhen overnight. Although she was nice to everyone, she tried to avoid being with Gan Bi alone, while he expected it very much.

有一次,阿英又回来了,当她计划那天夜里仍如以往一样和秀珍同住时,甘笔来邀请她到他的房间去,因为叶明那天回娘家探望她的父母要到次日才回来,但被阿英拒绝了。不管他如何恳求,就连秀珍也在旁边劝说,她就是不接受。甘笔只得失望地离开。

One day, when Aying came again and planned to stay with Xiuzhen that night as usual, Gan Bi invited her to go to his room as Yeming had left for her parents' home and would not return until the next day. Aying turned down the invitation, no matter how much Gan Bi begged, even with Xiuzhen's encouragement. Aying simply would not accept. Finally, Gan Bi left in great disappointment.

可是甘笔并没有真正的离远,他躲藏在秀珍的房间外面。当阿英稍后到屋外去做点什么时,他突然冲上去一把将她紧紧抱着,放在背上想把她背回自己的卧房。起初,她想呼救,可是后来想到他们当初的恩爱生活时,她放弃了。

But Gan Bi did not go away too far. He hid outside Xiuzhen's room. When Aying came out for something later in the evening, he suddenly jumped out and held her tightly in his arms. He carried her on his back by force, trying to take her to his room. In the beginning, she thought of yelling for help, but when she remembered their loving days in the past, she gave up.

第二天早晨,当秀珍在餐厅吃早饭遇到阿英时,秀珍惊讶她还没有离开。阿英笑着解释她在昨天夜里被强盗绑架了,甘笔在旁边得意地大笑。

The next morning, when Xiuzhen met Aying in the dining room for breakfast, Xiuzhen was surprised that she had not yet left. Aying explained to her in a smile that she had been kidnapped the previous night. Gan Bi laughed heartily by her side.

饭后,阿英又化为鹦鹉飞去。

After the meal, Aying turned into a parrot and flew away.

不久,甘笔发现一只大猫从他的前院穿过,嘴里衔着一只美丽的鸟。甘笔认出那是只鹦鹉。立刻怀疑那可能是阿英,便连忙追上去,终于逼得猫将鸟放下逃跑了。甘笔将鹦鹉捡起发现已经受了重伤,便将它拿进房内,放在他的床上,并尽可能地细心调理。

Soon after that, Gan Bi saw a large cat passing through his front yard with a beautiful bird in its mouth. He recognized that the bird was a parrot and immediately suspected that it might be Aying. He quickly ran

聊斋精选

out and chased after the cat. Finally, the cat dropped the bird on the ground and fled. Gan Bi picked up the parrot and found that it had been badly injured. He put the bird on his bed and nursed it as carefully as he could.

第二天早晨,当他醒来后,很惊讶地发现鹦鹉已经不见了,可他在自己的书桌上看到了一张短笺,上面写着:"命运要我们分离,你违背了命运,使我几乎丧失了性命。"

The next morning, when he woke up, he was surprised to find that the parrot had gone, and he discovered a note on his desk with the following message on it: *Fate wants us to be separated. You violated the law and I almost lost my life.*

从此以后,阿英就没有再回来过。

Since then, Aying never appeared again.

The Woman in the Mirror

当刘策还是一个小孩子时,有一天,他在离家不远处经过一条小水沟,发现沟里有一条像水蛇样的小动物,可是有角也有脚。不过这个小动物好像已经死了。

One day when Liu Ce was a child, he passed by a dry ditch not too far from his home. There he happened to find a small animal that looked like a water snake but had horns and feet. It seemed that the animal was dead.

出于好奇心,刘策用根长树枝去拨弄一下这动物,发现它还在移动,这就表示仍是活着的,不过快要渴死也许是快要病死了。于是他爬下水沟将这个小动物提了起来,提到不远处的一条河边将它轻轻地放进水里。

Out of curiosity, he used a long tree branch to poke the animal, and found it moving a little bit. This indicated that it was still alive but must have been dying of thirst or sick, he thought. He climbed down and picked up the sick animal and carried it to a nearby river, and gently threw it into the water.

当这个小动物到了水里以后,它立刻涨大了好几百倍,变成了一条龙,而且精力充沛地游得无影无踪了。

Once it was in the water, the snake suddenly grew several hundred times bigger, becoming a dragon and swimming away vigorously.

刘策的家原本是富有的。他是父母的独子。在他十来岁时,他父母的背运接连而来,更糟糕的是,一场大火把他家的大房子烧得一干二净。他的父母不得不卖去部分土地,盖了一栋小的房子居住。当刘策二十一岁时,父母双亡。他继承了这栋小房子及四十亩耕地。

Liu Ce's family was a wealthy one at first. He was his parents' only child. When he was a teenager, his parents lost their fortune one after the other, and the worst of all, a fire burned down their large home. They had to sell some land and built a small house to live in. When Liu Ce reached twenty-one, both his parents died. He inherited from them the small house and forty acres of land.

他现在面临的前途有两种选择:勤奋地在田里劳动,做一个普通的农夫,就像大多数的农民一样简单地过其一生,或者努力研读经书去参加官府的考试,去当个官像一些胸怀大志的青年那样。

Now he had two options for his future: to work in the land diligently as a common farmer to make a simple living like most of the farmers did, or to study the classical books hard in order to pass the government examinations to become a government official like some ambitious young men did.

结果呢,他既不在田里勤奋干活,也不去努力读书。一有时间,他就穿着他父亲遗留下来的漂亮衣服,去参加社交活动和追逐美丽的女孩。

In the end, he chose neither to work diligently in the land, nor to study hard. Whenever he had time, he would like to wear the splendid clothes left by his father to attend social parties and chase after pretty girls.

他终于认识了一个美丽的女子名叫凤仙。他们迅速坠入爱河。由于她的父母住在很远的省份,而他的父母已经过世,他们不必要去向任何人商量,几个月后便结婚了。

He finally made acquaintance of a pretty young lady named Fengxian. Soon they fell in love. As her parents lived in a faraway province, and his parents had died, they did not have to consult with anybody. A few months later, they married.

婚后,凤仙帮助她丈夫下田干活。回家后她独自处理家务。她要他去专心研读经书,好去参加官府的考试,做个受人敬仰和美慕的政府官员。然而刘策是个懒惰的人,口头上他对他的妻子说,他会听从她的忠告的,可是事实上他从未认真读过书,这使得她非常失望。

After their marriage, Fengxian helped her husband work on the farm. After work, she took care of the household affairs alone. She asked him to concentrate on his studies of the Chinese classics to prepare for the government examinations to become a government official, respected and admired by everyone. But Liu Ce was a lazy man. He said to his wife he would take her advice, but he never seriously did, that made her very disappointed.

一天,这对年轻夫妇抓住了一只鸽子。事实上是这只鸟从开着的窗户飞进来落在他们的桌子上的。凤仙立刻认出这只鸽子是她父母的传信使者。她从这只鸟的绑腿上解下了一封信。读了后她告诉刘策,她的父母邀请他们去参加她父亲的七十岁生日宴会。

One day, the young couple caught a pigeon. Actually, the bird flew through their open window and landed on their table. Fengxian immediately recognized that the pigeon was her parents' message carrier. She removed a letter bound to the bird's leg and read it. Then she told Liu Ce that her parents had invited them to attend her father's seventieth birthday party.

刘策还没有见过他的岳父母。他告诉她,他们一定要去参加宴会,还要带一份礼品去庆贺他岳父的生日。他把家中祖传下来的一些比较值钱的东西拿去典当成现金作为旅费,并买了一份他所能负担的最昂贵的礼品。

Liu Ce had not yet met his parents-in-law. He told her that they must attend the party and bring a birthday present to his father-in-law. He pawned some of his leftover family valuables as traveling fees and bought the most expensive gift he could afford.

当他们到达凤仙的父母家中时,刘策发现那是一栋豪华巨宅,里面满堂宾客,包括凤仙的已出嫁的两个姐姐和她们的丈夫,他们四人打扮得像公主和王子一样,刘策和凤仙则是穿着最普通的衣服。她的两个姐姐和姐夫所送的生日礼品都是非常高档和昂贵,和他们的相比较刘策和凤仙所送的可就太寒酸了。

一时间刘策和凤仙感觉非常不安。

When they reached Fengxian's parents' home, Liu Ce found that it was a huge mansion filled with many guests including Fengxian's two married sisters and their husbands, who dressed like princesses and princes, while Liu Ce and Fengxian wore the most ordinary clothes. The birthday presents her two sisters and their husbands brought in were all precious and expensive. Compared to their presents, Liu Ce and Fengxian's appeared quite cheap. Suddenly, Liu Ce and Fengxian felt very uneasy.

在宴会中,这三个女儿和她们的夫婿被安排坐在首席与主人夫妇同桌。当这两位富有的夫婿知道刘策的低微身份后,他们故意炫耀他们的富贵身份。

During the dinner, the three daughters and their husbands had been assigned to sit with the host and hostess at the table of honor. When the two wealthy sons-in-law learned about Liu Ce's lowly status, they purposely showed off their dignified status.

当宾客们来到首席向主人夫妇敬酒时,他们也对三个女儿及女婿敬酒。知道刘策是个出身低微的农夫时,这些人对他讲话的态度就和对其他的两个女婿全然不同了。

When the guests came to the table of honor to toast the host and hostess, they did the same to the three daughters and their husbands. Knowing that Liu Ce was a lower class farmer, they spoke to him in a very different way compared to how they spoke to the other two sons-in-law.

甚至于她的父母对待他们的女儿及女婿们也有所差别。在宴会结束后,他们邀请凤仙的两个姐姐和她们的丈夫再多留数日,可就没有邀请刘策和凤仙。

Even her parents also treated their daughters and sons-in-law differently. At the end of the party, they asked Fengxian's two sisters and their husbands to stay for a few more days with them, but they did not invite Liu Ce and Fengxian.

在回家的途中,凤仙没有说一句话。当要进入家门时,她对刘策说她爱他,但现在要离开他了。她给刘策一面镜子,告诉他如果他思念她,他就可以从镜子中去寻找。最重要的是如果他继续如此下去,不努力研读经书参加官府的考试,非常可能她就会永远不回到他的身边了。

On the way home, Fengxian did not say a word. But before entering their house, she said to Liu Ce that she loved him but she wanted to leave him now. She gave him a mirror telling him that if he missed her, he could check the mirror. And the most important thing was that if he still acted the way he had, continuing to refuse to study the Chinese classics hard to pass the government examination, it was very possible that she would never return to him.

刘策非常震惊。就在他还没有来得及向她提问题时,她就在他的面前失踪了。

聊
斋
精
选

Liu Ce was shocked. Before he could ask her any questions, she disappeared right in front of him.

独自一人回家后,他立刻去照镜子,果然发现了里面有他那可爱妻子的形象,她是背向着他站立在好几尺远。想起她所催他做的,他开始一有空时就去研读经书。因为思念妻子,他每天都要去照这面镜子。

Entering his home alone, he immediately checked the mirror and indeed found his lovely wife's image in it, with her back toward him standing many feet away. Remembering what she had urged him to do, he started to study the classics whenever he had time. As he missed his wife, he checked the mirror everyday.

似乎是如果他努力研读经书,她在镜子里所站立的位置就靠他近一点。这真是一个鼓励! 于是刘策日夜苦读经书,终于他很高兴地发现她在镜子里不但站得靠他更近,而且又面向着他显现出她那美丽的面孔了。

It seemed that if he kept on studying hard, her standing position in the mirror would appear a little closer to him. What an encouragement! So Liu Ce studied the books as hard as he could day and night. Finally, he was happy to find that she not only stood much closer to him but also turned her head, showing her pretty face in the mirror.

刘策有几个酒友,他们以前常在一起喝酒。一天,一个酒友来看他,邀请他出去喝几盅。刘策已经好久没有这种乐趣了,为了好玩,他接受了邀请。从此以后,他就经常出去与酒友饮酒,而不像早先那样努力研读经书了。

Liu Ce had a few drinking friends. They used to drink together. One day, a friend visited him, inviting him out to have a few drinks. Liu Ce had not enjoyed it for a long time. For fun, he accepted the friend's invitation. Since then, he often went out with his drinking friends and did not study as hard as he had done earlier.

一天晚间,当他从酒席回家后,他又去照镜子。他非常惊讶地发现凤仙在镜子中又转回了头将背向着他,而且又站得很远了。他知道为什么。从第二天起,他谢绝了所有酒友们的邀请,像以前一样地努力读书。慢慢地,她在镜子中的位置又改变了过来,站得很近而且又显现出她那美丽的脸孔了。

One evening after returning home from a drinking party, he checked the mirror again and was surprised to find that Fengxian had turned her head and stood much further away with her back toward him again. He realized the reason why. From the next day on, he turned down all of his drinking friends' invitations and began to study as hard as he had before. Gradually, her position in the mirror changed, standing closer and revealing her pretty face again.

一年后,刘策终于通过了当地官府考试。当他获悉这个好消息后,他去照镜子。他兴奋地发现他那美丽妻子的脸上挂着愉快的微笑,而且她就好像是站立在他的椅子后面。他转过头一望,惊喜地发现他

聊斋精选

的妻子正站在他的面前,眼中还含着泪水。凤仙回来了! 他紧紧地拥抱住她。

A year later, Liu Ce finally passed the local government examination. When he received the happy news, he checked the mirror and was excited to find a joyful smile on his beautiful wife's face, and it seemed that she was standing right behind his chair. He turned around, and was elated to discover his wife standing right in front of him with tears in her eyes. Fengxian was back! He held her tightly in his arms.

因为凤仙的归来,刘策继续加紧学习。第二年,他又通过了省府的乡试。三年后,他更通过了京城里的最后的殿试,并被封为朝中高官。刘策与凤仙乃搬到京城居住去了。

With Fengxian's return, Liu Ce kept up his concentrated study. In the following year, he passed his provincial government examination again. And three years later, he further passed the final central government examination, and was appointed a senior official in the central government. Liu Ce and Fengxian moved to the nation's capital to live.

这时凤仙终于对刘策承认她不是人类。她是天上来的一条雌龙。多年前,因为她犯了天条,被罚下到凡尘渴死在一条小的干水沟里。是刘策把她提送到一条河中救了她的命。为了感恩图报,她来到了人间做他的妻子。

Then Fengxian finally confessed to Liu Ce that she was not human. She was a female dragon from heaven. Many years ago, because she had made a great mistake, she was given a punishment of thirsting to death in a dried ditch in the human world. It was Liu Ce who had picked her up and put her in a river and saved her life. In order to reward her obligation to him, she came to the human world to become his wife.

当她发现他是如此地懒于读书时,她编造了一只鸽子带来了一封邀请信去参加她父亲的生日宴会,并在宴会中遭受了很多的羞辱。最重要的是,她又造出了一面魔镜,使他不停地去努力读书。她之所以玩弄这些计谋无非是想激励他去努力研读经书,最后可以成为朝中的一名高官。

When she found that he was so lazy to study, she created a pigeon to deliver an invitation to celebrate her father's birthday and to receive that humiliating treatment during the party. Most importantly, she had also created the miraculous mirror to make him keep on studying hard. She had performed all of those tricks to inspire him to study the classics hard and eventually to become a senior government official.

他们在京城住了差不多四十年,一直到刘策从政务中退职之后才搬回了老家。此时他们已经有了很多的儿孙,刘策已成了一位老翁了。可是,凤仙仍然看起来如当初一样地年轻貌美。

They lived in the capital for nearly forty years until Liu Ce retired from the government service and they moved back to his native home. By this time, they had had many children and grandchildren. Liu Ce had become an old man, but Fengxian still kept her youthful pretty look.

聊斋精选

刘策在附近的山上建了一座小茅屋,每年夏季,他便带着凤仙去山上避暑。有一年,夏季已经过去了,可他们并未像往年一样地回家。这使得他们的孩子们很担忧。他们便到山上去寻找。找到了小茅屋,发现两人都已经自然死亡了。他们便将父母合葬在同一个墓穴里。

Liu Ce built a small hut in a nearby mountain and he took Fengxian there to spend every summer. At the end of one summer, they did not return home as they had done every year. It made their children very worry and they went to the hut on the mountain to check, and found that both had died a natural death. Their children buried their parents together in one grave.

但是有时候,一些伐木者仍然时常远远地看到刘策和他那美丽的凤仙夫人在山上愉快地散步。当他们想走近时,就又不见了这对夫妇的踪影。因此人们相信刘策和凤仙可能没有真的死去,而都变成神仙了。

But sometimes, some woodcutters still often spotted Liu Ce and his pretty wife, Fengxian, happily walking around in the mountain from a distance. When they tried to approach them, they would lose the couple's trace. It made people believe that Liu Ce and Fengxian might have not actually died, but had become immortals.

聊斋精选

十五、

董生

Escape of the Vampire

一天半夜,董世从一个酒席回家后,发现他家的前门没有关好。他记得离家时是锁了门的。他害怕曾经有小偷闯入过,便急忙检查四周,发现没有什么东西遗失。

One midnight, Dong Shi returned home from a drinking party to find his front door unlocked. He remembered that when he left home, he had locked it. He was afraid a thief might have broken in. Checking around quickly, he did not find anything missing.

于是他进入卧室准备睡觉。突然间,他很惊讶地发觉有一个女人躺在他的床上熟睡。他叫醒了她,问她是谁及为何睡在他的床上。女人坐了起来。在这油灯的光亮中,他看出这是一个非常漂亮的年轻女子。她的面孔看起来好像有点儿熟悉。于是他端详着她的脸,希望可以想出在哪里曾经见过这个女人。

So he entered his bedroom preparing to sleep. And suddenly, he was shocked to discover a woman lying on his bed, sleeping soundly. He woke her up, asking her who she was and why she was sleeping on his bed. The woman sat up. By the light of the oil lamp, he saw that she was a very pretty young woman. As her face seemed somewhat familiar to him, he kept on staring at her trying to figure out where he had met this woman.

"你怎么不认识我了?"她妩媚地对他说,"我是苏艺啊。"
"How could you not recognize me anymore?" She said to him bewitchingly, "I'm Su Yi."

突然间,他想起来她是谁了。
Suddenly, he remembered who she was.

大约在五六年前,苏艺和她的父母从外省搬入这个小镇,他们住在一栋租赁的房子里,就在他家的隔壁。那时董世不过二十岁刚出头,而她才十七八岁。董世几乎马上就爱上了这个漂亮的女邻居。而她似乎也喜欢他。这两个年轻人开始秘密约会。不久,她的父亲发现了,他强烈反对他的女儿与董世往来因为董世只是一个穷小子。他希望把他的女儿嫁给一个富裕的男人。

About five or six years ago, Su Yi and her parents moved into the small town from another province to live at a rental house next to his. Dong Shi was in early twenties while she was a late teenager at that time. Almost immediately, Dong Shi fell in love with the pretty neighbor, and it seemed that she was fond of him, too. The two young people started to date secretly. But when her father discovered it, he was strongly against his daughter's going with Dong Shi, who was but a poor guy. He wished to marry her to a wealthy man.

因为她不顺从父亲,老父就很生气,便严禁她外出。不久后,他们全家就搬出了城,而董世连和他的小情人说声再见的机会也没有。他很想念她,可就是不知道她和她的家人搬到何处去了。慢慢地,他也就把这段短时间的谈情说爱之事忘记了。

As she did not obey her father, the old man was angry and forbade her going out. Not too long

聊斋精选

afterwards, they moved out of the town, and Dong Shi did not even have a chance to say goodbye to his sweetheart. He had missed her, but had no way to find out where she and her family had moved. Gradually, he had forgotten this short romance.

如今她回来了，而且还睡在他的床上！根据她的说法，她与她的家人在那一年搬到了南部的一个大都市。不久，她的父亲就将她嫁给了一个富有的中年鳏夫。她和她的丈夫根本合不来，因为她从来就没有爱过他，他待她也很不好。可是她没有办法去反抗这个环境。

Now she was back and sleeping on his bed! According to her, she and her family moved to a big city in the south that year. Soon afterward, her father married her to a wealthy middle-aged widower. She and her husband did not get along well, as she had never loved him, and he did not treat her fairly. Yet she had no way to rebel against the situation.

上个月，她的丈夫死于肺病。他们没有小孩，她的父母又早已搬回老家去了。她变得无助了，可是她也自由了。她不愿意再回到她的父母那儿，决定回到这儿来依靠董世，看看他是否仍然单身并仍然爱着她。

The previous month, her husband died of lung disease. They did not have any children, and her parents had moved back to their native place. She was helpless but finally free. She did not want to return to her parents, deciding to come back to Dong Shi to see if he was still single and if he still loved her.

当她叙述完了她的故事，他告诉她，他等着这个美妙的日子已经很久了。他说他爱她之深一如往昔。

After she finished her story, he told her he had waited for such a wonderful day for a long time. He said he loved her as deeply as he had before.

从此以后，苏艺便和董世住在一起。两个人像一对新婚的夫妇愉快地生活着。

Since that time, Su Yi stayed with Dong Shi. They lived happily like a couple of newlyweds.

一个月后，他感染上了一种奇怪的疾病，觉得一天比一天衰弱。可是他不知道如何去处理，一直到有一天，他在街上碰巧遇到了一个道士，道士警告他假如他不能摆脱那个正在诅咒他的人，他的性命将很危险。

A month later, he became afflicted with a strange illness, feeling weaker day after day. Yet, he did not know what to do with it until one day, He happened to meet a Taoist priest on the street The priest warned him that his life was in grave danger if he did not try to get rid of whoever had cursed him.

董世正为自己的健康日衰所困扰，听了这个道士的话后，他开始怀疑是否真的有人在诅咒他，是苏艺吗？那是不可能的，因为她是他以前邻居的女儿，他在困惑着。他把苏艺的故事告诉了这个道士。道士对他说如果他能见到她的话，他就能很容易辨别她是否是妖怪。于是董世把道士带回了家。

Dong Shi was bothered by the deterioration of his health. After listening to the priest, he wondered if he was really under a curse. Could it be Su Yi? But that did not make sense, for she absolutely was his former neighbor's daughter. He was puzzled. He told the priest about Su Yi. The priest told Dong Shi that it was very easy for him to tell if she was a vampire or not once he had a chance to meet her. So Dong Shi took the priest home.

于是，一件奇怪的事情发生了。当苏艺发现董世把一个道士带回家来后，她立刻在他们面前失踪了，而且就发生在他们的面前。这使得董世相信她真的不是他以前所认识的邻居的女儿，而是一个妖怪所变的。

Then a strange thing happened. As soon as Su Yi discovered that Dong Shi had brought home a Taoist priest, she suddenly disappeared right in front of them. It made Dong Shi believe that she was indeed not his former neighbor's daughter as he had believed, but a vampire to be turned to.

道士便急忙布置了一个道坛，并从口袋中掏出了一个小瓶子。他站在道坛上念诵着道教的咒语。很快地有一缕白色的烟雾从开着的窗户中由外面穿入了瓶中。当烟雾不见后，道士就将瓶口封好，走下了道坛。他很高兴地告诉董世说苏艺是一个妖怪，他已经把她和她一家都捉进了瓶子中了。他要董世放心，他的健康在两个星期左右就会恢复了。

The priest quickly set up an altar and took out a small bottle from his pocket. He stood on the altar chanting the Taoist invocations. Soon a thread of white smoke streamed in from outside of the house through the open window and entered the bottle. After the smoke disappeared, the priest sealed the bottle, and stepped down from the altar. He happily said to Dong Shi that Su Yi was a vampire and he had caught her and her whole family and put them all in the bottle. He assured Dong Shi that his health would be improving in a couple of weeks or so.

为了报答救命之恩，董世邀请道士在家吃饭。饭后，道士去厕所方便。董世一人留在客厅里。看着这个神秘的瓶子，他很好奇这么一个小小的瓶子怎么可以把这个妖怪及她的一家锁在里面。他把瓶子放在他的耳朵边听。

To express his appreciation for saving his life, Dong Shi invited the priest to have dinner at home. After the meal, the priest asked to be excused to go to the restroom. Dong Shi was left alone in the living room with the mysterious bottle on the table. Out of curiosity, he was wondering how such a small bottle could hold the vampire and her entire family in it. So he put the bottle to his ear to listen.

突然，他听到了苏艺甜美的声音自瓶内发出。她埋怨他背叛了她。她说她爱他而他也爱她。她从没有任何念头想要夺取他的性命。她的甜美的声音使得他想起了他们在一起相爱的时光。他问她如何可

聊斋精选

以救她出来。她要他把道坛右边角落第七根小蜡烛吹熄了,她就可以溜出来。她向他保证一旦出来了,她就永远离开他,同时她将帮助他找到一个好的女孩做他的妻子。

Suddenly, he heard Su Yi's sweet voice from inside of the bottle. She accused him of betrayal. She said that she loved him and he loved her, too. She never had any intention whatsoever to take his life. Her sweet voice reminded him of their lovely days together. He asked her how he could help her out. She told him to blow out the seventh small candle at the right corner of the altar, and she would be able to sneak out of the bottle. She assured him that once she was out, she would leave him for good, but she would help him find a nice girl to be his wife.

董世立刻照着她的要求去做。一缕很短的白色烟雾从瓶子里出来后就不见了。

Dong Shi quickly did what she had asked him to do. And a short thread of smoke rose from the bottle and disappeared.

就在这个时候,道士回到了客厅。看到了刚才发生的情况,他立刻检查瓶子并用一道符重新加封了瓶口。他告诉董世一个母妖怪已经逃跑了。也许这个妖怪命中不该被关。幸好她的家人都还被锁在瓶子里。然后道士收了道坛就离开了。

Just at that moment, the priest returned to the living room. Noticing what had happened, he quickly checked the bottle and resealed it with an amulet. He told Dong Shi that a female vampire had escaped. Maybe this one was not fated for being locked. Luckily, her family was still kept in the bottle. Then the priest closed the altar and left.

苏艺遵守她的诺言,真的没有回来。董世的健康情况一天天恢复。两个星期后,他完全恢复了健康。他开始思念苏艺,特别是晚间,可是他无法知道她在何处。

Su Yi kept her promise. She did not return. Dong Shi's health began to improve day after day. Two weeks later, he resumed to be a healthy man. He started to miss Su Yi, especially in the evenings, but he had no way to find where she was.

六个月后一天晚间,苏艺突然回来了。董世非常兴奋,乃想拥抱和亲吻她,然而为她所拒绝。她说她已经明了她以前的所作所为都不是正确的,虽然她从没有害死过一个人。她这次回来的原因是来实践她对他的诺言的。她说她已经预测到将有一群无法无天的盗匪将在某一天来攻击这个城镇,他们将屠城三日。

One evening six months later, Su Yi suddenly returned. Dong Shi was elated, and tried to hug and kiss her, but she refused. She said that she realized what she had done before was not correct, although she had never actually killed a person. The reason she came back was to carry out her promise to him. She said that she had foreseen that a gang of notorious bandits would attack the town where he lived and plunder the whole area for three days starting on a certain date.

为了可以逃避这场灾难,她送给他两粒药丸。她说服下一粒药丸后,这个人将可以隐形三天。在任何时候,如果这个人将他的头连点三下,他的隐形情况就消失了。如果他连摇他的头三下,他的隐形情况则又恢复了。如果两个人都服下了药丸,他们两个人不管点头或摇头都可以相互看见彼此。她说她给他两粒药丸的原因是一粒用以救他自己的性命,另一粒是救他喜爱的女子的性命。因为他救了她的性命,她大概就会嫁给他为妻以作报答。那就是她履行她对他的诺言,帮他找个好女孩做他的妻子。

To escape the calamity, she gave him two pills. She said that after taking one pill, the person would become invisible for three days. The person could restore his visibility any time he wanted if he nodded his head three times. He could become invisible again if he shook his head three times. If two people took the pills, they could see each other no matter they nodded or shook heads. She said that the reason she gave him two pills was to save his life as well as that of the girl he loved. If he saved the girl's life, she would probably marry him in return. That was how she would live up to her promise to help him find a nice girl to be his wife.

董世感谢她,并从她手中接下了这两粒药丸。当他再想拥抱她时,她已经不见了,只有她那甜美的"再会"声在空中飘荡着。

Dong Shi thanked her. Right after he took her pills from her, she disappeared before he tried to hug her again. But her sweet voice saying "Goodbye" remained in the air.

苏艺的预测果然不错。在她所说的那一天,一群好几百人的盗匪攻击了这个城镇。他们击败了本地的执法武装占领了整个地区。他们捣毁了官府的机构,杀害了官员。正如同苏艺所警告的一模一样。突然间,这个城镇变成了一个活生生的地狱,每个居民的生命都在危险中。

Su Yi's prediction was right. On the first day she had indicated, a gang of several hundred bandits attacked the town. They defeated the local law enforcements and occupied the whole area. They destroyed the government offices, killed the officials just like what Su Yi had warned. Suddenly the town became like a living version of hell. Every resident's life was in danger.

董世立刻吞下了一粒药丸,他在街上行走,没有一个人看得到他。他目睹无数恐怖残忍的罪行发生在每一个地方。混乱中,在一条街上他发现了一位年轻的美丽女子正被一个盗匪紧紧地追逐着。这个女孩惊怕极了,拼命地狂奔。终于她进入了一栋空的建筑物里。董世紧跟在她的后面。他连摇他的头三下,显现在这受惊的女孩面前。他迅速自我介绍并表达了他想救她的意愿。他给她另一粒药丸,要她立即吞下。刚吞下后盗匪冲了进来。因为他看不见她也看不见董世,就非常失望地离开了。

Having quickly taken one of the two pills, Dong Shi walked around the streets totally unseen by others. He witnessed the most horrible and merciless crimes happening in everywhere. Amidst the great chaos, he noticed a pretty young woman being chased by a bandit on a street. The girl was terrified and tried to run as fast as she could. Finally, she entered an empty public building. Dong Shi followed her closely. He shook his head three times, appearing in front of the frightened girl. He quickly introduced himself and explained his willingness to help her. He gave her the other pill asking her to swallow it immediately. Soon after that, the bandit rushed into the building. As he could not see her or Dong Shi, he left in great disappointment.

女孩感激董世的救命之恩。在往后的两天毁灭性的日子中,这对隐形人躲过了这场大难。在他们的隐形失效前,官府大军赶来击败了盗匪,又恢复了当地治安。

The girl thanked Dong Shi for saving her life. Over the next two days of destruction, the invisible couple escaped the calamity. Before their invisibility was to expire, the government reinforcement troops arrived and defeated the bandits, reestablishing order in the area.

董世陪同这个女孩回到了她的家,悲哀地发现她的父母都已遇难了。他帮助她安葬了她的双亲后,她就嫁给了他。

Dong Shi accompanied the girl to her home, and sadly found that her parents both had been killed in the attack. With his help, she buried her parents and married him.

每当董世和他的妻子谈到苏艺时,他们两人都非常怀念这位神秘的女子,可是苏艺一直没有再出现过。

Each time Dong Shi and his wife talked about Su Yi, both of them would miss the mysterious lady very much. But Su Yi never showed up again.

聊斋精选

十六、小翠

A Foolish Boy

很久以来,中国人一直相信当一个有灵性的兽类在寻求成为正果时,天律规定这个精灵必须先行经过一项可能致命的灾难,最常遭遇的灾难就是雷打电击。假如这个动物能够预先安排一位命中注定会成为显贵的人及时来当它的保护人,它就可以从这场灾难中逃生。

It was long believed by many Chinese that when a spiritual animal was seeking immortality, according to the heavenly rules, the animal would meet a potentially fatal calamity. One of the most common calamities was a thundering and lightning strike. If the animal could find in advance a person who would be predestined for a dignitary to be its protector, it could survive the calamity.

当张总督还是六岁时,一天,在一场大雷暴雨中他看到了一只像大黄猫似的动物向他跑来,年幼的张家小孩便把这只像猫似的动物抱在怀里。就在这个时候,雷电交加一个接着一个好像就是专对着他和他的家人住着的房子似的。

When Governor Zhang was six years old, one day he saw an animal resembling a large yellow cat running toward him in a heavy thunderstorm. Young Zhang took the cat-like animal in his arms just as the bolts of lightning and loud thundering burst in the air one after the other, all seemingly targeting the house where he and his family lived.

雷暴雨后,这个动物跑走了,很快就不见了踪迹。小男孩找不到这个动物,他问他的父母是否曾看到它。他的父亲高兴地告诉他的母亲说,他预测他们的儿子长大后一定会是个贵人,因为他相信这个像大黄猫似的动物一定是个狐狸正在寻求正果,怕被雷电击中去找寻贵人保护的。

After the storm, the animal ran away and soon disappeared. As the boy could not find the animal, he asked his parents if they had seen it. His father happily told his mother that he predicted that their son would be a dignitary when he grew up, as he believed that the large cat-like animal must be a fox seeking a protector to save its life from the deadly lightning strike as it was seeking immortality.

小男孩长大了后成为一个非常聪明的青年,他勤读中国经典。数年间,他就通过了所有的官办考试,被封为京城朝廷中的一名高官。没过几年,他就被皇帝晋升为他所出生的那个省的总督。那一年,他不过是二十九岁。

When the boy grew older, he turned out to be a smart young man, and he studied the Chinese classics very diligently. In a few years, he passed all the government examinations and was appointed a senior official in the central government. Several years later, the emperor promoted him to be the governor of his own province. He was only twenty-nine years old that year.

当他通过第一个地方官府的考试后,他就和一位退职宰相的女儿结了婚。他的妻子不但是位美丽的女子也是位能干的家庭主妇。婚后一年,他们就生了个儿子。他为儿子起名少兴。

When he passed the first local government examination, he married the daughter of a retired prime

聊斋精选

minister. His wife was not only a pretty lady but also a capable housekeeper. One year later, they had a son. He named his boy Shaoxing.

似乎是所有的好事张总督都有了。可是当少兴稍稍长大了点后，总督夫妇发现他们的儿子智能不足。夫妇两人用尽各种方法遍寻良医帮助他们解除烦恼，可就是没有一个人可以办到。最后他们也只有放弃努力了。

It seemed that all the good things had come to Governor Zhang. But when Shaoxing grew a little older, the governor and his wife found that their son was mentally deficient. The couple tried every way they could to find a good doctor to help them solve the problem, but nobody could. Finally, they gave up trying.

当少兴到了该娶妻的年龄时，没有一个媒人可以为他找到一个对象做他的妻子，因为没有做父母的愿意将他们的女儿嫁给一个智能低下的男青年。因此每当张总督夫妇想起这桩事情时，他们就感到很难过。而这个难题日夜困扰着他们无法得以好转。

When Shaoxing reached marriageable age, no matchmaker was able to find a match for him to be his wife, as none of the parents wanted to marry their daughter to a young man who lacked intelligence. Therefore, whenever Governor Zhang and his wife thought of this issue, they would feel very sad, and the sad situation bothered them daily. And they could do nothing to improve it.

一天，一位中年妇人和一位十七八岁的女孩来到总督官邸寻求女佣的工作。她们身穿破旧的衣服像叫花子似的。她们自称是母女。总督夫人注意到这个年轻女孩虽然穿着破烂，却是非常秀丽而且其眉宇间还透露出一股高度的智慧。她半开玩笑半认真地告诉这两个女子，她不需要更多的女佣，可确实的需要一个媳妇。

One day, a middle-aged woman and a teenage girl came to the governor's mansion seeking employment as maids. Wearing shabby clothes like beggars, they introduced themselves as mother and daughter. The governor's wife noticed that the young girl, although shabbily dressed, was quite pretty and showed high intelligence in her eyes. She half jokingly and half sincerely told the two women that she did not need any additional maid, but she did need a daughter-in-law.

"那好极了，"这个年长的妇人微笑着说，"张夫人，如果你认为我的女儿有资格做你的媳妇，这将是我们极大的造化。"

"That's wonderful," the older woman replied with a smile, "Madame Zhang, if you think my daughter is qualified to be your daughter-in-law, it would be a great honor for us."

"你的女儿太有资格了，"张夫人回答道，"可我的儿子没有资格做你的女婿。他是个痴呆的男孩，缺乏智能。"

"Your daughter is very much qualified," Mrs. Zhang answered. "But my son is not qualified to be your son-in-law. He is a foolish boy, lacking intelligence."

"痴呆并不是罪恶。"这个妇人说。然后她又接着说,"一个心地善良的痴呆男子比一个心地邪恶的聪明男子要好得多了。"

"Being foolish is not a crime," the woman said. Then she added, "A foolish man with a good heart is much better than a smart man with a wicked heart."

她转过头来对着她的女儿,她问这个年轻的女孩,"囡囡,你难道不同意我的话吗?"

Turning her head toward her daughter, she asked the young girl, "Honey, don't you agree with me?"

当这个女孩柔声地应诺时,母亲又问女儿,"你是不是宁愿嫁给这样一个痴呆的男子而不愿嫁给那种聪明的男子?"

When the girl softly answered yes, the mother asked her daughter again, "Would you rather marry such a foolish boy than such a smart one?"

女孩低下头羞红了脸。她没有说是,也没有说不是。

The girl hung her head and blushed. She did not say yes, neither did she say no.

当总督夫人非常有兴趣地听她们的谈话时,这个母亲又问她的女儿,"如果你同意我的话,就点头好了。"

While the governor's wife was very much interested in the conversation, the mother asked her daughter one more time, "If you agree with my words, just nod your head."

于是这个女孩羞涩地点了点头。

Then the girl nodded her head shyly.

这下子张夫人兴奋极了。她立即要她的侍女把她的丈夫和儿子找来。这两个男子来到后,她把情况向这两个男子说明。霎那间,每个人对这桩婚事都很兴奋,总督夫妇兴高采烈。少兴根本不知道这究竟是怎么一回事,但是他似乎知道他将有一个新的玩伴了,所以他也很兴奋。

Mrs. Zhang was elated. She quickly asked her maid to send for her husband and their son. When the two men came, she explained the situation to them. Suddenly, everybody was excited about the marriage proposal. The governor and his wife were overjoyed. Shaoxing did not know exactly what was going on, but he seemed to know that he was going to have a new playmate. So he was also excited.

聊斋精选

这对母女很高兴,因为她们不需要找工作了。她们被邀请居住在总督的官邸,作为总督夫妇的贵宾。

The mother and daughter were happy, as they did not have to find jobs. They were invited to live in the governor's mansion as the governor and his wife's honorable guests.

因为害怕这对母女变卦,尤其是这个女孩,张总督夫妇迅速在家里安排了一个简单的婚礼。于是这个名叫翠翠的穷女孩摇身一变成了总督的媳妇了。

Fearing that the mother and daughter might soon change their minds, particularly the girl, Governor Zhang and his wife quickly arranged a simple wedding ceremony to be held at home. The poor girl named Cuicui suddenly became the governor's daughter-in-law.

女儿成婚了以后这个老妇人说,她要回她的家乡告诉她所有的亲戚朋友们。然后她就带着笑容走了。

After her daughter's wedding ceremony, the older woman said that she wanted to return to her native place to relay the happy news to all of her relatives and friends. Then she left with a grin on her face.

刚开始时,总督夫妇对他们的聪明而美丽的儿媳妇感到很抱歉,他们害怕当她发现她的丈夫是多么的呆傻时她一定会后悔这桩婚姻的。可是他们很快地发现翠翠一点儿也不感到后悔。她与她的丈夫整天玩耍。少兴根本不知道结婚的意思是什么,他很高兴现在日夜都有一个伴侣和他玩乐了。

In the beginning, the governor and his wife felt sorry for their smart and pretty daughter-in-law. They were afraid that she might regret the marriage when she discovered how foolish her husband was. But they soon found that Cuicui did not feel regretful at all. She played with her husband all the time. Shaoxing did not really understand the meaning of marriage. Yet he was glad to have a partner to play with him day and night.

少兴和翠翠不像一般的新婚夫妇,简直就像是两个小孩子,生活中什么也不懂只知道玩乐。在公开场所如果少兴不在身边,翠翠的行为倒也像个正常的妇人。如果她和少兴在一起,则她就也像一个傻女孩。

Shaoxing and Cuicui did not look like the usual newlyweds but rather like two small children, knowing nothing else in life but leisure and play. In the public alone without Shaoxing by her side, Cuicui would behave like a normal woman, but when she was with Shaoxing, she acted like a foolish girl, too.

因为他们是富有人家,不要去工作,还有很多女佣服侍他们,所以他们每日都在寻欢作乐。

As they were wealthy people, they did not have to work, and they had many maids to serve them, so they had fun every day.

有时候,翠翠将少兴打扮为一个判官,要他坐在一张桌子后面不要移动,而她则和一些婢女扮作罪犯和执法人。有的时候,她又将她的丈夫扮作一个店主,而她和一些婢女扮作来向他买东西的顾客。不管翠翠要他做什么,少兴总是很高兴地照办。他的妻子就像个导演,而他就像个永远听导演指挥的演员。

Sometimes, Cuicui dressed Shaoxing as a judge and asked him to sit behind a table without moving, while she and the maids acted like criminals and enforcement officers. Or she would dress her husband like the owner of a shop, while she and the maids acted like customers coming to buy merchandises from him. Shaoxing was always glad to comply with whatever Cuicui arranged for him to do. So his wife was the director and he was an actor, listening to the director all the time.

因为不管她要他说什么他都同意去说,有时候,他忘记了她教导他说的话而时常引得翠翠和婢女们哄堂大笑,于是少兴本人也跟着大笑。

Because he tacitly agreed to say whatever she taught him to say, sometimes he could not remember all the words she wanted him to say, and the game would often end in hearty laughter among Cuicui and the maids, as well as Shaoxing himself.

张总督任总督职务已经有很长一段时间了。一些本地的政敌乃暗中策划劝说新的宰相将他免职。他们知道张总督和新的宰相尚不相识,他们中间也没有政治关系。因而一项秘密的政治阴谋在进行中。

Governor Zhang had held the governorship for a long time. Some of his local political opponents secretly planned to persuade the new prime minister to remove him from the office. They knew that Governor Zhang and the new prime minister did not know each other and had no political relationship between them. So a secret political trick was being planned.

一天,总督的卫士报告新上任的宰相大人前来私访。张总督立刻整装走到前门去以最恭敬的态度迎接他的上司。他向新宰相大人躬身低头不敢仰视,迎进客厅恭请上坐。

One day, the governor's guards reported that the new prime minister was paying him a private visit. Governor Zhang immediately dressed up and went to the front door to greet his new superior as respectfully as he could. He lowered his head and humbly bowed to the new prime minister. He led his superior into his living room and tried to offer him a seat.

就在这个时候,张总督发现了这位新宰相是个冒充的。再近一步观察,他发觉这个宰相是他的傻呆儿子少兴所装扮的,而他的所谓秘书则是他的儿媳妇乔装的。显然,翠翠又是这段戏曲的导演而少兴是她的演员。

Just at this moment, Governor Zhang discovered that the prime minister was an impostor. Upon looking closer, he found that it was his idiotic son, Shaoxing, pretending to be the prime minister, while his pretended secretary was his daughter-in-law. Obviously, Cuicui was the director of the gag and Shaoxing was her actor.

聊斋精选

总督勃然大怒,他痛责他的儿子和他的顽皮媳妇。在这同时,他的政治对手已经探悉到了新任宰相私访张总督的新闻。他们猜想这两位政治人物必已建立了密切的关系,因此他们把原先想将张总督的总督职位除去的计划迅速放弃了。

The governor was furious. He thrashed his son and shouted at his naughty daughter-in-law. Meanwhile, his political opponents had received the news of the new prime minister's personal visit to Governor Zhang. Presuming that a sound relationship must have been established between the two men, they quickly dropped their plan to remove Governor Zhang from office.

由于少兴是他父母惟一的孩子,他的父母很想抱孙子。可是结婚已经两年了,翠翠还没有怀孕。最后张夫人终于知道了少兴和翠翠自从结婚后两人根本就没有同床过。每天晚上,不是少兴就是翠翠一人睡在床上,另一个则睡在长榻上。她便要她的儿子和媳妇来到她的房间,她命令这对年轻夫妇从这天起,必须每晚同睡在一张床上。

As Shaoxing was their parents' only child, they were anxious to usher in their third generation. But two years after her marriage, Cuicui was still not yet pregnant. Finally, Mrs. Zhang learnt that Shaoxing and Cuicui had never slept on the same bed since their marriage. Every night, either Shaoxing or Cuicui slept on the bed alone while the other one slept on a couch. She demanded her son and daughter-in-law to come to her room. She gave order to the young couple that from that day on, they must sleep on the same bed every night.

数日后,少兴来到他的母亲处抱怨翠翠每天夜里都把她的脚放在他的腹上,使得他很不舒服因而不能好好睡觉。他要求他的母亲仍让他们像以前一样单独睡。这个呆傻的抱怨使得全家人都大笑不已。

A few days later, Shaoxing came to his mother complaining that Cuicui always put one foot on his belly during the night, which made him so much uncomfortable that he could not have a good sleep. He begged his mother to let them sleep separately like before. The foolish complaint made the rest of the family roar with laughter.

没有人可以强迫少兴去使他的妻子怀孕。终于张夫人让步了,任由她的傻儿子和他的妻子分开睡,和以前一样生活得像小孩子。

Nobody could force Shaoxing to impregnate his wife. Finally, Mrs. Zhang gave up and let her idiotic son and his wife sleep separately as they preferred, living the way they wanted to like small children.

一天,这对像孩子样的夫妇玩捉迷藏的游戏。当该是翠翠躲起来的时候,她把身体缩成一个小虫子一样大小藏在一个小瓶子里,少兴找不到她而像个小婴儿一样大哭了起来。当她从瓶子中跳出来恢复她原来的样子后,他又兴奋得跳了起来。

One day, the childish husband and wife played hide-and-seek game. When it was Cuicui's turn to hide,

聊斋精选

she shrunk herself down to the size of an insect and hid inside of a bottle. Shaoxing could not find her and cried loudly like a baby. When she hopped out of the bottle and resumed her original size, he jumped up excitedly.

等轮到少兴躲起来的时候,这个傻小子找不到什么地方好躲,便躺到床上。为了不让翠翠找到,他用很多床被子把自己连头带脚都盖了起来。翠翠知道他藏身何处,故意装做不知道,还不停地叫着他的名字到处寻找他。终于她掀起了被窝,发现少兴因为窒息已经死亡了。

Now it was Shaoxing's turn to hide. The foolish young man could not find a good place to hide, but lay on the bed. In order not to let Cuicui find him, he covered himself from the head to feet with many blankets. Cuicui knew where he was hiding, but pretended that she did not, and kept calling his name to look for him. Finally, she pulled away all the blankets, but found Shaoxing had died of suffocation.

翠翠既不恐惧也不悲伤,她甚至于也不哭泣或叫人帮助。相反地,她将少兴扶坐在床上并且仍不停地和他说笑。

Cuicui was neither frightened nor sad. She did not even cry or ask for help. Instead, she propped Shaoxing up in a sitting position on the bed, and continued to talk and laugh with him.

当一个婢女碰巧发现了这个悲剧时,她连忙去报告总督夫人。惊吓的总督和他的妻子赶紧跑到房间里查看,极度震惊地发现他们惟一的小孩真的死了。他们控诉翠翠谋杀亲夫,可是翠翠对此否认,她坚持少兴仍在熟睡中。

When a maid happened to discover the tragedy, she hurriedly reported to the governor's wife. The frightened governor and his wife rushed to the room and were shocked to find that their only child was indeed dead. They charged Cuicui with the murder of her husband. But Cuicui denied it, and insisted that Shaoxing was in a deep sleep.

当这整座府里哭乱成一团好一阵子后,少兴突然睁开眼睛问这个房间里是怎么一回事。更奇怪的是少兴的言谈不再像一个不成熟的孩子。总督夫妇于是问了他几个问题,他回答得完全像一个正常的成熟男子。他告诉他的父母他感觉好像是从一个很长的睡眠中醒来。然后他问他的妻子何在,翠翠急忙上前。他紧握着她的手高兴地大哭了起来,翠翠也哭了。夫妻两人携着手又是哭又是笑的,少兴的父母和婢女们便出了房间。

While the whole mansion had been filled with cries and in great chaos for a while, Shaoxing suddenly opened his eyes asking what was going on in the room. More strangely, Shaoxing's speech indicated that he was not immature any more. The governor and his wife asked him a few questions and he answered like a normal mature man. He told his parents that he felt as if he had just awakened from a long sleep. Then he asked where his wife was. Cuicui stepped forward, and he grasped her hands and cried joyously. Cuicui

聊斋精选

cried, too. The husband and wife held each other's hands, crying and laughing, while Shaoxing's parents and the maids retreated out of the room.

现在屋里只有他们这一对了,他们热情地拥抱就像一对正常的恩爱夫妻一样。

Now the young couple was left alone in the room. They hugged passionately like any ordinary loving husband and wife.

因为少兴变成一个正常的男子,翠翠的言行也像一个正常的妇人,他们不再去玩那些孩子气的游戏了。

Since Shaoxing had become a normal man, Cuicui acted like a regular woman, too. They would not play childish games anymore.

少兴曾经死了,后又活了过来,他智能低下的情形完全消失了。一家人都在困惑着这究竟是怎么一回事。聪明的张总督怀疑这一切的一切都与他那神秘的儿媳妇有关系。他也记得不久以前她把少兴装扮为新到任的宰相来拜访他,这不是儿戏,那是精心设计的谋略,为去愚弄他的本地政敌,以使他们放弃将他解除总督职务。

Shaoxing had died, then revived, and his mental deficiency had disappeared. The whole family was confused about why and how these had happened. The wise Governor Zhang suspected that all of these involved his mysterious daughter-in-law. He also remembered that not too long ago she had dressed up Shaoxing to pretend to be the new prime minister paying him a visit. It was not a childish game. It was a delicate trick to fool his local political opponents to drop their plan to remove him from the governorship.

"翠翠绝对不是一个普通的女人。"他对他的夫人说。

"So Cuicui must not be a normal woman after all." he told his wife.

于是他们与翠翠私下交谈,少兴也在旁边。他们问她这究竟是怎么一回事以及她究竟是什么人。

They had a private conversation with Cuicui with Shaoxing by her side. They asked Cuicui what was behind all of those things and who she actually was.

翠翠终于承认了她不是人类。她和她的母亲都是狐狸。因为在若干年前当张总督还是一个小孩子时,他曾经在雷暴雨中保护过她的母亲不受雷电的袭击,她是代表她的母亲来感恩报答他们的。现在,她已经完成了她的任务使总督的独子变成了一个正常的男子。因此她要离开他们回到山上去,修炼成为正果。

Cuicui finally admitted that she was not a human being. Both she and her mother were foxes. Because Governor Zhang had protected her mother from a deadly lightning strike many years earlier when he was a

聊斋精选

child, she had come back to return the favor on behalf of her mother. She had now accomplished her mission to make the governor's only son become a normal man. She wanted to leave them and return to the mountains to pursue her goal of becoming an immortal.

这个承认使得全家震惊,特别是少兴。他深爱他的妻子,恳求她留下不走。她告诉他作为一个狐狸,她是不能为他生儿育女的。因为他是家中的独子,他必须要有孩子来传承他家的香火。她建议他再去和一个正常的女子结婚,让她为他生育儿女。

The confession shocked the whole family, especially Shaoxing. He deeply loved his wife and begged her to stay. She told him that as a fox, she could not bear children for him, and he must have children to carry on his family name, as he was his parents' only son. She suggested that he remarry a normal woman who could give birth to children.

可是少兴告诉翠翠,他宁愿没有小孩也不能在生活中没有她。他说如果没有她,他今日仍是一个痴呆和没有儿女的男人。因此,不管她如何解释,他只是紧抓住她的手哭着求她不要离开他。终于,翠翠答应暂时留下不走。

But Shaoxing told Cuicui that he would rather be childless than live without her. He said that without her, he would have still been an idiotic and childless man. No matter how she tried to explain, he just grasped her hands and cried and begged her not to leave him. Finally Cuicui promised to stay for a while.

随着日月流逝,翠翠开始日渐衰老。不过一年光景,她就从一个年轻貌美女子而逐渐成为一个老年妇人。但这丝毫不减少兴对她的钟爱。翠翠问少兴如果她死了他怎么办。他回答如果她先他而死,他将不再娶妻。

As time went on, Cuicui began to age at an accelerated rate. Only a year later, she had changed from a pretty young lady to an old woman. But that did not alter Shaoxing's love for her even a little bit. Cuicui asked Shaoxing what would happen if she died. He answered that if she died before him, he would not remarry.

于是她告诉他因为他没有兄弟,如果他到时候拒绝再婚而没有生儿子来传宗接代,根据中国的传统,他将被认为是一个不孝之子。如果是为了她的缘故,她是不愿意负担这个责任的。

Then she quickly pointed out that because he had no brothers, if he refused to remarry a woman to have a son to carry on the family name, he would be considered a disloyal son by the entire society, according to the traditional Chinese philosophy. If it was all to be because of her, she did not want to be responsible for that.

夫妻两人几乎每天都为这件事争辩不已。终于少兴很勉强地接受了一个妥协,让翠翠为他安排一个

聊斋精选

女孩作为他的侍妾来生育儿女。同时,翠翠也不要再提起离开他。

The couple argued about this subject just about every day. Finally, Shaoxing reluctantly accepted a compromise to let Cuicui arrange a girl to be his concubine to bear children. Meanwhile, Cuicui would not mention leaving him again.

翠翠找到一百里外一个贫穷人家的女儿作为她丈夫的侍妾。当成婚那天少兴掀起了他新娘的头盖时,他家中的每一个人都很惊讶,因为新人长得就像当年未衰老前的翠翠。于是大家急忙找翠翠来做比较,可是没有人可以找到她,她已经失踪了。

Cuicui found a girl from a poor family a hundred miles away to be her husband's concubine. During the wedding ceremony, when Shaoxing lifted the heavily embroidered bridal cover from his new woman's head, every member of the family was surprised to find that she looked exactly like Cuicui when she had not appeared aging. Then they hurriedly looked for Cuicui to come over for them to affirm the comparison, but nobody could find her. She had disappeared.

在她的卧室里,他们终于发现了翠翠留给少兴的一封信。在信中,她说当她决定代她的母亲来报恩时,她故意变化成这个侍妾的模样,因为她预测这个女孩将会成为他的妻子。她要求少兴将这个女孩在家中的地位由侍妾升为妻子。如此她也可以安心地去继续寻求成为正果之道。她希望少兴有了一个新的妻子长得和她以前一模一样可以使得他减少对她的相思之苦。

Hidden in the bedroom, they finally discovered a letter Cuicui had written for Shaoxing. In the letter, she explained that when she decided to return the favor for her mother, she purposely took on the image of the concubine, because she forecasted that the girl would be predestined to be his wife. She asked Shaoxing to promote the girl's status in the family from concubine to wife, so she would feel free in her mind to continue her quest of becoming an immortal. She hoped that having a new wife who looked identically like her would release him from the bitterness of missing her.

事实上,不管他的新人长得和翠翠是如何地相像,少兴永远无法将翠翠的情影从他的内心深处除去。终其一生,他都在怀念翠翠。

The truth was that no matter how much his new woman looked like Cuicui, Shaoxing could not wipe out Cuicui's image from his deep mind. He missed Cuicui for the rest of his life.

聊
斋
精
选

十七、

莲花公主

The Venomous Attacker

王瑜在二十多岁时就已经是位天才诗人。一个夏日午后,在写了两个小时的诗后,他感到有点疲倦,便决定闭上眼睛休息一下。

Wang Yu was a talented poet in his mid-twenties. One summer afternoon, having written poems for a couple of hours, he felt tired and closed his eyes to take a short break.

不久,他听到轻微的敲门声。他去应了门,发现一个穿着官府小吏制服的男子站在门外。这个人很谦逊地告诉王瑜他的主人派遣他来邀请王瑜先生到衙门去一趟。自忖没有亲友在任何衙门里工作及自己最近没有做过任何违法错事,他问这个男子他的主人在什么衙门里工作以及他的官阶是什么。

Soon, he heard a slight knock on his door. He opened the door and found a man dressed like a lower government officer standing outside. The man humbly said to Wang Yu that his master had send him over to invite Mr. Wang Yu to come to the office. Thinking of having no relatives or friends working at any government offices, and having done nothing wrong or illegal recently, he asked the man what office his master worked for and what position he held.

男子恭敬地回答他的主人是掌管皇帝及皇家事务的宗人府总管大臣。至于他的主人为什么要见王瑜先生,他就不知道了。

The man answered respectfully that his master was the chief official in charge of the affairs for the king and his royal family. As for why his master wanted to see Mr. Wang Yu, the man said he had no idea.

既然这是一项公务邀请,王瑜就跟随这个男子出去了。他带领王瑜穿过了很多高大的楼宇,最后停在一扇龙形的大铁门前。王瑜生长在这个街坊,他很惊讶他怎么从来没有注意到这儿有这么多的高楼还有一道大铁门。在他还没有发问前,这个男子打开了门请王瑜入内。王瑜犹豫了一下,要这个人先进去,他紧随在他身后。

Since it was an official invitation, Wang Yu followed the man out. He led Wang Yu through many tall buildings and finally stopped in front of a huge iron gate designed in the shape of a dragon. Wang Yu had lived in the neighborhood all his life. He was wondering how he had never noticed the tall buildings, or the huge iron gate in the area. Before he asked, the man opened the gate and asked Wang Yu to enter. Wang Yu hesitated, wanting the man to go first so he would follow closely behind him.

进入后,王瑜更为惊讶。这里面更为宏伟华丽了,每一栋豪华的大楼前面都有庭院。很多穿着制服的警卫在各栋楼间忙忙碌碌、进进出出。

After entering, Wang Yu was even more surprised. The inside was much more magnificent, with a courtyard in front of each splendid building. Many uniformed security guards were busily coming and going in and out of the buildings.

聊斋精选

这名男子带领王瑜进入了一栋楼房见到了一位中年男士。看到王瑜进来,这个人连忙站了起来和王瑜招呼,并自我介绍是宗人府总管大臣。

The man led Wang Yu into a building to see a middle-aged man. Seeing Wang Yu entering, the man immediately stood up to greet Wang Yu. He introduced himself as the chief official in charge of the royal affairs.

他请王瑜坐下并敬了茶。他告诉王瑜,国王陛下很久就仰慕他的文学才华,因此希望能见他一面。于是王瑜被带进了皇宫,这座最高的金銮殿。

He asked Wang Yu to sit down and offered him tea. Then he told Wang Yu that the king had admired his literary talents for a long time and wished to see him. So Wang Yu was brought into the kings palace, the tallest of all the buildings.

国王坐在金色的宝座上。王瑜立刻向国王跪下,就像一般的庶民和官吏在谨见国王一样以叩头致最高的敬礼。国王站了起来,诏示他站起并坐到他的身边。

The king sat on a golden throne. Wang Yu immediately knelt down toward the king, with his forehead touching the ground as every civilian and official did when they paid high respect to the king in an audience. The king stood up and beckoned him to stand and sit by him.

皇帝慈祥地告诉王瑜他久已听闻他的文名,接着他问起王瑜的家庭情况,尤其是他是否已婚或定了亲。当他报告仍是单身也没有定亲时,皇帝告诉王瑜他那最小的女儿也喜欢读他的诗。他想把他介绍给他的女儿。王瑜回答如能有幸认识公主,那将是他的莫大荣幸。

The king kindly told Wang Yu that he had heard of his literary reputation for years. Then he inquired about Wang Yu's family, particularly whether he had been married or engaged. When he reported that he was still single and had not been engaged, the king told Wang Yu that his youngest daughter also enjoyed his poems. He wanted to introduce him to his daughter. Wang Yu replied that it would be his great honor to meet the princess.

不久,公主被带了进来。王瑜注意到那真是他一生中所见到过的最美丽的女子。她的腰围更是出奇的纤细。她被很多的宫女陪伴着。皇帝正式把王瑜介绍给他的女儿莲花公主。当介绍时,她坐在父亲旁边,含羞地低着头。

Soon the princess was brought in. Wang Yu noticed that she was the most beautiful girl he had ever seen. Her waist was unbelievably slender. She had many royal maids to accompany her. The king formally introduced Wang Yu to his daughter, Princess Lotus. She sat by her father and shyly lowered her head when the introduction was conducted.

聊斋精选

国王问王瑜是否愿意指导他的女儿赋诗。王瑜被公主的美貌所迷住而没有注意到国王的问话,因此也没有作答,只是一味地傻笑。因为没有听到王瑜的答复,国王要他的总管大臣将王瑜先生带到客房去用膳。

The king asked Wang Yu whether he would like to tutor his daughter on the poetry. So charmed was Wang Yu by the princess' beauty that he did not pay much attention to the king's question and did not reply, just smiled foolishly. With no response came from Wang Yu, the king ordered his chief official to take Mr. Wang Yu to the guest lodge to have dinner.

在用膳中,总管大臣埋怨王瑜没有回答皇上的问话。他告诉王瑜很明显皇上想将莲花公主嫁给他,因为他的糊涂行为,是他自己将这个成为皇家一员的机会丧失了。王瑜回答总管大臣,他为公主的美丽所迷根本没有听到国王的问话。现在一切都已晚了,王瑜和总管大臣都为错失良机而婉惜不已。

During dinner, the chief official reprimanded Wang Yu for his failure to answer the king's question. He told Wang Yu that it was very obvious that the king planned to marry Princess Lotus to him, but he had ruined his chance to become a member of the royal family with his foolish behavior. Wang Yu told the chief official that he was so bewitched by the princess' beauty that he did not hear the king's question. Now it was too late. Both Wang Yu and the chief official lamented the loss of such a good opportunity.

餐后,总管大臣把王瑜送到前门,他就自行找路回家了。

After dinner, the chief official saw Wang Yu off to the front gate, and he found his way home.

突然间,他醒了过来,发现他刚才在小憩中得了一个奇异的梦。他于是走出门去,想找寻梦中那些高大楼宇及那座龙形图案的门,可是毫无所获,一切仍如平时一样。不久他也就把这个梦完全忘记了。

All of sudden, he woke up and found he had had a strange dream in his nap. He went out, trying to find the tall buildings and the dragon designed gate, but he was totally lost. He could find nothing unusual in his area. Soon Wang Yu forgot the dream.

三天后的夜晚,他刚上床去睡觉,听到有人叩门。他奇怪怎么这么晚了还有人来拜访他。他去应了门后,很惊讶地发觉来人是他上次梦中所见过的那个小吏。小吏说他的主人又要他来邀请王瑜先生去他的衙门一次。这次王瑜不再问他问题了,于是跟着这个男子又见到了那位总管大臣。

Three days later, one late evening, soon after he had gone to bed to sleep, he heard somebody knocking on his door. He wondered who would visit him so late. He opened the door and surprisingly discovered that it was the same lower officer in his previous dream. The officer said his master wanted him to invite Mr. Wang Yu to the office again. Without questioning this time, Wang Yu followed the man and again met with the chief official.

总管大臣立刻向王瑜贺喜。他高兴地告诉王瑜国王陛下已经明了了他是愿意与莲花公主成婚的。

聊斋精选

因此他们已经安排了一个盛大的婚礼，就在今天举行。这是多么的意想不到！王瑜大喜过望。

The chief official congratulated Wang Yu immediately. He happily told Wang Yu that the king had realized his willingness to marry Princess Lotus. They had arranged a grand wedding ceremony to be held on that very day. It was so unexpected! Wang Yu was elated.

不久，数位宫女来帮助王瑜更换正式的结婚礼服。

Soon several royal maids came to help Wang Yu change his clothes into the formal wedding dress.

此后王瑜被带到大厅去，在那里他发现上百位来宾都身着盛装等候新郎。总管大臣将王瑜引入婚礼礼堂，国王和王后站在主位为他们的小女儿主持婚礼。

After that, Wang Yu was directed to come to the grand hall where he found hundreds of guests all dressed in dignified clothes, waiting for the bridegroom. The chief official ushered Wang Yu into the wedding room. The king and the queen stood at the head of the room to be in charge of their youngest daughter's wedding ceremony.

王瑜终于与美丽的莲花公主结婚了。

Wang Yu finally married the beautiful Princess Lotus.

因为欢乐来得太突然及意想不到，王瑜开始怀疑他与一位公主成婚是不是真的抑或仍如以前一样不过是一场梦。他于是用尺去量他新娘的细腰以证实他不是在做梦。莲花公主笑他及告诉他这一切都是真的。

Because the happiness had come so suddenly and unexpectedly, Wang Yu started to wonder whether his marriage to a princess was a real or if he was in a dream like what he had been before. He used a measuring tape to measure his bride's slender waist to be sure that he was not dreaming. Princess Lotus laughed at him and told him that everything was real.

就在这个时候，一个宫女冲了进来，向他们报告国王和王后要他们立刻去晋见。王瑜和他的新娘急忙去见国王和王后。国王让王瑜看一份他刚收到的皇家御卫队统帅大臣的报告。报告中说一个奇怪庞大的恶毒妖怪正向京都攻击，已经杀害了无数的士兵和居民。统帅大臣深怕他与他的部队难以抵挡这个妖怪，他建议皇室赶快撤退到安全的地方。

Just at that moment, a royal maid rushed in, reporting that the king and the queen wanted to see them immediately. Wang Yu and his bride hurried to meet the king and the queen. The king showed Wang Yu a report that he had just received from his commander-in-chief of the royal guards. The report said that a huge, strange, venomous monster was attacking the capital and had killed countless residents and soldiers. The commander-in-chief feared that he and his troops might not be able to stop the monster. He suggested that the entire royal family retreat to a safe place.

聊斋精选

国王告诉王瑜他的统帅大臣是位勇猛的将军,如果情况不是非常危急,他是不会呈上这份报告的。他要王瑜立即带着莲花公主到他自己的家中躲藏起来。

The king told Wang Yu that his commander-in-chief was a brave general. He would not have sent such a report if the situation had not been critical. He wanted Wang Yu to take Princess Lotus to his home and hide there immediately.

王瑜告诉他的公主妻子他的家不过是一栋普通的房子,没有皇宫的豪华。她说她已经嫁给了他,她是不在乎的。不管他去哪里,她都跟着他。

Wang Yu told his princess wife that his home was but an ordinary house, not as splendid as the royal palace. She said that since she had married him, she did not care. She just wanted to follow him wherever he went.

王瑜别无选择,只好将他的新娘带回了家。虽然这是一栋低下简陋的住宅,却是安全的。一旦进入屋内,公主就要求他回到皇宫去把她的父母也带来。王瑜回答她怎么可以把国王和王后请到这么一个小房子里。于是她哭了。她泪流满面地说假如他不立即行动,她真害怕她将永远看不到父母了。他的新婚妻子的哭声使得他烦恼不已。

Wang Yu had no choice, but to take his bride home. Although it was a humble house, it was safe now. Once went inside, the princess begged him to go back to the royal palace to bring her parents here, too. Wang Yu answered that how could he invite the king and the queen to his small house. Then, she cried. She said tearfully that she was afraid she might never be able to see her parents again if he did act quickly. His newlywed wife's crying irritated him.

突然间王瑜醒了过来而发现他又做了一个梦。他仍躺在他的床上,可是他觉得梦中的一切栩栩如生。因为天色已亮了,他便起身。

Suddenly, Wang Yu woke up and discovered that he had had a dream again. He was still lying on his bed, but he remembered everything vividly in the dream. As the day was dawning, he got up.

他仍然清晰地记得梦中的每一事件,他想他听到了他那公主妻子的清柔的哭声。他仔细去听并顺着声音的方向,发觉了一只小蜜蜂停在他的长榻上。他打开窗户让它飞出去,可是这个小动物不愿意离开。它仍停留在长榻上嗡嗡地叫个不停。终于王瑜放弃了让它飞出的念头,而坐在它的旁边观察。于是蜜蜂便飞到前门并在那儿盘旋着,似乎是要王瑜跟随着它。他走到了门前,蜜蜂就飞了出去。

While still reflecting on the events of the dream, he thought he was hearing the sound of his princess wife's crying very softly. He listened carefully and followed the direction of the sound, and he discovered a small bee on his couch. He opened the window to let the bee fly out. But the little creature would not leave. It stayed on the couch, humming nonstop. Finally, Wang Yu gave up and sat down next to the bee to watch.

聊斋精选

聊斋精选

Then the bee flew up to the front door and hovered around there, seemingly wanting Wang Yu to follow it. He walked over to the door and the bee flew out of the house.

王瑜尾随着蜜蜂出去,它一直很慢地向前飞。它在引导着他去到什么地方? 他在想,并紧跟着它。终于它停留在距离他家数条街不远处一株低矮老树上的一个大蜂房上。在那儿,王瑜发现了好几千只蜜蜂疯狂地从蜂房中飞进飞出。

Wang Yu followed the bee out and it flew ahead slowly. Was it trying to lead him to go anywhere? He wondered and followed it along the route. Finally, it stopped at a large beehive on an old short tree a few blocks away from his house. There, Wang Yu discovered thousands of bees flying in and out of the beehive in a complete frenzy.

王瑜靠近一看,他看到了一条两尺长的青蛇正在恶毒地攻击这个蜜蜂窝,无数的死蜂躺在树干下面。突然间,他明了了这个蜂窝就是他梦中的皇宫,他被邀请到这个蜜蜂王国里与这个小动物的公主结了婚。这个所谓奇怪的庞然大妖怪不过是这条小蛇而已。

When Wang Yu took a closer look, he saw a two-foot-long green snake viciously attacking the beehive, with countless dead bees lying around the trunk. Suddenly, he realized that the beehive was the royal palace in his dream, and that he had been invited to the kingdom of bees and had married the princess of the tiny creatures. The so-called huge monster was but the small snake.

他毫不犹豫地捡起了一根粗树枝把这条小蛇打死了。然后他再去寻找他的蜜蜂妻子,发觉她早已消失在这千万只的蜜蜂群中。

Without hesitation, he picked up a rough tree branch and killed the snake. Then he looked around for his bee wife, but he could no longer distinguish her from the thousands of other bees.

王瑜回到家中后很惊讶地在他的桌子上发现一张短笺,上面写着:"谢谢你救了我们王国。"

Wang Yu returned home, but was surprised to find a note on his desk saying, "*Thank you for saving our kingdom.*"

虽然没有人签名,他很清楚这是谁写的。

Although there was no signature, he clearly understood who had written it.

从此以后,王瑜没有再梦到这个皇宫或他的公主妻子或她的父母:这个蜜蜂王国里的国王和王后。

Since then, Wang Yu never again dreamed of the royal palace or his princess wife or her parents, the king and the queen of the bee kingdom.

聊斋精选

十八、青蛙神

Kindness and Cruelty

数百年前在今日的中国湖南省境内,有一所小的庙宇供奉着一只巨大的木刻青蛙。没有人知道为什么这个木雕会在那儿,或者是谁制造的,或者当地的人何时开始把这只青蛙当神一样地去顶礼膜拜。这座庙宇就叫做蛙神庙。

Hundreds of years ago, in what is today's Province of Hunan, China, there was a temple with a huge wooden carved frog set on the altar. Nobody knew how or why it was there, or who built it, or when the local people started to worship the frog as a god. The temple was known as God of Frog Temple.

乡民们每月初一及十五就会以最美丽的花朵以及最好的食物去供奉蛙神,祈求保佑他们免除自然灾难。如果当地的人们有困难或者有争议性的问题,他们到庙里祈求帮助。然后这位神就会以种种方式来帮助他们解决困难或回应他们的问题。

The country folks offered the most beautiful flowers and their best foods to the God of Frog on the first and fifteenth day of each month with a wish that the god would protect them from the natural disasters. And if the people had a hard problem or controversial question, they would go to the temple and pray for help. Then the god would help them solve the problem or answer the question, in one way or the other.

萧奎自少年时就是当地公认的最聪明和最英俊的一个年轻男子。一天,一位陌生的中年妇人来拜访萧奎的父母。她告诉他们她是蛙神要她来提亲的,蛙神希望将他的小女儿嫁给萧奎为妻。萧奎的父母不要他的儿子去娶一只雌青蛙,因此在犹豫着,同时他们也害怕得罪这位神秘有力的神,便诡称儿子年龄太小还不可以结婚。妇人便很失望地走了。

Xiao Kui had been well known since his youth as the smartest and most handsome young man in the area. One day, an unknown middle-aged woman paid Xiao Kui's parents a visit. She told them that God of Frog wanted her to present a marriage proposal for the god's youngest daughter to Xiao Kui. As Xiao Kui's parents did not want their son to marry a female frog, they were reluctant to accept the proposal. Meanwhile, they were afraid to offend the mysterious and powerful god. So they pretended that their son was still too young to get married. The woman was disappointed and left.

数月之后,当一个媒人来为萧奎提亲和另一个村庄的一个女孩结婚时,这个女孩的父亲得了一个梦。在梦中,蛙神警告这个父亲说萧奎是他未来的女婿。女孩的父亲醒了后,立刻把这个婚约打消了。

A few months later, when a matchmaker proposed a girl of another village as Xiao Kui's wife, the girl's father had a dream. In the dream, the God of Frog warned the father that Xiao Kui would be his future son-in-law. After waking up, the girl's father hurriedly withdrew the proposal.

聊斋精选

两天后,萧奎也做了一个梦。他被邀请进入一座豪华的宫殿,在大厅里他见到了蛙神,看上去是一位威严的中年男子。这位男子和蔼地要萧奎坐在他的旁边。然后他派人去请他的小女儿来见客人。萧奎不敢乱动,坐在那儿。

A couple of days later, Xiao Kui also had a dream. He was invited to enter a splendid palace to meet the God of Frog, who appeared to be a dignified looking middle-aged man, in a large hall. The man kindly asked Xiao Kui to sit by him. Then he sent for his youngest daughter to meet the guest. Xiao Kui dared not move, but sat there.

不久,一位非常美丽的女子由很多侍女陪同着走来了。她含羞地坐在她父亲的另一边。蛙神把她介绍给萧奎,那是他的最小女儿云娘。萧奎立刻为她的美丽所迷醉。他们喝了茶并简单地谈了几句话,然后这个女子就退回到内室去了。

Soon an extremely beautiful girl accompanied by many maids showed up. She shyly sat by her father's other side. The god introduced her to Xiao Kui as his youngest daughter, Yun Niang. Xiao Kui was immediately charmed with her beauty. They had tea and a brief conversation. After that, the girl retreated inside.

她走后,蛙神告诉萧奎他曾经派他的侍女去拜访他的父母提议让他的女儿嫁给他为妻,可是他的父母拒绝了这门亲事。

After she left, the god told Xiao Kui that he had once sent his maid to visit his parents to present a proposal for his daughter to marry him and his parents turned down the proposal.

"现在你在这儿了,"蛙神对萧奎说,"我要直接问你:你愿意接受这门亲事吗?"

"Now that you are here," the god said to Xiao Kui, "I would like to ask you directly: Would you like to accept the proposal?"

因为这个女子秀丽的面貌早已深深地印入了他的脑海中,他迅速地回答:"我愿意。"

Because the girl's pretty face had been branded in his brain deeply, he quickly answered, "Yes, I accept."

蛙神大笑并站了起来。他告诉萧奎回家去准备婚礼吧。

The god laughed and stood up. He told Xiao Kui to return home to prepare for the wedding ceremony.

突然,萧奎从梦中醒过来了。可是他清晰地记得刚才梦中的所见所闻。他把梦中的情形禀告了父母。当这对老人还在犹豫如何不让他们的儿子去娶一只青蛙时,他们家的仆人跑进屋来报告:有很多穿

聊斋精选

着青色制服的男子拥着一位像仙女一样的年轻女子,还带着很多箱的珠宝来到了门外。萧奎的父亲便急忙走出去察看究竟。

Suddenly, Xiao Kui woke up from his dream. But he remembered clearly what he had seen and heard in the dream. He reported his dream to his parents. While the senior couple still hesitated not wanting their son to marry a frog, their servant came into the room to report that many men in green uniforms surrounding a fairy-like young lady with many trunks of treasures were at the front door. Xiao Kui's father hurriedly went out to find what was going on.

这群人的首领告诉萧奎的父亲说他们是护送蛙神的小女儿来与他的儿子完婚的,因为他的儿子已经答应了婚约。这些箱子里的珠宝是蛙神送给女儿的嫁妆。

The leader of the group told Xiao Kui's father that they were escorting the God of Frog's youngest daughter here to marry his son as his son had accepted the proposal. The trunks of treasures were the dowries presented by the god.

见到这么一位美丽的年轻女子坐在这么精致的花轿里,萧奎的父亲不再拒绝了。他邀请这位女子及她的随从们进入屋内。不久,萧奎的母亲也来到了客厅。这个女子便立刻恭敬地向这对老夫妇行了准儿媳妇的大礼。

Seeing such a beautiful young lady sitting in such a colorful delicate wedding cart, Xiao Kui's father could not refuse anymore. He invited the girl and her group to enter the house. Soon Xiao Kui's mother also came into the living room. The girl quickly and respectfully paid the senior couple the due respect as a future daughter-in-law.

在如此情况下,萧奎的父母亲改变了他们的初衷,愉快地为他们的儿子和蛙神的女儿云娘安排了一个婚礼。

Under such circumstances, Xiao Kui's parents changed their mind and happily arranged a wedding ceremony for their son and Yun Niang, the daughter of God of Frog.

婚后,云娘被证实是一位非常能干的家庭主妇,她对待萧奎的父母也克尽孝道。蛙神和他的妻子也常来看望他们的女儿。蛙神看上去像一位威严的男子,他的妻子也像一位慈善的贵妇人。他们对待萧奎及他的父母都很友善。每当萧奎或他的父母有什么困难时,蛙神就会帮助他们解决。终于,萧奎的一家日渐兴旺了起来。

After her marriage, Yun Niang proved to be a very capable housewife, and she treated Xiao Kui's parents with filial respect. The God of Frog and his wife often visited their daughter. The god appeared as a dignified man, and his wife as a kind noblewoman, and they were very nice to Xiao Kui and his parents. Whenever Xiao Kui or his parents had some hardship, the God of Frog would help them overcome the difficulty.

聊斋精选

Gradually, Xiao Kui's family became prosperous.

　　自从云娘进了家门后,就时常有一些青蛙出没在他们家的后院。萧奎的父母及他们家的仆人们都知道这些是云娘的亲友,所以他们不去伤害这些小动物。人们和青蛙倒也相处得很好。

Since Yun Niang had moved into the house, there were often some frogs coming and going in their backyard. Xiao Kui's parents and their servants all realized that those were the relatives or friends of Yun Niang, and they would not hurt the small animals. So the humans and the frogs got along well.

　　惟一有时对青蛙不友善的人就是萧奎,特别是当他与他的妻子发生争吵时,他就会用脚去踢青蛙。

The only person who sometimes was not friendly to the frogs was Xiao Kui, especially when he had a quarrel with his wife. Then he would kick the frogs.

　　"请不要去伤害这些小动物,"每当他踢青蛙时,她就会央求他,"它们是完全无辜的。"

"Please don't hurt the small animals," she would beg him when he did. "They are totally innocent."

　　萧奎是他父母惟一的孩子,早被娇惯坏了。每当他不愉快时,他就不听从任何人的话。因此他对她的话是充耳不闻,这常常使得云娘很难过。

Xiao Kui was his parents' only child and had been spoiled. Whenever he was not happy, he would not listen to anybody. He ignored his wife's words. This often made Yun Niang feel sad.

　　一天,在与云娘剧烈的争吵后,他冲出门去到了后院,故意踢死了一只青蛙并又踢伤了好几只。然后离家到朋友家去。

One day, after a severe argument with Yun Niang, Xiao Kui rushed out of the room and went to the backyard. He purposely kicked a frog to death and badly injured a few others. Then he left for his friend's house.

　　当他晚间回家后,发觉妻子不见了,同时院子里的青蛙也没有了。第二天,她还是没有回来。萧奎的父母埋怨儿子,要他到蛙神庙里去祈祷,可是这个年轻人拒绝了。

When he returned home in the evening, he found his wife had disappeared, and so did all the frogs in the yard. As she did not show up the next day, Xiao Kui's parents blamed their son and demanded that he must go to the God of Frog Temple to pray. But the young man refused.

　　不久,萧奎的父亲因为没有蛙神的帮助,在事业上遭遇了背运。萧奎的母亲也因为忧虑她的儿子与儿媳妇的关系而生了病。似乎是不幸的事故接二连三光顾萧奎家。因为没有云娘都助她的婆婆处理家务,家中的每一件事情都不顺遂。

Soon, Xiao Kui's father lost a fortune in his business as he received no help from the God of Frog, and Xiao Kui's mother became sick as she was too worried about the relationship between her son and her daughter-in-law. It seemed that the unhappy events visited Xiao Kui's home just about one after the other. And without Yun Niang helping her mother-in-law take care of the house affairs, everything went wrong in the house.

同时,萧奎也开始在想念他那美丽的妻子。他很后悔他的所为。有一个晚上,他偷偷地到庙里祈祷要求惩罚他而不要去惩罚别人,尤其是他的父母。他答应他将善待云娘并不再去伤害青蛙了,他只要求她回家。

Meanwhile, Xiao Kui began to miss his pretty wife. He regretted what he had done. One night, he secretly went to the temple and begged for punishment to be given to him instead of the other people, especially his parents. He promised that he would treat Yun Niang well and would not hurt the frogs anymore once she returned home.

回到家后,他很欣喜地发现云娘早已经回来了。全家人都很高兴,于是一切又恢复了正常。

When he returned home, he was overjoyed to find that Yun Niang had already been at home. The whole family became happy, and everything returned to normal.

萧奎喜欢喝酒,他有几个酒友。每次他出去喝酒,时常会喝醉了。云娘告诉他喝酒是可以的,但不要喝醉了。她也劝他集中精力去攻读经典,参加官府考试,或许可通过而被封官。可他从不接受她的建议。而她愈是劝他,他就愈是外出喝酒,常喝到醉倒为止。

Xiao Kui liked to drink and had a few drinking friends. Every time he went out to drink with his friends, he often became drunk. Yun Niang told him that drinking was all right, but not to get drunk. She also advised him to concentrate on his studies of the classics so he could perhaps pass the government examinations to become a government official. But he never took her advice. And the more advice she gave to him, he would go out to drink and become drunk more often.

一天,在这个问题上他又与云娘发生了重大的争吵,他忘记了他在蛙神庙里许下的诺言,而竟公开地宣称:"我想带一条蛇回家把院子里的青蛙都吃掉。"

One day, after a big fight with Yun Niang on this subject again, he forgot the promises he had made at the God of Frog Temple. He publicly announced, "I'm thinking of bringing a snake home to eat all the frogs in the yard."

聊斋精选

聊斋精选

聊斋精选

云娘发怒。她告诉他:"我很难过,我必须再离开你了,而且不再回来了。"
Yun Niang became furious. She told him, "I'm sorry, I must leave you again. And I'll not come back."

"好啊,"他冷冰冰地说,"我不在乎你回来与否。"
"Well," he said coolly, "I would not care if you return home or not."

于是,她立刻不见了,所有的青蛙也同时都不见了。
Then she disappeared immediately, along with all the frogs.

一个月后,萧奎又开始思念起他那美丽能干的妻子,而他也明白这一切还是他的错。在他父母的督促下,他又到蛙神庙中祈祷。他发誓他一定会戒除饮酒的坏习惯并且善待他的妻子,假如她能原谅他并回家的话。
A month later, Xiao Kui began to miss his pretty and capable wife again. And he again realized that it was still his fault. At his parents' urging, he went to the God of Frog Temple to pray. He swore he would quit his bad drinking habit and treat his wife well if she could forgive him and return home.

可是这次不灵了。又一个月过去了,云娘还是没有出现。
But it did not work this time. Another month passed. Yun Niang still did not appear.

萧奎的父母便亲自到蛙神庙中去祈祷,也是毫无效果。这对老夫妇所能做的只有与儿子日夜后悔不已。
Xiao Kui's parents went to the God of Frog Temple to pray too, but received no response. The senior couple could do nothing but join their son in deep regret every day and night.

事情更糟糕了。邻村一位英俊的年轻男子家突然来了一个访客。访客称是蛙神要他来说媒的。蛙神想将他的小女儿嫁给他问他是否愿意。这个男子兴奋极了,立刻接受了这个婚约。现在他的全家都在准备着这件喜事。
And things got worse. A young handsome man in a nearby village suddenly had a visitor one day. The visitor said that the God of Frog wanted him to send a marriage proposal to the man. The god wished to marry his youngest daughter to him. The man was elated. He accepted the proposal immediately. Now his whole family started to prepare for a splendid wedding ceremony.

不久这个消息传到了萧奎和他的父母耳里。对萧奎来说,这真是一个晴天霹雳,他突然病倒了,失去胃口,又拒绝接受他父母的安排去看医生,日夜躺在床上自怨自艾。在绝望中,他思念他的妻子,不断喃喃地唤着她的名字。这个情况延续了好几个星期,他甚至于都不想活了,只希望早点儿死,因此身体是一天比一天衰弱。一个夜晚,终于昏了过去而没有一个人知道。

Soon the news reached Xiao Kui and his parents' ears. It was a terrible blow to Xiao Kui. He suddenly fell ill. He lost his appetite. And he refused to accept his parents' arrangement to see a doctor but lying in bed, hating himself day and night. He longed for his wife and murmured her name in despair. This situation lasted for a few weeks. He even lost his desire to live and just wished to die. Day after day, he became weaker and weaker. One late evening, he fainted without anybody knowing.

不久,他被一只柔软的手摸在他的脸上弄醒了,同时他也听到了熟悉的女子声音叫唤着他的名字。睁开眼睛一看,他惊喜地发现云娘泪流双颊地坐在他的床上。他立刻坐了起来,夫妻两人抱头大哭而说不出一句话来。

Soon, he was awakened by the touch of a soft hand upon his face. And he heard a familiar female's voice calling his name. He opened his eyes and was overjoyed to find Yun Niang sitting on his bed with tears running down her cheeks. He quickly sat up, and the husband and wife hugged tightly without saying a word.

然后云娘泪水满面地告诉萧奎:"父亲要我再嫁给另一个村庄的男子,我拒绝了。他大怒,警告我如果我再回到你的身边,我将被你虐待致死。我告诉他我宁愿死在我的丈夫家也不愿意再嫁人。"

Then Yun Niang told Xiao Kui with tears on her face, "My father wanted me to re-marry a man in another village, but I refused. He was angry and warned me that I would be mistreated to death if I returned to you. I told him that I would rather die at my husband's home than get remarried."

她是在她父亲的强力反对下归来的。

So, she returned home in defiance of her father's strong objection.

萧奎感到非常羞愧。他大哭,他忏悔。他对妻子发誓:"如果我再虐待你和青蛙,我将遭雷电劈死。"

Xiao Kui was very much shamed. He cried with deep regret. He vowed to his wife, "If I ever mistreat you or the frogs again, I would be punished to be killed by the thunder and lightning."

云娘立即用手遮住他的嘴巴,于是这对年轻夫妇又拥抱痛哭起来。

Yun Niang quickly used a hand to cover his mouth, and the young couple hugged and cried together again.

云娘回来了。这一家人又重新欢快了起来。

Yun Niang was back. The whole family was cheerful again.

聊斋精选

虽然,蛙神夫妇仍是拒绝来看他们的女儿,一直到一年后云娘生了一个小孩后才再来拜访。

However, the God of Frog and his wife refused to visit their daughter again until a year later when Yun Niang gave birth to a child.

十九、西湖主

The Princess in Dongting Lake

洞庭湖位于中国的中东部,占地2432.5平方公里,是这个国家的五大湖之一。

Dongting Lake, located in east central China, covering 2,432.5 square kilometres, is one of the five largest lakes in the nation.

陈明是一位年轻的诗人和学者。他担任一位将军的秘书工作,很得将军的信任。

Chen Ming was a young poet and scholar. He worked for a military general as his secretary and had won the general's deep trust.

一天,陈明陪同将军出差渡过洞庭湖。他们远远地看见一条大鱼将嘴伸出水面呼吸。为了好玩,将军拉起他的弓箭向鱼发射,他的箭射中了鱼。鱼浮在水上,应该是死了。

One day Chen Ming accompanied the general on a trip across Dongting Lake. In the distance they spied a large fish with its mouth protruding out of the water. For fun, the general drew his bow and shot at the fish. His arrow hit the fish and it floated on the water. It must be dead.

当将军想把这条死了的鱼拉上船时,他发现一条小鱼用嘴将大鱼的尾巴衔住好像企图拯救大鱼。将军吓退了小鱼将大鱼拉上了船,发现它还是活的,不过已经受了重伤。

When the general tried to pull the dead fish onto the boat, he found a small fish biting the large fish's tail with its mouth as if trying to rescue it. The general frightened away the small fish and pulled the large one on the boat finding it still alive but badly injured.

这条受伤的鱼的眼睛一直看着陈明,好像在求救。陈明是个虔诚的佛教徒,他请求将军让他处理这条鱼,因为他们尚有公务在身不能将鱼带回家去烧着吃。将军答应他后就到船舱里面去休息了。

The injured fish looked at Chen Ming, seemingly begging for help. Chen Ming was a devout Buddhist. He asked the general to let him dispose of the fish, since they were on official trip and could not take it home to cook it anyway. The general agreed and went to the cabin to rest.

陈明用他的急救药品涂在鱼的伤处,然后把这条鱼放回了湖中。慢慢地它游到深水处后就很快不见了踪影。

Chen Ming used his first-aid supplies on the fish's injury. Then he put the fish back into the lake. It swam into the deep water slowly and soon disappeared.

一年后,陈明回家度假,他又要渡过洞庭湖。船行湖中突然遇到风暴,船翻了,船上的每个人都淹死了。

A year later, Chen Ming returned home for a holiday. He crossed the Dongting Lake again. Midway, an unexpected storm capsized the ship and everyone on board was drowned.

聊斋精选

死后,陈明的灵魂到了湖底。他很惊讶地发现在这水底下竟是别有洞天。不但有蓝色的天空,更有那像岸上一样的新鲜空气。他停留在一栋豪华宫殿的一角。因为看不到周围有任何人,他便溜到后院并进入了一座大的花园。

After death, Chen Ming's spirit went to the bottom of the lake. He was surprised to find that there was another world under the water with blue sky and fresh air just like the one above the water. He landed in a corner of a splendid palace. As he did not see anyone around, he sneaked into the backyard and entered into a large garden.

此时,他已是非常饥饿,真希望能找到一个人可以要点东西吃。可是他看不到任何人,这整座花园像死一般的寂静。

By this time, he was awfully hungry. He wished he could find someone to ask for food. But he did not see anyone. It seemed that the whole garden was dead quiet.

他正在徘徊时,听到了女孩子们的讲话声和嬉笑声从一座假山后面发出,他知道他可能误入了一个显贵人家的私人寓宅了,因此不敢露面,躲在一株高大的树后面偷看。

As he was wandering around, he heard girls' conversation and giggles from behind an artificial mountain. He knew he might have mistakenly come to a dignitary's private residence. He dared not reveal himself but hid behind a tall tree and peeked.

他看到好几个十多岁的女孩子围绕着一位十分美丽高贵而又愉悦的少女,少女颈子上系着一条粉红色的丝巾。她们正在玩着跳绳的游戏。陈明猜想这个少女一定是这所宫殿主人的女儿,而其她女孩子们可能是她的侍女。他继续躲藏观望。

He saw several teen-age girls surrounding a beautiful and dignified cheerful-looking young lady, with a pink scarf on her neck. They were playing jump rope. Chen Ming presumed that the young lady must be the daughter of the dignitary in the palace and the other girls might be her maids. He kept hiding and watching.

终于,这些女孩子们不玩而离开了。于是这座花园又沉寂了下来。陈明走了过来,发现刚才这些女孩子们游玩的地上有一条粉红色的丝巾,他把丝巾捡了起来。

Finally, the girls quit playing and walked away. Then the garden became quiet again. Chen Ming walked over and happened to find a pink silk scarf on the ground by the place the girls had played. He picked up the scarf.

坐在一块石头上,他把丝巾放近他的鼻子,他似乎可以闻到一股女性的芬芳在上面。他知道这条丝巾大概是那位美丽高贵的少女的,她的美丽早已深深地印入了他的脑海里,她那甜美的笑声也仍停留在他的耳边。可是她早已经走了,而且他很可能永远没有机会再看到她了。

聊斋精选

Sitting on a rock, he put the scarf to his nose. It seemed that he could smell a girlish perfume on it. He knew the scarf might belong to the beautiful and dignified young lady, whose beauty was still stamped in his brain, and her sweet giggles were still lingering in his ears. But she had left. He would probably never have a chance to see her again.

作为一个诗人，他突然有了灵感在丝巾上写了一首情诗。在诗中，他写着这个女子一定是位仙女，否则人间哪有如此美丽的女子？因为她是他有生以来所看到过的最美丽的女孩，他祈祷如果有朝一日能和她相识的话，不管他作出多大的牺牲，他都心甘情愿。

Being a poet, he suddenly had an inspiration and wrote a love poem on the scarf. In the poem, he wrote that the girl must be a fairy, otherwise, how could a human girl be so beautiful? As she was the most beautiful lady he had ever seen in his life, he prayed that if he could make her acquaintance some day, he would be willing to sacrifice whatever he had to.

当他闭着眼睛一遍又一遍地背诵他的诗篇时，不知道一个年轻女子已经走到了他的面前。他睁开眼时，看到一名女孩已站在他的面前。从这个女孩子的衣着上，他猜想她一定是刚才陪同她主子玩跳绳游戏的一个侍女。女孩问陈明："你曾否在地上看到一条粉红色的丝巾？"

While he was closing his eyes and reciting his poem over and over, he did not realize that a young woman had come to him. Opening his eyes, he found a girl standing in front of him already. From the girl's dress, he figured that she must be one of the maids who had accompanied her master to play jump rope. The girl asked Chen Ming, "Have you seen a pink silk scarf left on the ground a little while before?"

他明了他是不能再保有这条丝巾的了。于是他回答是的，便将丝巾交给了她。
He realized that he could not keep the scarf anymore, so he answered yes and gave her the scarf.

当这个女孩发现丝巾上写了很多字时，她很生气。指着这些字她问他谁写的。陈明回答那是他写的诗。

When the girl discovered some writings on the scarf, she was angry. Pointing at the writings, she asked him who did it. Chen Ming replied that it was the poem he wrote.

女孩责骂陈明："你做了一件大错事了。丝巾是洞庭湖王最小的公主的。你在丝巾上写了脏话，你将受到严厉的惩罚。"

The girl rebuked Chen Ming, "You have made a great mistake. The scarf belongs to the youngest princess of the king of Dongting Lake. You will be severely punished because you have spoiled the princess' scarf with your dirty words."

聊斋精选

然后她叫来了卫士。一个身着制服的男子很快地过来将陈明逮捕并投入了牢房。
Then she yelled for the security guards. A uniformed man quickly came over and arrested Chen Ming and put him in jail.

差不多十五分钟后,这个女孩到牢房来看陈明。她告诉他:"你也许没事了,因为公主看了你写的字后没有表示出一点儿不高兴。"
About fifteen minutes later, the girl visited Chen Ming in jail. She told him, "You might be all right, for the princess has read your writings but did not show a mood of any unpleasantness."

陈明谢了她,一时感到轻松了一些。
Chen Ming thanked her and felt a bit relieved.

大约半个小时后,这个女孩又回到了牢房。她告诉陈明:"事情有了变化。我肯定你一定会有大的麻烦,因为王后知道了这丝巾的事件,正在大怒。"
Another half an hour later, the same girl returned to the jail. She told Chen Ming, "Things have been changed. I'm sure you'll have a big trouble because the queen has heard about the scarf story and she is furious."

陈明紧张了,不知道他将受到什么样的惩罚。
Chen Ming was nervous, wondering what punishment he would receive.

这个女孩是对的,因为不久后,另一个女孩来到了牢房。她高声叫喊王后来调查一个陌生男子如何可以溜进皇家花园并在公主的丝巾上写脏话。
The girl was right. Not long afterward, another girl came to the jail. She loudly announced that the queen was coming to investigate how a strange man could sneak into the royal garden and write dirty words on the princess's scarf.

但是,当这个女孩子看到陈明时,她突然问他:"你是不是在一年前陪同一位将军渡洞庭湖的那个男子?"
But when the girl saw Chen Ming, she suddenly asked him, "Are you the man who accompanied a general crossing Dongting Lake a year ago?"

当陈明回答"是"以后,她就立刻跑走了。不久她陪同一位中年贵夫人回来。女孩告诉他这是洞庭湖王后。
After Chen Ming replied her "Yes" she ran away immediately. Soon she returned accompanying a

聊斋精选

dignified-looking middle-aged lady. The girl told him that she was the queen of Dongting Lake.

陈明欲向王后下跪致敬。就在他还没有跪下前，王后走向前去先向他跪了下来。这个料想不到的举动使得陈明及所有牢中卫士都大为莫名其妙。

Before Chen Ming tried to kneel down to pay the queen his respect, she walked forward, kneeling toward him first. The unexpected action left Chen Ming and all the jail guards in great confusion.

王后含泪告诉陈明："我就是一年前被将军射中抓住的那条大鱼。你拯救了我，并在把我放回湖中前还用急救药涂在我的伤口上。你救了我一命，我们全家都深深地感激你。那个问你是否曾经陪同过一位将军渡洞庭湖的女孩是我的婢女，她就是曾经想救我而没有成功的那条小鱼。"

The queen told Chen Ming in tears, "I'm the large fish, shot and caught by the general a year ago. It was you who rescued me and you even put the first-aid medicine on my injury before releasing me back into the lake. You saved my life. My whole family all deeply appreciated your great favor. The girl who just asked you if you were the man to accompany a general to cross Dongting Lake is my maid. She was the small fish who had tried to rescue me but failed."

王后急忙下令将陈明释放，并邀请他作为她的贵宾住在宫里。

The queen quickly ordered Chen Ming's release and invited him to live in the palace as her most honored guest.

当她问陈明是怎么来到花园时，他把船翻遇难的事如实告诉了她。王后立即下令搜索陈明的尸体。不到半个小时，一个卫士就把陈明断了气的躯体找来了。王后给了陈明一粒药丸要他吞下，然后要他扑向他的尸体。灵魂和身体复合后，陈明又成为一个人了。

When she asked Chen Ming how he had come to the garden, he told her the sad story of the shipwreck. The queen immediately ordered a search for Chen Ming's body. In less than thirty minutes, a guard brought in Chen Ming's lifeless body. The queen gave Chen Ming a pill asking him to take. After that, she wanted him to run toward his own dead body. Immediately, the spirit and the body combined, and Chen Ming revived as a human again.

当洞庭湖王从天上开会回来后，王后把陈明的事情告诉了他，他又来感谢陈明拯救他妻子的性命之恩。

When the king of Dongting Lake returned from a meeting in heaven, the queen told him about Chen Ming, and he came to thank Chen Ming again for saving his wife's life.

湖王和王后曾经看过陈明写在他们女儿丝巾上的诗。他们计划将女儿嫁给陈明，先来问女儿她是否

聊斋精选

愿意嫁给一个凡间的男子。女孩羞涩地回答:"我已经读了他的诗,我很钦佩他的文采。那也就是为什么在我发现他在我的丝巾上写了很多文字后我并没有生他气的原因。"

The king and queen had read the poem Chen Ming wrote on their daughter's scarf. They planned to marry their daughter to Chen Ming, so they asked the girl if she was willing to marry the mortal man. The girl replied shyly, "I have read his poem and admire his literary talents. That was the reason why I was not angry after I had found his writings on my scarf."

得到公主的同意后,一个豪华的婚礼不久便举行了,陈明变成了洞庭湖王皇家的一员。

With the princess' agreement, a magnificent wedding ceremony was soon held, and Chen Ming became a member of the royal family of the king of Dongting Lake.

婚后,公主带着她的夫婿游遍了湖中的每一处胜地。陈明很愉快地住在这湖底世界。

After their marriage, the princess showed her husband all the interesting places in the lake. Chen Ming lived happily in the world of underwater.

一年后,陈明告诉他的妻子他很怀念他的父母,想回到他的故乡去拜访他们。公主报告她的父母,湖王和王后都鼓励他们的女儿和她的丈夫一同去,并和她公婆同住以尽一个做媳妇的孝道。一场离别宴会不久就在宫中举行。王后又送了她的女儿一箱子湖里的珠宝作为礼品。

A year later, Chen Ming told his wife that he was missing his parents and planned to return to his native place to visit them. The princess reported her parents, and the king and queen encouraged their daughter to go with her husband, and live with her parents-in-law to pay her due respects as a daughter-in-law. A farewell dinner party was soon held at the palace. The queen presented her daughter with a trunk of lake treasures as gifts.

陈明回到家后,他的父母大为惊喜。翻船后没有听到任何消息,他们认为他早已遇难了。如今他不但回来,而且又带回一位美丽的妻子。卖了箱子里的一些珠宝后,这对年轻夫妇变成了富有的人家。

When Chen Ming arrived at his home, his parents were happily shocked. Having heard nothing from him since the shipwreck, they presumed that he must have been dead. Now he not only came back, but also brought a beautiful wife with him. After selling some of the treasures in the trunk, the young couple became wealthy.

每年,陈明和他的妻子总要回到洞庭湖去拜访湖王和王后,而每次湖王和王后都要赠送他们一些珍宝作为礼品。

Every year, Chen Ming and his wife would return to the Dongting Lake and visit the king and queen. And every time, the king and queen would present them with many rare valuable treasures as gifts.

聊斋精选

一天,陈明的一位老友乘着一条小船游洞庭湖,他看到一条豪华大船上面有很多美丽女子,她们面对坐在主位的年轻贵人模样夫妇载歌载舞。这位贵人模样的幸运男子与他那秀丽的妻子在喝酒聊天。

One day, an old friend of Chen Ming took a small ship to tour the Dongting Lake. He happened to see a large splendid ship with many beautiful girls singing and dancing in front of a young dignified looking couple sitting at the table of honor. The dignified-looking lucky man was drinking and talking with his pretty wife.

当这个朋友的小船靠近了大船时,朋友惊讶地发现这个幸运的男子竟是陈明。陈明邀请他的朋友到大船上来,并向他介绍了他的妻子。他们享有一个愉快的下午,然后朋友回到小船上就立即回家了。

When the friend's small ship was a little closer to the larger one, he was surprised to find that the lucky man was Chen Ming. Chen Ming invited his friend to his large ship and introduced him to his wife. They had a wonderful afternoon. After that, the friend returned to his small ship and went to home immediately.

朋友与陈明是邻居。在回家的途中,他经过陈明家听到了爽朗愉快的谈话声从里面传出,好像陈明就是其中的一个。他敲门后陈明来开门。他很惊讶陈明怎么回来得这么快。陈明邀请他进入,他遇见了很多位文友。他们告诉他举行写作研讨会已经好几天了。朋友很困惑,因为他刚才还和陈明在一起游湖。陈明怎么可以同时分身两处? 他要陈明解释,陈明只是微笑没有作答,请他的朋友喝酒。

The friend was Chen Ming's neighbor. On the way home, he passed by Chen Ming 's house and heard loud happy conversations from inside of the building. Seemingly Chen Ming was one of the loud talkers. He knocked the door and Chen Ming came to answer it. He was surprised how Chen Ming had returned home so quickly. Chen Ming invited him to enter and he met many of their literature friends. They told him they had been holding a writing seminar for several days. The friend was confused, as he had just met Chen Ming earlier that day on the lake. How could Chen Ming be present in two places at the same time? He asked Chen Ming for an explanation. Chen Ming smiled and did not reply but asked his friend to have a drink.

若干年后,陈明和他的妻子有了很多的儿孙。在他的九十五岁生日宴会后,陈明生病了,数日之后就过世了。死后不久他的妻子也死了,而且没有任何征兆。他们的孩子们便将他们的父母放入一个特别大的棺材里,计划去安葬。

Over the years, Chen Ming and his wife had many children and grandchildren. Shortly after celebrating his ninety-five-year-old birthday, Chen Ming became sick, and in a few days he died. Soon after that, his wife died too, without any symptom of illness. Their children put their parents' bodies together in an extra large coffin and planned to bury them.

聊斋精选

　　在赴墓地的途中,抬棺人奇怪怎么里面有两个死者的棺材竟是如此地轻,他们把这个怀疑告诉陈明的孩子们,于是把棺材打开一看,很惊讶地发现原来里面是空的。他们父母的遗体不见了。孩子们终于明白了他们的父母并没有真正地死亡,不过是回到洞庭湖与湖王和王后共同生活去了。

On the way to the funeral, the pallbearers wondered how the coffin with two corpses inside had become so light. They told Chen Ming's children about their doubts and they opened the coffin to check. They were surprised to find that it was empty. Their parents' bodies had disappeared. The children finally realized that their parents had not really died, but moved to Dongting Lake to live with the king and the queen.

聊斋精选

廿、公孫九娘

The Haunted Suicide

虽然年轻,林兰已经是当地一位著名的诗人了。他喜欢晚上写诗,如果那天诗兴很高灵感也多,他就会一直写到天亮。因为家庭富有,他白天不需要工作。

Although he was still a young man, Lin Lan was already a well-known poet in the area where he lived. He liked to write poems in the evening. If he was in high spirits and felt inspired, he would keep on writing throughout the night. He was wealthy, so he did not have to work in daytime.

一天午夜,当他连写了几个钟头的诗后,他躺在长榻上闭目休息一下。

One midnight, after having written poems for several hours, he reclined himself on a couch and closed his eyes, planning to take a short break.

不久他听到有人敲门。心想这么晚了谁会来拜访他,他去应了门,发现一位不认识的年轻男子站在门外。这个男子问林兰他可否进去,因为他来求他一件事情。林兰让这个访客进屋后并请他坐下。男子自我介绍姓胡名耿,他说他是林兰的外甥女瑾瑾的未婚夫。

Soon, he heard a knock on his door. Wondering who would visit him so late in the night, he went to open the door and found an unknown young man standing outside. The man asked Lin Lan if he could enter as he came to ask for a favor. Lin Lan let the visitor enter and asked him to sit down. The man introduced himself as Hu Geng, the fiance of Lin Lan's niece, Jin Jin.

当林兰还未开口说话时,胡耿解释他此行的目的,他请林兰在他们的婚礼上担任他的外甥女的监护人,因为瑾瑾还未成年。

Before Lin Lan said anything, Hu Geng explained the purpose of his visit. He asked Lin Lan to act as his niece's guardian in their wedding ceremony, as Jin Jin was still a minor.

林兰困惑了,因为瑾瑾和她的父母,林兰的姐姐和她的丈夫,都早在数年前的一场战争中过世了。他告诉胡耿他可能找错了和他同名同姓的人了,因为他的外甥女瑾瑾早已死了。胡耿说他没有弄错,他和瑾瑾都是鬼。因为瑾瑾的父母都已投胎转世为人了,而瑾瑾还未成年,按照冥律规定,她在婚礼中需要一位监护人,林兰是她惟一尚存的长辈。

Lin Lan was confused, as Jin Jin and her parents, Lin Lan's elder sister and her husband, had all died in a war several years ago. He told Hu Geng that he might have found a wrong person with the same name as his, for his niece, Jin Jin, had already died. Hu Geng said that he was not wrong, as both he and Jin Jin were ghosts. Because Jin Jin's parents had been reborn as people and Jin Jin was still a teenager, according to the laws of the nether world, she needed a guardian in the wedding ceremony, and Lin Lan was her only senior relative.

林兰仍然困惑,他问胡耿:"我是一个人,如何去为一个做鬼的外甥女当监护人?"

聊斋精选

Still being confused, Lin Lan asked Hu Geng , "As a human, how can I act as a guardian for a ghost niece?"

胡耿回答:"这很容易。只要跟着我到我家去就可以了。"
Hu Geng replied, "It's easy. All you have to do is but follow me to my home."

于是林兰关起了门跟着胡耿走了出去。不久他们走到了一栋房子面前。胡耿说那就是他的家。顷刻间林兰看见一个少女从屋子里跑了出来。虽然林兰有好几年没有见到瑾瑾了,可他还是认出这个女孩是他的外甥女。舅甥两个愉快地携手走进了房子。瑾瑾感激舅舅来参加她的婚礼,并代表她的父母做她的监护人。
So Lin Lan closed the door and followed Hu Geng. Soon they reached a house, and Hu Geng said it was his home. Almost immediately, Lin Lan saw a young woman running out of the house. Although Lin Lan had not seen Jin Jin for several years, he could still recognize that the girl was his niece. They happily held each other's hands and pleasantly walked back into the house. Jin Jin appreciated uncle's coming to attend her wedding ceremony as her guardian on behalf of her parents.

不久婚礼开始了。这对夫妇的很多朋友和邻居都来做他们的见证人。礼成后,有茶点招待。然后,林兰就回家了。
Soon the wedding ceremony was held with many of the couple's friends and neighbors attending as witnesses. After the ceremony, they had tea and cakes. Then Lin Lan returned his home.

突然他醒了过来,发觉这整个的经历只不过是场梦。
Suddenly he woke up and realized that the entire experience was a dream.

奇怪的是自此以后,他就时常在梦中被瑾瑾和胡耿邀请去到他们的家里,有时还和他们及他们的朋友们一起吃饭。瑾瑾是一个拿手的烹饪者,她烧的菜非常鲜美可口,而胡耿也是一个很好的主人。他能使每一个客人都很快乐,林兰每次去他们家里都感到很愉快。每当他醒来后,他总希望他的梦如能再长些那该多好。
Strangely enough, since then, he was often invited by Jin Jin and Hu Geng to go to their home, and sometimes shared a meal with them and their friends in his dreams. Jin Jin was a good chef who always cooked a delicious meal, while Hu Geng was a good host who treated everyone happily. Lin Lan had a pleasant time during every visit. Whenever he woke up, he would wish his dream could have lasted longer.

渐渐地,林兰于梦中在瑾瑾的家里认识了一位名叫孔媚的美丽女子。孔媚是胡耿的姑母,死了已经一年。她比瑾瑾大几岁。因为也是诗人,所以她和林兰一见如故,双方相互赏识对方的作品。

Gradually, Lin Lan made the acquaintance of a pretty lady named Kong Mei at Jin Jin's home in his dreams. Kong Mei was Hu Geng's aunt who had died a year ago. She was a few years older than Jin Jin. As she was also a poetess, naturally she and Lin Lan got along very well. Each of them admired each other's poems.

当孔媚还是人时,她曾经嫁给一个富有的男子,那是她父亲做的主。她的丈夫是个粗鲁的男人,喜欢吃喝嫖赌。每次当孔媚劝他戒掉那些坏习惯时,这个粗鲁的男子不但不听她,反而对她施暴。终于她无法再忍耐下去而自杀了。

While Kong Mei was a human, she had married a wealthy man, chosen by her father. Her husband was an unrefined man. All he liked was drinking and gambling as well as going with prostitutes. Every time Kong Mei asked him to get rid of those bad habits, the rough man not only would not listen to her, but also reacted with violence toward her. Finally, she could not stand the situation anymore and committed suicide.

因为有一个做诗的共同爱好,林兰和孔媚不久就成了好朋友,最后更是相爱了。

Because of having a common interest in poetry, Lin Lan and Kong Mei soon became intimate friends and fell in love.

林兰曾经结过一次婚。两年前,他的妻子在生产时死亡,婴儿也夭折了。此后,很多媒人来提亲,林兰也见过好几个女子,可就是没有一个合乎他的意。他想找一个女子,不仅美丽,还要和他一样地喜欢文学。孔媚正是这样的一位他在寻找中的女子。

Lin Lan had once been married. His wife had died while giving birth to a baby a couple of years before. And the baby had died, too. Since then, many matchmakers had tried to find a match for him, and Lin Lan had seen many girls, but none of them met his requirements. He hoped to marry a woman who was not only pretty but also fond of literature as much as he was. Now, Kong Mei was exactly the kind of woman he had been looking for.

不久,瑾瑾和胡耿都注意到了林兰和孔媚的恋情。一天夜晚,当林兰又在梦中被他的外甥女邀请去家吃饭时,他发现除了孔媚外还有另一位客人,是一位中年妇人。瑾瑾立刻把她介绍给林兰,她是孔媚的母亲。瑾瑾告诉她的舅舅因为孔媚的母亲最近已经接到了阴曹地府的通知,安排她于一周后投胎为人,所以她特别为她举行了这个离别宴席。

Soon both Jin Jin and Hu Geng noticed Lin Lan and Kong Mei's love. One evening in a dream, Lin Lan was invited to go to his niece's home for supper again. He found one more guest in attendance besides Kong Mei. It was a middle-aged woman. Jin Jin quickly introduced her to Lin Lan as Kong Mei's mother. Jin Jin told her uncle that because Kong Mei's mother had received a notice from the ghost government informing her that her rebirth as a person had been arranged only a week away, she held this special farewell party for her.

　　然后，她把林兰拉到另一个房间，偷偷地告诉她的舅舅如果他爱孔媚的话，他应当趁孔媚的母亲还在阴间的时候向她公开求婚。

Then she pulled Lin Lan to the other room and secretly told her uncle that if he loved Kong Mei, he should take this opportunity to openly make a marriage proposal while Kong Mei's mother was still in the ghost world.

　　宴席间，林兰被安排坐在孔媚和她母亲之间。这位中年妇人看来很慈祥，似乎是很喜欢林兰。饭后，林兰站了起来，含情脉脉望着孔媚公开求她嫁给他。孔媚含羞地红着脸接受了，她的母亲也微笑地表示同意。老妇人说她很高兴在她投胎转世为人前知道她的女儿又将嫁人了。她对她的丈夫以前安排孔媚嫁错了人表示抱歉。她希望也相信孔媚的这次婚姻一定会幸福。

During the dinner, Lin Lan was seated between Kong Mei and her mother. The middle-aged woman was very kind and seemingly fond of Lin Lan. After the meal, Lin Lan stood up, staring at Kong Mei with love in his eyes, and openly asked her to marry him. Kong Mei shyly accepted the proposal with a blush, while her mother smiled in agreement. The middle-aged woman said she was very happy to learn that her daughter was to marry again before her rebirth as a person. She felt sorry that her husband had picked the wrong man for Kong Mei as her first husband. She wished and believed that her daughter would be happy in this marriage.

　　于是一个简单愉快的婚礼就在孔媚的家中举行了，她的母亲、瑾瑾和胡耿都做了见证者。

So a simple, joyful wedding ceremony was held at Kong Mei's home with her mother and Jin Jin and Hu Geng attending as witnesses.

　　但是当林兰醒来后，他仍是单身。只有他睡觉时在梦中才可以快乐地住在他的新婚妻子孔媚的家中。于是林兰改变了他的生活习惯。他把所有的事情都在白天做完，夜幕一降临，他就上床睡觉以便与妻子在阴间相伴。他拒绝了所有媒人的提亲，声称他已过惯了单身生活。

But when Lin Lan woke up, he was still single. Only when he slept and dreamed he could live happily with his newly wedded wife, Kong Mei, at her home. So Lin Lan changed his living habits. He did all his works in the daytime. Soon after darkness descended, he would go to bed to sleep and be with his wife in the ghost world. He turned down all the proposals made by the matchmakers, saying that he enjoyed his bachelorhood.

　　不幸的是，林兰与孔媚的甜蜜夫妻生活过得并不太长。孔媚的前夫死于一场与赌徒的殴斗中，也变成了鬼。当他获悉他的妻子孔媚已经再婚时非常愤怒。他在冥府控告孔媚重婚罪。对于孔媚来说，这真像是一个晴天霹雳。当林兰在梦里与她相见时夫妻两人与瑾瑾及胡耿认真研究案情，结果发觉无计可施。

Unfortunately, Lin Lan and Kong Mei's sweet conjugal life did not last very long. Kong Mei's previous

human husband died in a fight with a fierce gambler and he also became a ghost. When he got the news that his wife Kong Mei had been remarried, he was furious, and sued Kong Mei for bigamy in the nether world court. It was a shock to Kong Mei. When Lin Lan appeared in his dream, the husband and wife discussed the situation with Jin Jin and Hu Geng seriously, but nobody had any remedy.

　　所幸的是,法庭中的判官也是一名诗人。在审查了全部案情后,他非常同情林兰与孔媚的情况。他将开庭日期延后一个月,同时他答应孔媚在他的权力范围内他将尽力使案件对她有利。
　　Luckily, the judge in the court happened to be a poet as well. After having reviewed the whole case, he sympathized with Kong Mei and Lin Lan's situation. He postponed the hearing for one month. Meanwhile, he promised Kong Mei that he would use whatever power he could to make the case favorable to her.

　　一个月将尽,判官告诉他们这惟一的办法就是找寻一个刚死的女子尸体让孔媚借尸还魂。如此这个做鬼的原告,孔媚的前夫,就对人间的婚姻无法抗议了。
　　As the month was about to end, the judge told them that the only way to solve this problem was to find a newly dead young girl's body to let Kong Mei be revived as a human again. In that case, the ghost plaintiff, Kong Mei's previous husband, could do nothing to protest a human's marriage.

　　经过了多日的寻找,鬼判官告诉孔媚一个美丽的女子刚在某处她的父母家中过世了。孔媚立刻跑去将她自己冲向死者。于是她借尸还魂了。
　　After many days of search, the ghost judge told Kong Mei that a pretty girl had just died at her parents' home at a certain address. Kong Mei quickly went there and rushed herself into the dead girl's body, and she revived as a human again.

　　这对父母非常高兴发现他们的女儿又活了过来。可是这个女子告诉他们她不是他们的女儿而是另一个名叫孔媚的女子。几经努力,孔媚终于使这对老夫妇明白了她说的是什么了。然而他们不相信,于是他们来拜访林兰,才明白了这整个的事情。
　　The parents were elated to discover their dead daughter revived. But the girl told them that she was not their daughter but another girl named Kong Mei. It took Kong Mei quite a while to make the old couple understand what she was saying. Yet they still could not believe it. Then they visited Lin Lan and finally got the whole story.

　　发现林兰是一个好青年,他们便接受了这个事实,于是一个愉快的婚礼不久便举行了。林兰与孔媚终于在阳间成了夫妻。
　　Seeing that Lin Lan was a nice young man, they accepted the fact, and a pleasant wedding ceremony was soon held. Lin Lan and Kong Mei became husband and wife in the world of humans as well.

聊斋精选

一年后，孔媚怀孕了。在她生产的那天夜里，瑾瑾突然来拜访林兰，告诉她的舅舅她和她的丈夫胡耿都已经收到了阴曹地府的转世通知。她要求生为林兰与孔媚的女儿。胡耿要求生为林兰的好朋友王先生及他妻子的儿子。瑾瑾请求她的舅舅在他们长大后安排她和胡耿在人间仍旧结为夫妻。林兰愉快地答应了，然后他醒了过来而发现那不过是一场梦。

A year later, Kong Mei was pregnant. The night she would give birth, Jin Jin suddenly visited Lin Lan, telling her uncle that both she and her husband Hu Geng had received notice of rebirth from the government of nether world. She asked to be born as Lin Lan and Kong Mei's daughter, while Hu Geng requested to be born as Lin Lan's good friend Mr. Wang and his wife's son. Jin Jin asked her uncle to make arrangement to make her and Hu Geng become husband and wife again in the human world when they grew up. Lin Lan happily promised. Then, he woke up and found it was a dream.

不久，产婆来恭喜他说他的妻子生了一个女儿。他快乐地告诉孔媚他们的女儿是瑾瑾投胎的。

Soon after that, the midwife came to congratulate him that his wife had given birth to a daughter. He happily told Kong Mei that their infant daughter was Jin Jin to be reborn.

第二天，林兰拜访他的朋友王君，果然确实知道王君的妻子在前一晚间生了个儿子。林兰于是把瑾瑾和胡耿的故事告诉了王君和他的妻子。他们都同意等这两个小孩长大了后，他们会故意安排机会让他们相爱。

The next day, Lin Lan visited his friend, Wang, and surely learnt that Wang's wife had given birth to a son the night before. Lin Lan told Wang and his wife the story of Jin Jin and Hu Geng. They happily agreed to purposely provide opportunities for the two youngsters to fall in love when the babies grew up.

十八年后，这两个婴儿长大了。在他们父母的精心安排下，他们恋爱了，也结婚了。他们的父母于是将瑾瑾和胡耿的故事一五一十地告诉了他们。这对新婚夫妻很兴奋地知道他们的婚姻原来在出生前就已经安排好了的。

Eighteen years later, the two babies grew up. Under their parents' deliberate arrangements, they fell in love and get married. Then their parents told them the story of Jin Jin and Hu Geng. The pair of young newlyweds were excited to learn that theirs was a marriage of destiny.

廿一、

阿纤

Outcast

秋生是一个批发商人。他经常到外地那些小的城镇经商。
Qiu Sheng was a wholesale merchant. He often made business trips to the small towns.

一个很晚的寒冬下午,当他到达一个不知名的小镇时,他发现这时所有的商铺、饭馆和旅店都已经关门了。更糟的是这冰冷的腊月天气告诉人们一场大风雪即将到来。他在街上看不到一个行人。
Late one evening, when he reached a small, unfamiliar town, he found that all the stores, restaurants, and hotels were closed by this time. Worse enough, the chilly December weather indicated that a heavy snow was imminent. No one else could be seen on the streets.

他在镇上徘徊,从一条街走到另一条街寻找着栖身之地。最后,他停步在一家旅店门前敲门求助,可是没有人应门。他站在那里一时真不知道如何度过这个寒冷的风雪之夜。
He wandered through the town from one street to the other looking for a place to stay. Finally, he stopped in front of a lodge and knocked on the door asking for help. But nobody answered. He stood there wondering how to spend the night in the chilly storm.

突然,街对面的一栋房子大门打开了,走出了一个中年男子招手要他走过去。秋生高兴极了,他赶快走了过去,并随着这个男子进入他的家中。这个男子说他从窗口看到他的窘境已经好一会了。出于同情,他让秋生在他家里过夜。他说虽然睡在他的家里不是很舒服,可总比在户外好多了。
Suddenly, the door of a house across the street opened, and a middle-aged man came out, beckoning him to come over. Qiu Sheng was elated. He quickly walked over and followed the man into his house. The man said that he had observed Qiu Sheng's dilemma from the window for a while. Out of sympathy, he would let Qiu Sheng stay overnight at his home. He said that although sleeping at his home was not very comfortable, it would be much better than outside.

秋生非常感激这个人的善意。当这个人问他是否吃过晚饭时,秋生回答他从早上起就没有吃过任何东西。男子说他的妻子和女儿都早已上床睡觉了,他自己对于烹饪是一窍不通。但是,他可以把他们晚饭剩留下来的饭菜让秋生充饥。由于饭菜已经冷了,他便生起火炉把它热一热。秋生再度表示感谢。于是这两个人交换了姓名。这个男子姓楚名理。
Qiu Sheng deeply appreciated the man's kindness. When the man asked him if he had had supper, Qiu Sheng replied that he had not eaten anything since the morning. The man said that his wife and his daughter were already in bed, and he himself knew nothing about cooking. However, he offered Qiu Sheng what was left over from their supper. Since the food was cold, he lighted a fire to heat it. Qiu Sheng accepted the offering and thanked the man again. Then the two men exchanged names. The man's name was Chu Li.

就在秋生将要吃饭时,通向里面的门开了,一个十七八岁的女孩走了进来,手上提着一壶酒及两只小酒盅。楚理把这个女孩介绍给秋生,说是他的女儿安安。他说他们的谈话声惊醒了睡着的妻子和女儿,所以她母亲要女儿送来一壶酒招待客人,因为天气很冷。秋生于是又向安安道了谢。

Before Qiu Sheng started to eat, the door to the inside opened, and a teenage girl came into the room carrying a pot of liquor and two small cups. Chu Li introduced the girl to Qiu Sheng as his daughter, Anan. He said that their conversation had awakened his sleeping wife and daughter, so the mother wanted the daughter to bring out the liquor for the guest because the weather was cold. Qiu Sheng thanked Anan.

安安不多说话,当他父亲介绍她时,她只是微笑。在灯光下,秋生发觉她很文静秀丽。她倒了两盅酒,很恭敬地将一盅放在秋生的面前,另一盅放在她父亲的面前。然后她就退出了房间。

Anan did not speak much, but smiled when she was introduced. Under the light, Qiu Sheng noticed that she was very gentle and pretty. She poured the liquor into the two cups and respectfully placed one cup in front of Qiu Sheng and the other one in front of her father. Then she retreated from the room.

吃了热饭又喝了几盅酒后,秋生觉得好过多了。因为楚理看来也是一个嗜酒和健谈的人,这两个男子一边喝酒一边聊天。一壶酒还没有喝完,两人就成了朋友。

Having finished a hot meal and a few cups of liquor, Qiu Sheng felt much better. As Chu Li seemed to be a good drinker and talker too, the two men drank and talked happily. Before the pot of liquor was consumed, they had become friends.

楚理说他和妻子只有安安一个孩子。最近数年来他与他的妻子两人的健康情形日渐衰弱,他们非常担心女儿的前途,因为很难找到一个可靠的少年男子可以和她匹配。

Chu Li said that he and his wife had only one child, Anan. As their physical conditions were becoming weaker and weaker with each passing month, they were worried about their daughter's future for it was hard to find a good match for her.

突然间,秋生想起了他的弟弟秋路。他告诉楚理他只有一个弟弟比他小十二岁。人很聪明也长得很英俊。他们的父母都已亡故,夫妻两人没有小孩,把弟弟一直当作儿子一样地照顾。秋生说如果楚理同意的话,这将是理想的一对。

Suddenly, Qiu Sheng thought of his younger brother Qiu Lu. He told Chu Li that his only brother Qiu Lu, twelve years younger than he, was a smart and handsome young man. Their parents had died. He and his wife had been taking care of his brother as dearly as their son as they had no children. Qiu Sheng said this would be a good match for Anan if Chu Li agreed.

楚理很兴奋。他又问了几个关于秋路的问题,秋生回答了。然后楚理说他要到内室去和他的妻子及女儿商量一下。不久他回到了客厅说他们都同意这个婚约。一时间,这两个人觉得很高兴。

Chu Li was excited. He asked a few more questions about Qiu Lu and Qiu Sheng answered. Then Chu Li asked to be excused, so he could go inside to consult with his wife and daughter. Soon he came back to the living room saying that they had accepted the marriage proposal. Both men were happy.

因为天色已晚,楚理便安排秋生睡在他们的长榻上,他又拿来了被子和枕头,然后他们互道晚安就去睡了。
As it was getting late, Chu Li arranged for Qiu Sheng to sleep on their couch and brought in a blanket and a pillow for him. Then they said goodnight to each other.

第二天早上,秋生离开前,他要付给楚理食宿费,楚理拒收。他说他们即将成为亲戚了,怎么可以收一个亲戚的一夜留宿费用?秋生谢过楚理,然后就又上路了。
The next morning, before leaving, Qiu Sheng tried to pay Chu Li for his hospitality, but Chu Li refused to take his money. He said that they were soon going to be relatives. How could he take a relative's money for only one night's staying? Qiu Sheng thanked Chu Li and went back on the road.

事务办完后,秋生回到家中,愉快地告诉妻子及弟弟关于安安及婚约的情形。他的妻子埋怨他这个婚约定得太快了,至少他应当让秋路及安安见上一面。秋生答应他下次做生意回到那个小镇时就如此安排。
After he finished his business trip, Qiu Sheng returned home and happily told his wife and his brother about Anan and the marriage proposal. His wife blamed him for making the proposal in such a rush, for he at least should let Qiu Lu and Anan have a chance to meet each other once. Qiu Sheng promised he would make such an arrangement when he returned to the small town on his next business trip.

冬天过去,春天来了,天气变得暖和多了。秋生决定再作一次商务之行,他特别计划再经过楚理的小镇。他决定去拜访楚理进一步商讨如何让秋路及安安先见上一面。
After the winter, the spring came, and the weather became much warmer. Qiu Sheng decided to make another business trip, and he particularly planned to go to Chu Li's small town again. He decided to visit Chu Li to have further discussions about how to let Qiu Lu and Anan meet each other first.

当他向楚理的家中走去时,途中遇见了一位中年妇人及一位十七八岁的女孩。当这个女孩看到秋生时,她向妇人耳语了几句,然后这位妇人拦住秋生,很有礼貌地问他是否曾于去年冬季在一个名叫楚理的中年男子家里待过一夜。
When he was walking toward Chu Li's home, he met a middle-aged woman and a teenage girl on the street. When the girl saw Qiu Sheng she whispered to the woman, and the woman stopped Qiu Sheng, politely asking if he was the gentleman who had happened to spend a night at a middle-aged man named Chu Li's house that past winter.

当秋生回答是时,这个妇人伤心地告诉他,她就是楚理的妻子,她的丈夫已经于一个月前被倒下来的墙头砸死了。她身旁的女孩是她的女儿安安。秋生立刻认出了她是那个文静秀丽的女孩,那天夜晚她曾

聊斋精选

经拿来一壶酒并倒了一盅给他。这就是他为他的弟弟秋路定下婚约的女孩。

When Qiu Sheng replied yes, the woman sadly told him that she was Chu Li's wife and her husband had been killed under a collapsed wall a month ago. The girl by her side was her daughter, Anan. Qiu Sheng immediately recognized her as the gentle and pretty young lady who had brought out a pot of liquor and poured the liquor for him that night. This was the girl to whom he had made a marriage proposal for his younger brother, Qiu Lu.

楚理的妻子把秋生带回了家。她说既然她过世的丈夫已经和他为她的女儿及他的弟弟订妥了婚约，她希望这对年轻人尽快结婚，愈早愈好。

So Chu Li's wife led Qiu Sheng to her home. She said that since her deceased husband and Qiu Sheng had previously made the marriage proposal for her daughter and his brother, she just wished that the young couple would get married as soon as possible.

眼见安安的确是个非常讨人喜欢的年轻女子，秋生相信他的弟弟秋路一定会接受他所安排了的婚约。于是他建议这对母女和他一起去他的家。楚理的妻子立刻愉快地答应，安安红着脸低下头没有说话。从她的表情上，秋生看出来她也是同意他的安排的。

Seeing that Anan was indeed a very winning young lady, Qiu Sheng believed that his brother Qiu Lu would accept his arrangement without question. So he suggested that the mother and the daughter come with him to his home. Chu Li's wife accepted the arrangement happily and immediately, while Anan hung her head, blushing and not saying a word. From her expression, Qiu Sheng could tell that she had accepted the arrangement, too.

秋生决定暂停未完的商务之行，把安安和她的母亲带回了家。他的决定是对的。秋路对安安是一见钟情，而秋生的妻子也喜欢安安。安安对于秋路及他的家庭也很满意。不久就举行了一个简单愉快的婚礼。秋路和安安成了夫妻。安安的母亲被安排住在离他们家不远处一栋租来的小房子里，安安可以随时去看望她的母亲。

Qiu Sheng decided to suspend the rest of his business trip to bring Anan and her mother home. He was right. Qiu Lu was elated when he met Anan. Qiu Sheng's wife was fond of Anan, too. And Anan was also satisfied with Qiu Lu and his family. Soon a simple and pleasant wedding ceremony was held. Qiu Lu and Anan became husband and wife. Anan's mother was arranged to live at a small rental house nearby so Anan could pay her mother visits as often as she wanted.

婚后，安安对待秋生和他的妻子很恭敬就像是对待公婆一样。他们共同居住在一起，是一个快乐的大家庭。因为安安对家中的每一个人包括仆人在内都很好，家中的每一个人也都喜欢她。她是一个能干的家庭主妇，特别对家庭财务方面很有才干。她帮助秋生的妻子料理家中财务，处理得井井有条。一年后，这户人家日渐兴隆。

After her marriage, Anan treated Qiu Sheng and his wife with respect as if they were her parents-in-law. They lived together as a big happy family. Because Anan was nice to everyone including the servants, everybody was fond of her. And she was a capable housewife, especially in the management of household financial affairs. She helped Qiu

聊
斋
精
选

Sheng's wife manage the family's financial affairs and she did very well. In one year, the family became prosperous.

安安暗地告诉秋路要他转告秋生再去那个小镇时，不要对任何人提及她和她的母亲。秋生答应了，不过他很快就忘记了。

Anan secretly told Qiu Lu to ask Qiu Sheng not to mention her and her mother's names to anyone in the small town if Qiu Sheng happened to pass by that town again. Qiu Sheng promised, but he soon forgot.

一年后，又是冬天了。因为商业需要，秋生又一次来到了楚理的小镇。这次他特别提早到达以便有把握订住到旅店。这天外面又下着大雪，秋生和店主坐在火炉边喝酒。他告诉店主在一年前的今天晚间，假如没有一个好心人在这家旅店街对面开门让他投宿在他家的话，那天夜里他就得露宿街头。

A year later, it was winter again. When Qiu Sheng was making a business trip through Chu Li's small town, he purposely arrived earlier so he could be sure to check into a hotel to spend the night. As it was snowing heavily outside, Qiu Sheng and the hotel owner drank wine by a fireplace. He told the owner that one evening a year ago, he would almost have had to sleep on the street right here in the middle of town had not a kind man from across the street of the lodging opened the door and invited him to spend the night with them.

店主人惊讶地告诉秋生这对街的房子是他的叔父的。因为里面经常有怪异的事情发生，房子空着有好几年了。据说这房子里闹鬼，没有人敢搬进去住。

Surprised, the lodging owner told Qiu Sheng that the house across the street belonged to his uncle. It had been vacant for several years because of frequent strange occurrences. As the house was said to be haunted, nobody dared to move in.

接着店主人告诉秋生另一件奇怪的事情。差不多八九个月前，邻居们在这栋房子前院倒下的墙头底下发现一只猫一般大的死老鼠，第二天这只死老鼠又不见了。于是秋生问这个男子他是否认识一对姓楚的中年夫妇和她的女儿安安。这个人说这是一个很小的集镇，他在这儿住了一辈子了，他可以说认识这里的每一个人，可就是没有遇到或听到有这么一个人家曾经在本地住过。

Then the owner told Qiu Sheng another odd thing. About eight or nine months before, neighbors discovered a huge dead mouse the size of a large cat under a collapsed wall in the front yard of the house, and the next day, the dead mouse disappeared. Then Qiu Sheng asked the man if he had known a middle-aged couple by the last name of Chu and their daughter named Anan. The man said that this was a small town where he had spent all his life. He knew just about everybody here, but he had never met or heard of such a family who had lived in town.

秋生突然怀疑安安和她的父母可能不是人类而是老鼠，因为她的母亲曾经告诉他，她的丈夫是在这栋房子里被倒下来的墙头砸死的，而这栋房子就是有鬼出没。大概那就是为什么安安请他不要在这个集镇里向任何人提及她的家人名字的缘故。否则为什么这个旅店的主人从来没有遇到或听到他们呢？他愈想也就愈相信他的猜测可能不会错。

Suddenly, Qiu Sheng suspected that Anan and her parents might not be humans but mice, because her mother told him that her father had been killed by a collapsed wall in the house which was haunted. That was probably the reason why Anan wanted him not to mention her family's names to anybody in the town. Otherwise, how could the hotel owner have never met nor heard of them? The more he thought of it, the more he believed what he suspected might be true.

到家后,他把所听到的及猜测的暗中告诉他的妻子及弟弟秋路,安安不是人类而是老鼠。因为秋路深爱自己的妻子,他拒绝相信,对于他哥哥的故事他完全不予理睬。

After he reached home, he secretly told his wife and his brother Qiu Lu what he had heard and his suspicion that Anan might not be a human, but a mouse. Because Qiu Lu loved his wife so deeply that he refused to accept this notion, and totally ignored his brother's story.

秋生将他的疑虑与他的妻子商议,他告诉她他相信他所听到的都是事实,不过他的妻子仍然怀疑。后来,秋生又把这个秘密告诉了他家的仆人。不久家中的每一个人都在窃窃私语安安不是人类,每当安安走过来时,他们就闭嘴不说了。

Qiu Sheng discussed his suspicion with his wife. He told her he believed what he had been told, but his wife still doubted it. Later on, Qiu Sheng told his servants the secret, too. Soon everybody else in the house was whispering to each other that Anan was not a human. When Anan approached, they would keep their mouths shut up.

终于安安觉察到了这些背后的比手画脚指的是什么。她对这个传闻的真实性是既不否认也不承认,不过感到非常伤心。终于,她不能忍受这个冷漠的对待,一个晚上,当她与秋路单独相处时,她要求秋路写张休书给她,这样她将永远离开这个家。秋路把她紧紧抱在怀中告诉她,他对这些谣言从不放在心上的。他不在乎她的出身是什么,他爱她只认她是他的爱妻。这对夫妇抱在一起哭成一团。于是安安也就不再要求离开而仍留下。

Gradually, Anan noticed all the murmuring behind hands and mouths. She neither denied nor admitted the rumor's veracity, but felt very sad. Finally, she could not stand the cool treatment. One evening, when she and Qiu Lu were alone, she begged Qiu Lu to write a paper of divorce to her so she could take it and leave the house for good. Qiu Lu hugged her tightly saying that he had never paid any attention to the rumor. He did not care what kind of background she had. He loved her and only cared that she was his beloved wife. That was it. The couple hugged and cried together. So Anan dropped her request and decided to stay.

因为安安仍然留在这栋房子里,似乎对于这个谣言不予理睬,几天后,秋生突然对家人宣布他将带一只大猫来家提防房子里有老鼠。那天晚间,秋路回家后,他发觉安安不在家。他想她一定是看望她的母

聊斋精选

亲去了,因为她以往常去。可是到夜深了她还是没有回来,他于是去岳母家察看,方才惊讶地发现这位老太太也不见了。显然,这对母女都已搬走了。

As Anan still insisted on staying in the house without any seeming reaction to the rumor, several days later Qiu Sheng suddenly announced to his family that he was going to bring in a large cat in case there was a mouse on the premises. When Qiu Lu returned home that evening, he found Anan had disappeared. He thought that she might have gone to visit her mother as she often did. As she had not returned later in the evening, Qiu Lu went to visit his mother-in-law and was shocked to find that the old lady was not there, either. Obviously, both the daughter and the mother had moved out all together.

现在安安走了,秋生似乎如释重负,可是秋路非常难过。他每天到处寻找他的妻子,可是没有一点下落。

Now, Anan was gone. Qiu Sheng seemed relieved, but Qiu Lu was very upset. He started to look for his wife just about everywhere every day, but met with no success.

时日一久,秋生建议秋路再婚。秋路拒绝了,他告诉哥哥,如果他找不到安安,无论如何,他是永远不会再和任何一个女子结婚的。

As time went on, Qiu Sheng suggested that Qiu Lu find another match, but Qiu Lu refused. He told his brother that if he could not find Anan, he would never remarry another woman no matter what.

自从安安离家后,秋生的妻子生病了,她大部分的时间都躺在床上。因为没有一个像安安一样的能干家庭主妇帮助她,家中的事务日渐混乱,财务情况更是每况愈下。

After Ann had left the house, Qiu Sheng's wife became sick and lay in bed most of the time. Without a capable housewife like Anan to help her take care of the home, the whole household affairs became disorganized, and the family's financial conditions worsened, too.

秋路有个表弟与他自小一起长大的。一天,表弟到省的北部去经商。天晚了将要上床去睡觉时,他听到了旅店隔壁一家有人哀泣。显然这哭泣的人是位年轻女子。声音很熟悉,可他不能确定究竟是谁,于是他问店主这个女人是谁以及她为什么哭得如此伤心。

Qiu Lu had a cousin who had grown up with him. One day, the cousin went to a city in the northern part of the province on a business trip. In the evening, just as he was going to sleep, he heard sad cries from the house next door to the lodging where he was staying. Obviously, the sad person was a young woman. As the sound of crying seemed familiar and he could not be sure who she was, he asked the owner of lodging, who the woman was and why she was crying so sadly.

旅店主人告诉他,她哭是因为她的母亲最近死了。她的父亲早已死了,她又没有兄弟姐妹,如今母亲一死她就更孤单了。没有人知道她结过婚没有,六个月前她与她的母亲从南方搬来的。

The owner told him that she cried because her mother had recently died. She would be more lonely as

聊斋精选

her father had died years before and she had no brothers or sisters. Nobody knew if she had married or not. She and her mother had moved from the south only six months before.

表弟怀疑这个哭泣的女人是秋路的失踪妻子安安。第二天一早,他去拜访这位年轻女子,发现果然是安安。他劝安安回到秋路的身旁,因为他还是非常思念她并到处在寻找她。她拒绝了,她不停地哭泣。表弟便急忙通知秋路,秋路立刻跑来会见安安。

The cousin suspected that the crying woman might be Qiu Lu's missing wife, Anan. The next morning, he visited the young woman next door, and found that it was indeed Anan. He advised Anan to go back to Qiu Lu as he was still looking for her and missing her desperately. She refused, and kept on crying. The cousin quickly went to tell Qiu Lu, and Qiu Lu ran to Anan right away.

夫妻两人抱头大哭没有说一句话。秋路请求安安与他回家,她只是哭泣没说是也没说不。秋路说如果她不跟他回家,他也将永远留在这里陪她不走。终于她同意跟他回家,不过有一个条件:秋路和他的哥哥秋生必须分家,将家产平分后单独居住。秋路答应照办。

The husband and wife hugged and cried without saying a word. Qiu Lu begged Anan to return home with him. She just cried and did not say yes or no. Qiu Lu said if she would not, he would not go home either but stay here with her forever. Finally, she agreed to go home with him under one condition: Qiu Lu and his brother Qiu Sheng must divide their family property and live separately. Qiu Lu promised.

回家后,秋路与秋生将家产平分。秋路搬出祖传的大房子,他与安安买了一栋小的老房子居住。他们将房子重新装修得像栋新的房子一样,快乐地居住在一起。安安建议秋路开个小杂货店。因为有安安的帮助,秋路自己经营店务,数年间,秋路和安安的家道变成了殷实小康。反观秋生,因为他的妻子常年卧病在床,家中缺少一个能干的主妇料理一切,家道日渐中落。

After returning home, Qiu Lu and Qiu Sheng divided the family property into half and each of them kept one half. Qiu Lu moved out of the big ancestral house. He and Anan bought a small old house. They remodeled it to make it like a new house and lived there happily by themselves. Anan suggested that Qiu Lu open a small grocery store. With Anan's help, Qiu Lu managed the store business himself. In a few years, Qiu Lu and Anan became sufficiently well-off, while Qiu Sheng's wife was sick year-round and due to the lack of a capable housewife, Qiu Sheng's financial condition got worse each year.

每次当秋生遇有经济困难时,安安总是要她的丈夫去尽力支援。她告诉秋路,如果当初没有他的哥哥秋生帮忙,她与秋路怎能相遇又哪会有今日的幸福。

Every time, Qiu Sheng was having a hard time financially, Anan would urge her husband to help his brother as much as Qiu Sheng needed. She told Qiu Lu that without his elder brother's help in the beginning, she and Qiu Lu would not have met and would not have been happy as they were.

聊斋精选

The Family on the Second Floor

顾处平以勇敢无惧称道于乡里。二十岁时家道开始中落,次年父母双亡。他独居于一栋很小的房子里。

Gu Chuping was a man well known for bravery in the area he lived. When he was twenty, his parents had lost their fortune and both died the next year. He lived by himself at a small house.

处平的叔父也就是他父亲的弟弟拥有很多房产出租。其中一栋是个二层楼的房子,根据住过这房子的人说,这栋房子在夜间时常有怪异的事情发生。结果没有人敢再住这栋闹鬼的房子。

Chuping's uncle, his father's younger brother, owned many rental properties. One of them was a two-story house. According to the people who had lived in the house, there were often many weird things happening there at night. Consequently, nobody dared to live in the haunted house.

一天,他的叔父和他谈起这栋房子,问他有无胆量搬进去住,看看究竟是怎么一回事。他毫不犹豫地答应并于第二天就搬了进去。

One day, his uncle mentioned the house to Chuping asking him if he dared to move in to find out what was wrong. Without hesitation, he answered he would love to. And he moved in the next day.

处平选择楼下的主室作为他的卧室。第一夜没有任何怪异发生,第二和第三夜也没有,他讥笑那些编造怪诞故事的人。

Chuping took the master bedroom on the first floor as his bedroom. No strange things happened the first night nor the following two nights, either. He laughed at the people who had invented the weird stories.

可是在第四天的深更夜半,处平被二楼上响亮的讲话声音吵醒了。他在奇怪楼上发生了什么,这栋房子里根本没有别人住,他起身后蹑手蹑脚地上了二楼。他很惊讶地发现四个人坐在餐厅一张餐桌旁吃饭,两个年纪大,两个年龄轻,好像是父母亲和一个儿子一个女儿在用餐。桌子上有一壶酒及很多盘菜放在他们的面前。

But in the middle of fourth night, Chuping was awakened by a loud conversation on the second floor. He wondered what could be happening upstairs as there were no other people living in the building. He got up and sneaked to the second floor. Being surprised, he discovered that four people, two seniors and two juniors, like parents and one son and one daughter, sat at a table eating and talking in the dining room with a bottle of liquor and many dishes of food in front of them.

处平很喜欢喝酒,只要有喝酒的机会他很少放弃。于是他大胆地走进餐厅,大声地质问这家人怎么不邀请房东喝几盅。

Chuping was very fond of drink and seldom missed a chance of indulging. He boldly walked into the dining room and loudly scolded the family for not inviting their landlord to have a few drinks.

他的突然出现惊吓了这两位女性,她们立刻退到内室,两位男子生气地站了起来。年纪大的男子向处平吼道:"我知道这栋房子是谁的。你不是我的房东!"

His sudden appearance frightened away the two females, who quickly retreated to the back rooms, while the two males stood up in anger. The older man barked at Chuping, "I know who owns the property. You are not my landlord."

"我是房东的侄子,"处平傲慢地回答,"我的叔父要我搬进来照顾他的产业。"

"I'm the nephew of the landlord," Chuping answered haughtily, "My uncle asked me to move in to take care of his property."

处平的回答使这个人哑口无言。他勉强地邀请处平坐下,并为他倒了满满一杯酒。处平端起酒杯一饮而尽。于是这个人又倒了一杯,处平又干了。连饮了两杯酒后,处平谢了这个人。两人便开始交谈并互道姓名。这个人的名字是胡准,指着坐在身边的少年,说那是他的儿子胡儿。

Chuping's answer rendered the man speechless. He reluctantly invited Chuping to sit down and poured him a full cup of liquor. Chuping picked up the cup and downed the contents right away. Then, the man poured him another cup, and Chuping downed it again. After having drunk two full cups of liquor, Chuping thanked the man and they started to talk and exchanged names. The man's name was Hu Zhun. Pointing at the young man sitting by him, Hu Zhun told Chuping that was his son Hu Er .

很快地处平发觉胡准也是一个好酒的人。他同时也发现他们两个人的性格很相近,都是爽直而无心机。胡准毫不隐瞒地告诉处平他和他的家人不是人类,他们都是狐狸。

Soon Chuping found that Hu Zhun was a good drinker, too. And he also found that both of them had similar personalities, open-minded and unrestrained. Hu Zhun told Chuping without concealment that he and his family were not humans. They were foxes.

处平回答只要相处得好,谁也不在乎谁的背景是什么。换言之,如果不能相处,就是关系非常密切甚至于亲兄弟,也会不停地相斗的。接着他又告诉胡准,他从一本书上看到历史上一个传闻,说的是一只雌狐曾经帮助过大禹王治理天下的故事。胡准从来没有听说过狐狸会有这么一个光荣的历史。他很兴奋地要他的儿子到内室去把他的母亲及妹妹带回饭桌,来听听他们祖先的伟大事迹。

Chuping answered that as long as they could get along very well, who cared what whose background was. On the other hand, if two people did not get along, even though they were closely related or brothers, they still fought all the time. Then, he told Hu Zhun a historical rumor, which he had once read from a book, about a female fox helping the Great Emperor Yu rule the kingdom. Hu

Zhun had never heard of such a glorious tale about a fox. He was excited and wanted his son to go inside to have his mother and sister return to the table to hear about their ancestor's great accomplishment.

不久,一位中年妇人和一位十七八岁的女孩回到了餐厅。胡准向处平介绍那是他的妻子及女儿小凤。处平一眼望去,发觉这个女孩是他一生中所见过的最美丽的女子。能有这么一个美女同桌,处平讲起话来也就更是妙趣横生了。小凤不喜欢多言,不停地站起身来为她的父亲及客人斟酒。她对处平的故事听得是津津有味。

Soon a middle-aged woman and a girl in her late teens returned to the dining room. Hu Zhun introduced them to Chuping as his wife and his daughter, Xiaofeng. Chuping took one look at them and found that the girl was the most beautiful young woman he had ever seen. With such a beauty sitting at the table, Chuping spoke much more engagingly. Xiaofeng did not like to speak much, but kept standing up to pour liquor for her father and the guest. She also listened to Chuping's story with great interest and admiration.

处平说得兴高采烈,他的酒也就一杯接着一杯地喝。终于他喝醉了。也许因为他血液中的酒精提起了他的勇气,也许因为这个女孩的脉脉含情眼神激励了他,当小凤为他斟酒时,处平突然握住她的手,大声求爱要她嫁给他。

While he was speaking in high spirits, Chuping kept drinking the liquor one cup after another. Finally, he got drunk. Maybe because the alcohol in his blood had raised his courage, maybe because the girl's affectionate look had inspired him, Chuping suddenly grasped Xiaofeng's hand while she was pouring liquor into his cup. He loudly asked her to marry him.

这个突如其来的贸然求婚之举使得这一家人非常惊讶。胡准很生气,他要他的妻子和女儿退回到内室。然后他站起身来,冷冷地告诉处平他喝醉了,应该回到他自己的房间去睡觉。一个愉快的聚会就这么尴尬地突告结束了。

The unexpected blunt proposal surprised everyone of the family. Hu Zhun was upset. He ordered his wife and daughter to retreat back to their rooms. Then he stood up, coolly told Chuping that he must have been drunk and should go to his room to sleep. The pleasant gathering thus ended abruptly in great embarrassment for all.

第二天夜晚,处平回到二楼,可没有发现有什么异常。
The next evening, Chuping went back to the second floor, but he did not find anything unusual.

失望之下,他回到了自己的房间。就在他将要上床睡觉时,他的房门突然被打开了,走进来一个相貌怕人的魔鬼。这个魔鬼向着处平走去,并两眼瞪着他。处平立刻用手指沾在砚台的黑墨上,把他的脸涂得也像魔鬼一样,然后他回瞪着这个魔鬼。

Disappointed, he returned to his room. Before he went to bed to sleep, his door was opened suddenly and in came a horrible-looking demon. The demon walked toward Chuping and stared at him. Chuping quickly dampened his fingers on his ink stone and rubbed them on his face making himself look like a demon, too, and he stared back at the demon.

一阵紧张后,魔鬼从房间里退了出去不见了。此后,那天夜晚没有发生任何事件,以后的晚间也没有发生什么。

After a minute of tension, the demon retreated from the room and disappeared. Since then, nothing else happened that night, nor the following nights, either.

怀念着这个美丽的女孩,处平仍然每天晚上到二楼去希望能再看到她。可他在楼上再也没有发现任何异常事情。

Missing the pretty girl, Chuping still went to the second floor every evening in hopes of seeing her again. But he just could not find any thing abnormal upstairs.

十天后的一个晚上,处平独自一人坐在二楼餐厅,他在那儿曾经遇到过小凤及她的家人。他在深思她那含羞的笑容及那多情的眼神。突然间门打开了,走进了一个人。借着烛光,他欣喜若狂地发现那正是他日夜思念着的女孩小凤。

One evening ten days later, Chuping sat by himself in the dining room on the second floor where he had met Xiaofeng and her family. He was in deep thought about her shy smile and affectionate eyes. Suddenly the door opened and someone walked in. By the light of an oil candle, he was overjoyed to find that it was Xiaofeng, the girl he had been missing day and night.

他走上前去想握她的手,她没有拒绝,两人携手坐下。她告诉他那个魔鬼是她的父亲装出来想把他吓跑的,结果证实他太勇敢了根本一点儿也不害怕。他的父亲于是决定将全家搬出这栋房子。她知道他在想念她,可是她那固执的父亲不准她来看他。她今晚溜出来是因为她的父母和哥哥都出城去了。

He went forward and tried to hold her hands, meeting little resistance. They held each other's hands and sat down. She told him that it was her father who had tried to frighten him away by impersonating a demon. Because Chuping proved to be too brave to run away, her father had decided to move the whole family out of the house. She realized that he was missing her, but her stubborn father prohibited her from coming back to meet him. She sneaked out because her parents and brother were out of town that night.

处平大喜过望能再次看到她,把她抱在怀里,她把头放在他的肩膀上。当处平准备扶起她的头去吻

聊斋精选

她时,胡准突然冲了进来。这位保守的父亲大怒。他大声命令小凤立刻回家。当她离去时他紧跟在后面。等到处平跑出去时,他们已经无影无踪了,只有那父亲责骂女儿的声音还在远处回荡。

Chuping was overjoyed to see her again. He hugged her in his arms, and she put her head on his shoulder. As Chuping tried to lift her head and kiss her, Hu Zhun suddenly rushed in, the conservative father became very angry. He loudly ordered Xiaofeng to leave for home immediately, and he himself followed after her closely when she was exiting. When Chuping ran out of the house, they had disappeared, but the loud scolding the father gave to his daughter could still be heard in the distance.

自从这次事件后,这栋房子就变得安静和正常了。处平去报告他的叔父,这位富有的叔父便把这栋房子赠送给了处平,奖赏他的勇敢无惧。

After this incident, the house became quiet and normal. Chuping went to report to his uncle. The wealthy uncle gave the house to Chuping as a reward for his bravery.

六个月后,一天处平去拜访一个住在山脚下的朋友。当他走过荒野时,他看到一条猎狗正在追赶两只狐狸。一只狐狸跑上了山,这条狗便向另一只狐狸追去。当这只惊吓的狐狸发现处平时,它急速向他跑来并停留在他的脚下就像是遇到了救星一样。处平决定去帮助这只可怜的小动物,他轻轻地把它抱起放进了他的旅行袋里而带回了家。

Six months later, Chuping went to visit a friend who lived by the foot of a mountain. Walking through the wilderness, he found a hunting dog chasing two foxes. One fox ran up the mountain, so the dog pursued the other one. When the frightened fox spotted Chuping, it rapidly ran toward him and stopped right by his feet as if it had found a savior. Chuping decided to help the poor small animal. He easily picked it up and put it in his traveling bag and carried home.

到家后他打开袋子,这只狐狸从里面跳了出来,立刻变成了一位美丽的年轻女子,那是他日夜思念着的小凤。处平紧紧地把小凤抱在怀里,告诉她是如何害怕可能永远没有机会再看到她了。

After reaching home, he opened his bag and the fox jumped out and instantly turned into a pretty young lady. It was Xiaofeng, the girl he had been missing day and night! Chuping hugged Xiaofeng in his arms, telling her that he had been so much afraid he might never have a chance to see her again.

小凤回抱他,感谢他救了她的命。她说当她和她的表姐去散步时,她们不巧遇见了一条猎狗。假如她没有见到处平的话,她一定会被这条凶猛的狗所扑杀。她又告诉他她的表姐可能已经回去告诉她的父母她已被狗扑害了。既然如此,她也就不必再担心她的父亲反对她与处平交往了。从此以后,小凤与处平生活在一起就像一对新婚的夫妇一样。

Xiaofeng hugged him back and thanked him for saving her life. She said that when she and her cousin were taking a walk, they happened to come across the hunting dog. Had she not met Chuping, the fierce

聊斋精选

204

dog would have killed her. Then she told him that her cousin might have gone back to tell her parents that she had been murdered by the dog. In that case, she would not have to worry about her father's objection to her being with Chuping anymore. Since that time, Xiaofeng and Chuping lived together like a pair of newlyweds.

一年后，当处平正在家中读书时，他听到有人敲他家的前门。他去应了门，很惊讶地发现来人是小凤的哥哥胡儿。看到处平，胡儿立刻倒头跪下恳求帮助。处平把他扶起问他是怎么一回事。胡儿含泪说当他的父亲以狐狸原形在山中时，被一名猎人捕获。他已经打听出来了这个猎人是处平的好朋友名叫莫华。莫华将在回家途中于次日来拜访处平。他恳求处平在他的猎人朋友来访时救他的父亲一命。

A year later, when Chuping was reading at home, he heard a knock on his front door. He went to answer and surprisingly found that it was Xiaofeng's brother, Hu Er. Seeing Chuping, Hu Er immediately knelt down in front of Chuping begging for a big favor. Chuping helped him stand up and asked for details. Hu Er said in tears that while his father was in his original form of a fox in the mountain, a hunter captured him. He had found that the hunter was Chuping's good friend whose name was Mo Hua and that Mo Hua would pay Chuping a visit on his way home the next day. He begged Chuping to save his father's life when his hunter friend visited him.

回想起当初胡准强烈反对他与小凤的交往，处平故意回答说假如小凤来求他，他一定会乐于为之的。胡儿悲伤地说："我的妹妹已于一年前被猎狗扑杀了。"

Remembering Hu Zhun's strong objection to Xiaofeng's going with him, Chuping purposely replied that he would be glad to do it only if Xiaofeng could come to ask him. Then Hu Er said sadly, "My sister had been killed by a hunting dog a year earlier."

"既然你的妹妹已经死亡，"处平冷冷地答复访客，"我也就没有兴趣做了。"

"Since your sister has been dead," Chuping replied his visitor coolly, "I'm not interested in doing that."

他甚至于也没有邀请他的客人进屋内。胡儿没有办法只好泪流满面地离开了。

And he did not even invite his visitor to enter. Hu Er had no choice but to leave with tears running down both his cheeks.

送走客人之后，处平回到内室，告诉小凤刚才是谁来拜访他。

After seeing him off, Chuping went back inside and told Xiaofeng who had just visited him.

"你真的不救我的父亲吗？"小凤含泪地问。

聊斋精选

"Are you really not going to save my father's life?" Xiaofeng asked in tears.

处平告诉她:"当然我会为你去做的。"
Chuping told her, "Of course, I will do it for you."

接着他又说,"假如你真的死了,当我想起你父亲强烈反对我们的相爱时,我也许不会去做。"
Then he added, "But if you were truly dead, when I think of your father's strong objection to our love, I probably would not want to do it."

第二天,处平的朋友莫华果然来访。这位猎人捕获了很多的野兽放在不同的笼子内。处平注意到其中有一只黑色的老狐狸,伤得很重,被单独关在一个笼子里。当莫华骄傲地向处平炫耀他的猎物时,处平问莫华他是否可以买这只黑狐狸来修补他的破旧皮大氅。因为他们两人是好朋友,莫华把这只狐狸当礼品送给了处平。处平把笼子提到内室,小凤在那里等着,然后他回到客厅招待莫华吃饭。
The next day, Chuping's friend, Mo Hua, indeed came to visit him. The hunter had captured many wild animals and put them in different cages. Chuping noticed that among them was an old black fox, badly injured and locked in a small cage all by itself. While Mo Hua was proudly showing his captives to Chuping, Chuping asked Mo Hua if he could buy the fox from him, for he could use its fur to repair his old fur coat. Since the two men were good friends, Mo Hua gave the fox to Chuping as a gift. Chuping carried the cage back to his inner rooms where Xiaofeng was waiting for it. Then he returned to the living room to treat Mo Hua to a dinner.

莫华走后,处平走到内室,他发现小凤的父亲胡准坐在一张椅子上,脸上和颈上都是伤痕。看到处平走进来,老人立刻起身准备向处平磕头感激救命之恩,处平连忙止住了他。胡准为他以前反对小凤与他恋爱郑重向处平道歉,处平说这些事情都早已过去了。
After Mo Hua departed, Chuping went into the inner rooms. He found Xiaofeng's father, Hu Zhun, sitting on a chair with many bruises on his face and neck. Upon seeing Chuping, the old man immediately stood up, trying to kneel down to thank Chuping for saving his life. Chuping quickly stopped him. Hu Zhun apologized deeply to Chuping for his objection to letting Xiaofeng go with him. Chuping said that those things had been all over now.

父女团圆了,处平邀请胡准和他的妻儿都搬回来仍和以前一样住在二楼,处平和小凤住在楼下,胡准立即接受了这个邀请,他们又搬回来了。
Since the father and the daughter had had a happy reunion, Chuping invited Hu Zhun and his wife and their son to move back still living on the second floor like before, and Chuping and Xiaofeng lived on the first floor. Hu Zhun quickly accepted the invitation, and they moved back.

聊斋精选

聊斋精选

除了处平的叔父,他的朋友们都不知道他的妻子小凤和她的父母与哥哥不是人类。相反地,他们都很羡慕处平有这么一位美丽的妻子。

Aside from Chuping's uncle, none of his friends knew that his wife Xiaofeng and her parents and brother were not humans. Instead, they all envied Chuping for his having such a pretty wife.

聊斋精选

白于玉

Immortal

伍青安是一位非常聪明优秀的年轻学者,他相信他一定可以顺利地通过各级官府考试,先在地方官府中谋得一个官位,最后升任为京城朝廷里的高官。

As a notably bright young scholar, Wu Qingan believed that he would smoothly pass all the government examinations, and obtain a nice position in the local government, eventually becoming a senior official in the central government.

寇干是当地最富裕的男子。他很赏识青安的才华,预测这个年轻人定会有个光明的政治前程。他与青安达成一项协定,当青安通过第一个地方官试中了秀才后,他就把他的女儿嫁给他。寇干的女儿是地方上闻名遐迩的美人。青安有一次到寇干家的豪宅里参加一个慈善午餐会时曾经遇到过她,所以他很愉快地接受了这个婚约。

Kou Gan was the richest man in the area. He admired Qingan's talent and predicted that the young man would have a bright political future. He made a proposal to Qingan that after he passed his first local examination, Kou Gan would pledge to marry his daughter to him. Kou Gan's daughter was a well-known beauty whom Qingan had once met when he attended a charity luncheon at Kou Gan's splendid mansion. So Qingan happily accepted the marriage proposal.

结果出乎每一个人的意料之外,青安在他的第一次考试中就落榜了。他要求寇干将婚约延后两年,他将在两年后再去应试。如果他再失败,婚约就取消。在与妻子及女儿商量后,寇干答应青安的要求。青安再度苦读经典几乎日以继夜。

But to everybody's surprise, Qingan failed in his initial examination. He asked Kou Gan to defer the marriage proposal for two years and he would take the same examination again two years later. If he failed again, the marriage proposal would be voided. After consulting with his wife and his daughter, Kou Gan gave Qingan his agreement. Qingan once again studied the classics as hard as he could, day and night.

一个夏日的晚上,在读了几乎一整天的书后,他到附近的一个池塘旁边去散步。这个池塘很大,差不多像个小湖一样,有成百上千盛开的莲花飘浮在水面。白天有很多人来此赏花,现在天色已晚,池塘边静悄悄的。青安一个人沿着池边独自在那皎洁的月光下散步。

One summer evening, after having studied all day long, he went to a nearby pond to take a walk. The pond was large, almost like a small lake, with hundreds of blooming lotuses floating on the water. Many people came to the pond to enjoy the beautiful flowers in the daytime. But as it was late, the waterside was quiet. Qingan took a walk along the side of the pond all by himself in the full moonlight.

突然他听到了一个男子朗诵诗歌的声音。四周一望,发现了一位身着白色衣服的年轻男子坐在不远处的一块石头上悠闲地诵诗,可是他所诵的诗篇青安都从未听到过。他于是走近这个男子,两个人便交谈了起来。这个男子的名字叫苏彬。苏彬说他路过此地被这美丽的莲花所吸引,决定停下来休息一下。

聊斋精选

Suddenly he heard the voice of a man reciting poems. He looked around and found a young man in white clothes sitting on a rock not too far away, leisurely reciting poems that Qingan had never heard. He approached the man and they talked. The man's name was Su Bin. Passing through the area, Su Bin said he was attracted by the pretty lotuses and decided to take a rest.

青安不久更发现苏彬是个知识非常渊博的学者。两个人越谈越投机,真个是相逢恨晚,一见如故。

Qingan soon discovered that Su Bin was a learned scholar with extensive knowledge. And the more they talked, the more they admired each other's talents. In other words, they got along very well and wished to become friends.

因为青安住在当地,他便邀请苏彬回家住一晚。苏彬接受了邀请,于是他们来到青安的家。坐定后,苏彬将他所携带的书籍给青安看。青安发现没有一本是经书,都是些陶冶情操,教人如何修炼成仙的书,青安对这些书毫无兴趣。青安向苏彬吐露他现在最希望的是如何能够通过官府考试,然后迎娶寇干的美丽女儿。

Since Qingan lived in this area, he invited Su Bin to spend the night at his home. Su Bin accepted this invitation. So they went to Qingan's home. After being seated, Su Bin showed Qingan the books he had brought with him. Qingan noticed that none of them were the classics. Rather, they were all the books of spirit guides telling people how to become an immortal, which Qingan was not interested in at all. Qingan confided in Su Bin that all he wished was to pass the government examination so he could marry Kou Gan's beautiful daughter.

苏彬问青安寇干的女儿是如何的美丽,青安骄傲地回答她可能是中国最美的女子。苏彬大笑。他说他将来有一天邀请青安到他住的地方去看看所谓美丽的女子是个什么样子。青安问他住在什么地方。苏彬笑着回答,等他去了那儿他就知道了。

When Su Bin asked Qingan how beautiful Kou Gan's daughter was, Qingan replied with pride that she might be the most beautiful woman in China. Su Bin roared with laughter. He said that someday he would invite Qingan to the place he lived, so Qingan could observe the pretty women in his area. Qingan asked Su Bin where he lived. Su Bin smiled and replied that when he got there, he would know.

第二天早上早餐后,当他们坐在一张餐桌旁聊天时,一只小小的蜻蜓飞落在餐桌的一角。苏彬站了起来告诉青安,这是他离开的时候了。他给青安一道符,告诉他如果他想拜访苏彬并去看那里的美女,他可以在就寝前将这道符烧掉。说完了后他将身体缩得很小很小,然后跳在蜻蜓的背上,让这只小虫带着他飞出了窗户而不见了踪影。

The next morning after breakfast, when they were sitting by a table to chat, a small dragonfly flew in and landed on the edge of the table. Su Bin stood up and told Qingan that it was time for him to leave. He gave Qingan an amulet and told him to burn it before going to sleep if he wanted to pay him a visit to observe the beautiful women in his area. Then Su Bin shrank his body into a tiny size and jumped on the dragonfly's back. The insect took him flying out of the window and disappeared.

青安楞住了。他明了苏彬不是凡人,很可能他就是神仙。

Qingan was shocked. He realized that Su Bin was not an ordinary man. It was very likely that he was an immortal.

一天下午,在连续读了好几个小时的经典后,他感到疲倦了,想小睡片刻,然后继续攻读。突然他想起了苏彬的邀请,他把苏彬给他的符烧了,然后躺在长榻上等待。

One afternoon, Qingan felt tired after having studied the classics for several hours. He planned to take a nap, then, continue with his studies. Suddenly he remembered Su Bin's invitation. He burned the amulet Su Bin had given him, and lay down on a couch to wait.

刚躺下,一个十多岁的男孩来禀报,他的主人派他来请伍先生到天堂去一游。青安问他的主人是谁,男孩回答苏彬先生。青安跟随这个男孩走了出去,发现一只白色仙鹤停在他的前院。男孩跨上了鹤背后要青安也跨上,青安怀疑这么一只小鸟怎么可以负载两个人。经不住男孩催促,他决定一试。当他骑上鹤背后,很惊讶地发现这上面还有多余的地方。

Just after he had lain down, a teenage boy came to him reporting that his master had sent him to invite Mr. Wu to heaven. Qingan asked the boy who his master was. The boy replied, "Mr. Su Bin." So Qingan followed the boy out and found a white crane in his front yard. The boy got on the bird's back and wanted Qingan to join him. Qingan hesitated, as he wondered how the small bird could carry two people. Upon the boy's urging, he decided to have it a try. After he got on the crane's back, he was surprised to find that there was still plenty of space there.

白鹤平稳地飞向天空。青安向下望去,发觉他家的房子和其它的楼宇在地面上就好像一粒粒沙子一样大小。

The white crane flew up smoothly into the sky. Qingan looked down and found that his house and the other buildings on the ground all looked like tiny grains of sand.

终于仙鹤停在一座巨大的金色门前,门的上端刻有三个大字"南天门"。两只硕大无比的老虎守在门的两边。男孩用手轻拍一只老虎的头,就把青安带进了天堂。

Finally the crane landed in front of a huge golden gate with big Chinese characters that spelled out "Southern Heavenly Gate" engraved at the top. Two gigantic tigers stood guard at each side. The boy patted a tiger's head, and led Qingan go into heaven.

进入后,青安发现很多的豪华的宅第都是用各种不同颜色的玉石砌成的。主道是由半透明的玛瑙铺

聊斋精选

成的。路两边房子中间的树上都开着不知名的大花,停着五彩缤纷的鸣禽,路上的行人都呈现着愉快的神情,没有忧愁不悦的脸色。

Inside, Qingan found many splendid mansions built from different colors of jade. The main boulevard was a semi-transparent amber road. Between the houses on both sides there were trees adorned with large unfamiliar flowers and colorful singing birds. The people walking on the road all wore pleasant faces. Nobody showed signs of worry or unhappiness.

终于男孩停在一栋房子面前,发现苏彬站在那儿热情地欢迎他。

Finally, the boy stopped before a house and found Su Bin standing there warmly greeting him.

为庆贺他们的团聚,苏彬为青安设了一道宴席。有十二位年轻的女主人穿着代表一年十二个月的不同的彩色衣服。宴会上所有的器皿都是光亮的黄金或白玉制成的。食物精美无比,可青安辨不出它们的配料。

To celebrate their reunion, Su Bin ordered a banquet in Qingan's honor. There were twelve young hostesses in twelve different colored dresses representing the twelve months of the year. All the utensils were made of shiny gold or white jade. The foods were extremely delicious, but Qingan could not discern the ingredients.

宴席进行时,由多位少男少女组成的乐队轮番轻歌曼舞。每位少男都异常的英俊,每位少女都是非凡的美丽,人间的凡人是无法与之相比的。寇干的女儿如与这栋房子里的任何一位女子相比,她是不配称为美女的,只不过是一个极为平常家的女孩而已。

While the dinner was in progress, a band of teenage boys and girls took turns presenting dances and songs. Every young man was remarkably handsome, and every young woman was incredibly beautiful. None of them could be matched in the world of human beings. If Kou Gan's daughter was compared with any one of the young women here in the house, she could not be called a pretty woman, but a very homely girl.

宴席中,苏彬告诉青安在数百年前青安也是一位神仙,他们本是好友。因为青安犯了一个极大的错误,他被罚为凡夫。苏彬建议青安去努力进修,也许有朝一日他可以又有机会重返天堂再成为仙人。

During the meal, Su Bin told Qingan that hundreds of years ago, Qingan had also been an immortal, and they were good friends. Because Qingan had made a great mistake, he was punished to be a mortal. Su Bin urged Qingan to improve himself so maybe someday he would have a chance to return to heaven again as an immortal.

享受着如此美好的食物,望着如此美丽的仙女,听着如此美妙的音乐,青安喝了很多杯的酒。当宴席结束后,他醉倒了。苏彬吩咐一个穿着红色衣服的跳舞女孩带他去卧室睡觉。

Eating such delicious foods, watching such beautiful fairies, and hearing such wonderful music, Qingan drank many cups of wine. When the banquet was over, he was drunk. Su Bin ordered one of the dancing girls in red clothes to help Qingan go to the guest room to sleep.

聊斋精选

这个女孩是个活泼健美乐天型的美人。她帮青安脱去了外衣和鞋子,他邀她同床,她含羞地接受了。

The dancing girl was a buxom, happy-go-lucky beauty. She helped Qingan take off his clothes and shoes, He invited her to sleep with him, she shyly accepted.

第二天早上,当青安醒来,这个女孩早已起身并且穿好衣服了。她告诉他,一个凡人是不可以在天堂里停留超过一天一夜的。他必须起身回到他自己的世界。青安是依依不舍,她告诉他这是天律,他们别无选择必须遵守。

The next morning, when Qingan awoke, the girl was up and dressed already. She told him that as a mortal, he would not be allowed to stay in heaven for more than a day and night. He had to get up and leave for his own world. Qingan was unwilling to part with her, but she told him that they had no choice but to obey the heavenly rules.

在青安离开房间前,他要求这个女孩给他一件私人信物作为他们一夜情的纪念,女孩脱下她的粉红色手镯交给了他。青安立刻将之放入口袋内。

Before Qingan left the room, he asked the girl to give him a personal token for him to remember their night of love. The girl took the pink bracelet from her arm and gave it to him, and Qingan put it in his pocket immediately.

女孩将青安带到餐厅,苏彬又招待青安一顿早餐。餐后,苏彬吩咐那个把青安带上天堂的男孩再把青安送回人间。苏彬一直看到青安跨上了白鹤的背方才道别。

The girl led Qingan to the dining room and Su Bin treated Qingan to breakfast. After that, Su Bin ordered the boy who had picked up Qingan the day before to take Qingan back to the world of humans. Su Bin saw Qingan off when he got on the white crane's back.

在天上,当青安发现了在地上的他的家时,他非常兴奋以致一不小心从鸟背上摔落到地上。

High in the sky, when Qingan spotted his home on the ground, he became so excited that he slipped off the bird's back and fell to the ground.

突然间,他从梦中醒了过来,发觉他仍躺在家中的长榻上。

Suddenly, he woke up from a dream and found that he was still lying on his couch at home.

他告诉家人他到天堂里去了一趟,可是没有一个人相信他。于是他的手伸入口袋,拿出一个粉红色的手镯,向众人炫示,大家都承认这真是一件神奇的手镯,既不是金制的,也不是玉制的,可却具有两者的特性,没有人曾经看到过这么一件稀世宝物。

He told his family that he had made a trip to heaven, but nobody believed him. Then he reached into his pocket and took out the pink bracelet and showed it to them. Everybody admitted that it was indeed a marvelous bracelet, made of neither gold nor jade, but possessing the qualities of both. Nobody had seen such a unique treasure before.

　　自从这场梦后,青安变成了一个完全不同的人。他感到人世间的任何东西都是临时性的。与他在天堂里所见的相比,在他身边的每件事物都是庸俗的。他原来计划努力攻读经典之书去通过官府考试,然后迎娶寇干的女儿,现在这些计划都是毫无意义的了。一个高官可以随时被皇帝免职或送进牢房。寇干的女儿不能再称为美女,而且她会老去,最后死亡,尸体腐烂。就是贵为帝王,也将会死亡和腐烂。所有的欢乐、喜悦和荣耀都是空虚的。在人间,没有东西是永恒的。

After the dream, Qingan became a totally different person. He felt that everything in the human world was only temporary. In comparison with what he had seen in heaven, every object around him seemed vulgar. Originally, he had planned to study the classics hard, pass the government examination, and marry Kou Gan's daughter. Now these plans were completely meaningless. A senior official could be dismissed or imprisoned by the emperor. Kou Gan's daughter could not be called a beauty anymore, and she would grow old, eventually die, and her body would rot. As dignified as an emperor, he would die and rot, too. All joy, pleasure, and glory became hollow. Nothing in the human world was eternal.

　　青安告诉寇干他放弃了参加官府考试的计划,他请寇干将女儿嫁给别人,因为他甚至于不想结婚了。

Qingan told Kou Gan that he had given up his plan to take part in the government examination. He asked Kou Gan to marry his daughter to somebody else, as he did not even want to get married.

　　可是寇干的女儿不接受青安的突然变卦。她告诉她的父亲因为人人都已知道她的婚约,她仍要嫁给青安,不管他是否去参加官府考试。结果一个简单的婚礼便举行了。

But Kou Gan's daughter did not accept Qingan's sudden change. She told her parents that since everybody had known of her betrothal, she would marry Qingan whether he would take the government examination or not. Consequently, a simple wedding ceremony was held.

　　可是婚姻并不能改变青安。青安把他的所有经典书籍都搁置一边,他一心一意地去研究如何成为一个仙人。

However, the marriage did not sway Qingan. Putting aside all his classical books, Qingan concentrated only on his studies of how to become an immortal.

　　九个月后的一天下午,当青安在他书房长榻上小睡时,有人敲他的门。他去应门后,一位年轻女子走了进来。他欣喜万分地发现这个女子就是天堂上的那位丰满健美的女孩。她提着一只篮子,里面有个婴儿。在他还没有开口说什么话前,她把篮子交给了他,告诉他这是他的儿子。她说自从那次的一夜情后,她就怀孕了。孩子刚在数天前出生。按照天律凡人的孩子是不可以留在天堂的,所以她特别来此将婴儿

聊斋精选

交给他抚养,因为他是婴儿的父亲。

One late afternoon nine months later, while Qingan was taking a nap on his couch in his study, a person knocked on the door. He went to answer and in came a young woman. He was overjoyed to find that the woman was the buxom girl in heaven. She carried a basket with a baby in it. Before he could say anything, she handed the basket to him telling him that the baby was his son. According to her, she had gotten pregnant from that night of love with him. The baby was born only a few days earlier. As the heavenly laws did not allow a mortal's child to live in heaven, she had come here to give the baby to him to take care, as he was the baby's father.

青安兴奋地接过了篮子,把它放在他的长榻上,然后他就想去拥抱她,可是被她拒绝了。她说她不能重复她的错误,她必须立刻回到天堂去。不过她告诉青安,如果他能够不停地修炼他的正果作业,也许有一天,他和她可能在天堂里欢聚团圆的,说完了她就不见了。

Qingan excitedly took over the basket and put it on his couch. Then he tried to hug her, but she refused. She said that she could not repeat her mistake again and must return to heaven right away. However, she told Qingan that if he could continue to improve in his studies of how to become an immortal, maybe one day, he and she could have a happy reunion in heaven. Then she disappeared.

婴儿的哭声惊醒了青安,他发现他做了一场梦。虽然是场梦,可是婴儿在他的身边啼哭。他把婴儿送给他的妻子并把他的梦告诉她。他的妻子没有生育过子女,于是将这个婴儿视如己出当宝贝一样对待。

The baby's cry woke up Qingan, and he found he had had a dream. Although it was a dream, there was the baby crying by his side. He carried the baby to his wife and told her the dream. As his wife had never given birth to a child, she became very fond of the baby, and treated him as her own given son.

在庆贺小男孩一周岁生日后,青安决定到一座深山中去完成他成为神仙的最后修炼。他的妻子明白她是无法留住他的,只有勉强同意。

Soon after celebration of the boy's first birthday, Qingan decided to go to a high mountain to complete his final lesson in his immortality studies. His wife realized that she could not keep him stay at home, but agreed unwillingly.

道别后,青安一直没有回家。

After his farewells, Qingan never returned home.

二十年后,这个男孩长大成为一个聪明的男子。他通过了所有的官府考试,那些都是他的父亲一度想做而没有成功的。年轻人在京城朝中获得了一个职位。

聊斋精选

Twenty years later, the boy grew into a bright man. He passed all the government examinations that his father had once planned to do but had not accomplished. The young man obtained a position in the central government.

一天,这位年轻官员从京城回家去探视那住在老家的母亲,途中遭遇到一群盗匪。盗匪把他的卫士们打败了并把他的行李都抢了去,更想把他和他的卫士们都杀绝灭口。

One day, when the young official was returning home from the nation's capital to visit his mother in his native place, he met a gang of bandits, midway. The bandits defeated his security guards and took all of his belongings. Furthermore, the bandits wanted to kill him and his guards so nobody could become eyewitnesses to their crime.

就在这个时候,一个中年男子突然出现。他用手指向盗匪,盗匪的武器立刻掉落地上,就好像被一种神秘的力量重击一样。盗匪大惊,立刻弃下那抢来的东西及官员与他的卫士们,赶紧逃跑了。

Just at this moment, a middle-aged man suddenly appeared. He used a finger to point at the bandits. And immediately, all of the bandits' weapons dropped on the ground as if a mighty and mysterious power had hit them. The bandits were scared and left the official's belongings and the official and his group, and fled.

当这个年轻官员转身来向这位中年男子道谢救命之恩时,这个男子微笑地对他说:"我很高兴你已经成为一个有为的官员了。"于是他给年轻官员一个小包裹,请他把它转交给他的母亲。就在这个官员还未来得及询问这个男子的姓名以及他是如何认识他的母亲时,这个男子已经不见了。

When the young official turned to thank the man for saving his life, the man smiled and said to him, "I'm glad you have become a bright official." Then he gave the young man a small package, asking him to pass it to his mother. Before the official asked the man's name and how he had known his mother, the man departed and quickly disappeared.

年轻官员回到家后,把这整个的经过告诉了他的母亲,并将这个小包裹交给了她。打开包裹后,她发现里面是一只精致的粉红色手镯。她立刻认出这个手镯是天堂上的仙女送给她的丈夫的。她告诉她的儿子这位中年男子是他的父亲,他用神通救了他的儿子的性命。泪水还含在眼里,她对她的儿子说:"我知道你的父亲一定是达到他所追求的目的,成为一个仙人了。"

The young official returned home and told his mother the story and gave her the package. After opening the package, she found inside a delicate pink bracelet. She immediately recognized it as the bracelet was given to her husband by the fairy in heaven. She told her son that the middle-aged man was his father, who had used his supernatural powers to save his son's life. With tears in her eyes, she said to her son, "I realize that your father must have finally become what he had for so long sought to be: an immortal."

全书完
End of the Book

聊斋精选